Praise for THE ESCAPE ROOM

"The pages turn themselves . . . *The Escape Room* delivers all that it promises. It is a sleek, well-crafted ride to a surprisingly twisty conclusion." **—The New York Times Book Review**

"*The Escape Room* works as the ultimate locked-room mystery . . . Goldin excels at illustrating the pressures of a Wall Street career." —The Associated Press

"Addicting." **—Time magazine**

"A shrewd, brilliantly structured thriller doubling as a takedown of corporate culture." **—Shelf Awareness**

"There is clearly no happy ending likely for the four colleagues trapped inside [the escape room]; but fans of JP Delany and Ruth Ware will want to be right in there with them . . . a nail-biting tale of a corporate team-building exercise gone horribly wrong." **—Booklist**

"Riveting . . . [a] tale of greed and revenge set on Wall Street . . . Thriller fans will eagerly turn the pages to see what happens next." **—Publishers Weekly**

"Cancel all your plans and call in sick; once you start reading, you'll be caught in your own escape room—the only key to freedom is turning the last page!" **—Kirkus Reviews (starred review)**

THE
ESCAPE
ROOM

MEGAN GOLDIN

St. Martin's Griffin
New York

Published in the United States by St. Martin's Griffin, an imprint of St. Martin's Publishing Group

THE ESCAPE ROOM. Copyright © 2018 by Megan Goldin. All rights reserved. Printed in the United States of America. For information, address St. Martin's Publishing Group, 120 Broadway, New York, NY 10271.

www.stmartins.com

The Library of Congress Cataloging-in-Publication Data is available upon request.

ISBN 978-1-250-21965-7 (hardcover)
ISBN 978-1-250-24185-6 (international, sold outside the U.S.,
                          subject to rights availability)
ISBN 978-1-250-21966-4 (trade paperback)
ISBN 978-1-250-21967-1 (ebook)

Originally published in Australia in 2018 by Penguin Random House Australia

First U.S. Edition: July 2019
First International Edition: July 2019

First St. Martin's Griffin Edition: 2020

10 9 8 7 6 5 4 3 2 1

For everyone who has ever been made to feel powerless, trampled upon, or scorned, this book is for you.

*The supreme art of war
is to subdue the enemy
without fighting.*

—SUN TZU

PROLOGUE

I t was Miguel who called 911 at 4:07 A.M. on an icy Sunday morning. The young security guard spoke in an unsteady voice, fear disguised by cocky nonchalance.

Miguel had been an aspiring bodybuilder until he injured his back lifting boxes in a warehouse job and had to take night-shift work guarding a luxury office tower in the final stages of construction. He had a muscular physique, dark hair, and a cleft in his chin.

He was conducting a cursory inspection when a scream rang out. At first, he didn't hear a thing. Hip-hop music blasted through the oversize headphones he wore as he swept his flashlight across the dark recesses of the lobby.

The beam flicked across the classical faces of reproduction Greek busts cast in metal and inset into niches in the walls. They evoked an eerie otherworldliness, which gave the place the aura of a mausoleum.

Miguel paused his music to search for a fresh playlist of songs. It was then that he heard the tail end of a muffled scream.

The sound was so unexpected that he instinctively froze. It wasn't the first time he'd heard strange noises at night, whether it was the screech of tomcats brawling or the whine of construction cranes buffeted by wind. Silence followed. Miguel chided himself for his childish reaction.

He pressed PLAY to listen to a new song and was immediately assaulted by the explosive beat of a tune doing the rounds at the dance clubs where he hung out with friends.

Still, something in the screech he'd heard a moment before rattled him enough for him to be extra diligent.

He bent down to check the lock of the revolving lobby door. It was bolted shut. He swept the flashlight across a pair of still escalators and then, above his head, across the glass-walled mezzanine floor that overlooked the lobby.

He checked behind the long reception desk of blond oak slats and noticed that a black chair was at an odd angle, as if someone had left in a hurry.

A stepladder was propped against a wall where the lobby café was being set up alongside a water fountain that was not yet functional. Plastic-wrapped café tables and chairs were piled up alongside it.

In the far corner, he shone his flashlight in the direction of an elaborate model of the building complex shown to prospective tenants by Realtors rushing to achieve occupancy targets in time for the building's opening the following month.

The model detailed an ambitious master plan to turn an abandoned warehouse district that had been a magnet for homeless people and addicts into a high-end financial and shopping precinct. The first tower was almost finished. A second was halfway through construction.

When Miguel turned around to face the elevator lobby, he was struck by something so incongruent that he pushed his headphones off his head and onto his shoulders.

The backlit green fluorescent light of an elevator switch flickered in the dark. It suggested that an elevator was in use. That was impossible, because he was the only person there.

In the sobriety of the silent echo that followed, he convinced himself once again that his vague sense of unease was the hallucination of a fatigued mind. There was nobody in the elevator for the simple reason that the only people on-site on weekends were the security guards. Two per shift. Except tonight, Miguel was the only one on duty.

When Stu had been a no-show for his shift, Miguel figured he'd manage alone. The construction site was fenced off with towering barbed-wire fences and a heavy-duty electric gate. Nobody came in or out until the shift ended.

In the four months he'd worked there, the only intruders he'd encountered were feral cats and rats scampering across construction equipment in the middle of the night. Nothing ever happened during the night shift.

That was what he liked about the job. He was able to study and sleep and still get paid. Sometimes he'd sleep for a couple of hours on the soft leather lobby sofa, which he found preferable to the lumpy stretcher in the portable office where the guards took turns resting between patrols. The CCTV cameras hadn't been hooked up yet, so he could still get away with it.

From the main access road, the complex looked completed. It had a driveway entry lined with young maples in planter boxes. The lobby had been fitted out and furnished to impress prospective tenants who came to view office space.

The second tower, facing the East River, looked unmistakably like a construction site. It was wrapped with scaffolding. Shipping containers storing building materials were arranged like colorful Lego blocks in a muddy field alongside idle bulldozers and a crane.

Miguel removed keys from his belt to open the side entrance to let himself out, when he heard a loud crack. It whipped through the lobby with an intensity that made his ears ring.

Two more cracks followed. They were unmistakably the sound of gunshots. He hit the ground and called 911. He was terrified the shooter was making his way to the lobby but cocky enough to cover his fear with bravado when he spoke.

"Something bad's going down here." He gave the 911 dispatcher the address. "You should get cops over here."

Miguel figured from the skepticism in the dispatcher's cool voice that his call was being given priority right below the doughnut run.

His heart thumped like a drum as he waited for the cops to arrive. You chickenshit, he berated himself as he took cover behind a sofa. He exhaled into his shirt to muffle the sound of his rapid breathing. He was afraid he would give away his position to the shooter.

A wave of relief washed over him when the lobby finally lit up with a hazy blue strobe as a police car pulled in at the taxi stand. Miguel went outside to meet the cops.

"What's going on?" An older cop with a thick gut hanging over his belted pants emerged from the front passenger seat.

"Beats me," said Miguel. "I heard a scream. Inside the building. Then I heard what I'm pretty sure were gunshots."

"How many shots?" A younger cop came around the car to meet him, snapping a wad of gum in his mouth.

"Two, maybe three shots. Then nothing."

"Is anyone else around?" The older cop's expression was hidden under a thick gray mustache.

"They clear out the site on Friday night. No construction workers. No nobody. Except me. I'm the night guard."

"Then what makes you think there's a shooter?"

"I heard a loud crack. Sure sounded like a gunshot. Then two more. Came from somewhere up in the tower."

"Maybe construction equipment fell? That possible?"

A faint thread of red suffused Miguel's face as he contemplated the possibility that he'd panicked over nothing. They moved into the lobby to check things out, but he was feeling less confident than when he'd called 911. "I'm pretty sure they——" He stopped speaking as they all heard the unmistakable sound of a descending elevator.

"I thought you said there was nobody here," said the older cop.

"There isn't."

"Could have fooled me," said the second cop. They moved through to the elevator lobby. A light above the elevator doors was flashing to indicate an elevator's imminent arrival. "Someone's here."

"The building opens for business in a few weeks," said Miguel. "Nobody's supposed to be here."

The cops drew their guns from their holsters and stood in front of the elevator doors in a shooting stance——slightly crouched, legs apart. One of the cops gestured furiously for Miguel to move out of the way. Miguel stepped back. He hovered near an abstract metal sculpture set into the wall at the dead end of the elevator lobby.

A bell chimed. The elevator heaved as it arrived.

The doors parted with a slow hiss. Miguel swallowed hard as the gap widened. He strained to see what was going on. The cops were blocking his line of sight and he was at too sharp an angle to see much.

"Police," shouted both cops in unison. "Put your weapon down."

Miguel instinctively pressed himself against the wall. He flinched as the first round of bullets was fired. There were too many shots to count. His ears rang so badly, it took him a moment to realize the police had stopped firing. They'd lowered their weapons and were shouting something. He didn't know what. He couldn't hear a thing over the ringing in his ears.

Miguel saw the younger cop talk into his radio. The cop's mouth opened and closed. Miguel couldn't make out the words. Gradually, his hearing returned and he heard the tail end of a stream of NYPD jargon.

He couldn't understand most of what was said. Something about "nonresponsive" and needing "a bus," which he assumed meant an ambulance. Miguel watched a trickle of blood run along the marble floor until it formed a puddle. He edged closer. He glimpsed blood splatter on the wall of the elevator. He took one more step. Finally, he could see inside the elevator. He immediately regretted it. He'd never seen so much blood in all his life.

ONE

THE ELEVATOR

Thirty-four Hours Earlier

Vincent was the last to arrive. His dark overcoat flared behind him as he strode through the lobby. The other three were standing in an informal huddle by a leather sofa. They didn't notice Vincent come in. They were on their phones, with their backs to the entrance, preoccupied with emails and silent contemplation as to why they had been called to a last-minute meeting on a Friday night at an out-of-the-way office building in the South Bronx.

Vincent observed them from a distance as he walked across the lobby toward them. Over the years, the four of them had spent more time together than apart. Vincent knew them almost better than he knew himself. He knew their secrets, and their lies. There were times when he could honestly say that he'd never despised anyone more than these three people. He suspected they all shared the sentiment. Yet they needed one another. Their fates had been joined together long before.

Sylvie's face bore its usual expression, a few degrees short of a resting-bitch face. With her cover-girl looks and dark blond hair pinned in a topknot that drew attention to her green eyes, Sylvie looked like the catwalk model that she'd been when she was a teenager. She was irritated by being called to an unscheduled meeting when she had to pack for Paris, but she didn't let it show on her face. She studiously kept a faint upward tilt to her lips. It was a practice drummed into her over many years working in a male-dominated profession. Men could snarl or look angry with impunity; women had to smile serenely regardless of the provocation.

To her right stood Sam, wearing a charcoal suit with a white shirt and a black tie. His stubble matched the dark blond of his closely cropped hair. His jaw twitched from the knot of anxiety in his guts. He'd felt stabbing pains ever since his wife, Kim, telephoned during the drive over. She was furious that he wouldn't make the flight to Antigua because he was attending an unscheduled meeting. She hated the fact that his work always took precedence over her and the girls.

Jules stood slightly away from the other two, sucking on a peppermint candy to disguise the alcohol on his breath. He wore a suave burgundy-and-navy silk tie that made his Gypsy eyes burn with intensity. His dark hair was brushed back in the style of a fifties movie star. He usually drank vodka because it was odorless and didn't make his face flush, but now his cheeks were ruddy in a tell-tale sign he'd been drinking. The minibar in his chauffeured car was out of vodka, so he'd had to make do with whiskey on the ride over. The empty bottles were still rattling around in his briefcase.

As they waited for their meeting, they all had the same paranoid notion that they'd been brought to a satellite office to be retrenched.

Their careers would be assassinated silently, away from the water-cooler gossips at the head office.

It was how they would have done it if the positions were reversed. A Friday-evening meeting at an out-of-the-way office, concluding with a retrenchment package and a nondisclosure agreement signed and sealed.

The firm was considering unprecedented layoffs, and they were acutely aware they had red targets on their backs. They said none of this to one another. They kept their eyes downcast as they worked on their phones, unaware they were the only ones in the lobby. Just as they hadn't paid much mind to the cranes and construction fencing on their way in.

Sam checked his bank account while he waited. The negative balance made him queasy. He'd wiped out all the cash in his account that morning paying Kim's credit-card bill. If he lost his job, then the floodgates would open. He could survive two to three months without work; after that, he'd have to sell assets. That alone would destroy him financially. He was leveraged to the hilt. Some of his assets were worth less now than when he'd bought them.

The last time Sam had received a credit-card bill that huge, he'd immediately lowered Kim's credit limit. Kim found out when her payment for an eleven-thousand-dollar Hermès handbag was rejected at the Madison Avenue store in front of her friends. She was mortified. They had a huge blowup that night, and he reluctantly restored her credit limit. Now he paid all her bills without a word of complaint. Even if it meant taking out bridging loans. Even if it meant constantly feeling on the verge of a heart attack.

Sam knew that Kim spent money as much for attention as out of boredom. She complained that Sam was never around to help with the twins. He'd had to point out that they'd hired a maid to give her all the help she needed. Three maids, to be truthful. Three within the space of two years. The third had walked out in tears a week ago due to Kim's erratic temper.

Kim was never satisfied with anything. If Sam gave Kim a platinum necklace, she wanted it in gold. If he took her to London, she wanted Paris. If he bought her a BMW, she wanted a Porsche.

Satisfying her unceasing demands was doable when his job prospects were good, but the firm had lost a major account, and since Christmas word had spread of an impending restructure. Everyone knew that was a euphemism for layoffs.

Sam never doubted that Kim would leave him if he couldn't support her lifestyle anymore. She'd demand full custody of the girls and she'd raise them to hate him. Kim forgave most of his transgressions, she could even live with his infidelities, but she never forgave failure.

It was Sam who first heard the footsteps sounding through the vast lobby. The long, hurried strides of a man running late to a meeting. Sam swung around as their boss arrived. Vincent's square jaw was tight and his broad shoulders were tense as he joined them without saying a word.

"You almost didn't make it," observed Sylvie.

"The traffic was terrible." Vincent ran his hand over his overcoat pocket in the habit of a man who had recently stopped smoking. Instead of cigarettes, he took out a pair of glasses, which he put on to examine the message on his phone. "Are you all aware of the purpose of this meeting?"

"The email invite from HR wasn't exactly brimming with information," said Sam. "You said in your text message it was compulsory for us to attend. That it took precedence over everything else. Well, we're all here. So maybe now you can enlighten us, Vincent. What's so important that I had to delay my trip to Antigua?"

"Who here has done an escape-room challenge before?" Vincent asked.

"Are you fucking kidding me?" Sam said. "I abandoned my wife on her dream vacation to participate in a team-building activity! This is bullshit, Vincent. It's goddamn bullshit and you know it."

"It will take an hour," said Vincent calmly. "Next Friday is bonus day. I'm sure that we all agree that it's smart to be on our best behavior before bonus day, especially in the current climate."

"Let's do it," said Sylvie, sighing. Her flight to Paris was at midnight. She still had plenty of time to get home and pack. Vincent led them to a brightly lit elevator with its doors wide open. Inside were mirrored walls and an alabaster marble floor.

They stepped inside. The steel doors shut behind them before they could turn around.

SARA HALL

t's remarkable what a Windsor knot divulges about a man. Richie's Italian silk tie was a brash shade of red, with thin gold stripes running on a diagonal. It was the tie of a man whose arrogance was dwarfed only by his ego.

In truth, I didn't need to look at his tie to know that Richie was a douche. The dead giveaway was that when I entered the interview room, a nervous smile on my pink matte painted lips, he didn't bother to greet me. Or even to stand up from the leather chair where he sat and surveyed me as I entered the room.

While I categorized Richie as a first-class creep the moment I set eyes on him, I was acutely aware that I needed to impress him if I was to have any chance of getting the job. I introduced myself and reached out confidently to shake his hand. He shook my hand with a grip that was tighter than necessary—a reminder, perhaps, that he could crush my career aspirations as easily as he could break the bones in my delicate hand.

He introduced himself as Richard Worthington. The third, if you don't mind. He had a two-hundred-dollar haircut, a custom shave, and hands that were softer than butter. He was in his late twenties, around five years older than I was.

When we were done shaking hands, Richie leaned back in his chair and surveyed me with a touch of amusement as I settled into my seat across the table.

"You can take off your jacket and relax," he said. "We try to keep interviews informal here."

I took off my jacket and left it folded over the back of the chair next to me as I wondered what he saw when he looked at me. Did he see a struggling business-school graduate with a newly minted MBA that didn't appear to be worth the paper it was written on? Or was he perceptive enough to see an intelligent, accomplished young woman? Glossy brown hair cut to a professional shoulder length, serious gray eyes, wearing a brand-new designer suit she couldn't afford and borrowed Louboutin shoes that were a half size too small and pinched her toes.

I took a deep breath and tried to project the poise and confidence necessary to show him that I was the best candidate. Finally I had a chance at getting my dream job on Wall Street. I would do everything that I could humanly do not to screw it up.

Richie wore a dark gray suit with a fitted white shirt. His cuff links were Hermès, arranged so that the *H* insignia was clearly visible. On his wrist was an Audemars Piguet watch, a thirty-grand piece that told everyone who cared that he was the very model of a Wall Street player.

Richie left me on the edge of my seat, waiting awkwardly, as he read over my résumé. Paper rustled as he scanned the neatly formatted sheets that summed up my life in two pages. I had the impression that he was looking at it for the first time. When he was done, he examined me over the top of the pages with the lascivious expression of a john sizing up girls at a Nevada whorehouse.

"You look cold. Do you want me to turn off the air-conditioning?" he asked with a half smirk as he meaningfully lowered his eyes. Confused by the question, I looked down to where his eyes had settled. They were lingering on my nipples, the outlines of which were visible through the fabric of my top. I immediately turned red. His smirk turned into a full-blown grin. He was enjoying every second of my discomfort.

The line had sounded rehearsed. Richie had deliberately cranked the meeting room's thermostat to the coldest setting to provoke that physiological response. It was a cheap parlor trick. I guessed that he'd played it before with other female candidates.

I blushed again. Richie reveled in my embarrassment as he ran his eyes over the rest of my body. My cup size and the shape of my crossed legs, visible under the glass table. To Richie, I wasn't a high-potential graduate for the firm to recruit. I was fresh meat.

I faked ignorance of his little joke as best I could and ignored his intimate appraisal of my body. I was there for a job interview and I would damn well keep the interview on track.

I had prepared for the interview for days, I'd even researched Richie. He'd graduated from Princeton with an undergraduate degree, but he'd never gone to graduate school or received an MBA, which made him less qualified than I was. But then, he was Ivy League. My business school had a national reputation, but nothing compared to the cachet of Princeton.

Being a Princeton graduate automatically gave Richie a gold ticket in life. And didn't he just know it! He'd probably used his network to get himself into his first job and never looked back. That had been seven years ago, when the markets were red-hot and any bozo could climb the corporate ladder so long as he wasn't stupid enough to wear the same tie two days in a row. And if he had connections.

I was nervous as hell as I waited for Richie to ask the first question. I needed to sound the part; I already knew that I looked the part. I had gone into debt to afford the designer suit that I was wearing.

It was the nicest outfit I'd ever owned, and the most expensive. I saw that suit as an investment. If it got me the job I wanted, I'd get my money back and then some. I'd be earning seven figures in under a decade.

When I first tried on the suit, back home in Chicago, I was concerned it made me look too feminine. Too sexy. I wanted to be taken seriously. It's hard getting that balance right when you're a woman going for a job interview. Was the skirt too short? The jacket too tight? As I examined myself in the dressing room's mirror, the department store assistant assured me that I looked like a high-powered executive. When I handed her my credit card at the cash register a few minutes later, a lump in my throat at the huge bill, I reassured myself that my first paycheck would more than cover the cost.

Since I'd maxed out my credit card to buy the suit, I used my rent money to get my hair colored and cut into glossy brown tresses, which I flicked off my shoulder nervously under Richie's blistering scrutiny.

On paper, I was an ideal candidate. I ticked all the boxes of the job description. I'd graduated summa cum laude. My GPA was pure gold. I'd done an internship at an investment bank in Chicago. My references were practically sycophantic. My professors loved me and they weren't shy about expressing it in their reference letters. They described me as smart, driven, an original thinker, and an asset to any firm that hired me.

I had been confident that I had a good chance of getting the job until the moment I looked into Richie's bored blue eyes at the start of the interview.

"So you're from Chicago," he said, as if it were a different country. I nodded. He glanced at his watch. Bad sign.

"I was just in Chicago on a business trip," he said.

I swallowed the impulse to say "I know." My interview was supposed to have taken place in Chicago during Richie's visit. It was canceled at the last minute with the explanation that, unfortunately, he couldn't fit it into his packed schedule. Four days later, the recruiter called me again, as if nothing had happened. "Mr. Worthington would like to meet with you on Wednesday at our New York office." She made it sound as if I were being granted an audience with the pope.

There was no offer to fly me to New York. I didn't feel comfortable asking. I was too broke to buy a plane ticket. It was peak travel season and prices were exorbitant. So I took the train all the way to Penn Station. Twenty-one hours of Amtrak hell. The guy next to me snored so loudly that I barely slept.

"I went to the Cubs-Yankees game during my trip. It was my first time at Wrigley Field. Amazing experience." Richie was so self-absorbed he didn't immediately realize he'd effectively divulged that he'd stood me up on his supposedly jam-packed trip to Chicago in order to watch a baseball game. My expression must have reminded him, because he hastily added, "The baseball game was a networking event for our clients."

Yeah, right, I thought. You didn't need to graduate from Princeton to know a junket when you saw one.

I kept a sappy smile pasted on my face. But everything that had transpired so far told me that my chance of getting the job was precisely zero. You don't treat a candidate with such disrespect if you're planning on recruiting her.

The only reason that I scored the interview was because one of my college professors heard that I was still looking for work. He was baffled as to why his best student was scrambling around for a job months after graduation. He contacted an old friend with connections at the firm and called in a favor. That's how I landed interviewing with Richie.

I squeezed my fingernails into my palm to remind myself to be on my best behavior. Shut up and smile, I told myself. The pain of my nails in my flesh would be nothing compared to what would happen if I didn't get this job. I'd be broke and my career would be dead before it ever began.

I was a few months out of graduate school and, despite stellar grades, I was still unemployed. If that went on for much longer, I would be entirely unemployable by the time the next batch of graduates left business school. A graduate on the job market for too long is like a piece of rancid meat. Nobody wants to touch them.

It was bad luck that I graduated at the same time as a downturn hit the markets. There had been talk of a mini recession. Confidence was down; financial industry shares plummeted. Firms immediately slashed their hiring. There were plenty of graduates just like me who were struggling to get jobs.

"We get thousands of candidates applying for jobs every year. We have the pick of the crop. Why should we hire you?" That was Richie's first question.

I knew from his air of overindulged entitlement that he wouldn't understand what it meant to work your guts out through college and graduate school to get straight A's for a chance at a career he took for granted. He would have stumbled into his job as if it were a birthright.

I took a deep breath. I had prepared for questions like this all the way on the train ride over. And it was one long train ride. I'd memorized a clever answer for this question word for word. It was articulate, well reasoned, and, most important, relatively succinct. Nobody wanted a job candidate who rambled.

As I began to answer his question, Richie reached into his brief-case. My eyes followed his movements as I continued speaking, doing my best not to sound too rehearsed. Richie was digging around in his briefcase, looking for something. I figured he wanted a note-book or a pen. I found out what he was looking for when he trium-phantly removed a foil bag and ripped it open.

The sound of crinkling packaging was almost deafening as he shoved his hand inside the packet and scooped out a handful of mixed nuts, which he promptly shoved into his mouth.

I powered through my response to his question even though it was distracting, talking to someone who was shoveling nuts into his mouth.

Richie crunched so loudly that all I could hear was the crack of teeth on nuts. Crack, chew, swallow. Crack. All the while I was giving my best sales pitch.

I looked into his eyes and realized that it was deliberate. His chis-eled, venal face had the same look of amusement it'd had when he played his air-conditioner trick.

When I finished my answer, he took another handful of nuts, began chewing, and asked his next question with his mouth full. "Have you ever worked in a high-stakes environment? How did you deal with the pressure?"

I answered that question. And then another. It was hard to be eloquent when all I could hear was Richie's teeth crunching al-monds and cashews with the mechanical efficiency of an industrial grinder. I couldn't hear myself talk and was pretty sure that he couldn't hear a word I was saying, either. I inadvertently raised my voice slightly so that I could be heard over his crunching. He crunched more loudly. With a straight face.

It was plain as day that he didn't have the slightest intention of hiring me for the job. It didn't matter how well I presented, how eloquently I spoke, or how good my experience was. I was there purely as a box-ticking exercise.

The thought occurred to me that Richie probably had to interview a woman or two as part of the hiring process. I fit the bill. It was all about covering his ass. He was asked to bring me in for an interview; that didn't mean he had to treat me as a serious candidate. He just had to go through the motions, and that's what he was doing.

I had an overwhelming urge to stop talking, get up, and walk out. I didn't have the luxury. I had student loans to pay off, mounting credit-card debt, and rent to pay. I had more than enough to keep me in the red for the next decade unless I landed a good job. I couldn't risk burning my bridges by making a fuss over the way that Richie treated me. Who would believe me anyway?

In my sad reality, I had little choice but to answer Richie's dumbass questions while he all but gave me the finger as he shoved another handful of nuts into his mouth.

When it was finally over, he told me someone would be in touch. Then he walked out and left me alone in the meeting room to show myself out.

I left the interview feeling sick to my stomach. Sick that someone could treat me with such contempt. Sick at the fact that I had another twenty-one-hour train ride back home. Sick at the thought I had to cover a huge credit-card bill for my suit and was short of next month's rent money.

I returned my visitor's pass to the reception desk and walked in a daze into an elevator. Before the doors closed, some guy pushed his way in. I didn't pay him any attention. I'd had enough of his kind for one day. Another suit with an overpriced haircut and a watch that cost more than my parents' car.

There was a film of tears in my eyes from frustration. I was still holding my résumé—I'd intended to hand it to Richie to make sure he had a hard copy. I resisted the urge to rip it up.

"I hear that Michigan State has an excellent finance program." I looked up in surprise at the man who was breaking elevator etiquette by talking to me. He was tall, with a broad frame, and dressed in a de rigueur charcoal suit with a light blue shirt and a dark tie. There was something about him that made me realize he was the exact opposite of Richie. He didn't flash his success, but he oozed presence.

His English was flawless except for the vague hint of a European accent. His eyes were the lightest shade of blue I'd ever seen. Blue chips of ice.

"I graduated from the program recently," I said. "It was excellent. They have John Baker running it. He was one of my faculty advisers." Baker was a former Federal Reserve economist who cemented his reputation by predicting the previous financial crises when everyone was still bullish on equities.

I was a little creeped out that this man peeked over my shoulder to read the first page of my résumé. He must have known what I was thinking, because he gave me a rueful, slightly apologetic smile, which was infectious. I smiled back.

"I follow Professor Baker's analyses closely. He has a brilliant mind. I admire him for going back to his alma mater to head its research institute rather than taking an Ivy League position," he said.

"He's a strong believer in giving back to the community he

came from," I replied as the elevator rapidly descended toward the lobby.

"Professor Baker must have thought highly of you if he was your faculty adviser."

"He's one of my referees," I replied modestly.

"Impressive. I gather you're looking for work?"

"Yes, I'm looking for a graduate position."

"May I take your résumé, since you have it handy?" he asked. "I'm always looking for finance hotshots."

"Of course," I said, handing it to him and taking the business card that he offered in return.

"No promises," he said, looking directly at me with his piercing blue eyes. I didn't have a chance to respond—the elevator doors opened and he walked out without looking back.

I glanced at his business card before sliding it into my handbag.

"Vincent de Vries. Senior Vice President, Stanhope and Sons," it read.

THREE

THE ELEVATOR

All the lights in the elevator turned off at once. It happened the moment the doors shut. One moment they were in a brightly lit elevator; the next they were in pitch-darkness. They were as good as blind, save for the weak fluorescent glow from a small display above the steel doors showing the floor number.

Jules stumbled toward the elevator control panel. He pressed the button to open the doors. The darkness was suffocating him. He had to get out. The elevator shot up before anything happened. The jolt was unexpected. Jules lost his footing and fell against the wall with a thud.

As the elevator accelerated upward, they assumed the lights would be restored at any moment. In every other respect, the elevator was working fine. It was ascending smoothly. The green display above the door was showing the changing floor numbers. There was no reason why it should be dark.

Without realizing it, they shifted toward one another, drawn together by a primordial fear of the dark and the unknown dangers that lurked within it. Jules fumbled for his phone and turned on the flashlight setting so that he could see what he was doing. He frantically pressed the buttons for upcoming floors. They didn't appear to respond to the insistent pressure of his thumb.

"It's probably an express," explained Sylvie. "I saw a sign in the lobby that said something about the elevator running express until the seventieth floor."

Jules pressed the button for the seventieth floor. And the seventy-first. And, for good measure, the seventy-second, as well. The buttons immediately lit up one after the other, each button backlit in green. Jules silently counted the remaining floors. All he could think about was getting out.

He loosened his tie to alleviate the tightness in his chest. He'd never considered himself claustrophobic, but he'd had an issue with confined spaces ever since he was a child. He once left summer camp early, in hysterics after being accidentally locked in a toilet stall for a few minutes. His mother told the camp leader that his overreaction was due to a childhood trauma that left him somewhat claustrophobic and nervous in the dark.

"I don't know about the rest of you, but I'll be taking the stairs on the way down," Sam joked with fake nonchalance. "I'm not getting back into this hunk of junk again."

"Maybe the firm is locking us up in here until we resign voluntarily," Jules said drily. "It'll save Stanhope a shitload of money." He swallowed hard. The elevator was approaching the fortieth floor. They were halfway there. He had to hold it together for another thirty floors.

"It would be a mistake if the firm retrenched any of us," said Vincent. "I told the executive team as much when we met earlier this week." What Vincent didn't mention was that several of the leadership team had avoided looking at him during that meeting. That was when he knew the writing was on the wall.

"Why get rid of us? We've always made the firm plenty of money," Sylvie said.

"Until lately," Vincent said pointedly.

They'd failed to secure two major deals in a row. Those deals had both gone to a key competitor, who had inexplicably undercut them each time. It made them wonder whether their competitor had inside knowledge of their bids. The team's revenue was lower than it had been in years. For the first time ever, their jobs were vulnerable.

"Are we getting fired, Vincent?" Jules asked as the elevator continued rising. "Is that why we were summoned here? They must have told you something."

"I got the same generic meeting invite that you all received," Vincent responded. "It was only as I arrived that I received a text with instructions to bring you all up to the eightieth floor for an escape-room challenge. The results of which, it said, would be used for 'internal consultations about future staff planning.' Make of that what you will."

"Sounds like they want to see how we perform tonight before deciding what to do with us," said Sylvie. "I've never done an escape room. What exactly are we supposed to do?"

"It's straightforward," said Sam. "You're locked in a room and have to solve a series of clues to get out."

"And on that basis they're going to decide which of us to fire?" Jules asked Vincent in the dark.

"I doubt it," Vincent said. "The firm doesn't work that way."

"Vincent's right," said Jules cynically. "Let's take a more optimistic tack. Maybe they're using our escape-room performance to determine who to promote to Eric Miles's job." Eric had resigned before Christmas under something of a cloud. They'd heard rumors the firm was going to promote someone to the job internally. Such promotions were highly sought after. At a time when their jobs were in jeopardy, it offered one of them a potential career lifeline.

The green display above the door flashed the number 67. They had three more floors to go until the elevator finished the express part of the ride. The elevator slowed down and came to a stop on the seventieth floor. Jules exhaled in relief. He stepped forward in anticipation of the doors opening. They remained shut.

He pressed the OPEN button on the control panel. Nothing happened. He pressed it again, holding it down for several seconds. The doors still didn't budge. He pressed the button three times in quick succession. Nothing. Finally, in desperation, he pressed the red emergency button. There was no response.

"It's not working," he said.

They looked up at the panel above the door that displayed the floor numbers. It had an *E* on its screen. Error.

A small television monitor above the control panel turned on. At first, they didn't think much of it. They expected to see cable news or a stock market update, the type of thing usually broadcast on elevator monitors.

It took a moment for their eyes to adjust to the brightness of the white television screen. After another moment, a message appeared in large black letters.

WELCOME TO THE ESCAPE
ROOM. YOUR GOAL IS SIMPLE.
GET OUT ALIVE.

FOUR

SARA HALL

I received the phone call on my first day off in a week. Six straight days working double shifts at Rob Roy. My lower back ached from carrying pitchers of beer and heavy griddle pans with sizzling meat to an endless stream of hungry customers. I was so exhausted by the end of each shift that I had to make a concerted effort to make sure I was taking things to the right table.

It was midmorning. I was fast asleep, with my head under my pillow to block the sunlight streaming through the half-open blind. I'd forgotten to pull it closed when I'd collapsed into bed in the middle of the night.

I ignored the ring of my phone. That wasn't easy to do, given that it played on full blast the theme music from *Curb Your Enthusiasm*. I'm a heavy sleeper, and most days, if I put my mind to it, I could sleep through the noise of a marching band.

But that morning, I couldn't shut out the insistent drone of my phone no matter how hard I tried. Even in my deeply exhausted state, I worried that it was my mom calling about my dad. He was in the hospital again after another procedure on his heart. In the end, that nagging worry about my dad made me roll over, grab my phone, and take the call under the covers.

"Hello," I croaked, my voice muffled by sleep.

The long pause that followed suggested that whoever was on the phone line wasn't my mom.

"Sara." It was a man. Deep voice. Clipped accent. Maybe British? No, not British. There was a hint of something else. European. I was too groggy to think who it might be.

"Yes, this is Sara," I responded. I tried to clear my throat surreptitiously. "How can I help?"

"This is Vincent de Vries. From Stanhope and Sons?" A pause for recognition. I almost choked when I heard his name. My voice was like sandpaper. It was obvious that I'd just awakened. He'd think that I was an unemployed bum who lay in bed all day. This was a disaster. I scrambled into a sitting position and, while he spoke, squirted water from the drinking bottle next to my bed into my throat.

"We met in an elevator at my office about two weeks ago," he continued.

"Of course, Vincent," I responded with as much animation as I could manage, given that I'd been in a deep sleep ten seconds earlier. "You offered to take a look at my résumé. That was so nice of you."

"I'm not sure if I mentioned at the time that I might have an opening coming up on my team. That has now happened. After looking at your résumé, I think you might be a good fit. I'd like to ask our recruitment manager to arrange for you to be interviewed. That is, if you're still looking for work."

"Yes," I said, with the overenthusiasm of the unemployed. "I'd be very interested in interviewing for the position." As I spoke, reality set in. Another twenty-one-hour train ride to New York. Another three days of lost tips. Another train ticket and set of interview clothes that I couldn't afford. More debt. More lost income. More inevitable rejection. Why bother when it was only going to end in heartache?

"Great. I'll ask our recruitment team to fly you out for interviews on Friday. If that suits you?"

I paused to absorb Vincent's words. He'd said he'd fly me out. I wouldn't need to take Amtrak at my own expense. I felt encouraged that he'd said they'd bring me there for interviews, plural. It sounded as if I was a serious candidate. I actually had a chance.

"That would be absolutely fine," I replied smoothly. "Thank you so much for calling, Vincent. I really appreciate the opportunity."

I was ecstatic. Before the call, I had been facing what felt like a lifetime of waitering hell at a franchise restaurant, with a boss who siphoned tips and blamed his staff for his own mistakes.

Not to mention having to share an apartment with Stacey, a spoiled twenty-two-year-old who let her deadbeat boyfriend, Gary, stay over almost every night, left dirty dishes in the sink to attract roaches, and hung her bras and panties to dry in the shower stall, so that I had to shower with her underwear hanging in my face.

Vincent's call potentially meant a chance to get my career on track, financial security, a new life in New York. Maybe I'd even be able to have an apartment to myself. I was high as a kite just from thinking of the possibilities.

I jumped on my bed in my candy-striped pajamas like a hyperactive kid at a trampoline park, shrieking with excitement. All of a sudden, life was sweet.

Once my initial euphoria died down, reality set in. I knew from bitter experience how it would probably play out. I'd feel good during the interview and return to Chicago hopeful of a job offer. Eventually

I'd get rejected by another recruiter letting me down gently with a generic excuse from a prepared script. I'd been through that scenario with Richie and it had left me feeling despondent.

Richie's recruiter had called me two days after the interview to tell me that I hadn't made it into the final round. "The hiring manager has opted for another candidate more suited to his requirements."

"How, specifically, was I not suited? I met every requirement in the job description." I tried to keep my tone nonconfrontational, but I could tell that she was annoyed by my persistence.

"Richie, er, Mr. Worthington felt you lacked gravitas," she said in a pointed tone, as if her words actually made sense. "Gravitas is such an important quality at our firm."

I wanted to tell her that if gravitas was so important, then they should teach their hiring managers not to stuff their mouths with snack food during job interviews. It was a struggle to finish the call without telling the recruiter where Richie could shove his gravitas. The way that I saw it, gravitas was a masculine quality. A characteristic of men in suits. Men like Richie, minus the bad table manners.

I later found out that Richie hired the brother of a college buddy for the job. I was the decoy. Or one of several. He had to pretend to look at other candidates to cover for the fact that he was hiring a friend for the job. Good old-fashioned cronyism. It's how half the jobs in the city are filled.

The episode with Richie had left a sour taste in my mouth. I wasn't sure if I had the resilience to go through it again with Vincent. To lie awake at night filled with anticipation, counting my chickens before they hatched. That's what I'd done before the interview with Richie. I'd even looked up apartments listed for rent, so I could figure out where I'd want to live. Talk about being overconfident.

A few days would pass after I returned home from my interview.

I'd make excuses as to why I hadn't heard back from the firm. I'd tell myself the recruiter was ill, or Vincent was away on business. But at some point there would be no reasonable explanation for the time lapse other than the obvious: I didn't get the job. A form email would arrive in my in-box, sent by a recruitment manager.

"We were impressed with your skills and experience. However, we had a strong field of candidates and have found a candidate who better matches the skill set we were seeking in this position." Whatever that meant. Or it would say the position had been frozen, offered to an internal hire, changed in scope. Or one of a hundred other excuses that I'd heard ad nauseam.

I decided that I had to believe that I had a chance. Otherwise, I might as well curl up and die. The firm flew me to New York, just as Vincent had promised. My flight arrived in the afternoon, the day before the interviews were to be held. The firm had booked me into a five-star hotel within walking distance of the office.

It was the first time in my life that I'd stayed at a hotel that had more than three stars to its name. The closest I'd come to that level of luxury was working a summer job doing room service at a resort hotel on Lake Superior when I was nineteen. I was the girl in the hotel uniform who carried the breakfast trays and newspapers up to the rooms in return for tips.

That's why I gave a generous tip to the bellboy who showed me to my room in New York. Even though I was hardly flush with cash, I knew what it was like to end a shift with barely enough money for a ride home and dinner.

I grew up in a family in which every month, every week was a financial struggle. My father had health issues. He tired easily and was constantly ill. A mechanical engineer by training, he hadn't been able to carry a stable job since my early teenage years. My mother, who'd worked as a schoolteacher before I was born, struggled to get work once she had to step in to help support the entire family.

My childhood had been distinguished by scrimping and saving and struggling to get scholarships for my schooling, all while trying to hide our dire situation from everyone we knew. My parents were terribly ashamed at having failed to achieve their dreams, other than having me. Whatever money they had to spare went straight into paying for my education. We rarely went on vacation, and when we did, we certainly never had the money to stay at five-star hotels.

I relished my first experience of luxury travel. I was given a large room with turndown service and a bed big enough for five people. There were Belgian chocolates on the pillow and a basket of snacks by the window with a card that said it was compliments of the firm. It also said that Stanhope and Sons would cover up to two hundred dollars of food and beverage costs during my one-night stay.

I lay on the bed and reveled in the luxury. I checked out the pillow menu and selected one for the night, then played around with the music and entertainment system like a kid. In the bathroom, I found a vanity bag with expensive French-label products and body scrubs. I tried them all before soaking in lemongrass-scented water in the tub while watching TV, calming my nerves.

I couldn't resist ordering room service for dinner that night: steak, salad, and fries delivered on a white cloth–covered trolley, complete with silverware. I ate dinner cross-legged on the bed while rehearsing my interview responses.

The next morning, I ate a continental breakfast in my room, wearing a white robe and watching the early-morning Manhattan congestion through my window. The disorderly line of cars gridlocked on the street below resembled a piece of abstract art. The lines were unruly. The colors clashed against the asphalt gray. The hint of movement was so vague that it looked like an illusion.

When I was done drinking my second cup of coffee, I dressed in the suit that I'd worn for the interview with Richie. I paired it with a new lilac satin shirt and a filigree gold necklace.

I walked to the Stanhope and Sons offices two blocks away, passing throngs of Wall Street types striding into work in their two-thousand-dollar suits. The platinum blond assistant at the reception desk had been supercilious when I'd interviewed with Richie. This time, she couldn't do enough for me.

"Vincent told me to expect you," she gushed as she led me to the interview room. "Let me know if you need anything. Anything at all." She smiled as she closed the door and left me alone to await my first interview.

The meeting room was larger than the one used for my disastrous interview with Richie. It had a long white table that could seat eight people. There was no transparent glass tabletop like the one through which Richie had ogled my legs. The air conditioner was on a comfortable setting.

I would do five rounds of interviews in a single day, all in that interview room. I left only to use the bathroom and to go down for a half-hour lunch at midday. That was further proof that Richie's interview had only ever been for show. If he'd considered me as a serious candidate, he would have arranged for the other interviews to take place on the same day. He'd never intended for me to get past the first round.

The firm required a minimum of four interviews before an offer was made. It was an ironclad rule. Sometimes that number could rise to six. Or even seven, for very senior positions. But nobody was ever hired before passing at least four rounds. That went for everyone from senior executives down to mailroom clerks.

The first interview of the day was with Donna, a recruiter who had a master's degree in organizational psychology. Donna had long, dark hair that fell in waves below her shoulders and a wide, sincere smile. She went through a series of preliminary questions, mostly asking why I wanted the job and what value I thought I could bring to the firm. I had all those answers down pat. I ran through them confidently and in a clear voice. She took notes frequently and, thankfully, didn't throw me any curveballs.

The next interview was with Deepak. He wore wire-rimmed glasses over a fine-featured face that matched his thin, delicate frame. He said that he was originally from Bangalore. He told me the interview would focus on checking my knowledge of financial modeling. He gave me a few financial scenarios that he seemed to expect me to solve in my head, because he didn't offer me any paper.

I was so nervous that at first I couldn't keep up with the numbers. I paused and sipped my water to calm down. Then I answered all his questions without any mistakes. I could tell from his pleased expression that I'd done well.

After Deepak was Lance. Lance looked like an advertising executive. He had the chiseled face of a Ken doll, which belied the fact he was insanely smart. He bombarded me with questions, probing how I would handle certain situations. When I'd answered that first volley of questions to his apparent satisfaction, he moved on to another set of questions, which was even tougher.

"There's no right answer," he told me. "I just want to get an idea of how you think."

I nodded that I understood.

"How would you find a good Szechuan restaurant in downtown

Manhattan without access to the internet?" It wasn't exactly the type of question you prepare to answer in an interview at an investment bank.

"I'd walk through Chinatown and look for the busiest one that I could find," I replied.

He wrote something down with an inscrutable expression. There were other questions along those lines. He asked me to calculate how many tennis balls would fit into an eight-seater car, how I would go about finding a needle in a haystack. I told him I'd use a magnet.

The fourth interview was with Mitch. He was a sharp-faced lawyer from the risk and regulatory team, who needled me until I felt like a pincushion. "If you saw a colleague steal a dollar, would you report him?" he asked. "Come on," he prodded when I hesitated. "What's more important to you, Sara, ethics or getting along with your colleagues?"

The question stumped me because every possible answer seemed wrong. "Ethics," I said. "But I wouldn't report someone over a dollar."

"How much would someone have to steal for you to report him?" he fired back.

I squirmed under his expectant gaze. I didn't have a ready answer.

He took the conversation into a new direction. "Tell me about a time you screwed up royally."

It went on and on, until a trickle of sweat ran down my back as I fielded his questions like a batter facing off against a fastball pitcher.

I didn't show my discomfort, though. I kept my cool.

"You didn't do too badly," he said at the end of the interview. He was intimidating, but his hardball interview questions were a walk in the park compared to being drowned out by Richie crunching nuts to throw me off.

The interview with Vincent was the last for the day. Before it started, the receptionist from earlier brought me a coffee and a muffin. I scoffed them down, grateful for the sugar hit and caffeine kick. I was starting to flail. My voice was almost hoarse from talking nonstop all day.

Vincent came through the door not long after. "Good to see you again, Sara," he said.

He was taller than I'd remembered. And better-looking. I hadn't seen him properly when we met the first time in the elevator. I noticed that he had wide cheekbones and hair so short, it looked almost shaved. His eyes I remembered from our first meeting. They were like shards of light blue crystal in the afternoon sunlight streaming through the meeting room window.

He sat with his hands pressed together in front of him as he asked me preliminary questions to break the ice. He barely took his eyes off me as I responded. I found it both disconcerting and strangely appealing that he showed that much interest in me. After I finished talking, he contemplated my answer and then pulled over his notepad.

"Don't mind me," he said without looking up as he put on reading glasses and wrote notes in distinctive longhand. He was the only one who handwrote his notes. The others used laptops.

"Go ahead," I said.

After a while, he put down his pen. "I'm confused," he said.

"Confused about what?"

"You studied premed. Your subjects included chemistry, biology, and math. Your results were excellent. I'm sure you would have been welcome at any medical school in the country. Yet you studied for an MBA. And you're interviewing for a job in finance with an investment company." He waited for an answer, even though he hadn't actually asked a question.

"You want to know what prompted me to abandon the sciences for finance?"

Nobody had asked me that question in all the interviews I'd gone through. It was the one question I hadn't prepared for. I didn't have a clear answer myself.

By all accounts, I should have gone to medical school instead of business school. I had the prerequisites and the marks. In fact, I'd received two offers from well-regarded medical schools. I rejected both of them.

"Why the change of direction in your career?" he asked.

His eyes held mine. They reminded me of a blue ocean on a sunny day. It was obvious that he wanted a considered answer. He didn't want some lame response about how I'd always dreamed of working on Wall Street; how I saw myself as a female Gordon Gekko.

He wanted the truth. But I hadn't even been able to tell myself the truth about that decision.

"My mother had a stroke when I was in my senior year at college," I said. "And my father has had major health problems for as long as I can remember. I'm an only child." My voice trembled with the effort of holding in my emotions. "Not a day passes where I don't wonder if that's the day I'm going to get a call telling me that Mom or Dad has died, or that one of them is in the hospital, needing treatment their health insurance won't cover."

I willed away the tears forming in the corners of my eyes. I sensed that Vincent noticed them glistening. I cleared my throat. "That's a long way of telling you I wanted a career path where I would earn well from day one, because I'll need to help them with their medical expenses."

"Instead of within three to five years after graduation, which is how long it takes a doctor to start making money," he observed. "And of course business school takes half the time of medical school."

"I was given a partial scholarship for women in finance to cover the cost of my MBA. It cost far less than medical school. Somehow it made sense." I hesitated. "And I spent so much time in hospitals with my parents . . . I loathe hospitals."

"But you didn't anticipate there would be an economic downturn after you graduated. You figured you'd walk into a job," he said. "You didn't have the faintest idea that MBAs would be a dime a dozen by the time you left business school."

I was embarrassed by how much he knew about me. "I read the crystal ball all wrong. I figured that I'd be financially independent by now." Left unsaid was the fact that it had turned out to be about the dumbest thing that I'd ever done in my life.

Vincent didn't respond. He was writing in his notepad again. Minutes passed before he looked up at me. I wanted to kick myself for having been so blunt. I should have told him that I fainted at the sight of blood, or something else predictable.

"Don't worry," he said, reassuring me. "I've heard worse reasons for wanting to work here."

FIVE

THE ELEVATOR

Sam had done an escape-room challenge about ten months before, as part of a bachelor party for an old college friend. They'd
done two different rooms at the facility that night. The one he liked
best was a room laid out as a Learjet, complete with a replica of the
cabin, windows, and seats taken from a decommissioned executive jet. The scenario they were given was that there was a bomb on
the plane and they had an hour to defuse it.

It took them fifty-eight minutes to figure out the code to disarm the
virtual bomb, using clues they gathered by solving various puzzles
onboard the fake aircraft. A boarding pass from a previous "flight"
led them to a particular seat, under which they found a laptop requiring a three-digit code to disarm a bomb. They figured out the
code by solving various word games and math problems scrawled
in the back of a magazine, under a drink coaster, and in the text of a
flight safety card they found in a seat pocket. There were other clues
along the way, some of which led them to dead ends. With two minutes to go, they entered the code to disarm the fake bomb. It was the

wrong code. They heard the deafening sound of an explosion followed by a prerecorded announcement telling them they had failed in their mission and everyone was dead. A second later, the lights turned on and the door opened. They were back in the warehouse where the escape rooms were located.

In contrast, the elevator escape room was claustrophobic, dark, and frighteningly real. It took the concept up a notch by putting the experience in an actual elevator instead of one built from plywood in a warehouse.

"What happens now? You've done these before, Sam." Jules betrayed his nervousness by speaking too fast. He pressed his hand to Sam's shoulder, ostensibly to get his attention but really to make some human contact in the dark. Sam whirled around.

"How the hell do I know!" Sam snapped. "This is too fucking real for my liking."

Before doing the Learjet escape room, he and his friends had received fifteen minutes of instruction. In this one, apparently, they needed to figure out everything themselves. There was only the message on the television monitor. "Welcome to the escape room. Your goal is simple. Get out alive."

"When I did the other escape rooms, we had to find puzzles and solve them," said Sam. "Maybe we should start by looking around for instructions or clues. They could be hidden anywhere."

He remembered how on the Learjet he had found a major clue on the safety card in the pocket of a seat. But in the spartan elevator, there seemed to be no obvious place to hide clues. There were no nooks or crannies. No furniture. No props. Only the four of them standing in the dark, unsure of what to do.

"Apparently, we won't need to find a clue," said Sylvie dramatically. "I believe a clue has found us."

The original message on the television screen had been replaced with a new one.

Dead but not forgotten.

ASLHARLA

"What the hell does that mean?" asked Jules.

"It's an anagram," said Sylvie with a slight eye roll. Sylvie had never been one for games or team-building activities. She kicked herself for not declining the meeting invitation with an excuse that it clashed with her flight to Paris. But Vincent had made a point of texting them all to tell them attendance was compulsory. He would not have been pleased if she hadn't turned up.

"We can spend the next twenty minutes figuring out this anagram," said Sylvie. "Or we can get the answer in two seconds and get out of here."

She opened the internet browser on her phone. She didn't give a damn if that was considered cheating. Showing initiative to get ahead was an integral part of the firm's ethos. Plus, she was pressed for time. Sylvie wanted to get out of the escape room as fast as possible so she could get home and pack for her midnight flight.

Sylvie's phone displayed a message saying there was no connection. She tried again, with the same result. She checked her phone settings.

"I don't have a signal on my phone and there's no Wi-Fi," she said to nobody in particular. "Does anyone else have a connection?"

"No," the others said a moment later, almost in unison, as they checked their phones.

"How's that possible?" asked Sylvie.

"Maybe the escape-room people blocked our phone signals

because they didn't want us looking up answers on our phones?" suggested Sam.

"You give them too much credit," Vincent said dismissively. "If we're in the express part of the elevator, then we're in the equivalent of a long concrete tunnel. Except ours is vertical. Internet and phone signals can't get through reinforced concrete. And there's no Wi-Fi connection," he said. "In short, we're cut off from the outside world. We're going to have to figure this out without any help from Google."

"I don't have the time or the patience for stupid games," snapped Sylvie. "I have a flight to catch."

"You'll make your flight. We'll all be let out after an hour," Sam reassured her. "At my friend Phil's bachelor party, we did a couple of escape rooms. One of them was really tough and we couldn't figure it out—they still let us out after an hour."

They'd gone to a strip joint straight afterward, where they got plastered and encouraged the groom to get down and dirty in a private room with one of the strippers. The best man alluded to their strip joint visit in his drunken speech at the wedding reception. It hadn't gone down too well with the bride, who'd hoped the bachelor party would begin and end with the escape rooms, which is why she'd suggested it.

"We're all stuck here for the next hour," said Vincent. "We might as well try to play the game. The firm sent us here for a reason. It's a test of some sort. I think we should give it everything we've got."

"Let's get going, then." Sylvie sighed, thinking about Paris.

"Don't worry," said Jules, reading her thoughts, "there'll be plenty of time for you to make your flight to visit, uh, what's his name again?" Everyone shifted about awkwardly.

"It's Marc," said Sylvie coldly. "I introduced you to him at the Christmas charity dinner."

"Of course," replied Jules, as if he'd genuinely just remembered. "The art dealer. Short. With a nose that looks broken but isn't and hair that's too thick for a man his age. I presumed he has hair plugs. He's married, isn't he? With a daughter around your age?"

"Shut up, Jules. You're being an ass," said Sam.

"To answer your question, Jules," said Sylvie. "Marc's separated. His daughter's in junior high. Not that being a married father ever stopped you."

Jules smiled to himself but said nothing more. He'd hit his mark beautifully. But then, he always did know how to press Sylvie's buttons.

"'Dead but not forgotten,'" Sylvie repeated the clue, determined to ignore Jules's barbs. "Who do we know that fits that definition?"

"John Wayne," said Jules flippantly.

"What about Abraham Lincoln? Or Kennedy?" suggested Sylvie.

"It might be a pop-culture reference," said Sam. "How about Jimi Hendrix or Kurt Cobain?"

"You've all forgotten about the anagram. None of those suggestions fit with the letters in the anagram," Vincent said. "Let's work backward. Who do we know whose name is made up of the letters A-S-L-H-A-R-L-A?"

There was silence as everyone contemplated possible answers.

"Well, that's a blast from the past," said Jules in a tone that told them he'd figured it out.

"What's the answer?"

"If you rearrange those letters," Jules explained, "it spells out Sara Hall. Dead but not forgotten. Sara Hall. It fits, right?"

SIX

SARA HALL

Despite my best efforts at keeping my hopes in check, I was practically packing for New York the moment I returned home after my interviews with Vincent's team. I was on a massive high. I looked at apartment rental listings and read forums for people relocating to New York.

Two weeks passed. I didn't hear back. It was obvious that I hadn't gotten the job. I crashed back to Earth. Hard. I was devastated that I'd blown my chance a second time. First with Richie and then with Vincent. I ran through the final interview over and over again in my head.

I shouldn't have allowed Vincent to corner me about medical school. I should have given him a banal answer. And I should have held my emotions in check. He didn't want to hear about my personal problems. And he certainly wouldn't hire an analyst who might quit the firm a year into the job to chase a dream of studying medicine. Maybe that was why I hadn't heard back. Whatever the case,

I had screwed up what was probably my last chance to get my career on track before it was too late.

I increased my shifts at Rob Roy, took on double shifts on weekends, when tips were bigger. Anything to distract me and make a dint in my credit-card bill. I worked from noon to midnight for so many days in a row, I felt permanently jet-lagged.

I resumed my job search, focusing on second- and third-tier jobs in finance. There wasn't much around. Recruiters told me that positions were frozen due to the downturn and that people were getting jobs largely through their networks. "Don't take it personally. Even people with experience are struggling to find work," they told me.

I was reaching the point where I didn't care where I worked. I wanted a job that didn't involve being nice to rude customers, an aching back from carrying heavy trays, and chefs who would grab my ass in the restaurant kitchen whenever I had my hands full with dishes, knowing I couldn't swipe their hands away without dropping everything.

Three weeks after my interview with Stanhope and Sons, I was working the afternoon shift at Rob Roy. I was tired, annoyed with every single aspect of my life. Leo, the short, balding shift manager, chewed me out over a customer who threatened to put up a negative review online because there were only five baby tomatoes in her salad. She insisted that there were eight tomatoes in a photograph of the salad in the menu.

"I can't believe the lady counts tomatoes," I muttered as I carried her plate into the kitchen.

"If she wants to count baby tomatoes, then that's fine by me," Leo barked. "The customer is always right!"

"Why are you lecturing me, Leo? Talk to the kitchen guys. I just take the food out."

He looked at me for a moment longer than necessary, as if he wasn't sure how to answer. "The problem with you, Sara, is that you should smile more," he said. "If a customer wants more tomatoes in her salad, put a smile on your face and ask how many more tomatoes she would like. Mario will find you tomatoes. We have plenty of tomatoes. We have so many fucking tomatoes that our trash cans are overflowing with them by the end of the day."

I knew how Mario found extra tomatoes. It usually involved picking them out of the unfinished meals collected from tables, or taking them out of those same trash cans Leo mentioned. I shut up. I didn't want to get on Leo's bad side. He was already annoyed with me as it was. Rent was due soon, and I needed the extra shifts.

"And Sara, if you want better tips, take my advice: Wear a shorter skirt," Leo advised sagely.

I looked down at my black skirt. It seemed short enough to me. It was well above my knees.

"I thought this was a family restaurant," I said sweetly.

"It is." He nodded. "But a bit of leg never hurt anyone. It definitely would be good for tips."

"I'll remember that, Leo." I made no effort to hide my sarcasm. Everything was getting to me that night. The tomato lady. Leo. The customers who'd taken up one of my tables for two hours and left me spare change instead of a proper tip. My roommate, Stacey, who'd left another sinkful of dirty dishes in our apartment for me to take care of.

Being taken to task over tomatoes and the length of my skirt was not the career that I'd envisaged when I graduated top of my MBA class. I headed back to the restaurant floor, feeling lousy, when my phone vibrated in my back pocket.

A woman with frizzy red hair waved her hand in the air to signal to me that she was ready to order. I pretended not to see her as I bee-lined toward the restrooms. I answered my phone as I went into a stall so that Leo wouldn't give me a hard time about taking personal calls.

It was the recruitment manager from Stanhope and Sons. I'd spoken to her a few times when she'd arranged the flight and hotel for the interviews with Vincent and his team. "I'm about to send you an email, but I wanted to call to explain first."

I felt suddenly sick. She was calling to tell me that I hadn't gotten the job.

"Explain what?" I asked in a thin voice.

"I'm pleased to tell you that we'd like to offer you a job with the firm. It would be an analyst role, which is a great starting position. The only issue is that we need an answer within twenty-four hours and we'd need you to start next week. Vincent is hoping that might be possible."

"Sure, that's definitely possible." Someone flushed a toilet and I hurriedly cupped my hand around the phone's microphone to block the sound.

"Great," she said. "Congratulations. I'll email you the formal offer now. I need you to sign it and email it back by tomorrow."

Her message arrived a minute later. I opened the attachment while still in the toilet stall. The salary alone made me weak in the knees. They were starting me at $130,000, not including an annual bonus if I met certain targets. If that wasn't enough, they were paying me thirty thousand dollars as a sign-on bonus, and they would cover my moving costs.

I wanted to cry and laugh at the same time. I wanted to walk into the damn restaurant and buy every customer a drink. Even the crazy tomato lady, who'd been glaring at me ever since I served her the salad.

Instead, I did what I'd dreamed of doing since the day I graduated. I took off my Rob Roy apron and threw it in the trash and left without a word to Leo, Mario, or anyone else. I walked out of the place a free woman.

That same night, I gave notice to Stacey as she and Gary noisily slurped Chinese noodles in take-out containers while watching TV. "You'll have to pay the rent until I can find someone else to move in," Stacey told me, her eyes fixed on the television screen.

"No, I won't," I responded. "The contract says I have to give you two weeks' written notice."

I leaned over and wrote on her restaurant napkin "I hereby give two weeks' notice that I will be moving out." I signed and dated it. "Here you go," I said, tossing the napkin into her lap.

I went into my bedroom to pack. I was sure that Stacey was secretly relieved I'd be leaving. She had wanted Gary to move in permanently without any change to the way we divided our rent. I'd resisted. Gary was a pig, and our apartment wasn't big enough for three people. Also, the two of them had the loudest sex I'd ever heard. There was no way I could cope with Gary as a permanent fixture in my life.

My closest friends threw me a small farewell party. I'd hardly seen them for weeks, given all the extra shifts I'd been working. We all became teary when they brought out a bottle of champagne to toast me.

"To the most determined, tenacious person I've ever met," said Jill. She had been my best friend all through high school and was herself moving to Seattle to live with her fiancé. "I know more than anyone how hard you've worked for this, Sara. You deserve every bit of your success."

"Sara," said Lisa over a glass of orange juice. She was three months pregnant and wasn't drinking alcohol. "You have some nerve moving halfway across the country just as I'm about to have twins. I was counting on you to baby-sit!" We all laughed. "But seriously. You've always been an amazingly generous friend. You had a box of Kleenex and a pint of my favorite cookies and cream ice cream whenever I had a bad breakup. You never ever complained, even though I know you secretly hated cookies and cream," she said, laughing as she wiped her wet eyes. "And especially when things were tough for you. You're an inspiration, and I'm so happy for you—I could just scream!"

I burst into tears when I unwrapped the gift they gave me. It was a silver-framed photograph of us as teenagers, alongside a recent photo of us together at Lisa's wedding reception. The party broke up with long hugs and promises to stay in touch—always.

For the two days before I was due to fly to New York, I moved into my parents' place. I wanted to spend a longer stretch of time with them. I hadn't done that since leaving for college. Things had changed so much since then. I was no longer their little girl. And they'd become more reliant on me than ever before as they grew old and sickly almost before my eyes. Sometimes I felt as if our roles in the family had reversed without any of us noticing. My parents were thrilled about the new job, although I sensed an unspoken anxiety that their only child would be living so far away. My dad was on dialysis, and it would be hard for him to travel all the way to New York.

As I climbed into the cab to go to the airport, I promised to come back and visit regularly. I felt enormously sad as I watched them wave to me from the curb with their arms interlinked, as if to prop each other up. Saying good-bye to my folks was the hardest thing I'd ever done.

The firm flew me business class. That was another first. As I drank a glass of chilled French Chablis and ate a salmon frittata, I marveled at the surreal change in my fortunes. I had gone from taking the train to New York and getting splattered by a guy with sleep apnea to reclining on a leather seat while leisurely selecting cheese and dessert from a business-class lunch menu.

When the plane landed at La Guardia, I was met by a liveried driver holding a sign with my name printed in thick black letters. He drove me to another five-star hotel, this time with a view of the city skyline and a bedroom the size of the entire apartment that I'd shared with Stacey. On the desk was a fruit bowl and a box of chocolates, courtesy of Stanhope.

I took a selfie standing by my living room window, against the Manhattan skyline, biting into a red apple. "Living the dream," I captioned the photo.

SEVEN

THE ELEVATOR

The thin beams of light from their phones turned the elevator a hazy gray. It was enough for them to see one another's uneasy expressions as they waited for the escape room to give up its secrets. They looked toward the television screen for another clue. It was blank.

They'd received no instructions on what to do with the anagram they'd solved, spelling out Sara Hall's name. They didn't even know what they were looking for. Were they supposed to find a code? And if they did, where were they supposed to key it in? They had no idea what puzzle they were supposed to solve, and they were stumped about where to find the next clue.

"It could be anywhere," said Sam. "A Post-it note. Anything."

The mirrored walls shimmered as they shone their phones around to look for clues. They found nothing. Aside from the walls, there was nowhere to look. They were in an elevator. Sterile, spotless, and empty. Where could one hide a clue in an elevator?

They shifted about restlessly, frustrated by the fruitlessness of the exercise. They'd been in the escape room for five minutes and they'd already hit an impasse.

"What's this, then?" Vincent picked up a small piece of crumpled paper from the floor. It was a chewing-gum wrapper. Cinnamon flavor, judging from the smell. "There's writing on the inside."

"The Latin word for nephew," he read out loud, "is the origin of an English word for gaining an advantage. Someone you know has benefited from this practice. Find their name, which is two characters longer than that English word, and you will be one step closer."

"You have got to be kidding me. Latin?" Sylvie snatched the paper out of Vincent's hand to read it herself. She crumpled it up in disgust. "Who knows Latin in this day and age? It's ridiculous."

"Not as ridiculous as you might think," said Vincent. "I learned Latin at school. In Holland, it's compulsory. I have three years of Latin. It's been a while, but . . ."

Sylvie crossed her arms as they waited for Vincent to recall his high school Latin lessons. She'd known him for so long that she sometimes forgot that Vincent had been born and raised in Holland. Rotterdam, then The Hague. He'd served in the Dutch army before completing his undergraduate degree in London and moving to Boston for his MBA.

"It's *nepos*," said Vincent. "The Latin word for nephew is *nepos*."

"The clue says we need to find an English word," Jules responded.

"Yes, thank you for stating the obvious, Jules," said Vincent. "*Nepos* is the origin of the English word *nepotism*. The question is, who do we know who has benefited from nepotism?"

"Where do you even start in this industry?" groaned Sylvie. "We're spoiled for choice."

"Let's start at the firm," said Sam. "After all, the clue says that we know the person in question."

"It also says the person's name is two characters longer than our answer," Sylvie said. "Nepotism is eight characters. That means we need to think of someone we all know whose name is ten characters long."

"That's easy, then," said Jules. "Eric Miles is the most obvious candidate and his name is ten characters, if you count the space."

Eric Miles was the nephew of a board member and the great-grandson of one of the original Stanhope family founders. He'd joined Stanhope straight out of graduate school by virtue of those family connections. He wasn't much of a student, and he certainly wasn't much of an investment banker.

Word was that his family gave a large endowment to get Eric accepted into his Ivy League business school, where he'd made it through with the help of handsomely paid tutors who ghostwrote his papers and drilled him to within an inch of his life before exams. Eric's rise at Stanhope was nothing short of meteoric. And completely undeserved. Vincent considered him to be as sharp as a doorknob, a somewhat generous assessment. But within three years of his being hired, Eric's job grade and salary were above that of Jules, Sam, and Sylvie, even though they'd all started a few years before he joined the firm and were considerably more talented.

It wasn't just that Eric was borderline incompetent; he was downright mean. He had a nasty streak a mile wide. He was rude to the support staff, and had a reputation for wandering hands. The admin staff knew to be wary of Eric, especially when he drank at parties.

He was at his most lecherous when they were pulled into group photos. Eric's hands would inevitably wander south—from over a female colleague's shoulder to down her back to squeezing her ass. One time, he hiked up a woman's skirt from behind and splayed his hands inside her lace underwear.

Eric seemed to take a special satisfaction in being crude around women. One story that did the rounds came from a woman who'd been riding up in an elevator with Eric and a male colleague. Without batting an eyelid, Eric turned to his male colleague and loudly said, "Jenny gave me a blow job last night. That tells me one thing."

"What?" his friend asked.

"That I have to check my Amex account."

That summed up Eric. He was lazy, arrogant, and sleazy. Despite his many flaws, nobody ever complained. Eric was untouchable. He was able to get away with murder, and didn't he just know it.

Eric was well on the road to another major promotion when, just before Christmas, he abruptly left the firm. Before he resigned, he told a few people in the London office that he'd been forced to stay in England longer than expected because he'd perforated an eardrum, rendering him unable fly.

But gossip from the London office suggested that the real reason was that Scotland Yard had advised him not to leave the country until they finished investigating allegations that he'd sexually assaulted a recent graduate at the firm.

It transpired that the woman who'd made the allegation changed her mind, refusing to cooperate with police. The investigation was closed. But Eric returned home weakened politically, enough for some of his enemies in the firm, such as Vincent, to finally get rid of him.

At least that was the version Jules had heard. He'd also heard that Eric had sworn he'd get even with Vincent. "I'll cut Vincent's balls off. It could be next week. It could be a year from now. He won't see me coming until it's too late" were Eric's exact words, according to a secretary Jules was sleeping with at the time.

The internal communications team published a note in the weekly newsletter. "It is with regret that we advise that Eric Miles has left the firm to work as managing director at the Miles-Newton Venture Capital Fund. We wish Eric great success in his new role." It sounded impressive to anyone who didn't know that the fund was owned by his family and the job was nothing more than a gesture to save face. Eric had, for all intents and purposes, been fired.

"Let's assume that clue number two is Eric Miles, who surely must go down as the king of nepotism in an industry that's turned it into an art form," said Sam. "That means we have Sara Hall for clue number one and Eric Miles for the second clue."

He paused to consider the implications. One colleague was dead; the other had recently been fired. "I don't know about the rest of you," he said, "but I'm not sure I like where this is going. They're not exactly standard escape-room clues. They seem very . . . well, personal."

EIGHT

SARA HALL

The night before my first day, I tossed and turned for hours, until I fell asleep from sheer exhaustion. I woke to the furious ring of my alarm and blundered into the shower, still groggy from sleep. It took me ages to fix my hair and makeup and then dress in the clothes that I'd laid out the night before.

I'd blown a good chunk of my sign-on bonus buying a new wardrobe, with the help of an in-store fashion consultant who claimed to know everything there was to know about how Wall Street women should dress.

"Men barely need to think about what to wear to the office. They throw on a Ferragamo suit and tie and they're instantly classy. Women have it tougher. We have to be feminine and yet professional. Fashionable yet conservative. It's hard to navigate all the contradictions." As she spoke, she pulled out items for me to try on from racks of designer suits with prices that made my eyes water.

I left the store carrying eleven shopping bags, including five suits and five pairs of shoes. I can't bring myself to say how much it all cost. Let's just say that I earned enough frequent-flyer points on my credit card for a round-trip flight to Tokyo.

I arrived at the Wall Street office by taxi, flustered by the slow, gridlocked journey downtown. Entering the building's opulent lobby, I had first-day-at-work butterflies in my tummy. I was directed by a concierge to an express elevator that went directly to the Stanhope office on the ninetieth floor.

Two men followed me into the elevator, deep in conversation. "There's no way that I'm getting married until I'm forty. Between you and me, my future wife is probably still in elementary school," said the guy with short blond hair while looking at my ass as if he were analyzing a financial chart.

"I wish I'd held out. I don't have time for all this wedding shit. Everything about getting married is an argument," his friend complained. "Lisa wants a church wedding—I think her parents are behind it. I told her, 'No fucking way. I don't believe in God.'"

"The only thing that you worship is your investment portfolio," the other said, laughing. "You'd think she'd know that by now."

"Exactly. I pointed to the fucking rock on her finger and told her that investment bankers don't need religion. We don't need to wait for the next life to enjoy paradise, not with the money we make."

My first taste of that paradise began when I stepped out of the elevator into the Stanhope and Sons reception area. A Human Resources assistant met me and took me to the room where the weeklong induction was being held. Her curls bounced on her shoulders as she led me up a central balustrade staircase to the exclusive luxury of the executive floor.

I was escorted along a wide corridor where priceless artworks were displayed under security-glass panes. I didn't have a chance to look at the art itself as the assistant led me directly to a double door, which she opened to reveal a large executive lounge. At the side of the room was a long buffet with fruit platters, mason jars of granola with berry coulis, and pastries arranged alongside old-fashioned soda bottles filled with an assortment of freshly squeezed fruit juices and health shakes.

Nine other recruits were sitting on chairs around a long table, flipping through the pages of their welcome packs. They all looked up as we entered. The men were clean-shaven, with new haircuts, neatly pressed suits, and shoes that had been polished until they shone. The only other woman sat in the far corner. We smiled at each other encouragingly. Her name was Elizabeth and her thin smile suggested that she was almost as nervous as I felt.

It struck me that we were like kids on the first day of elementary school, wearing brand-new outfits and shiny shoes. Except our outfits cost a fortune and we didn't need a single Kleenex among us; quite the opposite: None of us could wipe away our smile.

Induction was like boot camp with a corporate twist. Maybe that's why they chose Janet to host the sessions. She'd been a naval officer before graduating from Harvard and joining the firm. She had cropped blond hair and wore a fitted gray suit that told us that she wasn't to be messed with.

"Congratulations. You've achieved the career equivalent of winning the lottery," Janet told us in her opening address. "You won't need to buy lottery tickets now that you're at the firm. You've already won." Everyone laughed.

We didn't need Janet to tell us that we'd hit the jackpot. We only had to stroll through the executive foyer, where a Ming dynasty vase was in an alarm-protected glass cabinet, and where a gilt-framed Picasso sketch of his mistress hung under a glass panel opposite a Monet oil painting. It was a small one, but a Monet is a Monet. In the corner of our meeting room was a bronze dancer tying her ballet slippers as she looked up at us with sympathetic eyes.

"You can see in these charts"—Janet clicked through to a colored bar graph—"just how tough it is to get to where you are sitting right now.

"Over the past year, we've received over nine thousand applications for graduate positions." She used a red laser to point to the relevant section of the graph. "Some were formal applications. Others were referred by current staff and alumni, who are always on the lookout to ensure that we hire the best.

"We short-listed nine hundred candidates, who were all sent online tests. These were analyzed by a complex algorithm developed by psychologists who are leaders in their field. That helped us refine that short list to two hundred and fifty candidates. Those candidates went through an initial telephone screening interview with external consultants, who we have trained to understand our exacting requirements. Just one hundred candidates were invited for a first round of formal interviews at one of our global offices. From that number, we chose fifty for the full gamut of our intensive interview process. That meant, as you all know, four rounds of interviews at a minimum. Of that number, thirty candidates were offered jobs, including yourselves." She paused to let her words sink in.

"It's quite an accomplishment for you all to be here today. Congratulations." Janet clapped her hands in slow-motion applause. "You belong to an exclusive club."

With that resounding endorsement, she introduced the lineup of speakers due to present to us for the rest of the week. Janet said they were all current staff or former executives who had moved on to start their own funds, or retire at forty to manage their investment portfolios. That was the investment banker's dream.

Their speeches over the course of the week covered a range of top-ics, such as legal issues, strategy, and crisis management. They came from a range of disciplines and backgrounds, but they all had one thing in common: They spoke about the firm in superlatives.

"We only hire the smartest people." "Our remuneration is the most generous in the industry." "The firm handles the biggest deals in the world and has the most prestigious client list."

Every speaker parroted variations of the same hyperbole.

"You won't find another company anywhere that will give you this level of experience from the get-go," said Max, a forty-something former senior executive. He told us that he kept busy in his semire-tirement by doing consulting work and flying to London for five days a month to teach an executive MBA course. "One day at Stan-hope is like a month anywhere else in terms of experience."

All the other new recruits had only just graduated from busi-ness school. I was the only one who had been looking for work since Christmas. I was well aware that I was there by the merest fluke of fate; if it hadn't been for the accidental meeting with Vincent, I would never have been hired.

Over the five-day induction, I was transformed from a disillu-sioned business graduate who'd spent months waiting tables for tips to an entry-level graduate at one of the world's leading financial houses.

The message they pummeled into us was that our world revolved around money: making it, accumulating it, spending it—in that order. It was Stanhope's version of the Holy Trinity.

"I feel like I'm joining a cult," someone whispered as we stood around drinking coffee during a break. "And let me tell you, I, for one, am more than happy to drink their Kool-Aid."

"I don't know why they call it an induction; it's more of a full-blown indoctrination. But hey, I'm not complaining. Stanhope is every-thing I ever imagined," said another.

The firm spoiled us rotten during induction week. We didn't re-alize that we were being wooed for a long, heady love affair with greed. By the end of the week, any ideals we'd held before we started working at the firm, whatever half-baked notions we'd held on every-thing from climate change to social justice were wiped away in one fell swoop.

On each chair was a gift bag filled with corporate gifts. Silk ties for the men; Italian silk scarves for the women. We were presented with leather organizers on the second day. On the third day, we en-tered the meeting room in the morning to discover Samsonite com-pact suitcases arranged against the wall. Each was monogrammed with the recipient's initials.

"You'll all be doing lots of traveling, so we thought we'd get you started with the right gear," said Janet as we located our own suitcase.

Inside the suitcases were fitness watches, the best wireless head-phones on the market, and a bunch of other stuff that probably cost a couple of grand altogether. The next day, we were presented with memberships to the fitness center on the third floor of the building. On the final day, we were given tickets to a Broadway musical as the guests of Harrison Stewart, a board member. That night, we sat in his box and afterward went for drinks at his private members club.

Even the most cynical among us was seduced by the five-star treatment. A waiter came in and out of our training room to bring us cold-pressed fruit juices and coffees made by an in-house barista. In between sessions, he would serve an assortment of tasty amuse-bouches prepared by the firm's executive chef.

Lunch was served in a private dining room on the executive floor.

"You should lose that tie," Brad whispered to Luke on the first day. He shut up as the waiter brought them both oversize plates with the entrée of lobster tail and browned butter.

"Why?" Luke asked when the waiter had gone. "I heard everyone who is anyone wears Hermès."

"That's exactly the problem," said Brad. "I worked here as an intern last summer. One day, my boss turned to me during a stand-up meeting with our entire team. 'Brad, I don't give a fuck if you can afford to buy Hermès. In this place, you have to fucking earn the right.' He cut off my tie with scissors in front of everyone and made me go downstairs to buy another one."

Luke turned pale. He slipped away after lunch and returned late to the next session wearing a striped navy Gucci tie.

The second day, we had a presentation by Steven Mills, a department head with sandy hair and a propensity to punctuate his words by jabbing his finger into the air.

"If you work hard," said Mills, "you'll be rewarded. We pay well at Stanhope. Better than our competitors. We take care of you so that you can put all your talents into taking care of our business, and our clients' business. That means growing wealth. *Everyone's* wealth, yours included."

He pressed PLAY to begin a series of profile videos of staff members we were supposed to see as role models.

"They were in the same graduate intake," said Mills. "Eight to ten years ago, every one of them sat exactly where you are now." Footage appeared on the screen of a man wearing aviator sunglasses. His dark blond hair was ruffled by wind. He spoke to the camera while driving a black Lamborghini along a coastal road.

"When I left grad school," said the man, whom the graphics identified as Dean, "I never imagined in my wildest dreams that my life would look like this."

The video cut to aerial drone shots of his car going up a curving, tree-lined driveway and stopping outside a white colonial-style house with blue accents, a manicured garden, and an Art Deco swimming pool. It cut back to Dean in his leather fighter-pilot jacket getting out of his car and walking up to the porch. A woman with long pale-blond hair embraced him. She was holding a photogenic toddler in a knit sweater. It was as if they were all taken straight from central casting.

The video for Joe was the same, except at the end of his car trip, he stepped onto a yacht and gave instructions to a captain. In the last shot, the camera pulled back, showing Joe with his arm around his cover-girl wife, who was dressed in a white evening gown that covered only one shoulder and enhanced her ebony complexion. The shot dissolved as they sailed off into the night.

The only video that was different was also the only one showing a woman. When she climbed out of her silver Mercedes convertible, outside an English manor house, she was embraced by an older man with salt-and-pepper hair and two young children holding on to the lead of a playful beagle.

"She must have used a surrogate to have those kids," Elizabeth whispered to me. As the only women in our induction group, we'd gravitated to each other. "My sister's best friend worked here and she had to hide her pregnancy until she was in her sixth month. When she came back from maternity leave, she had no clients left. She said that getting pregnant killed her career."

I had no intention of having kids for years, probably not until I was well into my thirties, but I still felt uncomfortable at the thought that I'd have to hide my baby bump until I was in my final trimester. It wasn't enough to put me off the firm. I figured that I'd cross that bridge if I came to it.

Our first week at the firm was nothing short of full-blown

seduction—the generous gifts, the deferential treatment, the endless little perks. We embraced it all with the unbridled enthusiasm of the young and ambitious. And why not? For me, it was a hell of an improvement on eating doggie bags of leftovers from Rob Roy.

By 12:30 P.M., on the dot, we'd all be salivating in anticipation of our 1:00 P.M. gourmet lunch: sous-vide Wagyu beef served with potato fondant and char-grilled asparagus, or Atlantic salmon with a thyme infusion paired with parsnip mash, or whatever other culinary delight the executive chef had cooked up for the day. Each meal was matched with vintage California wines.

On the last day, we were each given bound copies of *The Winning Way*, with instructions to memorize key passages.

"At the firm, we quote *The Winning Way* with the same reverence that my grandmother used to quote Scripture," Janet explained. "Think of it as your road map to success."

It was a one-hundred-page book that detailed the firm's history and philosophy of creating value, going back to the thirties. Whenever anyone at the firm used the term *value*, they really meant money. The terms were used interchangeably, but it was considered crass to talk just in terms of money. We were supposed to pretend that we were delivering a service to the community, beyond making Stanhope and its clients exceedingly rich.

The book had lines such as "Our people are exceptional because, to be the best in the business, you need the best people in the business, solving the toughest problems in the business."

It took ten pages to spell out the firm's founding vision, complete with black-and-white photographs of the original Mr. Stanhope and his sons, who were treated like demigods at the firm. Their portraits hung in every one of the firm's forty offices across the country and in twenty-one offices around the world.

"For every two of you who will make it, one of you will fall short," Janet told us in the final session. She didn't seem to care that she was completely contradicting her assurances on the first day, when she'd said that we'd all won the lottery. It turned out that only some of us got to take home the prize.

"Thirty percent of all our graduates leave in the first year because they aren't up to scratch," she said. "If you want to stay, then you're going to have to work harder than you've ever worked before."

By the time we walked out of the training room fully "inducted," we were like trained dogs. I thought of the eagerness with which we'd anticipated the gourmet lunches. We had been conditioned to do whatever the firm needed in return for a reward.

In the blind, cultlike reverence that followed the induction, each and every one of us would have taken a bullet for the firm. If truth be told, I think that most of us would have killed for Stanhope.

NINE

THE ELEVATOR

W arm air wafted out of the ceiling vent in a relentless stream of heat. At first, they welcomed it because it took the edge off the cold. As time went on, in the tight confines of the escape room, the heat became intolerable.

Sweat trickled down Sylvie's neck and between her breasts. Her legs itched under her nylon hose. It became so bad that she slid off her shoes and unrolled her stockings. They were stuck to her thighs with sweat. She tugged at her stockings to get them off, her nails tearing through the nylon fabric until her legs were stripped bare and the sheer nylon was shredded beyond recognition.

"There must be a way to turn the heating off." Sylvie fanned her hand in front of her face to cool herself down. Her hair was damp and limp; her makeup was melting. She was far from maintaining her usual impeccable appearance. For the first time since they'd stepped inside, she was grateful for the darkness. It shielded her from their prying eyes.

"We tried," said Vincent. "It won't turn off. The screw heads on the control panel aren't standard, so we can't even get at the wires."

"It's unbearable. I'm not sure how much more I can take."

"Well then, let's find the rest of the clues so we can get out of here before the hour is up," said Vincent. "The quicker we solve this puzzle, the faster we get home."

"I can't believe they brought us to such a dump," complained Jules. "Everything is malfunctioning. No lights. The heater is set too high. We're stuck on God knows what floor. And there aren't even any more clues to solve! How do they expect us to get out?" He tried to sound funny rather than hysterical. He didn't want the others to know how anxious he felt in the dark.

"I'm sure there are more clues," said Vincent. "We need to try harder. If we work together, then we'll figure it out."

He turned on his cell-phone flashlight and ran the narrow beam across the floor of the elevator, looking for more crumpled-up pieces of paper or anything else that might provide a clue. All he could see were Sylvie's shoes, neatly arranged next to each other by the wall.

Sweat poured down his face. He mopped it up with his handkerchief. The heat really was unbearable. Vincent removed his jacket and hung it next to Jules's jacket on the chrome handrail on the back wall. He loosened his tie and opened his shirt collar.

"This isn't like any other escape room that I've done," observed Sam. "This is hardcore. There's no staff. No instructions. No obvious clues. It's hot, dark, and we're halfway up a skyscraper in a real elevator."

Sylvie pushed wisps of hair away from her face and straightened her jacket, which she refused to remove, despite the heat. If this really was an exercise to determine who in their team might be laid off, she would be damned if she'd look like a mess when they finally got out. The men could get away with wearing loose ties and open shirt collars, but if the elevator doors opened and her shirt was unbuttoned, or her hair was a mess, then people would assume she'd had a meltdown. That she hadn't been able to handle the pressure.

With that thought, she decided to slip her feet back into her high heels. It would hurt like hell to stand in them for so long, but she absolutely refused to look like a barefoot hippie in front of her superiors. It was bad enough that she wasn't wearing stockings. Putting on her shoes, Sylvie lost her balance and fell against Jules. He grabbed her with pretend gallantry so that she wouldn't fall. His touch was like acid. She flinched and pushed him away with more force than intended. She could feel his surprise at the violence of her reaction.

Sylvie instinctively stepped farther back to get away from him, until her back hit the handrail hard enough that she winced. "Ouch." A bruise would form later, but she didn't mind. Even a bad bruise was better than Jules's touch.

The mere thought of being in physical contact with Jules made her want to retch. It was bad enough that over the past eight months she'd had to see Jules, work with him, talk to him, as if nothing had happened. Touching him was more than she could handle.

She moved as far away from Jules as she could manage in the tight space of the elevator, but it was pointless. Regardless of where she stood, she would always be within touching distance. It was tiny. They were so close that she could hear the others breathing. Her nostrils filled with the earthy scent of their perspiring bodies.

Sylvie slid along the handrail to get farther away, accidentally knocking off a jacket that had been folded over the rail. It fell on the marble floor with a metallic clang.

"What the hell was that?" Vincent asked.

"I dropped someone's jacket," said Sylvie, bending to pick it up.

She groped around on the floor in the dark to find it. Instead of grabbing hold of fabric, she touched something else. It was cold and hard. The shape was distinct. She knew exactly what it was the moment she ran her fingers over it.

"Why is there a gun here?" Sylvie asked.

"What do you mean, a gun?"

"I mean a gun, Vincent," said Sylvie. "A pistol, a handgun. It fell out of the jacket that I knocked down. Here," she said, handing it to Vincent. He examined it under the light of his phone.

"It's a Glock," he said. "And it's loaded."

He turned to address everyone.

"Who the hell brings a loaded Glock to a work meeting?"

TEN

SARA HALL

E veryone, say hello to Sara." Vincent stood behind me with his
hand on my right shoulder in what he probably intended to be a
reassuring gesture. The team was spread around a large table in a
meeting room, immersed in work.

As Vincent's words registered, their eyes shifted from their laptop
screens to me. I stood hesitantly in the doorway. I secretly cringed
under their piercing scrutiny. It gave me that awkward new-girl-at-
school feeling.

"Hi, Sara." I turned with relief in the direction of the first
friendly voice in the room.

"I'm Sam." Sam sat on a black swivel chair with his arms crossed
and a cynical twist to his lips that belied the friendly tone of his voice.
He had closely cropped blond hair that you could tell would be curly
if he let it grow, and large blue eyes that never missed a thing.

It was 9:00 A.M. on a Saturday morning and they'd taken small
liberties with the strict dress code. Jackets were flung over the backs
of chairs. Ties were loosened. Shirt collars were unbuttoned.

That was about as casual as it got at Stanhope and Sons. The firm was old-school. Casual clothes and jeans were banned in the office even on weekends.

Vincent guided me into the meeting room with his hand pressed against the small of my back. I felt led like a lamb to the slaughter. I would have wriggled away, but I was afraid of offending him. It was a relief when he let go of me to close the door.

The blinds had been pulled down over the glass walls as well as the floor-to-ceiling windows, which I only much later discovered had a partial view of the Statue of Liberty. The lack of natural light made the place gloomy even with the overhead lights turned on.

I'd arranged to go apartment hunting that morning, but Vincent quashed those plans with a single telephone call on Friday evening.

"Sara, I'm going to have to throw you into the deep end," Vincent said. "I was planning on moving you between different teams for a few weeks until you got the hang of things, but we don't have that luxury. We have a bake-off and we're under the gun."

"A what?"

"You'll get a hang of the jargon," he said, amused. "A bake-off is when we are competing with other banks to submit a proposal. In this case, it's for a possible acquisition. It means all hands on deck for the next two weeks, until the submission deadline."

"Oh," I said, mortified at my ignorance.

"Don't worry about it, Sara. You'll catch on quickly. That's why I hired you," he said. "I am done with arrogant, entitled Ivy League graduates who don't know the meaning of the word *scrappy*. Listen, the team is looking forward to meeting you. I'll see you at the office at nine A.M. tomorrow. Sharp."

It wasn't a request.

I texted the Realtor to cancel the rental viewings I'd booked. I was sorry to miss my appointment for a studio apartment in the East Village that sounded ideal. The Realtor had warned me that it would be snapped up quickly. Losing that dream apartment was my first taste of how the firm took precedence over everything. We had to be available as and when we were needed, short of a birth, death, or marriage. And sometimes even then.

Other than Sam, nobody else bothered to greet me as I entered the meeting room. They were absorbed in whatever they were doing on their laptops. I wasn't sure whether they didn't want to interrupt their train of thought by talking to me or if they didn't give a damn.

"Introduce Sara around, won't you." Vincent instructed Sam as he flicked through a file while still standing.

"Of course." Sam bounced up from his chair with an explosion of friendly charm that I sensed was never much more than skin-deep. "I have the dubious honor of leading the team on this project. Under Vincent's supervision, of course," Sam said, with a cheeky wink at Vincent.

"It goes without saying that everything that takes place between these four glass walls is strictly confidential," he told me. "We don't discuss it with wives, or husbands, or lovers, or mothers. Or roommates, for that matter. There are potential SEC violations for insider trading and other considerations that could get a person into very hot legal water if he or she decided to shoot his or her mouth off."

He took a deep breath to allow his words to sink in. "Do you understand where I'm coming from, Sara?"

"Of course," I said a bit too vehemently. I was offended that he thought it was necessary to tell me the obvious. I was not a college freshman. I had two degrees, including an MBA, with a major in corporate finance and investment banking. I knew the consequences of SEC violations. "We spent an entire day with legal during our induction discussing insider trading and other legal risks." I tried not to sound offended by his patronizing attitude.

"I hope they scared the living daylights out of you," he responded.

"They sure did."

I shifted my gaze across the room. Laptops were open, with power cords running everywhere, and document boxes were piled up against the back wall. Across the table were files heaped in piles threatening to spill over.

"I'll get introductions out of the way quickly so that I can put you to work." Sam gestured toward his other colleagues. "Sitting across the table on the left is Jules. He's the lawyer. That means you can't tell lawyer jokes when he's within earshot. Jules has very good hearing and very thin skin. You'll work closely with him—he's the guy usually telling us what we can't do. Right, Jules?"

"Hello, Sara," Jules said, looking at me with inscrutable smoky black eyes that contrasted sharply with his pale face. He flicked back a dark tuft of hair that had fallen across his forehead. "I won't come around to shake your hand. Too lazy and too tired to get up. We were here until two A.M. and then back again at seven this morning."

"You must all be exhausted," I said sympathetically.

"Nothing a Red Bull can't fix," he said, picking up an empty can and tossing it into the nearest wastebasket. "Your timing is perfect, Sara. We're thrilled to have you." I didn't miss the trace of sarcasm in his tone.

"I'm looking forward to getting to work," I responded.

"Good. We have about two months of work to do in twelve days, which means that you can forget about eating, sleeping, or, sadly, satisfying any carnal desires. At least until deadline day."

"Vincent warned me that I was in for a marathon few days," I said with a confident smile that I hoped conveyed that I wasn't daunted. "I eat very little, I'm good with virtually no sleep, and I don't know a soul in New York, unless you count the doorman of my hotel."

"Well, that never stopped anyone," muttered a leggy blond woman. She was sitting away from the table, with her long legs stretched out onto a second chair. Her skirt had hiked up onto her thighs, displaying her tanned and incredibly toned legs. She wore a crème-colored silk shirt. She had a navy jacket hanging on the back of her chair. The fabric of her shirt was sheer enough that I could see the outline of her bra.

Her long caramel blond hair fell in a curtain, covering her face as she worked on her laptop. She didn't bother looking up at me even when she spoke.

"Sylvie. Take a second to say hello to Sara, won't you? We've been begging Vincent for an extra pair of hands for weeks. Now that we have one, be nice to her, or she may run off to play with someone else."

"She'd be crazy if she did," said Sylvie, speaking about me as if I weren't there. "This is the most interesting project at the firm. I hope you're a fast learner, Sara. The last thing we want is someone who is needy and asks lots of questions. We told Vincent to find us an analyst who can get up to speed straightaway or not bother. We don't have time for stupid questions and hand-holding. Vincent seems to think that you're capable." Her tone suggested she was not convinced.

"She is," said Vincent, without looking up from the documents he was reading. "Sara will be great."

Sylvie lifted up her head for the first time and surveyed me. Her dubious expression turned into burning contempt. I felt as if I'd been slapped across the face.

Sylvie had a narrow chin and wide cheekbones that made her

look both fragile and exotic. She was tall, thin, and intimidating in her beauty.

Sylvie rose from her seat to her full height. Only Vincent was taller than she was. I assumed that she was standing up to shake my hand, and I stepped toward her like an exuberant puppy excited at being shown a crumb of affection. She ignored me and leaned over to take a bottle of Evian from a tray on the table.

She'd chosen a bottle of water that was just out of reach. She extended her hand to the bottle in a long, exaggerated feline stretch. She held that pose for several seconds, until the eyes of every man in the room, Vincent's included, were fixed on the tight fabric of her shirt. It had pulled across her breasts and left almost nothing to the imagination.

I had the impression that only Sylvie and I knew what was really going on. It was a primitive demonstration of power—her way of telling me that she was the alpha female and I shouldn't challenge her. Frankly, I don't know why she thought I'd be a threat. I'm five foot six, with shoulder-length brown hair and what I've been told is a dimple when I smile. Sylvie, by comparison, was a leggy goddess: a Barbie doll with brains and attitude.

When Sylvie knew that she had everyone's undivided attention, she twisted open the metal cap of the bottle, lifted her head back, and took a long sip. Then she put the bottle back on the table, flashed a victorious smile at me, and sat down to resume her work without bothering to drink any more of the water that she'd made such a fuss about seconds earlier. Nobody except for me noticed that Sylvie hadn't actually said hello to me or spoken to me directly. That turned out to be classic Sylvie—bitchy, hierarchical, and highly manipulative.

"Sara hasn't met the runt of the litter," said Sylvie once she'd settled back into her chair. "Shouldn't we introduce her?"

"My bad," said Sam as he turned toward a dark figure in the corner of the room. I'd briefly noticed her when Vincent and I first walked into the room. She was so silent and reserved that she blended into the background. I'd totally forgotten she was there.

"Last but not least, meet Lucy. She might not look like much, but she's probably the smartest person in the firm. Yours truly not withstanding, of course," said Sam.

At the sound of her name, Lucy looked up momentarily from her computer. She either hadn't heard or didn't care about the backhanded compliment. She had a pale, expressionless face, with eyes obscured by thick glasses that reflected the overhead lights. She was shorter than I, slight, with straight dark hair that she wore loose.

"I'm sorry. I don't mean to be rude." Lucy spoke in a monotone, without any inflection. "I'm working on some calculations and don't want to lose track. I look forward to having a coffee with you later and hearing your life story," she said in a slightly robotic tone, not meeting my eyes.

"She won't," whispered Sam.

"Won't what?"

"She always says that, but it won't happen. You should know Lucy's on the spectrum. She's learned to say what's expected, but she doesn't ever follow through. She's . . . awkward in social situations. I've known her for three years and we've never once had a coffee, or talked about anything other than work."

Lucy wore a black jacket over a pale shirt and a skirt that reached her knees. The outfit was drab. I found out later that Lucy was colorblind. Her mother came to her apartment every few weeks to make sure her clothes were properly paired up with suitable shirts and accessories. We could always tell when her mother was away, because Lucy would come to work in increasingly mismatched clothes. It was rumored that the head secretary for our department had instructions to call Lucy's mother when things started going downhill with her wardrobe. It was one of the concessions that was made for Lucy's idiosyncrasies, and her brilliance.

On that day of our first meeting, Lucy struck me as a computer nerd with Goth tendencies and an obvious inability to connect socially. She also seemed to be the most sincere person on the entire team. That said more about the team than about her.

"Find a place to sit and plug in your computer," Sam told me.

Vincent had slipped out while we were talking, without my noticing. I didn't see him again for almost five weeks. That was how it worked with Vincent. He traveled constantly and was highly secretive. He never gave anybody more information than he felt was absolutely necessary.

"I've emailed you a report, Sara," said Sam. "You'll need to print it out, proofread it, and fix every mistake. I don't care how small. I also need you to double-check all the calculations. Make sure the commas and decimal points are in the correct places. The firm lost a deal last year over an incorrectly placed decimal point in one fucking figure. Just one. The entire team responsible was fired. We have zero tolerance for mistakes."

"Sure," I said, opening the document on my computer. It was fifty pages long, with page after page of tables filled with numbers. It looked like it would take days to check it all. "How long do I have?"

"Five P.M.," said Sam.

It would be a hell of a job to go through the document with the detail he was asking for, redoing hundreds of calculations, by that afternoon. I wasn't actually sure it was humanly possible.

"Sara, just to be clear." Sylvie's voice was patronizing. "Your job is to make sure that everything written here is perfect. If there is so much as an unnecessary space after a period, you will be responsible for the consequences."

"Of course." I was irritated by her immediate assumption that I would screw up. Sylvie had blithely made it clear that I was a gopher. I'd do all the grunt work and take all the blame.

Over the weekend, when the secretarial staff were away, I did coffee and take-out runs. I sprinted to the copy room to collect printouts. It was my job to double-check everyone's numbers and proofread every word of the report the team was pulling together. We were going to go through a dozen drafts before we had the final document. I had to check each and every single line in every version.

Vincent was away somewhere in London, then Dubai, and after that Tokyo. He called in all the time and sent emails with instructions, both to the whole team and to some of us individually. Figures that he wanted pulled so he could look over them, reports retrieved from archives, or whatever else he needed on any given day. He knew what was going on to the last detail even though he was in a time zone on the other side of the world.

Sam spoke to him on the phone several times a day. Never in front of us. He'd disappear into an adjoining room and shut the door. Sylvie would bristle at being left out. Through the slats of the blinds, I'd see Sam pacing across the room while he spoke.

A couple of times, Sam and Jules would argue quietly about an issue. "We need to discuss this with Vincent." They would both storm out together to call him in the adjacent room.

Everything was secretive. Nobody updated me on the background of the deal that we were working on, or provided any other information. Everything that I knew, I gleaned from the report I was proofreading. I was new and untested. I had to earn their trust.

Late one night, Sylvie whispered loudly to Jules in the back corner of the room. "Vincent said that he didn't want her to know." They both stopped talking when I raised my head slightly.

They left, ostensibly to make coffee. Through the half-open door, I saw them standing in the corridor, having an animated discussion. They seemed to be at loggerheads. I tried not to look up. They silently disappeared into a meeting room down the corridor, where they remained for ages. When they came back into our meeting room, not a word was said. The secretiveness left me on edge.

We were constantly reminded about being discreet. The meeting room blinds were permanently down. Nobody except for us was allowed to come in, not even the admin staff helping us. The room was always locked when we weren't in it. That was a strict rule. There was a sign on the door to remind us.

For close to two weeks, I would leave work at two or three in the morning, returning to my hotel room for a shower and five hours' sleep. Six if I was lucky. Then I was back at the office for another day.

It was mentally grueling, especially because I was terrified that any mistake might get me fired before the probation period was over. Everyone was too busy to provide much in the way of explanations. Sylvie had made it clear that none of them would waste time answering dumb rookie questions. It was sink or swim. I swam.

"Does Sylvie not like me, or is she like this to everyone?" I asked Jules when he joined me on a late-night take-out run the night before our deadline.

"Sylvie is Sylvie," said Jules. "You'll get used to her. She's tough as nails, but that's probably because of what she's been through."

"What do you mean?"

"Haven't you heard of her?" There was a slightly incredulous note to his voice. "She was famous once, a top teenage model. The face of some brand like Miss Dior. You would have seen her face on the cover of magazines. She was cast in a Hollywood movie!"

"Really, which one?"

"Oh, I can never remember, but it doesn't matter. She never made the movie. Sylvie was damaged goods by then. In more ways than one."

"What do you mean?"

"Her twin brother, Carl, was killed in a car accident when they were seventeen. A witness said Sylvie made no effort to pull her brother clear of the wreckage before it was enveloped in flames. Sylvie denied it. Said she'd been drunk and couldn't get to him before the fire became too dangerous. I guess the cops bought her story. They didn't charge her. Maybe they figured that the burns were punishment enough; they killed her modeling career."

"What burns?"

"Haven't you noticed that she never wears anything sleeveless? Doesn't matter how hot it gets. Even when we traveled to Delhi and the weather was close to one hundred and twenty degrees, she still wore long sleeves."

The two of us walked into the Chinese restaurant across the street from our office building. The lady by the cash register passed Jules a paper bag with our order.

"How did Sylvie get into investment banking if she started off as a model?" I asked as we headed back to the office.

"Sylvie's smart. Well connected. Our clients think she's hot and they like working with her. But mostly, I think Sylvie's addicted to the adrenaline. We all are."

"She certainly seems to know her stuff," I said. We got into the elevator to go up to our office.

"I know she can be a bitch, but don't let it bother you," Jules advised. "It's par for the course in this business."

"I think I've grown a second layer of skin in the two weeks that I've been here," I joked.

Wasn't that the truth! They were a cliquey bunch. Jules, too, despite the occasional friendly overtures. Jules was a gossip. He loved getting information and then spreading it around to see what would happen. Jules was like a kid poking a stick into an ant nest to see how the ants responded.

None of the team made much of an effort to let me feel as if I belonged. They didn't once ask me if I'd found an apartment or how I'd settled in. They went out together sometimes, all of them except Lucy. I was never invited. Sylvie was the coldest of all of them. I had hoped that she and I could be allies. There were few enough women at the firm, you'd have thought we'd all stick together.

But that wasn't Sylvie's style at all. I had the distinct impression that she saw other women as a threat. Even me, despite the fact that I was a wet-behind-the-ears new recruit, while she'd already been at Stanhope for close to three years.

We had rare moments of friendship. The first was the day after the project had been submitted to the leadership team for approval. It was a Friday night and we were finishing off supplementary material for the submission. We both left work at 10:00 P.M. and found ourselves alone together in the elevator on our way out.

I'd moved into my new apartment two days earlier and hadn't had time to unpack, due to the killer hours we'd been working. A 10:00 P.M. finish was relatively early, and I figured that I'd spend what was left of the evening sorting out my bedroom, which was a mess of boxes. I smiled in the friendly way that you do when you have to stand in close proximity to a colleague in an elevator. Sylvie looked through me. Didn't say a word.

I thought to myself that was ridiculous. I'd spent more time with Sylvie over the previous days than I'd spent with Stacey, my roommate in Chicago, in over a year. Yet Sylvie and I weren't capable of having a superficial conversation in an elevator for two minutes.

Someone had to break the ice; I decided it would be me. Worst-case scenario, she'd rebuff me, which she'd already done so many times that I was immune to her snubs by that point.

"I'm not used to getting home this early," I joked. "Do you want to get a drink?"

She looked up from her phone in surprise. She hadn't expected me to say a word.

"Why not," she replied. "I know a place around the corner."

It was a bar, down a set of stairs, with a twenties vibe. A brass plaque alongside the red door said it had been a speakeasy during Prohibition. I ordered a margarita with lime. "I'll have the same," Sylvie told the bartender.

We drank two margaritas with silver sea salt from France on the rim, followed by a couple of shots. While we were drinking, a guy with a two-toned collar came in with a friend. They made a beeline for us.

You could tell he was a broker and thought he was hot shit. He wore Gordon Gekko–style suspenders to hold up his pants, and a brash tie.

"I'll cover their bill," he told the bartender as he pulled up a seat next to Sylvie at the bar.

"Thanks," I said. "We've already paid."

"Then I'll buy you more drinks," he offered, speaking too loudly.

"The night's still young, ladies," he said, checking his Rolex Submariner, despite the fact that there were clocks behind the bar for five cities around the world, including New York.

"We're done for the night," Sylvie said, getting up.

"Hang on." He put his hand on Sylvie's arm. "We've only just met. Jimmy and I would like to get to know you two girls a little better."

"We would have liked that," said Sylvie, without making much effort to disguise the sarcasm. "But we have an early-morning meeting."

"On a Saturday? The markets aren't even open. Give me your boss's number. I'll explain that his beautiful secretary needs some time off."

"You're not very good at hearing the word *no*, are you?" I said, pushing his hand off Sylvie. "She was trying very politely to let you down easy. You're not her type. You're at least ten years too old and thirty pounds too heavy. Plus, you're at least two inches too short. Probably in more than one department." And with that, we walked out.

Suspenders man and his sidekick shouted something after me. I think it was something to the effect of us being lesbians, but we couldn't really hear them because we were laughing so hard.

"Oh my God," said Sylvie when we'd climbed the steps back to street level. "That was hilarious. I haven't laughed this hard in ages. Now I have to pee!"

"Well, you'd better do it at my place. No way we're going back in there."

We took a cab to my apartment. It was five blocks away. Much closer than Sylvie's place, which was all the way uptown.

I'd taken up the lease from a colleague sent on a ten-month assignment to another company. I saw the ad on the notice board in the lunch area at the office and figured I might as well take it. I realized there would be no spare time to go looking for places.

I shared the apartment with Amanda, a management consultant who was on the road five days out of seven. It was decorated with Ikea furniture and felt more like a cheap hotel than a cosy apartment. It was a place to sleep—I already understood that most of my waking hours would be spent at work, so the lack of character and back-alley view from my bedroom window made little difference to me.

Amanda wasn't home that night; she was in Atlanta for two weeks. Sylvie and I ended up watching a movie and drinking homemade hot chocolate. Sylvie went home by cab sometime after 1:00 A.M.

I was back at work the following morning at 8:00 A.M. It was my three-week anniversary at the firm, but it felt as if I'd been there for six months. I supposed that was almost accurate if I added up all the hours that I'd worked.

Sylvie waltzed into the office not long after I arrived. In contrast to my washed-out face and hair tied back into a severe knot, Sylvie looked amazing, as if she'd had twelve hours' sleep and a morning facial.

I went out for a coffee run and brought lattes back upstairs for everyone. The seat near Sylvie was empty, so I figured I'd sit near her. After all, we were buddies now. The ice had well and truly melted when she'd vomited into my toilet bowl while I held her hair away from her face.

Before I could sit on the chair, she pulled it over and slipped her legs onto it. It was the exact pose she'd been in on the first day we'd met. There was no apology. She didn't even look in my direction.

Sylvie picked up a two-inch-thick report and began to work with her laptop on her knees. All morning, she didn't so much as turn her head to acknowledge me. I didn't know if she was more embarrassed that she'd socialized with me or that she'd shown me she was human.

In retrospect, I think she didn't give a hoot either way. That was Sylvie. One day she was your best friend and the next she was your mortal enemy.

ELEVEN

THE ELEVATOR

Vincent held the cold metal grip of the Glock in his hands as he surveyed the shadowed faces of his colleagues. "Would someone please answer my question? Who brings a loaded gun to a meeting?"

The ceiling vent noisily pumped out a fresh cycle of warm air. An awkward silence hung over them.

"I do," said Jules finally. More silence followed. "I was mugged a few months ago," he added defensively. "Pistol-whipped. You saw the bruises, Vincent. After that, I bought a gun for protection. When I received the message about this meeting, telling me—no, let's be more precise here—ordering me to turn up at night, in a remote part of the South Bronx . . . there was no way that I was going to come to this neighborhood unarmed."

"I don't actually think it's legal for you to carry a concealed weapon," Vincent replied. He tested the weight of the gun in his hands, moving it from one hand to the other. There was a magazine in the gun. It was loaded and ready to fire.

"What, are you, a cop now? Vincent, give it back." Jules hated the pleading note in his voice. It was his damn gun and he shouldn't need to beg. Everything felt out of control in the dark, choking claustrophobia. Jules suddenly needed that gun desperately. He'd do anything to get it.

"I'll give it back to you when we get out," Vincent promised.

"You have no goddamn right," hissed Jules.

He stepped toward Vincent in a fury. He tried to snatch the gun from Vincent's hand, but his boss shifted the gun to his other hand faster than Jules could seize it in the dark. He passed it back between his hands as Jules lunged for it again. They scuffled over the gun like children fighting over a favorite toy.

"Give it to me, Vincent," Jules practically shouted. The claustrophobia and incessant heat had made him lose all restraint. "You can't confiscate my property. It's my gun and I want it back."

Vincent pushed Jules's hands away once more and took a step back to evade him. It was a mistake. Vincent had backed himself into the corner of the elevator and now had nowhere to go. He was trapped. Jules came up so close, their faces were practically touching. Vincent put the hand holding the gun up above his head.

"It's mine," Jules said again. He grabbed for the gun but instead knocked Vincent's glasses off his face. They fell to the floor before either of them realized what happened. Jules lunged for the gun again and they all heard the glasses crack under his shoe.

Jules knew that without his glasses, Vincent was at a disadvantage in the dark. He tried again to grab the gun, reaching behind Vincent's back. "You don't have any right to—"

Vincent kneed him in the groin before he could finish his sentence. Jules fell to his knees in agony.

"You bastard," Jules half-whispered when he was able to speak again. "You brought us here deliberately, didn't you? Vincent? It's another one of your sick games. Always pitting us against one another. Always testing us."

Vincent tucked the gun into his belt at the small of his back. He put out his hand and helped Jules up. "Think whatever you like," Vincent said as he lifted him to his feet. "I didn't set up any of this. But I can tell you one thing: No way in hell am I letting anyone as short-tempered as you hold on to a loaded weapon in an elevator."

Sylvie stood between Jules and Vincent. Both men were breathing heavily after their confrontation. She knew Jules well enough to know that he was gone but not out. He'd get his strength back and, when Vincent least expected it, Jules would hit back in the only way he knew how—below the belt.

She'd been almost as shocked to see how Jules had confronted Vincent as she'd been to find his gun lying on the floor. Jules had always held Vincent in the highest regard. It wasn't just because Vincent was his boss and the center of power in their division; it was a respect that ran deeper than that. Jules craved Vincent's praise. When he received it, he glowed with pleasure. When Vincent gave him a dressing-down, it was like watching a dog getting beaten with a stick. She always felt bad for Jules when that happened. Even after she'd come to hate him.

Sylvie suspected that Jules saw Vincent as a father figure, even though there was only a nine-year age gap between the two men. Jules's father had lost interest in him after his mother died. He was sent to boarding school a few months later, and from there he went straight to college. His father was on to wife number four by the time he graduated. All of Jules's stepmothers produced copious offspring.

Jules had gone from being the sole heir to a sizable family fortune to being one of many beneficiaries of a dwindling inheritance, which his father had squandered on alimony and bad investments.

Jules barely spoke to his father. He was bitter that he'd have to share whatever remained of his beloved grandfather's fortune with seven half siblings he barely knew.

Vincent pointed Jules's Glock toward the floor. He removed the magazine in one smooth motion with a loud click of metal. Then he pulled back on the slide to empty the chamber. A clatter echoed as a bullet fell to the floor. Vincent shoved the gun back in place under his belt.

"That should never have happened," he said. "Now let's get going. So far we've only figured out two clues."

"Vincent, I'm sorry about your glasses," said Jules, suddenly contrite. "I'll reimburse you. I shouldn't . . . I shouldn't have reacted like that. I don't like being in enclosed places. It makes me jittery. And it's so damn hot in here that I can't think straight."

"All the more reason for you not to be carrying a loaded weapon," said Vincent. "Now come on, everyone, let's look around again. We have just over thirty minutes left to solve this thing."

Vincent had been a lieutenant in the Dutch forces in Afghanistan. He'd done a two-year tour before his university studies. It had given him an authority and confidence that other students his age lacked. It was one of the reasons why he'd quickly risen up the ranks after joining Stanhope, first as an intern and then as a graduate recruit. He had leadership qualities that were unteachable at any place of higher education, an authority that came from being responsible for the lives of other soldiers from a young age.

Vincent's authority also came from his physical appearance. His height was imposing—he was close to six foot three—and he had wide shoulders and blue eyes so piercing that people looked away because it felt as if he were stripping down their soul.

Vincent always wore pristine shirts and suits to work. He bought top-of-the-line Zegna. People mistakenly thought it was because he was status-conscious, but he didn't much care about labels. What he cared about was efficiency. With Zegna, it was a one-stop shop. Once a year, he'd walk into a store, put down thirty grand, and sort out his wardrobe for the next twelve months. While he looked like a well-dressed businessman at the office, at the gym, where Vincent did mixed martial arts each morning, he looked like a street fighter. He had a tattoo with Chinese characters snaked around the bicep of his right arm, and in the middle of his chest he had the insignia of his unit in the Royal Netherlands Army, a sword pointing upward, with the initials of each of his men underneath. Nobody at work had ever seen his tattoos.

After two years at the firm, Vincent had been chosen to lead his own dedicated team. It was part of a strategy to set up crack, multi-disciplined teams that were small and nimble. Jules, Sam, and Sylvie had all been assigned to Vincent from the start.

Vincent had dark blond hair in those days. In recent years, he kept his hair so short that it looked almost shaved. He had a wide face, with broad cheekbones and a sculptured chin. To those he cared about, Vincent was principled and fair, and he showed patience that was unusual for someone of his stature.

But to his enemies, he was utterly ruthless. People were wary of crossing Vincent. They could sense a violent streak underneath the surface. He lived by a strict moral code of hard work and diligence, which had been the values of his childhood. Vincent drank but never to the point of excess. In an industry in which popping pills to cope with grueling hours and stress was par for the course, Vincent's only pick-me-up was a glass of organic wheatgrass each morning. He never drank coffee. His only caffeine was from green tea.

Vincent had changed in the years since she'd first met him, Sylvie thought. He'd weakened. His authority had eroded. Perhaps it was because Mitch Graves, one of his biggest supporters on the board, had retired. Or maybe it was because the last six months had been brutal for the team. They'd had a bad run of losing key accounts.

Vincent had been getting increasingly frustrated recently. Office gossip suggested the executive team was losing confidence in him. He'd been nervous lately. Volatile.

Sylvie considered it a further sign of Vincent's diminishing influence that Jules had felt confident enough to confront him so aggressively. Jules had reminded Sylvie of a young male gorilla challenging a silverback. Vincent had drawn first blood and Jules was suitably chastened. For now anyway.

Vincent had always been an enigma to his subordinates. He had an apartment in TriBeCa, and another in Amsterdam, which he rented out. Other than that, Vincent kept his private life just that.

When Sylvie occasionally bumped into Vincent at the theater or a restaurant, his dates were always pretty dark-haired girls. She always thought that his clear preference for brunettes explained why he'd never made a play for her, even before he became her direct manager. That was a rare experience for Sylvie; Vincent's lack of interest in her had always grated.

Many times, she'd telephoned him late at night or early in the morning for urgent work matters, and a few times, she had heard the movements of someone else in the background—the rustle of sheets or a running shower. He'd never brought his girlfriends to office functions. He'd always been circumspect about discussing his private life.

"I think I've found our next clue." Sam broke the silence abruptly. It made them all jump in surprise. He pointed the light of his phone up at a corner at the top of the elevator. When the others looked closely, they saw a string of letters written on the wall.

"Has that been there all this time, right above our heads? How didn't we see it earlier?" said Sylvie.

"I don't think it was there before," Sam said. "I could swear I looked there earlier. Maybe it's been revealed by the heat. It's right by the vent."

Jules wrote the letters down on a section of the mirrored elevator wall, using a marker pen that he took from his bag. The clue looked unsolvable. A jumble of random letters.

IPX NVDI EP ZPV USVTU FBDI PUIFS?

TWELVE

SARA HALL

S o what do you think about investment banking after your first
month on the job?"

Sam asked the question while cutting into a steak at Delmonico's.
Sam had been standoffish since I'd joined the team. After weeks of
being treated like a lackey, it felt strange to be sitting in an expensive restaurant, watching Sam cut into a sixty-dollar steak. As if he
really cared about my impressions of the firm.

"Is it everything you expected, Sara?"

"I'm loving it. Still getting used to the lack of sleep, of course. I
don't think I've slept more than six hours a night since I started."

"As my old man used to say, you can sleep when you're dead. Or
in our case, when you're retired at forty."

That was the fantasy of every investment banker I'd ever met: to
retire at forty. Few managed to pull it off. The men developed a taste
for trophy wives, expensive yachts, summer houses, and all the other
accoutrements of wealth. Not to mention the financial burden of multiple alimonies and child support.

Then there was the constant adrenaline rush that came with the work, which became almost as addictive as the drugs many took to get through the brutal hours. From the finest Colombian blow to a smorgasbord of amphetamines, from Adderall to Quaaludes and every letter in between. Those addictions kept people in the game long after they wanted to quit.

We had only forty minutes for lunch, so I was surprised that Sam insisted on going to Delmonico's, a steak house known for its long liquid lunches and oversize steaks. It turned out he'd taken all of that into consideration. Sam had ordered our meals on the way to the restaurant. Within thirty seconds of us sitting down, our food was brought out. He'd arranged it all with military precision.

Sam had ordered a medium-rare rib-eye steak. I had the grilled sole. I shook my head when he asked me if I wanted wine. We had a client meeting that afternoon and I didn't think it was a good idea to get soused.

"You're right." Sam sighed as he waved away the waiter holding the wine list. "This meeting will be tricky enough even if we're sober." It was with a Japanese consortium, and the nondisclosure agreements that we'd had to sign just to talk with them could have filled three volumes of the *Encyclopædia Britannica*.

I'd already been firmly instructed by Sylvie that during the meeting I was to sit at the back of the room and keep my mouth shut. She'd had a whispered argument the previous day with Sam about his decision to allow me to attend. "It's too soon," she'd hissed. "Sara doesn't know enough to be useful." In the end, they'd agreed that I could attend as long as I didn't say a word.

I suppose that I should have been honored that they were letting me near a client so soon. Lucy was never taken to meetings with clients. I overheard Jules once say that Lucy was "too weird to put in front of a client." They'd leave her at the office but covertly consult her by text message when they needed some quick number crunching. They cashed in on her genius without our clients ever knowing who the real brains behind all our sophisticated financial strategies was.

Most client meetings were held during the day, usually in the afternoons, or occasionally over lunch. Some evenings, Sam and Jules would disappear for drinks with clients. Sylvie was never invited. Just two nights earlier, Jules and Sam had left abruptly in the early evening for a client meeting. I asked Sylvie why she wasn't joining them. She stared at me. Shocked by my naïveté.

"They're going to a strip joint, Sara."

"Isn't that a bit, I don't know, circa 1955? Who conducts business at a strip joint in this day and age?"

"Sara, topless bars are where some of the biggest deals on Wall Street are cut," she said. "Right now their CFO is probably putting a fifty-dollar bill into a stripper's G-string while using his other hand to initial a billion-dollar takeover."

"Doesn't that mean you get left out of all the glory?" I asked.

"They'd feel awkward with women around," she said, without any irony. "And I would find it bizarre if they ever asked me to join them."

Just as Sylvie predicted, Sam and Jules arrived at work the following morning to brashly announce that the parameters of the deal had been finalized over the course of five hours of binge drinking and lap dances.

"You must have wrapped up early last night," said Sylvie, eyeing them both. They were freshly shaved, with healthy pink complexions.

"Not really. We finished at four A.M.," said Jules.

"You've had four hours' sleep! It doesn't show at all," I said. "What's your secret?"

"Tea bags," said Jules with a straight face. "I freeze used tea bags and put them on my eyes while I do my stomach crunches in the morning. Sam uses bee-venom serum, but I can't because I'm allergic."

It turned out that eye cream was a big topic of conversation among male investment bankers. Women at least had the option of putting on extra concealer when we looked run-down. In an industry notorious for long hours, it was probably our only advantage.

Despite Sylvie's apparent indifference to being excluded from the after-hours client meeting, I could tell from the tight set of her mouth that she was not happy they'd finalized the deal without her. I knew that she had done an incredible amount of work behind the scenes. She'd negotiated most of the key points of the deal through exhaustive meetings over several weeks. All Sam and Jules had really done was ensure the agreement was signed.

From their boasting around the office and at the celebratory drinks they arranged, most people without inside knowledge would have assumed Sam and Jules were the ones responsible for the deal.

Not that I felt bad for Sylvie. She was a big girl. She knew how to manipulate things better than most. I suspected that it wasn't so much our colleagues' credit that worried Sylvie. She was afraid that Sam and Jules would get a bigger share of the bonus from the deal, when all they'd really done was get the client drunk enough to sign a memorandum of understanding.

The atmosphere was tense for weeks afterward. Sylvie tried to undermine both of them in a dozen different ways to get back at them. It was nothing new. There was always an undercurrent of conflict in the firm. The air crackled with a permanent sense of distrust. In the firm's toxic worldview, conflict was good. Conflict made people work harder and act smarter. It made them ruthless.

"There are winners and losers in this world," Sam told me as he wolfed down his steak that day over lunch at Delmonico's. "So pick a side, Sara, and don't ever look back at the trail of people you've trampled into the ground. You don't owe them a thing. Success is not for the squeamish."

THIRTEEN

THE ELEVATOR

They stood together in the gloomy darkness, trying to decipher the letters of the next clue. Bunched together, they reminded Sam of canned sardines. Entombed in a small metal box. Cooking in their own juices, as it were, with the heater blasting on high and sweat pouring down their bodies. They were barely able to stretch or move without bumping into one another.

They went through the motions of trying to solve the code, but it was beyond their abilities. Sam knew it. They all did. If Lucy had been around, she'd have solved it in sixty seconds. He wasn't sure if they'd be able to solve it in a lifetime.

Sam wanted out. Not just from the elevator but from all of it. His life had been spinning out of control for a long time. Materially, he'd more than achieved his goals, but he wished he could go back in time and change many of the decisions that he'd made along the way.

He often thought back to the Sam Bradley he'd been as a kid. The idealist impatient to go out into the world and make a difference, like an overambitious home decorator who thought that a new roll of wallpaper would fix a crooked wall.

Sam had wanted to become a human rights lawyer. "Can you imagine!" he'd say, long after he'd grown out of his idealistic phase. How many people had he amused over the years with hoots of drunken laughter, telling that story at rowdy Wall Street parties?

He wondered how he'd let his optimism morph into a hard shell of cynicism. The Sam Bradley of his youth would have hated the man that he now was. As the years passed, he increasingly agonized over the possibility that he'd let himself down. Worse than that, he'd let down his dead father, who'd always put more store in values than in money.

As much as he despised his life, Sam was addicted to it. His salary had become his morphine. His designer watches, suits, shoes, ski trips, cars, homes, and wife had become his coke. His success had become his heroin. It was killing him softly. Brutal hours at work, backroom machinations. Not to mention the pulsating stress that was a constant undercurrent of his life.

Sam longed—with a nostalgia so sweet that it almost hurt—for the simple, modest world in which he'd been raised. At the same time, he shuddered at the very thought of ever returning to it.

Since hearing about the planned layoffs via the rumor mill, he'd been feeling anxious for weeks. He worried that it was the beginning of the end for him. That he'd hit his peak and his career would be all downhill from here.

He didn't believe Vincent's claim that their performance here might offer a reprieve. That solving mindless clues in an escape-room elevator would somehow reassure the firm that he, or any of them, for that matter, was worth keeping on the payroll.

For what felt like the dozenth time, Sam examined the jumble of random letters on the glass elevator wall, where Jules had written them in neat letters. IPX NVDI EP ZPV USVTU FBDI PUIFS?

"It's indecipherable," Sam complained in frustration. "I can't see how we can possibly solve it."

There was still a good twenty-five minutes until their time in the escape room was up, and, judging by everyone's expressions, nobody had the faintest idea how to solve this puzzle. He sensed that Jules and Sylvie had given up and were prepared to wait it out until the end of their escape-room session rather than make the effort of cracking the code transcribed on the wall.

"Let's all work on it separately," suggested Vincent. "We'll come together in five minutes and share what we've come up with."

Sam typed the letters into his phone. IPX NVDI EP ZPV USVTU FBDI PUIFS?

He was good at this sort of stuff, but his mind kept drifting to bigger problems. The conversation with Kim earlier had upset him more than he'd cared to admit.

He'd been sitting in the backseat of a chauffeured Town Car as it crawled through the traffic near the corner of Second Avenue and East Sixty-sixth. The cars around him blended into a kaleidoscope of colors as they snarled in the low light of dusk, waiting for the traffic lights to change. The oncoming headlights were almost blinding. He swallowed hard. He couldn't delay it any further. He had to call Kim to tell her that he wouldn't be able to make their flight to Antigua.

It wouldn't be the first holiday that he'd missed, though it was probably the most important. Kim insisted the trip to Antigua was "do or die" for their marriage. "It's time to show who you love more," she'd said, "me or Stanhope."

Kim was already at the airport with the twins, waiting for him to arrive, when he telephoned her. He gave her the bad news quickly.

Before she could say a word, he quickly promised to take the next flight or the one after that. He swore on his life that he'd get to Antigua by Saturday afternoon at the latest, even if he had to ride shotgun on a DHL flight.

"Honey." Pause. "Honey." His tone was placating.

"Honey. Let me explain." He put his phone on speaker and scrolled through his emails as he let Kim talk without interruption. Slight eye roll. He folded his arms as he was forced to endure another barrage.

"I know we've been planning this trip for ages. Kim. Honey." He interrupted her before she could get going again. His voice rose slightly in irritation. "I *know* how much you're looking forward to it." He opened an attachment to an email. "I've been looking forward to it, too."

He allowed a note of sincerity to enter his voice as he zoomed in to analyze the figures in a chart at the bottom of the email. "Believe me, Kim, I don't want to be here, but I didn't have any choice in the matter. It's an important meeting." Pause. "You're right, I do always say that, but this one really is. I wish I could get out of it. I tried. Honest to God, Kim, I tried. I read Vincent the riot act, but he absolutely insisted. I'll fly out straight afterward. I promise." Pause. "Kim? Honey?"

The line was dead. He was more relieved than angry that she'd ended the call without warning. It saved him the effort of lying to get off the phone. Plus, it gave him the higher ground.

Sam's phone vibrated. Kim was calling him back. He pressed the speaker button to answer it.

"Kim," he said. No response. He was about to disconnect when a foulmouthed torrent spat out of the speaker of his phone. Kim spoke so fast and with such fury that most of her words were unintelligible, except for the last few before she disconnected again.

"You *fuck*!" She yelled so loudly that his driver's head snapped back against the leather headrest. "You sad fuck!"

Sam had mulled over Kim's words all the way to his destination in the South Bronx. All the way into the escape room. All through their childish game of hunting clues in the overheated elevator with the vague promise it might guarantee them their jobs, though that felt like a cheap door prize to Sam.

Kim was right. He *was* a sad fuck. He'd become a slave—to Stanhope, to Kim, and, most of all, to his own ego. What price would he pay for being a no-show for their flight to Antigua? It would not come cheap, especially as Kim had made it a test of his commitment to their marriage. Kim had talked of little else since she'd been offered a place at the exclusive resort. It was usually booked up by movie stars or trust-fund kids. Kim said they were lucky to get in.

He wasn't sure if luck had anything to do with it. The resort charged eight thousand dollars a night for a private beachside villa with its own infinity pool. That wasn't including taxes or service charges, or meals.

He'd stood Kim up, but he assured himself that he had nothing to feel guilty about. After all, it was his work at Stanhope and Sons that produced the money that funded Kim's exorbitant holidays.

It wasn't a huge hardship for Kim to fly alone to the Caribbean with their two-year-old twins. They were booked in business class and the resort had a baby-sitting service. Kim could enjoy herself, unencumbered by the toddlers. She'd barely be inconvenienced. Sam would arrive before she developed tan lines. Maybe even before dawn broke. He'd pay whatever it took. It would still work out cheaper than if it pushed Kim over the edge and she followed through on her frequent, thinly veiled threats of divorce.

That thought reminded Sam to focus on the escape room. He needed to play the game. He needed to show that he was an asset to the firm so that Stanhope wouldn't retrench him, and might even promote him to Eric Miles's vacant job.

He thought about how he'd make it up to Kim. He'd buy her jewelry. That's what he usually did. Last time it had been earrings, the time before a bracelet. There'd need to be at least one diamond. Kim's taste in jewelry was as extravagant as her temper.

Sam looked at the jumble of letters on the wall once more. IPX NVDI EP ZPV USVTU FBDI PUIFS? It made no sense whatsoever. He reworked the letters into a different order on his phone. The result was as mystifying as the original had been. As mystifying as my marriage, he thought.

They'd had many arguments about the same thing: Kim barely got to see him. He racked up eighty to ninety hours a week at work. He routinely missed dinner parties, weekend trips, and holidays. When he did get home, he barely had enough time to screw Kim and get five hours' sleep before he had to turn around and go back to the office.

It had been like that since they were first married. They'd been married for six years and had only managed to spend three anniversaries together. He'd almost missed the birth of his daughters two years ago. He was in Toronto, with a blizzard about to hit, when Kim had gone into labor three weeks early. He'd pulled in every favor he was ever owed, and then some, to get a seat on the last flight out. It went to Boston. He took a train back the rest of the way. Kim was being prepped for a caesarean at Mount Sinai when he burst through the delivery room's doors. Three hours later, he was back on the phone, discussing the finer points of a credit swap with a client.

"You promised that you wouldn't do this to me," Kim rasped once she'd come out of surgery.

"I'm sorry, Kimmi." Back then, those words still meant something.

Later, when Kim was in her five-star maternity suite, he reminded her, and his guilty conscience, that she lived the life of a princess purely because of the work that he did and the schedule that he kept. Without him, she'd be a preschool teacher in Queens, wiping kids' snotty noses. He hadn't said that, but he'd thought it often enough. He knew that deep down she thought it, too.

"Kim, listen." He was cradling their baby daughters in his arms, sitting on the edge of her hospital bed. "If you want me to quit my job and find work in consulting, then I'll do that. The hours will be better. We can cut back on our expenses to manage on a smaller salary. Maybe that's better, if it means that I get to spend more time with you and our beautiful babies."

It worked. Kim hadn't raised the issue of his punishing work schedule since. Not until recently. When she did, he knew that she wasn't upset about his long hours. She was upset because she suspected he was having an affair.

Sam could tell from the suspicious tone in her voice whenever he called to tell her he was staying overnight at their apartment in the city. Recently, she'd taken to phoning at odd hours. It was obvious that she was checking up on him.

Kim's instincts were good. They always had been. The only thing she'd gotten wrong was that he wasn't having an affair, at least not in the traditional sense. It was a transaction.

For the past year, he'd taken to hiring call girls every now and again. Maybe once or twice a month. He only ever booked with Magdelina's, a high-end agency that provided models for parties and for what was euphemistically called "private entertainment." For a substantial fee.

Sam was never particular about which girl he ended up with. From his experience, every girl on the agency's books was a stunner. He had a preference for girls with long legs and big tits. He was less concerned about their coloring. There were blondes, brunettes, and redheads. It suited him well; he liked variety. There were girls from California, the Midwest, Brazil, and France, and quite a few from Russia. Whichever girl turned up at his door at midnight was always sexy as hell and showed him a good time.

Then he met Trixie. After that, he wanted only her. She was blond, originally from Georgia. She had an authentic Southern accent to prove it. She charged one thousand dollars for a two-hour session. Three times that rate if he wanted her to stay all night, and he usually did. He felt no guilt. Compared to the other guys at work, he was practically a saint. They went through girls the way Kim collected handbags. The lies they told their wives and girlfriends were pure artistry. Until recently, Sam had never thought he was capable of that level of guile.

He never imagined that he'd cheat on Kim when he said his vows on their wedding day. He'd imagined they'd have the "till death do us part" Catholic marriage that his parents had shared. But eventually he came to the conclusion that was impossible. His parents had been married at a different time, in different circumstances. His father hadn't faced the sort of temptation that Sam experienced on a daily basis.

Sam worshipped his dad, though he was the first to admit that there was little he did to follow in his footsteps. His dad had been devoted to his mother until his dying day; Sam barely lasted two years before he first cheated on Kim. That's if he didn't count an encounter before their wedding with one of the bridesmaids, Kim's closest childhood friend. He didn't. It was after the rehearsal dinner and they were both drunk. He felt awful about it afterward.

In his first three years at the firm, Sam earned more than his dad made in his entire lifetime. He'd never imagined earning that kind of money when he was a kid growing up in the poorest neighborhood in Suffolk County. His dad was a high school math and physics teacher who taught at the best public school on Long Island to support his wife and five sons. Sam was the eldest. While his father gave other people's kids the best education on the island, by virtue of their school district and their father's meager salary, his own children were forced to attend the worst school on Long Island. The locals called Sam's school "Rikers High."

If it hadn't been for his easy charm and sharp mind, Sam might well have fallen over the edge, like so many of his school friends. Meth addicts. Petty thieves. Rap sheets for breaking and entering.

Sam had done some stupid stuff after his dad died—smashing headlights, small-time shoplifting. He was never caught, but his mother found out. That was worse. She reminded him that he had four younger brothers who would follow whatever example he set.

He made a concerted effort to reach a 3.9 GPA. He nailed it. He applied to three colleges and was accepted at all of them. In the end, he opted for a small Roman Catholic school in New Hampshire that offered him a generous scholarship. There he completed his four-year undergraduate degree in three years, thanks to extra subjects that he took at summer school. His stellar marks won him a place at Wharton. He paid his MBA fees with a combination of scholarships, financial aid, and income earned tutoring and driving cabs at night. He was recruited as an analyst at Stanhope and Sons two months before graduation.

It took years for Sam to claw his way up the ladder at the firm. He still had a few more rungs to go to reach the top. Like Everest, the final ascent was the toughest. His rivals were all cut from the same cloth. Political animals—ambitious and ruthless. They'd sell out their grandma in a heartbeat if that's what it took to cut a deal or get a promotion. Sam was no different. His Catholic guilt had long fallen by the wayside. Money, he learned, absolved even the guiltiest conscience.

Sam looked down at his dark gray shoes. They'd cost him twelve hundred dollars. He had a dozen pairs just like them in his closet. They were his way of giving the finger to the austerity of his childhood.

Lately, he'd had nightmares that he was flat broke. The more he earned, the more Kim spent. He was making stinking amounts of money, but it barely covered their expenses. He made enough for them to live like millionaires. The trouble was that Kim wanted to live like a billionaire. He couldn't pull it off. God knows, he'd tried.

He bought a house in Westchester. Kim wanted to live near her friends. Their house was a faux French château. It had six bedrooms. They used only two of them. The roof was gray slate, with protruding attic windows reminiscent of a Parisian mansion. When he bought the house, he thought it more classy than kitsch. He soon came to realize he was mistaken. It was kitsch on steroids. Just like his life. He cringed every time he drove through its black cast-iron gates.

In no time, Kim began to complain that the house was too small, too dark. There was a smell of mildew in the front living room. The pool wasn't long enough to swim laps, not that she ever used it. The kitchen was old-fashioned, and there was no space for a tennis court.

"You should move to Queens," Sam's mom advised him. He was driving her to the train station after a weekend visit, during which

Kim had complained incessantly about the house. "Better to have the biggest house on the street than the smallest." His mother always had a knack of putting things in perspective. So had his father.

Shit, he thought. He needed to focus. His mind returned to the jumble of letters in front of him. IPX NVDI EP ZPV USVTU FBDI PUIFS?

He asked himself what his dad would have done in the same situation. Ever the high school teacher, his dad had always espoused the concept of Occam's razor: The simplest answer is usually the right one.

It gave him an idea. What if the letters were one before the real ones in the alphabet, or one after? They would be the obvious options in the absence of any key to the code.

He tried transposing the letters on the screen of his phone. Instead of *I* he tried one option with a *J* and another with an *H*. He went through the sentence, testing both options. The first option, he quickly realized, resulted in gibberish. The second produced a coherent sentence.

"I have it," he called out, as if he'd just won a race. "I've solved the code."

"What does it say?" Jules asked.

Sam turned his phone around so they could all see the solution to the code on the screen.

"How much do you trust each other?"

FOURTEEN

SARA HALL

Professor Niels, an economics professor at my business school, once asked the class a question that not even the smartest students could answer. "What's the scarcest resource in the world?"

Students put up their hands and had all sorts of answers. Rhodium, osmium, and iridium were among some of the more educated guesses.

"You're all wrong," he said when we'd run out of guesses. "The scarcest resource in the world is time."

It was only when I started working at Stanhope that I understood what he meant. It was basic arithmetic, really. If you were working eighteen hours a day, that meant you had six hours to get home, sleep, and somehow arrive at work the next morning looking the part. For those with wives or husbands, and kids, that effectively meant seeing their families only on weekends. They'd get home long after their loved ones had gone to bed, and they'd leave long before they woke up.

Maintaining a semblance of a personal life required remarkable multitasking and time-management skills. I once overheard a guy from our bonds desk tell a colleague how he fits in twenty minutes a day with his two-year-old daughter. He did it by putting her on his lap while he did stomach crunches. She'd hold a picture book and he'd read it while lifting up and clenching his abs for the time it took to read a page. He said it was the only way he could read to her and maintain his washboard stomach.

It wasn't said purely out of vanity. Looking good was a huge deal at Stanhope. It was practically a requirement of the job. Our senior management didn't want a bunch of fat schmoes representing the company. We had to look as exclusive as the brand.

That meant looking fit, toned, and tanned. That was ironic, given everything about our lifestyle was unhealthy. Long hours and stress were just the tip of the iceberg. Some people sat glued to their trading screens for most of the day; they barely moved. We had little to no opportunity to go outside and get a natural tan because we were working from dawn to dusk. So we had to fake it with visits to tanning salons and by slathering on tanning cream any chance we got. Everyone was neurotic about eye lotions. Nobody wanted to come to work with dark rings under their eyes, even if they were working almost around the clock. Everything we did was to project the impression of vigor. Inside, we were withering.

"The fact is that twenty-four-hour days aren't enough for people in our line of work," said Sam during a catch-up over lunch. He had appointed himself my unofficial mentor. Since our first steak lunch, he'd met with me weekly to share useful tips to navigate the confounding complexity of our firm and its mysterious social mores and hierarchies.

"Yeah, there aren't enough hours in the day," I agreed. "Especially lately."

"This is nothing," said Sam. "People these days are pussies. When I started, it was even tougher. We had three major M&As and the markets were going wild. There were times when I would come into the office on a Monday morning and I wouldn't leave until midnight on Wednesday. If I was lucky, I would grab a few hours on a couch somewhere. Go down to the fitness center for a shower in the morning, pop some Adderall, and, wham, it was a new day."

"Sounds like crazy times," I said, unsure whether he wanted sympathy or praise. "I don't mind the hours. I'm footloose and fancy-free! My parents know they'll have to wait until Thanksgiving or Christmas to see me."

Sam cut me off, waving his fork in the air as if foretelling the future. "You shouldn't count on going home for the holidays. Nine times out of ten, there is something that comes up on the eve of a holiday and you have to cancel. I know people who've missed their sister's wedding, the birth of a son, and almost their own funeral. When the firm snaps its fingers"—he snapped his fingers to emphasize the point—"we drop everything."

I hoped he was wrong. My parents missed me terribly. If I didn't turn up for the holidays, then it would be the two of them grimly going through the motions of Thanksgiving with a store-cooked quarter turkey and a side of stuffing prepared from a box.

But it was made crystal clear to us when we first joined the firm that we were expected to work weekends whenever the need arose. And while that turned out to be more often than not, the hours were usually laxer on the weekend—we'd work eight to ten hours instead of eighteen. Holidays were, apparently, notional. Sick leave was for sissies.

At college, it was a badge of honor for people to return from summer internships at investment banks and consulting firms to boast about working eighteen-hour days. The reality of the constant, never-ending grind was different. My work hours were barely within the limits of human endurance.

One night when I was working late, I walked into the ladies' restroom and almost slammed right into Elizabeth, the other girl from my induction group. She was standing near the sink, snorting a line of coke off the leather organizer we'd received during our induction. When I'd first met her, Elizabeth was a Goody Two-shoes who refused to drink wine during our lavish lunches. After three months working with the fixed-income team, she was snorting coke like she'd been born doing it. I was probably among the few who didn't medicate myself to survive our grueling schedule.

The executive team, on the other hand, came in late and left early. It was an open secret that they spent most of their time at long champagne lunches or taking corporate jets for golf trips with clients. I suppose the argument was that, when you reached their level, schmoozing clients was bringing the firm billions of dollars in business. Still, it created a certain unspoken resentment among the rest of us on the front lines, sweating it out while the executive team lived it up.

We ran and reran numbers. Built one-hundred-page deal books in the space of days, then had them torn up by someone from the executive floor and started all over. We plotted and strategized about takeovers and mergers. We spent our days and nights figuring out ways to squeeze more value by planning layoffs at target companies and devising creative asset-stripping schemes. The executive team had a sweet deal; they just signed off on our work and collected the lion's share of the bonuses.

"We work the deals; they take the credit—and most of the bonus," griped Jules during one marathon all-nighter.

"That's how the system works," Sam said. "If you play your cards right, then one day you'll rake in all the money while a twenty-something grunt who's barely outgrown acne breakouts burns out before your eyes doing all the work."

"It's a blessed life. I can't wait. Drunken lunches with their brokers. Sneaking off to conduct affairs in penthouses stashed away in private trusts so their wives can't get them when they divorce," said Jules. He turned to Sylvie with a smirk. "Will you enjoy reporting to me when I get bumped upstairs?"

"What they're trying to tell you, Sara," said Sylvie, putting a manicured hand on my forearm, "is that if you're a woman at Stanhope, then you're going to have to get used to watching male colleagues who are dumber than you get promoted."

"There's hope for you yet, Sylvie. Didn't you read the latest newsletter?" Sam said. "Diversity is now one of Stanhope's core values." I had seen the article about Stanhope's big diversity push. It struck me as more about capturing headlines in the business papers than actually tackling what was a real problem in the firm.

But the fact that he'd read it shed light on Sam's eagerness to mentor me. The newsletter noted that experienced managers who mentored women and ethnic minorities in their divisions would get a component added to their annual bonuses. Knowing Sam, he figured he might as well cash in and suck up to Vincent at the same time by offering to mentor me.

You could count the female investment bankers at the firm on two hands, and the number of female executives on one finger. The head of Human Resources was a woman and there was a woman on the board—a great-niece of the original Stanhope founder. That was it.

Most of the women employed at the firm were in support roles—marketing, communications, HR, and admin. The army of personal assistants was almost entirely female. Without them, the firm wouldn't function.

The firm's senior executives paid lip service to diversity, just as they gave lip service to corporate social responsibility, another buzz-word they bandied about in employee communications and brochures. All they really cared about was making money. It was the firm's raison d'être, and it was ours, as well.

FIFTEEN

THE ELEVATOR

Sylvie rolled her eyes as Sam high-fived Jules and Vincent. He'd deciphered a simple transposition code, but from the way he acted, you'd have thought he'd just discovered quantum theory.

As the men celebrated, she leaned back against the elevator wall with her arms crossed. All Sam had produced was the cryptic sentence "How much do you trust each other?" It's not as if the doors immediately opened to let them out. Nothing had changed. They were still locked inside and it was still pitch-dark.

All they'd found so far were random clues that made little sense, fragments of a larger puzzle that none of them understood. There were still no instructions on what to do with the clues they'd solved. Sylvie had the feeling they were being toyed with. They were no closer to getting out of the escape room. Even if they'd known what they were looking for, it was virtually impossible to find anything in the dark.

Sylvie checked the time on her phone. There were twenty minutes left. It couldn't go fast enough. She still needed to get home and pack for Paris. Thanks to the stifling heat, she also needed to shower and wash her hair before her flight—there was no way she was flying to Paris all grimy and sweaty.

Marc was picking her up at Charles de Gaulle and they were driving straight down to the Loire to have dinner with his parents. The timing of the trip was lousy, with all the uncertainty at work as they headed into bonus week. If it hadn't been Marc's birthday, Sylvie would have flown over on a different weekend.

They planned to check into their hotel in Blois to freshen up before dinner. Sylvie had been reluctant to stay with Marc's parents at their converted farmhouse just outside the town. Marc had only recently divorced his wife, Cecile, after a twenty-year marriage. His folks had taken the breakup hard. Sylvie was going to have to use every scrap of charm to win them over, and she didn't think it was a smart idea to spend all weekend holed up with them at their country retreat.

The trip was important to her. Marc was important to her. Their relationship was at that delicate stage where it could go either way. She absolutely had to make her flight, and she shouldn't have put herself in a situation where she might have to rush. She berated herself yet again for turning up.

In truth, she'd felt compelled to attend once she knew the others were going. In the current environment, it would have been a bad move to miss the meeting if everyone else was there.

Sylvie touched the television monitor in the hope that it would display the next clue. The screen remained as lifeless as it had been every other time she had tried it. This time, though, perhaps because of the angle that Vincent held his phone flashlight in the dark, Sylvie noticed something underneath the monitor. It looked like tightly rolled plastic. It had been taped in such a way that it was disguised as part of the frame of the panel.

It came loose when she tugged on it. It was a roll of small square pieces of cellophane.

"What's that?" asked Sam.

"Cellophane," said Sylvie. "I found it taped under the monitor."

"Let me take a closer look." Sam snatched the squares from Sylvie and held them under the beam of his flashlight, looking for writing. All he saw were three sheets of cellophane, two purple and one blue.

Sylvie was annoyed. She'd already checked for that. There was no writing on the cellophane sheets. No fresh clues. Sam's small success at solving the code had gone to his head; now he was acting as if he were a leading authority on escape rooms. As far as Sylvie was concerned, that would have been fine if he'd been able to get them out. But he hadn't.

"They're blank," complained Sam, as if Sylvie were somehow to blame.

"I don't think they're a clue," said Vincent. He took the sheets of cellophane, studied them for a moment, then arranged them one over the other. He held the combination of them tightly over the flashlight of his phone, producing a darkish blue beam. "I think this is like a black light."

He moved the beam against the back wall of the elevator. It was very faint under the filtered light, but there was writing that had been invisible to them before. Under the filtered light, a number of messages were revealed all over the walls, as well as what looked like doodles and other illegible graffiti.

At the top of the back wall, painted in large letters, were the words "WELCOME TO THE ESCAPE ROOM." That was innocuous enough. When Sam ran the flashlight over the area underneath, they all fell into an awkward silence.

Underneath the words "Wider Feedback" was a series of quotes that appeared to be taken straight out of their annual reviews.

"Sylvie needs to learn that her looks will only get her so far," read one of the quotes on the wall. "Sylvie should be less critical of her colleagues and focus more on the quality of her own work," said another. "Sylvie needs to step up. She's the weakest link."

Another message, written on an angle, read "Jules seems to be distracted by his personal life and hasn't been productive this year." "Jules is a great sounding board for his teammate's ideas" said a slightly more diplomatic backhanded comment.

"Sam needs to lose his negativity and display some leadership qualities if he wants the respect he thinks he deserves." "It was good to see Sam buckle down and do some work this quarter, for a change."

A large message in capital letters read: 'IT'S NOT SURPRISING THAT WE'VE HAD THE WORST YEAR ON RECORD, GIVEN THAT VINCENT IS DISTRACTED AND INDECISIVE.'

There were other quotes, too, covering the wall in a swirl of the team's poisonous remarks about one another. The quotes had obviously all been taken from their annual reviews, in which they were asked to submit feedback about their colleagues anonymously. They'd traditionally used the opportunity to score points and undermine one another, sometimes subtly, sometimes more directly.

Stanhope had a way of pitting people against one another. After all, bonuses, salaries, and promotions were a zero-sum game at the firm. Even best friends would throw each other under the bus if it raised their chances of getting a bigger bonus.

But there was a difference between suspecting that nasty things were being said about them behind their backs and actually seeing the words in front of their eyes. They could feel one another's anger boil to the surface. The veneer of camaraderie was dissolving.

Jules turned the flashlight beam away from the wall in embarrassment. There were still plenty of comments they hadn't read. They'd seen more than enough.

Sylvie was particularly crushed. Nobody had had a good word to say about her. It was all cruel and reductive. The comments tapped into Sylvie's worst suspicions that her colleagues saw her as the token female on the team. Literally just a pretty face.

Sylvie had grown a tough skin over the years. She'd put up with an awful lot. Not just the "bro talk" but constant passes made by men angling to turn her into a notch on their bedpost.

When she was a junior analyst, she'd attended a dinner at a steak house to celebrate closing a lucrative deal. One of the young bankers at her table called over a pretty waitress with a pixie hairstyle to ask about a particular steak on the menu. "It's a tenderloin," the waitress explained earnestly.

"Is it juicy?" he asked, hiding a smirk.

"Yes, it's considered a juicy cut," explained the waitress before moving over to another table to take an order.

"I'd like to put her over a chair and give her tenderloin something very juicy," said the guy who'd asked the question, drawing uproarious laughter from everyone except Sylvie. The waitress had looked in their direction at the laughter and then quickly averted her eyes, a slight flush on her cheeks. She didn't have to hear the words to know pretty much what had been said.

Sylvie felt bad for not saying anything. She hadn't wanted the men to call her "touchy" and make lewd comments about her instead, so she'd kept her mouth shut.

She was used to the sexism. It was par for the course. A few years ago, when she'd returned from a holiday with a new boyfriend, she'd found torn, sexy lingerie on her desk with a note that said something along the lines of "Hope you had fun!" Sylvie pretended not to be bothered by such things. Not even after she found a drawing of her naked from the waist up on a notepad left behind after she'd presented to the leadership team.

The comments on the wall proved what Sylvie had always suspected. She'd fooled herself into thinking that they took her seriously. What infuriated her most about the comments was that they were completely dismissive of her contribution. She'd come up with strategies that had won significant business for the firm.

In her opinion, her contribution was larger than that of Jules and Sam combined. Those two were great at greasing palms and playing politics. They were excellent at taking credit for other people's work and pontificating about their views. They were extremely tactical in their approach. They did things that looked good in the short term. But she came up with strategies that actually worked, rather than just whatever looked good on paper.

When Sylvie thought about it, her achievements were never acknowledged. At best, they were considered to be a team effort. When Sam, Jules, or even Vincent did something minor, there were rounds of drinks and high fives. The congratulatory emails would flow thick and fast. It had been the same with other women who'd been on the team over the years. Lucy, especially, never received due credit for her financial wizardry even when it literally earned the firm hundreds of millions of dollars.

If the elevator had felt small before, it felt impossibly tiny after they'd read what they all thought about one another. They wanted to get as far away from one another as possible. Instead, they were so close, they could almost hear their quickening heartbeats. They stood around awkwardly, angry and embarrassed, smelling one another's sweat and frustration in the rising heat.

Nobody spoke. The silence was thick. It was almost a relief when the television screen came to life again and red letters scrolled across the bottom like a caption for a breaking story on a cable news broadcast. Above the red bar was a virtual keyboard with four empty boxes where they were obviously supposed to enter a code.

A Greek god has a message for you, said the text on the screen. Find an object that starts with *E*, ends with *e*, but has only a single letter in it. Enter the third digit of each number in the message and you shall be free.

SIXTEEN

SARA HALL

I was ambling through Central Park about two months after starting work at Stanhope, enjoying the Sunday-morning sunshine filtered through the golden rust of fall leaves. It was a rare day off work and I felt liberated to be in jeans, a sweater, and sneakers instead of a suit and heels.

I saw a sign for the zoo at Central Park. I'd last been to a zoo when I was eleven. I had a sudden urge to visit, whether from nostalgia or loneliness, I wasn't sure.

I strolled along the main path that looped around the zoo, watching moms and dads taking photos of their kids in front of various animal enclosures, or pushing drowsy toddlers in strollers while enthusiastically pointing out the animals they passed.

I stood by the sea lion enclosure for a while, watching the keepers throw fish into their greedy whiskered mouths. Next to me was a little girl with a blue foil helium balloon, which kept getting caught up in her hair. Eventually, I arrived at the snow leopard exhibit, where a young leopard was sunning himself on a rock. I sat down on a bench next to someone in a black sweatshirt and an oversize baseball cap who was drawing quite expertly on a large sketch pad.

The leopard was flapping its tail comically to swat away a persistent fly. I instinctively turned to share with the stranger my amusement at the leopard's unwitting comedy. With surprise, I realized that the stranger was not a stranger at all. It was Lucy Marshall, my colleague.

As she sketched the snow leopard, Lucy was in a state of such deep concentration that I suspected she didn't even realize that I was there, although you couldn't always tell with Lucy. She didn't acknowledge me as she drew the contours of the leopard with a charcoal pencil.

At work, Lucy was obsessed by numbers, statistics, and financial modeling. I would never in a million years have imagined that she had any interest in art, let alone any talent. It was a shock to see Lucy drawing a monochrome sketch that could easily have been framed and sold at a gallery.

"You're very good," I said eventually, feeling awkward that I'd been sitting right next to her for some time and hadn't made myself known.

Lucy immediately panicked. She half-covered the drawing with a cupped hand. Her eyes darted around as if to look for an escape route. I felt awful.

"I'm sorry, Lucy. I didn't mean to give you a fright. I shouldn't have disturbed you." I stood abruptly and was about to walk off, when she called out to me.

"Stay, Sara."

I hesitated for a moment and then decided to sit and watch her work. It was a chance to establish a semblance of a relationship with Lucy. She and I had barely exchanged two words since we met the day that I was introduced to the team. It wasn't personal. I'd quickly learned that Lucy didn't talk to anyone unless it was work-related. Even then, she generally preferred to chat via messenger.

Lucy was the least friendly member of the team, aside from Sylvie, who blew hot and cold, with a distinct tendency toward the latter. It wasn't that Lucy was intentionally rude; she genuinely didn't know how to handle social interactions. It was like a foreign language to her. Jules had told me that Lucy had Asperger's. While her social skills might have been poor, when it came to smarts, Lucy was in the stratosphere.

Lucy never joined the cynical repartee that Sylvie, Sam, and Jules engaged in as they sat in the cluster of desks where our team was located. She didn't join us for lunch or drinks after work. On business trips, she returned straight to her hotel room, where, I gather, she ate room-service meals and went to sleep.

The others subtly mocked Lucy. They liked to pretend they were ribbing her, as if they were older siblings giving their younger sister a hard time, but it wasn't genuine. There was an underlying nastiness to their comments that made me wonder what it was they said about me behind my back.

Even as they made fun of Lucy's otherworldliness, there was a grudging respect for her brilliance. Lucy was a genius when it came to finance. Her ability to see patterns and opportunities was unparalleled, which made her work critical to the team's success.

By the same token, she was an outcast. She did not comply to the firm's standards for looks, or dress, or social skills. But she more than made up for her deficiencies in other departments. Sam once told me that Lucy had an instinctive, uncanny ability to make money. "She doesn't realize how good she is."

The only time that I ever saw Lucy doing anything that involved a social interaction was when she went for lunch with Vincent, who was officially her mentor. Nobody really understood his ongoing interest in her, other than the fact that he'd plucked her out of obscurity and brought her to the firm.

The others would make cynical, nasty remarks when they watched Vincent and Lucy disappear for their catch-ups. Sometimes there was sexual innuendo. I had the impression they felt that Vincent was favoring Lucy. In the firm, that meant an awful lot, because it had implications for salaries, bonuses, and career progression. Their resentment created a nasty undercurrent, but I don't think that Lucy noticed or cared.

"Did you know that they're blind when they're born?" Lucy's comment was so unexpected that I almost jumped at the sound of her voice.

"Sorry?" I said, unsure what she meant. "Who's blind?"

"Snow leopards are born blind," she said. "It's ironic. They're born blind, but eventually they develop acute vision—among the best of any mammal. Humans, by contrast, are born with the ability to see but become blind—figuratively speaking. We learn to block out the things that we don't want to see."

I was going to ask her what she meant, but Lucy was engrossed again in her drawing. She'd already forgotten about me. Her hands became progressively darker from the charcoal dust. She took out a wet wipe and cleaned them before turning the page and starting a new sketch.

I watched Lucy draw the outline of the snow leopard's right front paw. It stretched out on a boulder near the leopard's face. When she was finished with the paw, Lucy drew the torso and head of the cat, along with its facial features, including a remarkable cat's-eye iris.

She didn't say another word to me as she worked on her drawing. It wasn't personal. When we got to know each other better, I realized that her brain became so immersed in work that she blocked out everything else as background noise. She compared her mind-set to an airplane landing: It was only once she landed that she was able to engage with anything else.

You'd think that Lucy didn't hear a word, or take in anything, and then hours later she'd respond to a comment or question that had been posed earlier in the day. It was like watching a computer come to life. Lucy would suddenly spout out an analysis based on information that you didn't think she'd overheard, because she hadn't said a word at the time. But Lucy missed nothing. Tone of voice, body language, comments, information—it was all data to her. And if there was one thing that Lucy knew, it was how to decipher data.

When Lucy was done sketching the leopard, she tore the page out of her sketch pad and handed it to me. It perfectly captured the leopard's languid mood, lying on the rock and gently flapping its tail.

"It's stunning, Lucy. You're very talented." She didn't respond, though I noticed a flush of pleasure on her face. "What were you saying before about snow leopards?" I was hoping to engage her in conversation again. It was so hard to find common ground with Lucy.

"Snow leopards are born blind. They get their sight when they are seven days old. At eighteen months, they leave their mothers, and for the rest of their lives they live and hunt alone. Doesn't that remind you of someone?"

"Who?"

"Vincent," she said, as if it should have been obvious to me. "He's a loner. An apex predator surrounded by enemies waiting for the first sign of weakness so they can take him out. It's the law of nature. Eventually, the predator becomes the prey."

"Who do you think Vincent's enemies are?"

"The same as yours and mine," said Lucy. "The rest of the team.

You wouldn't believe the things they say while I work quietly in the background. They think I'm autistic—and for some reason they have decided that means that I'm also deaf. So they speak quite freely around me. I don't show it, but I take in everything. And not just the horrible things they say about me."

"I'm sure they don't mean anything by it," I said, embarrassed that she'd heard their nasty banter.

"They talk about you behind your back, as well, Sara. That they should leave you a tip when you bring them coffee," she said. I flinched. "You should be careful, Sara. They're not just nasty; they're dangerous."

"What do you mean?" I asked hesitantly. Her words made my eyes sting. I felt like I had in high school—rebuffed by the cool crowd. I honestly thought I'd started breaking into their clique. There had been signs of progress—Sam ostensibly taking me under his wing to mentor me, Jules sharing office gossip, late-night drinks with Sylvie.

"I'm sorry, I shouldn't have said that," said Lucy. "It doesn't matter what they say or think. It doesn't bother me, and you shouldn't let it bother you." Lucy wiped the charcoal dust off her hands. "Never think you're inferior or that the firm did you a favor by hiring you. They'll only see it as a weakness and use it against you. I've seen your work, Sara. You're good. Stanhope is lucky to have you."

"Thanks," I said, swallowing hard with emotion. They were the kindest words anyone had said to me since I'd started working at Stanhope.

"Let them underestimate you. It'll give you an advantage." Lucy packed her charcoals and sketch pad into a shoulder bag. She stood abruptly and turned to me. "'Pretend inferiority and encourage their arrogance.' Sun Tzu, *The Art of War*."

Before I could think of a response, Lucy had disappeared beyond a twist in the tree-lined path.

For someone with limited social skills, Lucy was remarkably perceptive. She was right, of course. I carried my inferiority complex with me wherever I went. It was a permanent appendage. I didn't need a shrink to know that it was the result of my childhood.

No matter how much I achieved, I always saw myself as unworthy. If I hadn't met Vincent, then I wouldn't have had a job at Stanhope. Some people took that sort of luck in their stride; they believed it had been written in the stars for them, that it was their destiny. Me, I felt as if I was a fraud, terrified that one day someone would figure out I was an impostor.

A few days after our meeting at the zoo, Lucy invited me over for pizza at her place. It was the start of a somewhat strange friendship.

We met up occasionally, mostly at Lucy's apartment to watch movies and eat dinner. Lucy tried to teach me chess. I was horrible at it. Eventually, she gave up and we took to playing checkers instead. Or poker, though that wasn't much fun for me. It was like playing against a human calculator. Lucy worked out probabilities in her head as she played. Unsurprisingly, she won almost all the time.

Sometimes we'd go to a museum or gallery. One time I convinced Lucy to go with me to an Off-Broadway experimental show. Needless to say, she didn't like it much. Lucy had little interest in the abstract.

I valued the time that I spent with Lucy. I had little opportunity to make friends, given the hours that I worked, and it was refreshing to spend time with someone who was nonjudgmental. Sure, Lucy was idiosyncratic, borderline obsessive-compulsive, and often immersed in a world of numbers and concepts that were beyond my comprehension. But she was loyal, and that was a rare quality in our line of work.

When I went out with other people from work, we had a great time, but the atmosphere crackled with an underlying sense of distrust. I could never let my guard down or relax. I definitely couldn't confide in them or show any vulnerability. I had to be überconfident. I was constantly under scrutiny. Anything I said or did could, and would, be used against me if it helped them get ahead.

At work, Lucy's attitude toward me remained the same. We barely spoke when we were in the office. I told her that I thought it was weird that we hid our friendship there. She said it was for my protection, that it was better people didn't know we were friends. She was quite adamant about it. I figured that it was another quirk, like the way she avoided touching door handles and only ever drank coffee out of one particular mug.

I didn't see any point in arguing, and so I followed her lead at work. She barely acknowledged me, and I did the same. Most of our interactions went via the rest of the team. I had no reason to deal directly with Lucy. She churned out complex forecasts, statistical analyses, and modeled scenarios for Vincent. She reported to him directly. The others bristled that Lucy could circumvent them at any time to deal directly with Vincent.

Lucy was full of contrasts. Outside of work, I found her to have an amusing, self-deprecating sense of humor. She was more savvy about people than she let on at work. It was true that she lacked social skills, but not at all on the level that one might have imagined from the way she acted in the office.

There, she was shy and introverted, usually buried in her own thoughts or immersed in mental calculations. She had a habit of not acknowledging anyone until she needed their input, at which point she'd abruptly ask a question without so much as a hello.

People thought that she was rude, but that wasn't intentional.

Lucy tended to work on autopilot. She was free of guile; a loner more comfortable working by herself than with a team.

Her intuition was remarkable and her memory was even better. Lucy was like a human tape recorder. She remembered everything. Nothing escaped her. Nothing. In the end, that's what got her killed.

SEVENTEEN

THE ELEVATOR

The clue teased them as it ran across the bottom of the screen. "A Greek god has a message for you. Find an object that starts with *E*, ends with *e*, but has only a single letter in it. Enter the third digit of each number in the message and you shall be free."

"A Greek god? The only god I can think of is Hades," said Sam. "That's fitting, given how dark and hellishly hot it is in here. The lord of the underworld?"

"Very cute," said Sylvie dismissively. "But let's try to be serious here. Vincent, you're the self-confessed classics expert. Which Greek god could it be?"

"Zeus," Jules said. "The god of lightning. If we could see what we were doing, then we would find the damn clue."

"Shut up, Jules," snapped Sylvie. "Vincent will do the gods part. You can focus on figuring out the second part of the riddle. 'An object that starts with *E*, ends with *e*, but—'"

"Hermes," Vincent said, interrupting. "Hermes is the Greek messenger of the gods."

"That's it," Sylvie said, elated.

"What are you getting excited about?" Jules's tone was derisive. "There's no Greek god in here."

"Yes there is," Sylvie said, quickly turning to the others. "Who has anything by Hermès with them?"

"We all wear Hermès ties," said Sam. "Vincent has a Hermès briefcase, I believe."

"And I bet that inside his briefcase is the envelope we're looking for," said Sylvie. They all looked at her in confusion.

"What makes you think that we're looking for an envelope?" Sam asked.

"'An object that starts with *E*, ends with *e*, but has only a single letter in it,'" she said, repeating the riddle. "The answer, of course, is an envelope. And it's carried by Hermes."

Jules swiveled around to confront Vincent. "Is there an envelope with a code in your briefcase?"

"How would a clue for the escape room get into my briefcase?" Vincent asked.

"Humor us, Vincent," said Sylvie. "It's the only thing we have to go on right now."

"I keep my briefcase locked. Always. Nobody can put anything in it," said Vincent, irritated.

"Come on, Vincent," said Jules, some of the earlier menace back in his voice. "Open your briefcase."

Vincent reluctantly complied, unlocking his ebony Hermès briefcase and pushing it into the middle of the elevator so they could all look for themselves under the beams of their flashlights. He had nothing to hide.

His briefcase contained a thin silver laptop and charger, a sealed bottle of water, two energy bars, a few sticks of nicotine gum, and his security pass for the Stanhope offices. There was no envelope inside. Vincent sighed, as if to say, I told you so.

"What about the outside pocket?" Sam asked.

"Go ahead," offered Vincent.

Sam slid his hand into the external pocket. When he removed it, he was holding a white envelope. On the front were the words "Annual Bonuses: Private and Confidential." Next to it was a drawing of the Greek god Hermes, wings on his Grecian sandals.

"I didn't put that there," said Vincent, trying hard not to sound defensive. They all looked at him skeptically, as if they'd caught him out in a lie.

Jules took the envelope from Sam and began to tear open the sealed flap.

"You can't open that envelope," Vincent commanded. "The firm's rules are clear. No one is to be advised of their bonus early, and there can be no sharing of bonus information among staff. Sharing remuneration information is a firing offense."

"We have to open the envelope," Sylvie said, surprised by Vincent's reluctance. "It's our next clue! I'll do anything to get out of here, even if it means breaking a company rule. Come on, Vincent. They'll never know."

The roar of the ceiling vent emphasized the urgency. The temperature was still rising. The heat was melting their self-control. They were acting out of instinct rather than with their usual careful calculation; normally, none of them would have considered defying Stanhope's cardinal rules.

"Stop and think for a moment," said Vincent. "This might be the key test of the escape room. It might be why they sent us here in the first place. To see whether, even under extreme provocation, we observe the rules." Vincent's point was persuasive.

He looked at his watch. "The hour will elapse in exactly eleven minutes. We don't need the code. We can just wait until they let us out."

"Fine." Sylvie relented. "Since the hour is almost up anyway, we'll wait." She leaned against the steel elevator doors with her arms crossed. It was dark again. They'd turned off their flashlights to conserve their batteries, which were starting to wane after almost a solid hour of near constant use.

Without his glasses, Vincent perceived the darkness as thicker than it had been earlier. It didn't help that he had sweat pouring down his forehead and into his eyes. The last time he'd been this hot was when he'd had to stay in a ditch for three days straight, in high summer in Afghanistan's Helmand Province, while a U.S. bomb-disposal unit swept the road ahead for IEDs.

As they waited to be let out of the escape room at the end of the hour, they thought about their plans for the rest of the evening. Sylvie mentally packed her suitcase. Jules wondered if there would be time to call his kids before they went to bed. He liked to read bedtime stories to his four-year-old daughter, Annabelle, over the phone. She'd taken the divorce hard.

Sam decided he'd take a cab straight to the airport and get on the first flight to Antigua. Kim had taken his suitcase to the airport, so he needed nothing except for a ticket.

Vincent decided that he wouldn't suggest they go for drinks once they got out, as he'd initially intended when he'd received the message they were doing an escape-room team-building activity. He didn't want to spend the evening making small talk with them at a bar. After seeing the wider feedback comments, he didn't want to be with any of them for a moment longer than necessary.

"Right," said Sylvie when the final minute elapsed. "The hour's up.

Let's get out of here." She stepped forward. She was so close to the elevator doors that she practically touched their smooth steel.

They didn't open. Perhaps their watches weren't synchronized. They waited a little longer, but the doors remained shut.

"Well . . . it doesn't look like they're gonna open," Jules said finally.

"I want. To get. Out." Sylvie spoke with the demanding tone of a little girl on the verge of a major tantrum. They waited a few minutes more. Nothing happened. Everything was as dark and still as it had been. The lights remained off. The doors remained closed. The elevator remained paralyzed. Their disappointment was palpable. Their ordeal wasn't over.

"Sorry, Vincent, we tried it your way," said Jules, turning in his direction. "We're going to need to open that envelope after all so we can get the code to get out," he said.

"Wait a little longer," Vincent ordered. He gripped the envelope.

"We did what you wanted, Vincent. We waited for the hour to elapse. We've played the game the way you wanted. Now it's time to go home." Sylvie's voice rose with each word. "Open the damn envelope!"

"Sylvie," warned Vincent, "you know Stanhope's salary-disclosure rules are very strict. Maybe this isn't a sixty-minute escape room. Maybe it goes for seventy minutes, or ninety. We should wait longer. The firm takes a very dim view of sharing remuneration information. It's an ironclad rule. We need to stick to it."

"Rules?" Jules spat out. "Did you just say we should stick to the rules? It's so hot in here that I'm sweating like a stuck pig. It's so dark that I'm practically blind. It's so stuffy that I feel like I'm suffocating. I never signed up for this. It's cruel and inhumane punishment." He paused to take a deep breath. "I'm tired of rules, Vincent. We all are. We're getting cooked in here."

The growing hysteria in Jules's voice was contagious. Sam and Sylvie began to feel it, too. Until now, Jules had used every ounce of self-control not to give in to his childhood phobia of being trapped in a dark, airless place. But he could exercise only so much self-restraint when there was no sign it was going to end.

"The final clue is in that envelope. All we have to do is open it. And you have the nerve to tell us that we can't because we have to play by the firm's rules?" He took a step toward Vincent. "You seem to be intimately acquainted with the rules of this escape room. Vincent? It's almost as if you designed it yourself to mess with us. Maybe that's why the final clue was in *your* briefcase."

Vincent couldn't see Jules in the dark, but he could sense his approach. He knew that he had to take charge of the situation, or he'd have a mutiny on his hands.

"How about I look at what's inside and tell you what the third digit of each number is, and we put that into the keypad on the screen?" suggested Vincent. "That way, we aren't breaching the firm's rules, and we still get out of here."

"I don't see why you should see it and not us," complained Sam. He was still angry about the comment he'd seen on the wall about his lack of leadership skills. It had obviously come from Vincent. He'd always shown Vincent loyalty—clearly his boss had not returned the favor. Vincent had screwed him with his comments in his annual appraisal. Sam wondered if he'd screwed him on his bonus, as well. Maybe that was why Vincent was so reluctant to let them see the figures.

Vincent opened the envelope containing the letter with their bonuses. It was blurry. He tried to focus his eyes but still couldn't see a thing. Not without his glasses. He didn't want everyone to know just how useless he was in the dark. It was a sign of weakness. It would be a mistake for them to see his vulnerabilities.

"All right, I'll tell you what. Sam, you do the honors," he said, handing him the papers.

The others crowded behind Sam and read the document over his shoulder. There was only one page that seemed pertinent. It was a single page with the bonuses they'd received, listed in order of how much they'd each been given.

Nobody was surprised to see Vincent had earned the biggest bonus. They were surprised, though, to see that his bonus was $1.25 million. It had been a bad year for their team. In terms of revenue generated, their worst ever. If Vincent earned a seven-figure bonus in a bad year, it made them wonder how big it must have been in the good years. Sam came next, with $850,000, followed by Jules, who received $585,000. Sylvie burned with anger when she saw her bonus: a mere $378,000. She'd received half the amount that Sam had and more than 30 percent less than Jules.

Sam entered the third number from each bonus amount, using the virtual keypad on the monitor: 5-0-5-8. They all held their breath as he pressed ENTER with a dramatic flourish, as if the elevator doors would open the moment the button had been pressed.

Nothing happened. The screen froze. And then it turned off, casting the elevator back into complete blackness.

EIGHTEEN

SARA HALL

B onus day was traditionally on the third Monday of January. By
close of business, you would either be floating on air or getting
filthy drunk. In the run-up to the day, people ingratiated themselves
with whoever had influence, in a bid to shore up a bigger bonus.

"You have to kiss ass. That's the game. Just try to keep it taste-
ful," said Sam over a lunch of pasta and salad.

"How, exactly, do I do that?" I asked.

"Buy Christmas presents. It's the fastest way to get people on your
side, and"—Sam examined me dubiously over his glass of white
wine—"in your case, reminding them that you exist."

"So what do I buy? Chocolates? Wine?"

"Sara, do me a favor; don't make a rookie mistake." Sam was shaking his head. "It reflects badly not only on your personal brand
but also on mine as your mentor. Whatever you do, don't *ever* skimp
on the cost. Buy big. Be generous and don't think about the price.
Make a list of people with influence; it could be a personal assistant,
it could be someone in HR. Make sure to buy gifts for everyone on

that list and anyone else you think might be worth it. And I mean *anyone*."

"You mean like you?" I said cheekily.

"Sara, please. You don't have to worry about me, I already have your back. Save your presents for someone who doesn't give a rat's ass about you, which is pretty much the rest of the firm. Even if it doesn't help you this year, it'll build your brand for the future."

"So how much do people spend?"

"I spent close to fourteen grand last year," he said matter-of-factly.

I held my fork in the air in stunned silence. "Fourteen grand." I gulped.

"You're still entry level, so you could get away with half that," he added with a twinge of something akin to sympathy.

I was still paying off my student debts as well as helping my parents with their medical bills. And then there was my insane rent.

"Consider it an investment," Sam said. "Get a loan to cover the cost of the gifts until your next paycheck if necessary. It will more than pay off in the end. Trust me."

Sam asked me to trust him a lot. In this instance, though, he was right. It was an investment for my future. Unfortunately, I wasn't the only person who thought so. In the week before the holidays, the office was inundated with the most lavish Christmas giving imaginable. Everyone vied to give the most original gift, or the most expensive. If they could swing both, then better still.

First-year analysts spent two hundred dollars on a bottle of aged Johnnie Walker Blue, with the label engraved with a message of thanks to their boss. Others bought day-spa treatments for the personal assistants of executives who had their boss's ear. Not a day passed without a delivery of Cuban cigars, monogrammed silk ties and cashmere socks, and boxes of intricately iced cupcakes from Brooklyn bakeries. You name it and people gave it.

As much as Sam tried to warn me about the insanity, nothing he told me in our informal lunch or coffee mentoring sessions prepared me for the nail-biting tension of the day itself.

Bonuses were handed out in order of seniority. I was pretty low on the totem pole, which meant I was on edge for much of the day as I waited for my turn.

It was hard getting any work done that day. I couldn't concentrate. Nobody else could, either. Productivity was almost nonexistent. Everyone was too busy watching each other surreptitiously, looking for signs of how well colleagues had fared and clues as to how their own bonus might shape up. Those who'd already had their meetings with their managers did their best to maintain a poker face. No matter how hard they tried, you could get a sense of who'd done well and who'd gotten shafted.

Bonuses were first delivered on the executive floor. By midmorning, the bonus conversations had moved down to our floor. We knew that it was our turn when Vincent entered a meeting room at the end of our section of desks, carrying a small cardboard box that contained our bonus letters.

My desk happened to face the glass-walled meeting room, so I was able to watch his meetings unfold while pretending to do valuations on a twelve-tab spreadsheet.

Vincent kept the blinds up. I suspected it was a deliberate ploy to show everyone that the process was transparent. In reality, from what I gathered from Sam, it was as murky as a mangrove swamp.

Sam was the first from our team to go in. He tried to act nonchalant as he rose from his desk and walked down the corridor to the meeting room. I could tell that he was nervous by the way he tapped his finger against the side of his leg. It was a mannerism that I'd picked up on over the months that we'd worked together. He always did that when he was uncomfortable about something.

Sam came out five minutes later. His facial expression was deliberately neutral, but he couldn't hide the euphoria that flared in his eyes as he left the meeting holding a white envelope. He winked at me as he passed my desk. I guessed the exorbitant amount of money that he'd spent on gifts had paid off handsomely.

Sylvie went into the meeting room a few minutes later with her usual graceful confidence. Her meeting took longer. It didn't look as if it was going well. I could tell from the defiant way she held her head and the stiffness of her back. Vincent repeatedly scratched the back of his neck. He was visibly uncomfortable. The door opened abruptly and Sylvie walked out.

She paused for a fraction of a second, put on a stony expression, lifted her chin, and walked down the carpeted corridor as if she were walking down the runway during Paris Fashion Week. Her eyes were like flint.

"It's your turn," she told Jules as she walked past him. Like Sam, she held a white envelope in her hand. Unlike Sam, she tossed hers onto her desk when she sat down.

I could hear Sylvie fiddling at her desk behind me. A couple of times, she picked up her desk phone and then hung it up again. She was fuming. I could feel her anger radiating.

Jules came out a few minutes later with his envelope. He tried to hide a smirk but failed miserably. I heard him telephone his wife not long after. "Find a sitter. We're going out for dinner tonight, honey," he whispered louder than necessary.

By the time he'd finished his phone call, Sylvie had left the office.

Initially, I thought nothing of her disappearance, until Jules stuck his head over the partition.

"You know how you tell when people get screwed on their bonus?" he whispered.

"No," I replied awkwardly. I'd been told that discussing bonuses was a firing offense.

"They leave the office, like Sylvie just did," he said. "She's not a happy camper."

He was right. There were a flood of impromptu coffee runs on bonus day. They were thinly disguised excuses to call headhunters from somewhere private. The headhunters knew better than anyone who was getting shafted come bonus time. Who was leaving, who was looking. And, perhaps most important, what other firms were paying.

"They're sounding out their options. They can hardly do it from the office," said Jules.

Bonus time was peak season for headhunters. They didn't have to go looking; business came to them. All they had to do was wait for their phones to ring.

"Don't worry," Jules whispered. "Sylvie won't leave the firm. She has too much invested in it. Vincent was trying to teach her a lesson. He'll make it up to her next year. And she knows that, too."

Lucy was called in to meet with Vincent not long after. She stayed for a while. When she came out, she had the usual inscrutable expression on her face. It was impossible to tell whether she was happy or disappointed. Her dark eyes were expressionless behind the thick frames of her glasses.

"Lucy did well," Sam messaged me. "I can tell."

"How do you know?"

"There's a skip in her step. Believe me, I can tell when a woman is satisfied."

When I received a chat message from Vincent, I rose from my seat and walked self-consciously to the meeting room. My legs quivered. I tried to fight it. I reminded myself that I wasn't intimidated by Vincent. He'd always been good to me. My nervousness was from the tension that had built up over the course of the day.

"I haven't been around much over the past months to help you settle in," Vincent said when we were both seated. "I hope that Sam and the others have made you feel welcome and helped you get up to speed."

"They have," I responded. "It's been a great few months. I've really enjoyed it."

"I've certainly heard good things about your work, Sara. HR gave me a hard time about hiring you because you're not from an Ivy, but I told them to trust my judgment. I'm very good at reading people. From what I've seen so far, you've more than proved my faith in you. You're a quick study. I like that in my people."

Vincent handed me an envelope with my name on it. I held it awkwardly, not sure whether I was supposed to open it in front of him or wait until afterward.

"It's okay," Vincent said. Amusement danced in his ice blue eyes. "You can open it."

I tore it open and read the letter. It thanked me for my work and told me that I would be getting a bonus of $26,000 that year. That far exceeded my expectations. I'd only worked at the firm for six months. I hadn't expected anything close to that figure.

"Thank you, Vincent." I was thrilled.

"Don't thank me," he replied. "It's the firm's money. You deserve it for all the work you've put in. We've had a lot of deals since you came aboard, and the team would have struggled if they hadn't had your help."

"I really appreciate your faith in me, Vincent. And your generosity."

I didn't know it at the time, but my bonus that year was pretty ordinary, even for a newbie analyst. By the time I'd become more experienced at the firm, I realized that Vincent had screwed me over. I cringe when I think about how pathetic I acted, all flustered and grateful, as if Vincent had done me a huge favor. I'd earned that bonus with long hours of hard work. Sam told me afterward that I'd made a mistake by being so gushing in my thanks.

"Managers always remember if you're grateful. It tells them they can throw small change at you the next year and you'll still be thankful," he told me during our next catch-up.

"Men never act grateful; we always complain," said Sam. "It doesn't matter how much we're blown away by the amount, we always look disappointed. Like it's a major financial blow. Like we've been screwed over royally. Women act grateful, and that's a fatal mistake."

Men, he told me, were very adept at playing the heartstrings of their managers. In the run-up to bonus season, they talked about their wives and kids, the cost of prep schools and Manhattan rent. They griped endlessly about how hard it was to make ends meet with the crazy real estate market. Needless to say, that usually netted them more money come bonus time.

Not that any of us really knew what the others earned. It was all smoke and mirrors, speculation and misinformation. It was drilled into us that nobody should discuss his or her bonus. The punishment was immediate dismissal.

Even though people tried to keep a tight lid on their bonus amount, it was easy to tell who had done well. Within days, they'd be on the phone to luxury-car dealers, getting their name on waiting lists for the latest Porsches or Ferraris. Or talking to Realtors about investment properties. Or buying boats they'd never have time to sail.

In a good bonus season, the Rolex store would have six months' worth of back orders for the Daytona. The starting price for one of those was eighteen thousand dollars, rising to over eighty thousand for the high-end versions. Even more for some of the rare vintage ones. There were guys who wore a different watch for each weekday. It was not unheard of for a guy to have a hundred thousand dollars in watches.

On the flip side were the employees whose bonuses fell short. Maybe it was because their departments hadn't met their KPIs; maybe their bosses hated them. They were usually the ones who handed in their notice a few weeks later and moved to a rival firm. Otherwise, they'd spend the year tripping up their colleagues so they'd come out of it looking good for the next bonus season.

Bonuses were a cake-cutting exercise. Each manager was given a pool of money to divide up among his team members. If one person on the team received a large slice of the bonus pie, then someone else would have to receive a commensurately smaller slice. Usually, in the latter case, it was the most junior person, or the woman on the team.

On our team, it was me. Sylvie was way too smart to get seriously slammed on her salary. As for Lucy, she made so much money for the firm that I was sure that Vincent always made sure to give her a generous bonus.

Regardless, there was always enormous suspicion and resentment around bonus time. I once heard that in Finland, every individual's income is published annually. Everyone can find out what their relatives, or friends, or next-door neighbors earned. Not to mention the colleague sitting two seats away, the department manager, and the executives. There was full transparency.

I always figured that level of transparency would be dangerous at Stanhope. If we all knew the truth, it would bring out our worst, most primitive instincts. We'd turn into feral animals. We'd consume one another.

NINETEEN

THE ELEVATOR

When the code didn't work, a wave of cold fear ran through them all. They'd followed the instructions in the last riddle to the letter. "Enter the third digit of each number in the message and you shall be free." But they weren't free. They were still locked in the sticky heat of the elevator, with no idea what more they needed to do to get out.

They were paralyzed by the uncertainty of it all. No matter how they looked at the situation, they should have been freed already. They weren't sure whether they should wait it out or take matters into their own hands and try to escape.

Jules's chest tightened, until he felt as if the claustrophobia was choking the life out of him. He seethed like a wild animal trapped in a cage. His desperation to get out was overwhelming every last semblance of self-control. He kicked the steel doors in frustration—three blistering kicks that made the elevator jolt. Someone gasped. His violent loss of control made the others even more nervous.

They were crammed together in the dark. Whether they liked it or not, their fates were intertwined. It didn't help that they could barely see anything without the help of their phones. Jules couldn't take it much longer. He bounced restlessly on the tips of his toes, like a boxer. His heart beat rapidly and his mouth filled with the sour taste of fear.

Sylvie's rage was equally visceral. They could feel her anger in the way she clenched her fists and took in frequent sharp bursts of air, as if preparing for battle. Vincent worried that the situation would combust if they didn't get out soon. The revelations from the annual reviews and bonus letter would have been awkward at the best of times. In their current predicament, they'd turned the elevator into a powder keg.

It was unheard of for them to have such insight into one another's remuneration. The firm didn't need to make overt threats to warn staff off sharing their salary details. Nobody talked about their bonuses for the simple reason that the most valuable commodity around was information. One person's advantage was another's disadvantage. Even among close friends, bonus details were rarely discussed with any accuracy or honesty.

Sylvie was mortified to find out the extent at which the firm had been lowballing her. It wasn't about the money; she had plenty of that. What cut the most was that she now knew for a fact the firm valued her less than her male colleagues, despite all she'd done. And she'd done plenty for Stanhope and Sons—above and beyond anything her male colleagues had done. She'd always felt that she had to be twice as good as they were to get even half the credit.

"Is it a coincidence that the only woman among us got the smallest bonus?" Sylvie broke the silence. Her voice was emotionless—the calm before the storm.

"It's got nothing to do with gender," muttered Jules unconvincingly.

"Then what *does* it have to do with?" asked Sylvie.

"I don't know," he said. "The number and types of deals you handled."

"You don't think I've been as productive as you?" Sylvie spoke in a reasonable tone that masked her fury. She knew for a fact that she'd contributed way more than Jules, who'd spent most of the year in varying states of inebriation, ranging from mildly drunk to totally wasted.

"I'm certain that's not the case, Sylvie," said Sam, trying to sound conciliatory. He was thrilled with his bonus. It would tide him over nicely, provided Kim didn't ramp up her spending in celebration. "It's one of those things. There are always winners and losers. Honestly, it all evens out in the end."

"Are you serious?" Sylvie was astonished. "The person who has been screwed the most is the only woman and all you can say is 'it's one of those things' and 'it all evens out in the end'?"

"It has nothing to do with your being a woman," insisted Jules, sounding faintly exasperated. "It's bad luck. We've all been there. I don't know why you're complaining. Most women would be thrilled to earn what you earn."

"Really? *Really?* Most women would be happy? Oh well, that's all right, then," she said dramatically. "What a relief. You're right. I should thank you all. I'm such a lucky girl."

"That's not what I meant," said Jules. His hands trembled slightly. He really needed a drink.

"I've worked my ass off. For *years*," said Sylvie. They had to strain to hear her above the rattle of the heating vent. "The same hours as the rest of you. The same hard work. Do you have any idea how much money I've made for the firm? How many deals I've saved from disaster because I could see problems the rest of you didn't know existed? Yet I'm worth less than you all."

"Sylvie, the deals you handled over the past year weren't as lucrative as theirs," said Vincent. "It has nothing to do with the fact that you're a woman."

"Maybe not." Sylvie shrugged. "After all, poor Jules is trailing far behind the two of you in the bonus department. Perhaps it's just out-and-out favoritism."

Sylvie knew that Jules felt left out by what he sometimes called Vincent and Sam's "bromance," including lunchtime racquetball he was never invited to join. Sylvie was happy to rub salt into Jules's wounds. She needed an ally of sorts, even if it was one she couldn't stand.

Sylvie's words hung over the dark elevator long after she finished talking. Jules tried to block them out. It *was* unfair that Sam was getting paid more. Sam, who had been hired in the same intake as he had. Who worked on the same deals. And yet he had always been a step ahead of him because Vincent liked him better.

Sam was Vincent's unofficial deputy, including attending leadership meetings on Vincent's behalf when he was away. Jules was better qualified. He had a law degree, an MBA, and a family pedigree and connections that were way beyond Sam's modest, lower-middle-class background. Jules was better at his job than Sam. He'd proved it many times over the years.

But Sam was good-looking, with his fair hair and the blindingly white smile that made him look like a model in a toothpaste commercial. He was fast at taking credit. Like a fucking bullet train.

"Sylvie's right!" Jules exploded. "It doesn't make sense. Why does Sam get paid so much more than I do, Vincent?"

The heat and isolation were fraying tempers, making them lose control. They weren't thinking logically. Neither was he, Vincent realized. He should have torn up the bonus envelope the moment he found it. That information had unleashed a wave of jealousy, and he wasn't sure that he could contain it.

"Vincent." The bitterness in Jules's voice ripped through the darkness. "You told me a couple of years ago that I was earning in the highest tier possible for my job grade. You led me to believe that I was getting the biggest bonus of anyone on the team."

Vincent rubbed his temples. He hated having his words thrown back at him. He'd given his team plenty of platitudes over the years. He'd stretched the truth. Sometimes he'd told them outright lies. It was all well intentioned, to keep people motivated and prevent them from becoming disheartened.

"I still remember what you said, Vincent," Jules went on. He parroted Vincent's British-inflected Dutch accent. "I wish I could help you out more, but my hands are tied. Once someone reaches the top salary for their job, the only way to get more money is to be promoted."

Jules stepped toward the gray silhouette that he knew was Vincent's hulking frame. "If I'm in the highest salary tier, how come Sam is earning more than I am?"

No answer.

"Come on, Vincent. Admit that you lied to me." Jules raised his voice. He sounded drunk with aggression.

Still no answer.

Jules's kick was loud and vicious, shattering one of the mirrors on the wall. His next kick also came without warning. It hit Vincent in the solar plexus.

Vincent groaned as he fell to the ground. He was fully expecting

Jules to follow up with another kick, and then another. But Sylvie was holding Jules back—not by force, but by gently rubbing her hands on his arms to soothe him.

Vincent rose to his feet. He resisted the urge to remove the Glock holstered in the back of his pants and use it to remind Jules who was in charge. Through the pain, he knew it would be perceived as weakness. His stomach ached and he wanted to vomit, but he couldn't allow himself the luxury. His survival depended on what he did next. His instincts took over. In a single motion, he picked up a piece of shattered glass, grabbed Jules by the throat, and pushed him violently into the wall.

They all heard the thump of Jules's body hitting the wall. Vincent put the broken glass to Jules's throat. Jules couldn't swallow. He couldn't move. Vincent cut the skin under Jules's chin very slowly and deliberately. It was a superficial cut, but Jules could feel the warm blood running down his neck.

"If you ever raise a hand to me again," Vincent said in a matter-of-fact tone that made his message all the more chilling, "I will kill you, Jules."

TWENTY

SARA HALL

It's funny how you block out the things you don't want to see. All I saw in that first year at Stanhope was that I'd made it to the big time.

I was earning a small fortune. For the first time in my life, I'd walk into a boutique and buy whatever I wanted, without being concerned about the price. Professionally, I was working alongside the best and brightest in the business. I was getting unparalleled experience, working on major international deals. My career was exactly where I wanted it to be. I was on track to achieve all my ambitions.

The sniping, the backstabbing, the lack of women in senior roles, never mind people of color or other minorities—it was all there in plain view. But I didn't see it. I was busy enjoying the ride. Not to mention struggling with the grueling hours, which never seemed to let up. We went from one big deal to the next. They all blended together after a while, becoming indistinguishable in my memory.

The deals were little more than numbers, statistics, profit margins, rates of return. They never had a human face. They all generated huge amounts of money for the firm, which we were certain would translate into bigger bonuses for us all.

But one deal broke through the haze. We were working on a large automaker's acquisition of manufacturers in its supply chain. Among the companies being eyed was a small auto-parts factory in Michigan. It was a successful business—profitable, great products, healthy cash flow, and excellent productivity. The owners had no reason to sell. But buying their firm was a cornerstone of the strategy we'd devised for our client. Our client made the board of this company an offer that it couldn't refuse, And, indeed, didn't refuse. The company's board voted unanimously to sell to our client.

My team was involved in structuring the acquisition. Sylvie, who was the team's tax expert, figured out that if the production of the parts was taken offshore then we could take advantage of a tax incentive in the destination country that would save our client $110 million over five years. That alone would effectively pay for the acquisition. On the day the deal was signed, all 530 of the factory staff in Michigan were told they'd lost their jobs.

The night the factory layoffs went into effect, we were all working back in the office. We saw news footage that showed picketing workers scuffling with police outside the automaker's headquarters in Detroit. One guy had brought his baby in a T-shirt that said "My dad got fired. Who's going to feed me now?"

"Doesn't it make you feel bad?" I asked Sam.

"Why should I feel bad? We did our job. It's why they pay us the big bucks," he replied. "Why do you care?"

"They're regular people," I said. "People who have bills to pay. Mortgages. Kids to school and feed. We've destroyed their lives. We should have gone over the numbers until we found a way to do it without putting them on the street." My voice dropped off uncertainly.

"They're all dumb fucks for depending on an obsolete industry," Sylvie interjected.

"Sylvie's right," said Jules. "It's the people who are too stupid to know how dumb they are who drag us all down. Take my advice, Sara. Don't become one of them. There are winners and losers in this world. The winners are the one percent who get to live the dream. The losers are everyone else."

At home that night, I was unable to meet my own eyes in the bathroom mirror. I hated myself for not fighting harder to avoid those job losses. I should have made more of an effort to find an alternative. It was my first taste of disillusionment, the first twinge that maybe I didn't belong.

Despite my misgivings, I was addicted to the cachet and perks of my job. Cold-pressed fruit juices lined up in neat colorful rows in the office drinks fridge, free gym membership, vouchers for massages and facials that would suddenly appear on my desk as part of the employee-welfare program. The never-ending supply of free tickets to Broadway shows or prime seats at sports games. And, most importantly, the money they dangled in front of us.

It all gave me temporary amnesia, or perhaps willful blindness, at the damage we'd wrought on the lives of the nameless people at that factory in Michigan, or a hundred other places affected by our decisions. We used profit as justification for shattering lives. It was that simple.

"Never feel bad for doing your job," Sam told me during one of our unofficial mentoring sessions. "Your allegiance should be to our client, to the firm, and, above everything else, to your own net wealth."

I didn't know the people affected at the Michigan factory, but I knew people like them. My dad, for one. He had been a mechanical engineer and had spent half my childhood unemployed. He'd lost his job not long after his first health scare—after his third time in the hospital, his boss said he couldn't have him taking so many sick days. He needed someone reliable. Dad was fired and we lost our health insurance at the worst-possible time. I don't think that he ever recovered from the shame.

I knew firsthand the implications of putting someone in their mid-forties out of work. At that age, those factory workers would be very lucky to get another permanent job. They'd move from one itinerant job to another, one contract to the next, until the work dried up completely and they'd be left with nothing.

Nobody at Stanhope seemed to care. To them, all of life was a casino. As far as they were concerned, those factory workers had placed the wrong bets.

Three months later, I found out that a former foreman at the Michigan auto-parts factory had blown his head off with a hunting rifle. His wife had left him, and the bank was about to seize his family home. I was filled with self-loathing. His blood was on our hands.

"What do you think about it?" I asked Lucy later that night. I'd gone to her apartment after work. I was distraught over what happened and needed to talk it through with someone. "Do you think that we're responsible?"

"I've never understood why someone would do that," Lucy said in a rough voice.

It was the closest I'd ever seen her to being emotional.

"But at the same time," she went on, "I can't help but think that our actions pushed him into a corner."

I swallowed guiltily. I'd been thinking the same thing since hearing the tragic news. Lucy lifted up her head and glanced straight at me, which was very unusual. Usually, she avoided eye contact at all costs. I sensed that she wanted to confide something to me.

"Sara, there was another way of doing that deal. I showed Jules and Sylvie the numbers. They said I was being overly optimistic with my projections."

"Were you?"

"Of course not. Jules and Sam took the easy way out," Lucy said. "They wanted a sure thing."

That was the first time I realized why the firm gave us such generous perks and pay. It was to skew our moral compass so that we wouldn't hesitate, wouldn't flinch, when we had to be ruthless.

TWENTY-ONE

THE ELEVATOR

It's rather shortsighted of you, Vincent, to screw me on my bonus," said Sylvie sweetly, breaking the silence that had hung over them since his physical confrontation with Jules. "We know so much about each other. So many secrets."

"Is that a threat, Sylvie?" asked Vincent quietly. Everyone in the elevator froze. Jules licked his lips nervously. They'd now all seen what Vincent was capable of. Jules knew better than anyone. The cut on his neck still stung.

"No, it's not a threat, Vincent. I'm merely pointing out that it's best for us to be on the same team. Don't you think? And to tell you the truth, right now, I'm not feeling like a fully fledged member of your team." Sylvie was beyond caring about overstepping the mark with Vincent.

"What do you want?"

"I want it fixed," Sylvie said. "You still have time to amend my bonus before I get the official letter on Friday. If necessary, you can ask for your own bonus to be cut back and pass the difference on to me." Sylvie had never made such a demand before. She'd always been in awe of Vincent. In the dark, she felt no fear. Sylvie knew that Vincent would never lay a finger on her. He was old-school when it came to women.

They all waited for his reaction. Nobody ever gave Vincent an ultimatum—about anything.

"Is that how you feel, as well, Jules?" Vincent asked.

"Well, I would like to know why my bonus is so much lower than Sam's," mumbled Jules.

"You screwed up the Paragon deal. It really is that simple," replied Vincent. "By all rights, you shouldn't get a bonus at all. You should have been fired. You should be very grateful to be getting anything at all, let alone a bonus this substantial."

"There's nothing substantial about my bonus. Vincent, *you* have a substantial bonus. It's almost three times what I'm getting," Jules whined. "Sam's doing pretty nicely too. Meanwhile, I have alimony to pay, kids to support. It's not enough."

"I'm not discussing this further," Vincent said sharply. "I don't even know if the bonus figures on that sheet are accurate. I don't know where that envelope came from. They could easily be random numbers."

"The numbers are the real deal," said Jules. "I held the paper. It was on watermarked Stanhope letterhead."

Vincent knew Jules was right—he'd signed off on the amounts the previous day. But he had no idea how the envelope ended up in his briefcase. Bonus details were kept under lock and key until bonus day. He also knew that if any of them were retrenched, they wouldn't be getting their bonus; it would become part of their severance package instead. He didn't say a word. It was better for them not to know that unpleasant detail.

The revelation of their bonuses did not just generate animosity; it robbed Vincent of his power over them. He was usually deft at manipulating all of them with how he handed out their bonuses. He did it to keep people motivated and to keep the peace. Mostly, he did it because the system was opaque and he could get away with it.

"You've been lying for years, Vincent, telling us how you fight for us to get our rightful bonuses and salary increases," said Sylvie. "All the while, you made sure that you received the biggest share."

Vincent shut his eyes in the faint hope that it would improve his vision when he opened them again. His poor eyesight made him vulnerable. He tried to read their emotions through their voices. He could tell that Sylvie was furious but she'd get over it, and he felt he could still count on some loyalty from Sam. It was Jules who worried him most. He didn't have to see Jules to know he was as dangerous as a rabid dog.

"For the record, Vincent, I did most of the work on the Paragon deal," Jules insisted. "We had a few bumpy moments, but I pulled it together."

"That's rich," Sam said. "You left most of the work to first-year graduates because most days you were drunk by eleven A.M. Vincent and I didn't mind; we figured that first-year graduates, no matter how inexperienced, would do a better job than a drunk."

"That's not true," said Jules, sounding more vehement than he felt. How could they have known that he'd been drinking each morning? He only ever drank vodka. "I don't drink when I'm working."

"You were drunk when we got into this elevator!" Vincent said. "We might not have noticed if it had been a two-minute elevator ride, but it's obvious now. You smell like a distillery."

"Attack is the best defense, right, Vincent?" said Jules. "You smear me as an alcoholic so that we'll all forget that you've been robbing us blind for years."

"I don't need to smear you, Jules," hissed Vincent. "You *are* an alcoholic."

"Do you have any idea what I had to do to pull off that Paragon deal?" Jules said, pointing at his chest with his finger. "My wife walked out on me because of the hours that I put into that deal. It was my idea, I structured the whole thing. But you took the credit. As you always do."

"The Paragon deal was your idea," admitted Vincent. "But it would have come apart at the seams if Sam and I had left it to you. We had to intervene when you screwed up."

"Sam?" Jules gave a hoot of derision. "You're the only person who thinks that Sam adds any value to our work. Sam's a face man. A human handshaking machine. Sam wouldn't know a business strategy if it bit him on the ass. One day they'll build robots to replace the Sams of this world, shaking hands and greeting clients all day. Taking them to exquisite lunches on the corporate card like a sycophantic salesman incapable of an original thought. I didn't see my wife and kids for weeks! I sacrificed my marriage for the Paragon deal!"

"Do you really think that you're alone in making sacrifices, Jules?" Sylvie said. "I sacrificed my relationship for this job. Peter wouldn't marry me unless I agreed to have kids, but I'd seen what Stanhope does to women who get pregnant. They're sent to the equivalent of corporate Siberia until they quit." Sylvie paused. "Do you know what Peter did after we broke up? He got married. Five months later. To a twenty-six-year-old business school graduate. I see their kids on my Facebook feed constantly. Every burp gets shared. From the way they go on, you'd think their son had been nominated for a Nobel Prize for chemistry just because he pooped in his glow-in-the-dark potty for the first time. It drives me nuts."

"You should block them."

"I don't want Peter to know that I care enough to block him! Don't talk to me about sacrifices." Sylvie swallowed back tears. She was well aware of the fact that if they didn't get out soon, she wouldn't make it to the airport in time for her Paris flight. Marc wouldn't tolerate another no-show; he'd already warned her. She wasn't willing to sacrifice another relationship for Stanhope.

"Did it ever occur to you," said Jules, "that Peter walked out on you because he didn't want a manipulative bitch to be the mother of his children?"

"Leave her alone," spat Sam. "Stop attacking everyone else, Jules. Maybe you should use this as an opportunity to take a look at yourself."

"Shut up, Sam. You always were Vincent's whore. That's why you earned a higher bonus than I did," replied Jules. "Vincent pays you off for loyalty."

"When will you understand, Jules, that I don't decide the bonuses." Vincent's patience was wearing thin. He rarely raised his voice, but when he lost his temper, it was like a volcanic eruption. There were admin staff at the office who left meetings in tears when Vincent's legendary temper exploded.

"Oh please, Vincent. Stop acting like you have nothing to do with it," Sylvie said. "You decide our bonuses. Only you. The remuneration committee rubber-stamps your decision."

"I'll tell you what. If our team survives the layoffs next week, you're all welcome to quit in protest over your bonuses," Vincent suggested. "Stanhope pays far more generously than our competitors. You'll never even come close to these amounts anywhere else." Vincent's accent became more pronounced when he was angry.

"Do you really want us to quit?" asked Sylvie. "I always thought the only way out of this team was in a box."

"I am going to assume, Sylvie, that it's the stress of this situation that's making you talk like this." Vincent's voice was soft, but the threat was clear.

"Oh, I've barely begun," replied Sylvie. "While Jules was in a semi-permanent state of intoxication last year and Sam was hanging out with an endless procession of prostitutes and coke dealers, I was the one doing the bulk of the work. Yet come bonus time, they magically get way more than I do. All I am asking is why." She turned to Vincent. "Why? That's a fair question."

Vincent didn't answer. He wasn't going to get pulled any further into a line-item analysis of everyone's bonuses. Sylvie was way out of line. The dark was emboldening his subordinates to say things they'd never dare say to him in the cold, hard light of day.

"For the record, Sylvie, I resent your comments about my personal life. How dare you intimate that I'm cheating on my wife," snapped Sam.

"I'm not intimating." Sylvie laughed. "I saw you last week at a club with a quote, unquote 'model.' She was so full of silicone that she might as well have been a sex doll."

"You're not being fair to Sam," said Jules with thick sarcasm. "His wife is a shopaholic. His only consolation is hookers. Believe me, I've seen Kim in action. The woman is a bankruptcy lawyer's wet dream."

It was too dark to see exactly what happened, but they all heard the crunch of fist on jaw as Sam punched Jules. And then a thump as Jules violently pushed Sam against the wall.

Jules's nose spurted blood all over his white shirt. It didn't bother him. He was still laughing when the screen lit up with another clue.

TWENTY-TWO

SARA HALL

I was in Seattle on an assignment when Lucy died. By the time I returned to the office in New York, I knew the details of how it happened. What I didn't know was why.

The weekend before my Seattle trip, Lucy and I went to the Met to see the Leonardo da Vinci exhibition "Inside the Mind of a Genius." The exhibition displayed da Vinci's collection of papers, known as the Codex Atlanticus. It contained notes and drawings of inventions centuries before their time—parachutes, tanks, a crude version of a submarine.

Lucy was in her element. She was particularly entranced by da Vinci's use of mirror writing and the mathematical concepts he employed in his designs and his art. After a couple of hours, I was ready to leave. Lucy insisted on staying until the museum closed, and she told me she was going to come back the next morning when it re-opened.

The last time that I saw Lucy alive, she had her face pressed to an illuminated display case as she examined a da Vinci sketch. That is how I like to remember her.

Lucy was found dead in her bathtub. A power outage in her building had been traced to her apartment. When the janitor knocked on her door several times, there was no answer. Eventually, he let himself inside with his key, and he was the one who found her.

Lucy was electrocuted by a tablet device she was using in the bath. It was connected to a power outlet. It would have been thought an accident if it hadn't been for two things. For one, Lucy was too smart to sit in the bath with an electronic device plugged into the power, and, more important, she left a suicide note on her hall table. The authorities determined it was deliberate. Death by suicide.

I found out in the cruelest way possible. I clicked on a link to a breaking news story with the headline INVESTMENT BANKER DIES AS MARKETS PLUNGE. Lucy had died on a day on which the markets had a significant correction. It had nothing to do with her death, but I guess it was the sort of headline that went viral. I clicked on the link and discovered the investment banker in question was Lucy Marshall. It was so undignified and sad. Lucy would have been humiliated at the way her death was splashed across the tabloids with lurid headlines.

Vincent was in London when Lucy died. He flew back that evening, as did I, for a memorial service the firm organized at Trinity Church.

The church was filled with Stanhope staff who'd barely given Lucy the time of day when she was alive. All of a sudden they were publicly mourning her. Maybe they turned up because her death had been so public. Or maybe it was in deference to Vincent, who'd arranged the ceremony.

A poster-size framed photograph of Lucy stood on the podium, along with a large wreath. Lucy's narrow, intelligent eyes seemed to survey with surprise the sizable crowd that had gathered. In life, she'd known very few of them. And many of those she had known hadn't been particularly nice to her.

Several of Lucy's relatives attended the memorial service, too—an aunt, some cousins, and her mother, who spent most of the ceremony with her face buried in Kleenex.

Vincent spoke eloquently about Lucy's brilliance, her understated wit, and her enormous contribution to a number of successful deals. I noted that Vincent did not mention that those deals earned the firm close to a quarter of a billion dollars. Or that they might not have happened at all if it hadn't been for Lucy's work.

When Vincent was done, a Human Resources manager spoke in soft tones about how everyone at Stanhope was a large, extended family and how they all grieved the loss of one of their own. She offered free counseling assistance to anybody who needed help. In a final address, Thomas Nelson, a member of the executive team, announced that the firm would keep Lucy's memory alive by helping other talented students achieve their career goals.

"Because Lucy had a lifetime of achievement before her," he said, "it's only fitting that we help other brilliant graduates finish Lucy's work. That's why we're creating a scholarship fund in Lucy's name."

He presented Lucy's mother, Cathy, with a framed certificate announcing the annual Lucy Marshall Scholarship. He also gave her a check for Lucy's funeral expenses.

"Maybe she'll be able to have an open-coffin funeral now," whispered a guy to his friend in the row in front of me.

"It's the least that we can do," Thomas Nelson said, shaking Cathy's hand. Cathy looked fragile and numb throughout the ceremony. Vincent held her arm to support her as she rose to shake hands with people filing past to offer their condolences.

"Lucy was a greatly loved member of our team," Jules said as he took Cathy's hand and held it between his own. "I don't know how we'll manage without her.

"I really don't," he said as we walked back to the office. "Lucy made us all a lot of money over the years. It's a shame. A damn shame."

The police went through the motions of investigating Lucy's death, including turning her apartment into a crime scene for a few days and dusting for fingerprints. It was halfhearted. After all, Lucy had left a suicide note in her own handwriting. That pretty much wrapped up the investigation before it even began.

The coroner's report ruled definitively that Lucy's death was a suicide. A passing reference in the report to her having had sedatives in her system noted that the amount was not considered significant, even though her mother, Cathy, said that Lucy had an aversion to taking medication of any type—not even ibuprofen for her migraines.

With all the evidence pointing toward suicide, nobody imagined for a moment that Lucy had been murdered.

TWENTY-THREE

THE ELEVATOR

The new clue appeared in red letters in the center of the white screen. Vincent and Sylvie noticed it; Jules and Sam did not. They were splayed out on the floor, panting hard after their scuffle and attending to their wounds. Jules held a handkerchief to his nose to stem the bleeding. Sam was in agony. He'd hit the wall hard with his shoulder and was in so much pain that he couldn't make a sound.

> Let your plans be dark and impenetrable as night,
> and when you move, fall like a thunderbolt.

The sentence expanded until it almost filled the screen and then contracted until it could barely be seen.

"Is that supposed to be a clue or an observation?" asked Sylvie as she watched the sentence expand again.

"I don't know," said Vincent wearily. "I wish this place came with an instruction manual, because—" Vincent stopped talking. They all froze as they felt the elevator make a lumbering shift, like a monster waking up after a long hibernation. Their moods lifted. Their ordeal was ending.

The elevator jolted again. Then it fell into a sudden descent. It was so unexpected that their stomachs dropped as if on a roller coaster.

At first, they didn't worry when the elevator's descent gained speed. They assumed it was taking them down to the lobby. It was when their ears popped that they realized the elevator was falling so fast that it was virtually in free fall. They were plummeting to the ground.

Someone screamed, or maybe they all did. Sylvie clutched Sam's arm in a futile gesture.

"Oh my fucking God." Jules wasn't sure if he screamed it or thought it. His heart raced. The elevator kept falling faster and faster, still gaining speed.

When it stopped, it was sudden and brutal. It felt as if they were in a speeding car hitting a brick wall. Their bodies were tossed around like bowling pins. They tumbled and lay on the ground in a tangled pile, battered and bruised.

Jules was the first to move. He tentatively stretched his arms and legs one at a time. Nothing felt broken. That was a good sign. His nose was still dripping blood from being punched by Sam, but he didn't mind that.

He focused on finding his phone. The flashlight had become his lifeline. He found it next to him and turned it on, then waited until the screen was illuminated. He'd never seen anything as beautiful as his wallpaper. It was a photograph he'd taken during a ski trip with the beautiful Jana. They'd since broken up, but he enjoyed looking at her, which is why he hadn't deleted the photo. Jagged cracks now ran down the length of the screen.

"Are you all okay?" Jules pointed his phone around the elevator to assess the damage. They weren't okay. They were lying in contorted heaps on the marble floor, dazed and injured. Vincent was lying facedown and not moving at all.

Sylvie sat up slowly. A thin red gash ran vertically down her face. Jules curiously watched a droplet of blood roll down her cheek like a tear. The cut seemed out of place on flawless Sylvie. A human mannequin. It was hard to believe that she bled. She looked shattered and afraid.

Jules moved over to reassure her, but she immediately backed away like a wounded animal.

"You're hurt," he said more bluntly than he'd intended. He was offended by her rejection. He pointed the light at the trickle of blood that ran down her forehead to her mouth. "There's a cut on your temple. It's bleeding," he said callously.

She ran her tongue onto her skin and tasted salt. She scooped her dark blond hair behind her head, pinning it up as best she could without the benefit of a mirror. Then she ran her finger all the way down the wound to wipe off the trickle of blood. Unsure of what to do with it, she licked the blood off her finger. It left a lingering taste and stained her lips.

Sam lay on the floor in utter agony. His body was broken. He moaned faintly at the back of his throat like a wounded dog. He was in pain, but alive. Vincent still hadn't made a sound.

Jules slid over to him. His still body was lying facedown. "Vincent?" he said, shaking him roughly. "Vincent? Are you okay?" There was no response.

"Vincent?" He shook him by the shoulders. Still no response.

With the delicate touch of a pickpocket, Jules slipped his fingers behind Vincent's belt and slowly eased out the Glock.

TWENTY-FOUR

SARA HALL

Vincent arranged for the team to meet at a bar after Lucy's memorial. I suppose it was an Irish wake of sorts. "It will give those of us who worked closely with Lucy the chance to reminisce," he wrote in the invitation he emailed to the wider team, including junior analysts and support staff.

The cynical side of me suspected that our Human Resources department was behind the invitation. That it was a page from a playbook on how to deal with an employee's death. They'd had practice; there had been other deaths in previous years. One trader gassed himself in his garage. Another drove his car into a tree. There was some question as to whether it was deliberate or an accident caused by his exhaustion. He was a recent graduate who'd worked one hundred hours a week for three weeks in a row.

Lucy's death first truly hit home as I watched her portrait being taken away after the memorial ceremony. That's when the numbness that had kept the tears at bay dissolved.

When I returned to the office after the memorial, I noticed that

Lucy's desk had been packed up and wiped clean. The only thing left behind was an old calendar with quotes by Sun Tzu, which was pinned to her desk partition.

When I'd asked Lucy why she kept a calendar that was two years out-of-date, she told me Vincent had given it to her as a gift. He'd said that Wall Streeters love to quote Sun Tzu because they think it makes them sound badass, but that Lucy was the only one who'd actually read Sun Tzu's writings and applied them in her work, which made her a genuine badass.

Remembering that conversation made me want to cry. I stifled my tears while I rushed off to the women's restroom. I locked myself in a stall and sobbed until thin trails of mascara ran down my cheeks. I had to wash off my makeup before I could go back. I examined my red eyes and gaunt face in the mirror. I looked fragile and heart-broken even after I applied fresh lipstick.

When I returned to my desk, I noticed the Sun Tzu calendar wasn't hanging by Lucy's desk anymore. The last of Lucy's things had been taken away. It felt as if all traces of her had been erased.

I was relieved to get out of the office and into the fresh evening air for a solitary walk to O'Dwyer's for the drinks Vincent had orga-nized in Lucy's honor. He'd reserved two long booths at the back of the wood-paneled Irish bar. He ordered plates of finger food and a bottle of whiskey, from which he poured shots for the two dozen or so people who turned up.

"To Lucy," Vincent said when everyone had arrived. We all held up our glasses. "She'll be missed by all of us. May she find the peace that she never found in this world."

I'd always thought that Lucy had peace in this world. On her terms. That's why I didn't understand why she'd committed suicide. It struck me as strange, given what she'd said a few months earlier about the factory foreman's suicide. That she didn't understand why anyone would kill themselves. Now it seemed she had found herself in that same place.

"You look as if you're away with the fairies, Sara." Jules's face was flushed from drink.

"I was wondering how Lucy ended up at the firm," I replied, lying. "She was hardly the stereotypical Stanhope candidate."

"It was Vincent; he headhunted her," said Jules. "He insisted on hiring her even though Lucy didn't fit in. She ticked none of the boxes except for intelligence, where she was obviously off the charts. Nobody knew why he chose her. Maybe the stress of not belonging took a psychological toll on her."

Vincent hired Lucy for the simple reason that she was brilliant. He mentored her with a devotion that was markedly unusual for Vincent. He always made time to meet with Lucy no matter how full his schedule. Sylvie once told me that Lucy was Vincent's vanity project, that he saw himself as her Pygmalion. She sounded jealous.

Jules leaned across to me and whispered in a low voice. "Vincent took a risk when he hired Lucy. It paid off, until now. I hear the exec team is upset about the media coverage. There's a suggestion Lucy offed herself because she was overworked. That sort of publicity won't be good for Vincent's career. Up until now, he could do no wrong, but I think that's about to change."

"I'm sure the firm knows that hiring Lucy paid off many times over," I said. "Lucy's work was very lucrative for the firm."

He shrugged, as if he didn't agree. "They have short memories. All they see now are ugly headlines. It doesn't reflect well on Vincent."

I had no doubt that Vincent had known he was taking a risk by hiring Lucy. Lucy did not fit the template of a Stanhope recruit. The staff was their brand, and that meant we had to look the part. With over ten thousand applicants a year, the firm could hire candidates who had both intelligence and good looks. Stanhope had the luxury, as one internal recruiter once crudely put it, of having its cake and eating it, too.

Lucy, though, had pale skin, since she spent little time outdoors. She wore thick glasses to treat severe myopia. Her hair was cut in an unflattering style that added a decade to her age. She had never worked out in a gym in her life because she didn't see the point. As the Human Resources people would say, she was a poor cultural fit.

I observed Jules, Sam, and Sylvie nursing their drinks across the long table. Why was Lucy so afraid of them? She hadn't wanted them to know we occasionally watched a movie together or spent an evening listening to her extensive record collection. Our friendship seemed so trivial, but Lucy didn't want them to know. She was intent on playing the brilliant, clumsy, friendless fool.

I remembered what Lucy had said about keeping them off balance. "Pretend to be weak, so they may grow arrogant," she'd told me. She called it a "survival mechanism." At the time, I thought she was paranoid. Watching them whisper to one another across the table, I decided that maybe Lucy had been onto something.

"Did you know that Lucy only needed four hours' sleep a night," Sam said, interrupting my thoughts.

"That's true," said Vincent. "I'd often find her still at work in the morning, with the same focus that she'd shown the night before. I'd have to insist she go home to rest."

He proposed another toast.

"Lucy was quiet and self-contained, but she had an amazing work ethic and she was easily the best forecaster I ever worked with." He paused. "We were lucky to find her. To the greatest number cruncher in the business." He raised his glass and the others joined him.

"How did you find her, Vincent?" Sylvie asked. "You've always refused to say."

Vincent sighed. "I hired her straight out of college. She was still completing the final year of a master's degree in mathematics. I was giving an address to MBA students on job opportunities."

It was one of those talks that was organized by Stanhope's publicity department to raise the firm's profile ahead of recruitment season.

When he took questions after his presentation, Vincent told us, the students asked about starting salaries and training. There was even a question on what sort of hours were expected of graduates. Vincent said that he counted one moderately smart question among them: After the questions died down, a hand went up in the back of the auditorium.

"Go ahead," called out Vincent. "This will be the last question, I have to get back to work. The markets never rest." A titter of laughter.

"Are you aware that based on the Nash equilibrium theory, it makes no sense for the Atlantic Mining Company and the Western Metals Conglomerate to merge?" It sounded like the voice of a teenager. Everyone turned around to glimpse a young girl in jeans and a deep red wool sweater. She wore glasses and her hair was pushed back behind her ears, which stuck out slightly. She was in the aisle seat of the back row.

"I suppose everyone is entitled to an opinion," said Vincent. "You seem very certain about yours. If you oppose a merger, what do you propose instead?"

"I don't propose anything," she responded with surprise. "I don't care if the two companies merge or not. However, if they did not merge, but, rather, Atlantic Mining acquired Western Metals, then according to my calculations the share price would be eighteen percent higher. That figure would almost double after two years." Silence followed. "Of course, this is based on the publicly available financial information and on certain assumptions about future metals prices and demand. Maybe there's other information that I haven't seen that undermines my theory." Her comments were followed by a deep silence and then heads slowly turning back and restless shuffling of papers.

"Here she goes again," someone whispered. There was a ripple of laughter.

"Perhaps we should talk after this presentation and you can explain your thinking to me," Vincent suggested.

When the talk was over, Vincent was inundated by aspiring graduate recruits keen to impress him and make sure he remembered them. Some of them handed him business cards with their contact details. He always tossed them out afterward; from his experience, any college student who handed out business cards was cocky, conceited, and a potential liability if ever hired.

Vincent packed up his briefcase and scanned the room for the student who had asked him that last question. It had piqued his interest because he had come to the same conclusion when, weeks earlier, he'd presented the various options to the executive team. The executives chose the merger option despite his advice.

Lucy was standing back from the crowd with a backpack over her left shoulder, reading a book. As Vincent approached, he saw the title in silver type on the book's spine. It was Chekhov's *Uncle Vanya*.

Lucy looked up from the book at Vincent. "You want to know how I came to that conclusion?"

"I am curious," replied Vincent.

"I read about the deal in *The Wall Street Journal*. I've been testing the Nash equilibrium against real-life situations. I thought this deal would be a solid case study, so I took both company's annual reports for the past five years, compared them to industry reports, and ran various projections of their potential share prices depending on how a deal was structured and global metals prices. I can show you the calculations if you'd like and run you through some of the numbers."

"Unfortunately, I don't have time right now," said Vincent. "Come and see me before you graduate. We'll talk then."

"I graduate in two weeks," said Lucy.

"Well then, come and see me in two weeks," said Vincent, handing Lucy his business card. That was the only card he gave out at the event.

TWENTY-FIVE

THE ELEVATOR

Vincent lay facedown on the marble elevator floor like a felled giant. Sylvie crawled over to him in the dark. She grabbed his arm and ran her hands down it until she reached his wrist. There was a steady pulse.

"He's alive."

Sam heard the relief in Sylvie's voice as he lay motionless on his back, staring into the void. Every time he blinked, Sam wondered if he were dead. There was no difference between having his eyes open or closed. Everything was black.

He was afraid to move. He could tell that his shoulder was resting at an odd angle. He moved his arm and was immediately overcome by a wave of pain so excruciating that he fainted.

Sylvie stood up clumsily from the floor. She ran her hands across the walls to navigate to the steel elevator doors. She found the control panel and pressed the red emergency button at the bottom repeatedly. Nothing happened. The button felt loose, as if it weren't connected to anything.

When, after a half dozen presses of the button, there was no response, Sylvie slammed her palms against the metal doors. "Help us! We're stuck! Help!" she shouted. She pounded her palms furiously against the steel panels, filling the elevator with a frantic beat of metal percussion. "Someone help us! We need an ambulance!"

"Nobody can hear you," Jules said. "Help me pry open the doors—they might hear us if we call for help down the elevator shaft."

They each took a door and tried to push them open, but it was harder than they'd expected. The doors were stuck together like glue. Sylvie put her hands into the groove where the doors met. She winced with the effort of trying to pry them open. With every bit of her strength, she managed to break the suction that kept the doors together. She wiggled her foot into the small gap. She and Jules used the weight of their bodies to push the doors away from each other. As they did, a gust of cold air immediately hit them from the drafty elevator shaft.

"Help!" Sylvie shouted through the gap. "Help us!" All they heard was the echo of her voice. It sounded thin and pitiful.

Jules pointed his phone's flashlight through the gap. He hoped to see the outlines of external elevator doors, which they might force open as well to get out onto whichever floor they were stuck on. Instead of external doors, all he could see was concrete.

"I'm sure they're sending people to get us out," said Jules with more confidence than he felt.

"Do you hear anyone coming to rescue us?" snapped Sylvie. "Because I don't. I don't hear a goddamn thing."

She stopped talking so they could listen. The only sound they heard was the whir of the vent as it poured out streams of heat, and the whine of steel cables holding up the elevator. That was hardly reassuring.

"I'm going to sue them. I'll sue whoever owns this shitty escape room. I'll sue Stanhope for sending us here. I'll sue the owners of this building. I'll take them all to the fucking cleaners," Jules ranted.

"Don't be stupid."

Jules stopped talking. It was Vincent. He was awake.

"Are you all right, Vincent?" asked Sylvie, squatting down to check on him. "Is anything broken?"

"Just my head," joked Vincent weakly. He sat up and rubbed the back of his head. "Jules, stop chasing ambulances for once in your life. Threats won't get us anywhere. How about we all focus on getting out of here."

Vincent grabbed the handrail and lifted himself to his feet. His hands shook from the physical effort that it took to rise. When he was standing, he was hit by a rush of dizziness. He felt his legs buckle under him. It required every bit of strength that he could muster to stay upright.

He was glad for the dark. They couldn't see him like this, weak as a baby. He put his hand to his temple. His head ached awfully.

"The clue that came up before the elevator crashed. It's familiar," Vincent rasped.

"Not to me," said Sylvie. Jules looked up at the words still on the screen: "Let your plans be dark and impenetrable as night, and when you move, fall like a thunderbolt."

"I've never heard it before, either," said Jules.

"I'm sure I have," said Vincent, putting his hand to his temple again to stop the pounding that made clear thinking impossible. "Don't any of you know where it's from?"

"What does it matter? The escape room has obviously malfunctioned," said Jules. "Answering another stupid clue isn't going to get us out of here."

"It matters," replied Vincent. He didn't know why, but he knew that it mattered.

TWENTY-SIX

SARA HALL

A policeman and a grief counselor delivered the suicide note to Cathy three days after Lucy's death. They expected that she'd open it and read it in their presence so that they could comfort her.

She offered them coffee. They politely declined. They hung around for a while longer, sitting on the edge of the sofa and making small talk. She clutched the letter in her hand so hard that her knuckles turned white. Even standing at her living room window, watching them drive off into rush-hour traffic, she made no effort to open the envelope.

When they were out of sight, Cathy put the unopened letter inside a book on a shelf in her bedroom. A part of her still hoped that if she didn't read the letter, it wouldn't be true. Her daughter might still walk through the door and explain how it was all a big misunderstanding.

Cathy opened the letter three days later, not long before dawn after another sleepless night. She realized through the haze of insomnia that she would never sleep properly until she'd read Lucy's last words.

She climbed out of bed and found her way in the gray of night to her bookshelf. The book she'd placed the letter in was called *The Grand Secrets of Chess Masters*. It had been a present for Lucy's ninth birthday.

Cathy opened the envelope while sitting on the edge of her bed. The paper inside was folded with razorlike precision. She wouldn't be the first to read it; the police had told her they'd opened the letter and made a copy for their investigation. She'd bristled at the thought that others had read Lucy's last words before she'd seen them.

Cathy swallowed hard as she unfolded the paper. Her hands trembled. Lucy's familiar tight handwriting blurred as tears welled in her eyes. She wiped her tears on the polyester sleeve of her nightgown. Cathy curled up on her bed, with the letter pressed to her chest. She felt lost and alone. Dawn broke over her neighbor's rooftop laundry line.

Later that day, after considerable thought, she telephoned Vincent and asked him to meet her the following morning. There was something she wanted to ask.

Vincent suggested they meet at a café in Midtown, near the optometrist where Cathy worked. Knowing Vincent, he chose the sterile cafeteria-style café deliberately because he wanted to avoid a scene and wasn't sure what Cathy wanted, or how emotional she would be.

A slow news week had kept the story of Lucy's suicide in the media spotlight. One newspaper published what it called an "exposé" on the real life of bankers, the pressures and long hours that led to them dying young. Stanhope was not happy. It hated publicity at the best of times. It especially hated gratuitous tabloid stories that cheapened the exclusive cachet of its brand.

As Jules had predicted, there had been something of a backlash at the firm against Vincent after Lucy died. He was the one who'd hired Lucy, mentored her. He had to bear some responsibility for the consequences of her death, and any resulting damage to Stanhope's carefully cultivated image.

But from Cathy's point of view, Vincent was the only one at the firm who had acted decently, helping her after Lucy died. The only other contact she'd had from Stanhope was a brusque personnel manager who called her about Lucy's life-insurance policy and pressured her to collect Lucy's things from the office because she said there was nowhere to store them.

"Thanks for meeting me here." Cathy was visibly nervous when she sat down with Vincent. His stony expression and flint blue eyes could be intimidating. She was in her late fifties, with curly dark hair and glasses with bright purple plastic frames. "I know it's out of your way, and you must be very busy," she said, flushing as she realized that she was blabbering.

"Anything I can do to help," Vincent said to reassure her. "Tell me, how are you doing?" His eyes were filled with concern.

"I take each day as it comes," Cathy said, her voice unsteady. "It sounds trite, but I don't know any other way to keep going. It's like putting one foot in front of the other. Eventually, you realize that you're walking, but you don't know how you managed to move so far and you're not sure where you're going. That's how it feels right now."

"I'm sorry," he said simply, but his voice was thick with sympathy. A waitress stopped to take their orders. He ordered a coffee. Cathy asked for a double espresso. Caffeine had become her crutch.

"I wish I'd known that Lucy was going through a hard time,"

Vincent said once the waitress had left. "I would have done anything to help her."

"Lucy visited me the day before she died. I was blow-drying my hair when she came in. She dropped off clothes and other things she was donating to a charity store and then left," said Cathy. "It was my last chance to see her, and all I cared about was fixing my hair."

"You can't blame yourself, Cathy. You had no idea. None of us did." His voice was drowned out by the clatter of cutlery as a waitress served a table nearby. "I understand that Lucy left a note. Did it give any indication of her state of mind? Was she depressed? Worried about something?"

"You can have a look yourself. I have it here." Cathy took the note from her bag and handed it to him.

Mom, please forgive me. It's not because of you. You were the best mother I could have hoped for. It's always been a struggle for me to fit in, and now I am tired of trying. It's time for me to go. I never said it enough, but I want you to know that I love you. Your loving daughter, Lucy.

"Don't you find it strange?" Cathy asked when Vincent finished reading the note.

"In what way?"

"Lucy was never very affectionate. She didn't use words like *love*. I always knew that she loved me, but she never used the word. She hadn't called me 'Mom' for years, just 'Cathy.' And she never cared about fitting in. She once told me that there were too many interesting things to learn about in this world to care about what other people thought."

"I never realized that she wanted so much to be accepted," said Vincent, still thinking about the note.

"That's exactly my point," said Cathy, raising her voice slightly. "Lucy didn't give a damn about whether she fitted in or not. That's what's so strange about the note. It's all wrong. Lucy didn't have a sentimental bone in her body. Her mind didn't work that way. Believe me, I'm her mother."

"You don't think she wrote the note?" asked Vincent, slightly incredulous.

"It's Lucy's handwriting. She definitely wrote the note," Cathy said. "It's just that the language . . . They're not her words. I feel like someone—this is going to sound crazy—dictated it to her. I don't believe that she wrote it of her own volition."

Vincent said nothing as he digested her accusation. The inscrutable expression on his face did not betray whether he thought hers were the emotional words of a grieving mother still in denial or if he thought there was some truth in what Cathy had said.

"Have you told the police about your concerns?" asked Vincent finally. He picked up his teaspoon and stirred his coffee while he waited for Cathy to answer.

"I read the note for the first time yesterday. I called the police right away. I told them the note was overly emotional, that Lucy never communicated that way. That it was totally out of character for Lucy to write phrases like that. It just didn't ring true."

"What did they say?"

"They said that people sometimes get sentimental when they write suicide notes," she replied.

"Maybe that was the reason," he said, looking at her steadily.

"Maybe." She shrugged, without much conviction. "Did Lucy ever confide in you about anything troubling her at work? I need to know what she was going through before she died, because none of this makes sense." Cathy's shoulders shook from deep, heaving sobs. "I have to make sense of this. And no matter how hard I try, I can't do it."

Vincent poured Cathy a glass of water and passed it over to her, watching as she drank. It was only when she'd calmed down that he began to speak again.

"I was Lucy's mentor and we did talk regularly, but always about work. Never anything personal. I was actually away in the weeks before this happened. My only contact with Lucy was when we had team teleconferences. It's hardly the ideal way to gauge someone's mood, but I didn't have any sense that something was wrong."

"What about someone else from the office? Is there anyone else she talked to?"

"Lucy kept herself to herself," said Vincent simply.

"There was nobody at all?" Cathy's voice cracked as she absorbed the weight of Vincent's words. Her daughter had struggled to make friends her entire life. She might have killed herself because of it. "Lucy didn't have a single friend at work?"

"Not that I'm aware of," Vincent said awkwardly. He glanced at his watch. Cathy realized the meeting was coming to an end. "Is there anything else I can help you with?" Vincent asked.

"Maybe one thing," said Cathy. "Someone from Stanhope's Human Resources department left a voice mail asking me to collect Lucy's personal effects."

"I'll have it all sent to you," said Vincent.

"I'd appreciate that. I'm going to Lucy's apartment tomorrow to clear out her things. If you could have it sent over there tomorrow, I'll pack it for the movers," she said. "The landlord's already found a new tenant, so I have to get everything out by the end of the week."

"I could arrange for a packing company to help you," Vincent offered. "If you don't want to step foot in there . . ."

"No." Cathy sighed. "I'll have to go through Lucy's things myself at some point. Might as well get it over and done with. I've taken tomorrow off work to do all the packing." She took a sip of her espresso. "To tell you the truth, I'm a little bit nervous about going there. It'll be my first time there since it happened."

"You shouldn't go alone," said Vincent. "One of Lucy's colleagues has offered to help in any way needed, I'm sure she could stop by tomorrow for a few hours. I'll send Lucy's personal effects with her."

"That's very kind," Cathy said. "What's her name?"

"Sara," he said. "Sara Hall. She'll stop by late morning."

TWENTY-SEVEN

THE ELEVATOR

The buzz that pulsated in Vincent's ears intertwined with another noise—a whine of pain. Vincent scrambled across the floor toward the sound. It was Sam. He was whimpering softly, like an injured dog.

"Sam," Vincent called out in the dark. "Are you all right?"

"Don't know." Sam spoke through clenched teeth. "Something's broken."

Vincent's old army instincts kicked in. His own injuries were forgotten in the adrenaline surge. He gently ran his hands over Sam's body, examining him in the dark with the efficiency of an experienced battlefield medic. Sam flinched when Vincent reached his shoulder. Vincent didn't need to see it to know that it was dislocated.

What worried Vincent more than Sam's shoulder was the possibility that Sam was going into shock. His pulse was weak. His skin felt clammy and his breathing was labored and shallow.

"You've dislocated your shoulder. It's not a big deal," Vincent told him. The grim set of his jaw belied his dismissive tone. Vincent needed Sam to calm down so that his vitals would stabilize.

"Can you fix—" Sam's voice broke off as he was overcome with a spasm of pain.

"Yes." Vincent turned to the others. "Does anyone have pills, painkillers? I don't care what you've got, I'm not judging."

"I have some oxy in my wallet," said Sam weakly. "In my back pocket."

Vincent gingerly pulled the wallet from Sam's pants. Inside was a photo of Kim, with their twins on her lap—all flaxen hair and pastel linen sundresses. He found a tiny Ziploc bag with the green pills inside the coin compartment of Sam's wallet. There were a dozen tablets.

Vincent put two oxycodone in Sam's mouth and told him to swallow it with his spit. He figured that would probably have been enough opioids to endure an amputation. He sat next to Sam and waited for the oxy to take effect. He'd need the others to help. It wouldn't be easy getting Sam's shoulder back into place in the dark and without any medical equipment.

Vincent leaned his phone against the side of the elevator so the flashlight would let him see what he was doing. There were shards of broken glass on the floor from when Jules had kicked the mirrored wall earlier. Vincent slid the shards into the corner with his foot and sat down on the ground next to Sam.

"Jules, I need you to hold Sam's legs firmly so that he doesn't move his body. I need traction," instructed Vincent. He turned in Sylvie's direction. "Sylvie, hold his good arm and cradle his head as best you can. I don't want him to hit his head on the floor and do himself more damage. Can you two do that for me?"

"Yes," they said in unison.

"Good."

Vincent waited until Sam's eyes closed drowsily not long after. It was time. He folded up the sleeves of his shirt until they were at his elbow. He moved Sam's arm at an angle and held his wrist gently.

Even under the influence of the oxy, Sam flinched as Vincent began working. He rotated Sam's arm in a continuous motion, ignoring his muffled groans. Vincent was thankful for the oxy. Without it, Sam would have been writhing in pain.

Vincent kept rotating Sam's arm until his own became sore from the effort. It took minutes of continuous motion until they finally heard a soft pop. Sam's arm joint was back in the socket.

Vincent checked Sam again. Sam flinched when Vincent touched his upper arm. It was swollen. Probably a broken humerus bone, which he knew sometimes happened in tandem with shoulder dislocations. Vincent tossed his dress shirt aside and then pulled off his white undershirt, which he ripped into strips and tied together to make a sling, immobilizing Sam's arm.

When he was done, Vincent put his overcoat over Sam, who was shivering despite the heat. He propped Sam's feet up on his briefcase, which he pressed upright against the wall so that it wouldn't fall over. He put another folded coat under Sam's injured arm to elevate that as well.

"I think he'll be all right now." Vincent sounded more confident than he felt. Even if Sam's vitals returned to normal, he needed to get X-rayed and checked by a doctor soon, in case there was a bleed or other complications. For the moment, Sam's pain was under control and he was in a deep sleep. That was better than nothing.

Vincent's skin was slick from sweat. The stream of heat pouring out of the ceiling vent was relentless. Vincent didn't put his shirt back on, leaving his chest bare. It was cooler that way.

"The only thing that seems to work in this place is the heating system," Vincent muttered.

He was in severe pain himself. He had knifelike pains in the front of his head. Probably a seven out of ten, if he had to rate it. He would have loved an oxy to alleviate the pain, but he was pretty sure that he was concussed. Under those circumstances, it was better to stay awake. He put his head in his hands to dull the throbbing in his skull.

When he was able, he lifted his head and watched the red letters expand and contract on the screen, until they started looking like an optical illusion. "Let your plans be dark and impenetrable as night, and when you move, fall like a thunderbolt," he murmured. The words flickered on the white screen.

TWENTY-EIGHT

SARA HALL

Though I speculated, I never knew exactly why Vincent chose me to help Cathy pack up the contents of her dead daughter's apartment. Maybe it was because I was the most junior member of the team. Or perhaps he sensed my sadness. It hung heavily over me.

Vincent had no idea that Lucy and I were friends. I had never understood Lucy's insistence on keeping secret something as mundane as two colleagues getting together for downtime after work, but I'd always humored her paranoia on that front. I figured it was another one of her many quirks.

Following her death, I felt uncomfortable about making our friendship public. It seemed opportunistic, attention-seeking. I didn't want to fall into the category of colleagues who hadn't given Lucy the time of day when she was alive but were claiming to have been her greatest friends and supporters once she was dead. Jules, Sam, and Sylvie did just that after years of being cruel toward Lucy in their own inimitably vicious ways.

Vincent called me into his office a week or so after Lucy's death.

His invitation was unexpected and unusual. It did not bode well. In my role, I usually dealt with Sam or Jules on day-to-day issues, or Sylvie when she deigned to talk to me. They were the ones who spoke directly with Vincent.

I entered his office hesitantly and with trepidation. I was afraid that he'd called me in to tell me I was fired. About 30 percent of graduates never made it past the first year, and I was close to reaching that milestone. Most disappeared within months. They were either fired outright or performance-managed out of the firm. Sometimes they'd get nothing in the way of a bonus, which was another not so subtle way of the firm showing them the door.

"Sara," Vincent said grimly, tossing his horn-rimmed reading glasses onto a pile of folders. I sat down on the visitor's chair by his desk. I braced myself for bad news. He sat back and watched me from behind his desk. "I need a favor."

"Sure," I responded with relief. "Anything you need, Vincent."

I meant that sincerely. I was acutely aware that if he hadn't hired me, I'd probably still be waiting tables at Rob Roy. He knew it, too, I could tell. Sometimes I think that's why he chose me—he liked the thought that I would have a debt of gratitude that would make me eternally loyal. That's how strong men built their empires. "I promised to send Lucy's personal items to her apartment tomorrow. Her mother, Cathy, will be packing up before the movers come," Vincent said. "I imagine that will be quite traumatic for her—Lucy *died* in that apartment. Would you mind helping Cathy? Give her a shoulder to cry on, if she needs one? She has nobody else to help. . . . It was only the two of them."

Vincent cleared his throat. "I'd consider it a personal favor, Sara. You don't have to do it. It's way out of the scope of your job. Of course, we could arrange for a moving company to help her pack, but I don't think that's the sort of help Cathy really needs. It's emotional support."

"I'm fine to go," I reassured him. "What time should I be there?"

"A driver will be picking up Lucy's personal items tomorrow at ten. I'll arrange for him to swing by your building on the way. Thank you." He turned his eyes to his computer screen. The conversation was over. I headed toward the door.

"Oh, one other thing, Sara," he said, as I was about to walk out. I turned around, holding his office door open as I waited for him to speak.

"If you see any papers or files in Lucy's apartment that belong to the firm, please make sure you bring them back to the office. We don't want any confidential information floating about." Vincent's eyes were on his screen. He didn't look at me as he spoke.

"No problem," I said before closing the door.

I arrived at Lucy's apartment the following morning dressed in jeans and a plaid shirt, holding a box of Lucy's things from her desk at Stanhope. The apartment door was ajar. I pushed it open. Lucy's mother was sitting motionless on a sofa in the corner, a mug of steaming coffee cupped between her hands. She looked like a wax figure in a museum. Her eyes were empty, and sort of broken.

Cathy obviously hadn't done any packing. I had seen the flat boxes from the moving company in a pile on the landing outside the apartment. She hadn't even cut the twine binding them together.

"Who are you?" Cathy asked numbly when she saw me standing on the threshold.

"Vincent asked me to come by," I said by way of introduction. "I'm Sara. Lucy and I were colleagues. I'm so sorry for your loss."

Cathy nodded slowly in acknowledgment before noticing the large box in my arms. "You can put the box over there." She indicated a place on a rug next to the dinner table.

"Thank you, Sara. It was kind of you to come," she said when I was done. "Can I make you a coffee before you go?"

"There's no need, but thank you. I had coffee earlier. Besides, I didn't come only to bring you Lucy's things; I'm here to help you pack. Only if you'd like the help, of course."

"That's very kind of you, but surely you have more important things to do?"

"I don't, actually," I responded. In fact, I had a forty-page report to finish by the following day. But I couldn't think of a single thing more important than helping Cathy. "What would you like me to do first?"

"I don't really know where to start." Cathy was floundering, bewildered. "I've left it very late. I should have started packing days ago, but the police still had their tape up over the door and they wouldn't let me in. . . ." Her voice trailed off. She looked down at the floor, where a small pile of discarded police tape lay. "When the police finally gave me access, I was busy dealing with the medical examiner and funeral arrangements."

Lucy's funeral was a private ceremony. Her remains were cremated. Vincent attended, but nobody else from the firm was invited.

"You never think about everything that needs to take place when a person . . ." She couldn't bring herself to utter the word. "I arrived an hour ago. I was determined to pack without getting emotional," said Cathy. "The landlord needs me to clean out the apartment by the weekend. When I came in, I didn't know where to start. And that's when I noticed."

"Noticed what?"

"That Lucy's things seem to have been disturbed."

"I suppose the police must have gone through the place," I said, gesturing toward police tape still stuck on the bathroom door.

"I asked them," said Cathy. "They said they didn't go through Lucy's closet. They said their forensics team focused its work in the bathroom, where Lucy . . ." Her voice dropped off. "Lucy's bedroom closet is chaotic. Not at all like Lucy. The shelves were always arranged like a department store's. You do know that Lucy was on the spectrum?"

I nodded. "Yes, I was aware."

"She was also color-blind. I'd stop by to arrange her clothes so that she wouldn't accidentally wear clashing colors to work. I hung things in a certain order to help her know which shirt went with which suit and so on. She was vigilant about it. She didn't want to look out of place at the office. But when I looked in her closet, there was no order. Everything was"—Cathy paused, uncertain how to describe it— "flung all over the place. Lucy was fastidious. She'd never have left it like that."

Cathy was right. Lucy organized her closet with military precision because of her color-blindness, but also because she was inherently incapable of leaving a mess. She could see only black, white, red, and pinks. She had labeled her closet shelves with the names of colors. I knew this because she had once asked me to help her put away her laundry using that system.

I opened Lucy's closet doors and was as shocked as her mother when I saw the state it was in. Clothes half-hung from hangers. Others were tossed into balls or simply lay on the floor. The colors were all mixed up.

"What else looks different?"

"The bookshelf," said Cathy, taking me to the white floor-to-ceiling bookshelf that took up an entire wall of Lucy's living room.

Lucy kept an extensive collection of books and vinyl records and CDs. They were her main indulgence. Her books were arranged by category and then in order of size. When I looked closely, I noticed that some books had been removed and then put back in the wrong place. That sort of thing would have driven Lucy crazy. She was so particular that I never dared to take a book off her shelf—if I wanted to borrow one, I'd ask Lucy and she'd take it off the shelf for me.

"The police think it was a suicide. If they're right, then why did I find broken glasses and dishes in the trash? Why was Lucy's grocery cupboard a mess? She was obsessive about how she arranged everything, from pots and pans to her breakfast cereals."

"Is it possible," I said, choosing my words carefully, "that Lucy's emotional state was erratic before she died? That she didn't maintain the apartment to her usual standards?"

"Not at all," said Cathy. "That was what was so strange about it all. Lucy was upbeat before it happened. She told me that she'd been to an exhibit at the Met and it blew her away. She was fascinated by it. She'd been going every weekend."

"That must have been the da Vinci exhibition," I said. Cathy gave me a strange look.

"The first time she went to the exhibition, we actually went together," I explained. "She stayed until it closed and then texted me to say that she was going there again."

"So you and Lucy were friends," Cathy said with relief.

"Yes, we were."

"Tell me, Sara. Did something happen at work to upset her?"

"I don't know," I replied. "I was working from our Seattle office in the weeks before Lucy died and we hadn't spoken for a while," I said, tearing up. Ever since I'd heard about Lucy, I had an aching feeling that if I'd been around it would never have happened. "I'm sorry," I said, wiping away tears with the back of my hand. "I've come to help you pack. Let's get to work."

I carried in the pile of flat boxes and assembled them with duct tape. We worked together, starting by wrapping Lucy's dishes in newspaper. While we packed, Cathy told me about Lucy's difficult childhood. She'd raised Lucy alone after her husband walked out on them for another woman. It hadn't been easy for her or Lucy.

Lucy's teachers claimed she lagged far behind the other kids in class and didn't seem to understand the lessons. Even as a young child, Lucy rarely spoke and almost never engaged with her teachers or fellow students. Her teachers wanted to hold her back a year, and even suggested she be transferred to a special-needs school.

That seemed strange to Cathy because, without being taught, Lucy had been able to recite the alphabet backward from the age of two. One time, when they were in the supermarket, Lucy told her mother how much a shopping cart full of groceries would cost, before it was added up at the cashier. Lucy was correct to the last cent. She was seven at the time. That's when Cathy sent her to a psychologist to be assessed.

It was determined that Lucy's IQ was 151. Lucy told the psychologist that she was bored in class and spent most of the time doing math questions in her head. At the age of seven, she'd already taught herself quadratic equations.

"The psychologist was stunned that the mute child playing on the carpet in her office had a near-genius level of intelligence," Cathy told me as she packed the newspaper-wrapped plates into a small box. "You have to understand, in those days the medical under-standing of kids like Lucy was nowhere near what it is now."

What the teachers thought was a learning delay was a propen-sity to internalize her thinking. Lucy was diagnosed as having high-functioning autism, which explained her poor social skills, her obsessive nature, her hyperconcentration. And her brilliance.

Lucy stayed at her school but was allowed to drift off to the back of the classroom, where she'd work through textbooks with advanced math problems and other subjects that were years ahead of her level. The other children found her strange. The teachers found her unco-operative. They learned to leave her alone.

"Sports was the only subject Lucy failed," said Cathy as we began to work on the pantry. "She had no interest in running or kicking balls. She was clumsy and had poor hand—eye coordination. That's why her sudden passion for sports came as a surprise to me. In some ways, it was the making of her at school," Cathy told me. We were tossing perishable food into big trash bags.

It was on a sunny Wednesday afternoon in middle school that Lucy found her passion for sports. She was sitting on the sidelines, watch-ing her classmates play basketball. The gym teacher, Mr. Mason, had learned by then that Lucy was best left to her own devices. He'd stopped trying to get her to participate in gym classes.

As Lucy watched a practice basketball game, she found it par-ticularly interesting to calculate how many times a player would score a shot from a certain location. She began calculating in a note-book the probability of a shot going in based on the player, the lo-cation, the proximity of defenders, and various other factors.

Lucy drew up her calculations and presented them to the coach in a series of graphs. She was immediately offered a role as team statistician. They'd never before had a team statistician. It was, after all, middle school basketball.

Lucy was so good at forecasting the outcome of various plays that pretty soon the coach consulted her on player lineups and when drawing up plays at time-outs.

"The school team went from a string of defeats to making it into the finals for the first time in a decade. A great part of it was thanks to Lucy," said Cathy.

Lucy's experience working with the basketball team taught her the importance of social interaction. Not so much because she wanted such interactions, but because it helped her understand the benefits of being able to engage with the people around her. She won the grudging respect of her classmates. She didn't get shoved around or teased anymore as she walked through the corridors at school.

Lucy was a fast learner. Gradually, throughout the rest of her schooling, Lucy learned to mimic social conventions. She learned what to say in various circumstances. She absorbed the tones that one might use for those circumstances and the acceptable responses to common questions. She was still incapable of making close friends or interacting with people socially, but her role on the basketball team helped her integrate into the world.

"Lucy's journey was a long one," said Cathy. "Working at Stanhope was a daily battle. Every moment that she was there, she was outside her comfort zone."

"She never considered finding another job? Somewhere more supportive?" I asked, thinking that the environment at Stanhope was hostile even for people who were relatively well adjusted.

"She loved the work. She found it fascinating. And there was support—Vincent was good to her. He protected her," said Cathy.

Cathy was packing various tin cans into a box to give to charity. I removed Lucy's wooden spice rack from a cupboard and put it on the counter. The spices were arranged in alphabetical order: cardamom, cayenne pepper, cinnamon, and so on. Cathy took one look at the spices and burst into tears.

"Lucy always arranged things in alphabetical order when she was stressed. Something was going on with her. I just know it. None of this makes sense."

Cathy pointed to a laundry rack in the far corner of the living room, which still had clothes on it. "Lucy's laundry is hanging just the way she left it," Cathy said, looking into my eyes. "Why would Lucy wash her laundry, hang it out to dry, and then kill herself?"

I knew what she meant. I found it strange that Lucy stocked her fridge with yogurts and a gallon of milk on the morning that she died. The convenience store receipt was under a magnet on the fridge door. I didn't want to upset Cathy any further by pointing it out.

Cathy was visibly relieved to have someone telling her what to do. We threw out most of Lucy's food and packed away any unopened items for Cathy to donate to a soup kitchen. "Especially the spices," Cathy said. "Lucy would have loved to know that her spice collection went to good use."

When we were done in the kitchen, we moved to the bedroom. Lucy's bed was neatly made, with the pillows perfectly fluffed and the mint-striped quilt pulled out flat, without a crease.

Cathy took out all of Lucy's clothes and put them in a box for charity. On the dresser was a photo of Cathy and Lucy, who, at a guess, was about ten years old. Her hair was long and she had straight bangs. Cathy looked like a younger version of herself, with oversize earrings. Cathy wrapped the photo in bubble wrap and put it in her handbag.

She studiously avoided the bathroom, where Lucy had died. It was the only room still taped off with police tape. The door was shut. I had no desire to go in there, either. "The cleaners will take care of it when they come on Friday," Cathy said. "I've told them to throw everything out."

We finished cleaning out the contents of Lucy's bedroom, leaving only the bare mattress and bed frame. After that, we moved on to the living room, where Cathy wrapped Lucy's personal computer in bubble wrap and packed it away in a box, along with a mouse and other computer paraphernalia. The toughest job was Lucy's bookshelf. The bookshelf had been custom-made to house the bulk of Lucy's extensive book and record collection.

"She has more books at home," said Cathy. "My spare room is filled with Lucy's books and records. I don't know what I'll do with them all."

We made two piles on the floor. There was a pile of books that Cathy wanted to keep and a pile that she would donate. Cathy wanted to keep all of Lucy's vinyl records. Some of them were collector's items, she said.

"Why don't you have a look and see if there are any books that you might want," suggested Cathy.

I took a couple of novels that I'd wanted to read for a while and a nonfiction book that Lucy had spoken of highly. I packed the rest of the books in labeled boxes. The last thing to pack was a pile of sketch pads in an assortment of sizes. On the top of the pile was a clear plastic box where Lucy stored her charcoals and other drawing equipment.

"Lucy loved to draw," said Cathy as she flicked through the pictures in a large sketch pad from the top of the pile. I looked over her shoulder. There were sketches of city streets, buskers playing guitar. A man break dancing—Lucy had captured the essence of his movements with a few strokes of a pen.

In another sketch pad, Lucy had used a charcoal pencil to draw animals at the zoo, including a series of the solitary snow leopard. It reminded me of what she'd said that day, how the snow leopards reminded her of Vincent. There was also a sketch of a house cat curled up in an armchair. Cathy explained that it was hers, that Lucy had drawn it during an afternoon visit a few months earlier.

"Lucy was very talented," I said, kneeling down to pack a pile of books in a box.

"Oh, she sure was. Lucy was a remarkably—" I heard a sudden intake of breath, followed by a thump as the sketch pad fell to the floor.

I turned around. Cathy's face was gray. She looked unsteady on her feet, as if she was about to faint. She slowly lowered herself into an armchair.

"What's wrong?" I asked, kneeling next to her. "Are you okay? Can I get you some water?"

"I'm fine," gasped Cathy, with her hand pressed to her mouth. "I have medication in my purse. The inside pocket." I unzipped the pocket and handed her an aluminium strip containing blood-pressure tablets. They were wafer-thin, and Cathy took one without water. She was still shaking, but the color was slowly returning to her face.

"I'm sorry if I gave you a fright," she said in a daze.

Her eyes were large, the pupils dilated. She looked at me as if she were about to say something important. I saw hesitation flicker in her eyes and knew that she'd changed her mind. I bent down to pick up the sketch pad. Before I could open it, she snatched it out of my hands and slid it into a box.

TWENTY-NINE

THE ELEVATOR

Sylvie watched the words flash on the screen, until it almost seemed to pulsate with a life of its own. She sensed Vincent's mind ticking over as he tried to solve the puzzle.

From her perspective, she had no interest in solving any more escape-room puzzles. The only problem she wanted solved was whatever mechanical failure was preventing them from getting out. She should have been in the business-class lounge at JFK, preparing to board her flight to Paris.

Instead, they were in what was essentially, when she thought about it, a tin can. Cut off from the outside world. There must have been people working in the building; maintenance staff or guards doing the weekend shift. Why had nobody made contact with them? That frightened Sylvie more than the thought that they were hanging by steel cables, possibly hundreds of feet above the ground. There was nothing she could do except remain patient.

Sylvie was familiar with being patient. She'd mastered the art of patience over a lifetime. When she was a child, her father was posted to New Delhi as a commercial attaché at the U.S. embassy. The heat had been unbearable in the summer. Her mother, Marianne, had been a ballet dancer and achieved some success in a second-tier ballet company in Boston. She never adjusted to the heat or the cloistered life of a diplomat's wife. She found both oppressive.

Marianne used whatever excuse she could find to go back home, until she was spending more time in Boston than she was with her family in India. In the end, Marianne ran off with an old boyfriend, leaving Sylvie and her twin brother, Carl, with their father. The next time that Sylvie saw Marianne, her mother was approaching her at the cemetery after Carl's funeral. Sylvie turned her back on her mother and walked off.

Sylvie tried to suppress thoughts of Carl. She'd spent years blocking out the memory of the night her brother died. But in the dark and empty silence of the motionless elevator, there were no distractions. She had no choice but to remember.

Carl had been sick with a bad cold. He'd wanted to stay home in bed. "We had a deal," Sylvie said, cajoling her twin. "I went to your party last week. Now it's my turn." Carl had his driver's license; Sylvie was still working on getting hers. She needed Carl to drive her to the party.

Carl relented, as he usually did with his sister. He adored his twin. Sylvie gave him a cold tablet to perk him up. Neither of them realized the tablet that she'd given Carl was the night dose. It contained an antihistamine that caused drowsiness, especially when mixed with alcohol.

By the time they arrived at the party, there were people swimming in the pool, some still in their clothes after having been pushed in. Others were spread out on loungers, drinking beer from a keg.

Sylvie looked for Alex in the glare of the bright lights against the starlit navy sky. Music throbbed loudly and some people danced on the pool deck. Alex was her latest crush and the reason that she'd been so insistent on coming to the party. Eventually, someone poured her a beer, and then another. And then a few rounds of shots. She forgot all about Alex.

When Carl found her, she was dancing with a guy named Gary. He was a sleaze who did some petty drug dealing at their school. She wouldn't have gone near him if she'd been sober.

"Let's go," said Carl, pulling her away despite her drunken protestations. He helped her to the car. She was so messed up by the alcohol that she didn't realize Carl was groggy, too. He'd drunk two rum and Cokes. Along with the antihistamine, it was a fatal combination.

Carl fell asleep at the wheel on the drive home. Their car veered off the road and went down a grassy embankment. Sylvie was too drunk to do anything other than vaguely register that they were speeding toward trees. They hit a large oak tree with a loud crack. The collision totaled the front of the car. Sylvie unbuckled her seat belt and scrambled out.

She smelled the fire before she saw it. She assumed that Carl was getting out, too. Her shirt caught fire from a spark and she immediately patted out the flames. She didn't notice that Carl hadn't made his way out of the car. The crackle of the flames was so loud that at first, she didn't hear him scream for help.

When she turned back to check on him, she saw that he was still in his seat, desperately trying to get out. Flames licked the hood of the car. By the time Sylvie reached Carl's door, it was too late. The handle was too hot to touch and flames were everywhere. Her last memory of Carl was the way he looked at her through the crackle of orange flames, helpless.

Her dad and her shrink told her that she wasn't to blame for Carl's death. She knew that wasn't true. If she'd really wanted to, she could have saved him.

Sylvie spent weeks in the hospital burns unit. Her father initially had the room's television taken away and banned the nurses from bringing her any reading material other than the pile of books he left her. He didn't want Sylvie to see the tabloid coverage of the accident.

TEEN MODEL SUFFERS THIRD-DEGREE BURNS AS TWIN DIES IN FIERY CRASH. One of the more unsavory headlines said something like, TEEN MODEL RUNS TO SAFETY, LEAVES TWIN BROTHER TO BURN ALIVE. They always used the same photograph: a magazine cover of Sylvie on the water's edge in Bermuda, wearing a white bikini and pouting toward the camera.

It took Sylvie years of therapy to come to terms with what she'd done to Carl, wittingly or unwittingly. It didn't matter. That was nuance. She'd killed her brother as surely as if she'd put a knife in him.

Sometimes she thought it was liberating—to know what she was capable of doing. Once a person had killed, surely it wouldn't be too hard to do it again.

THIRTY

SARA HALL

It was about two months after Lucy died that my roommate, Amanda, convinced me to go with her to a party. Amanda was a management consultant at a Big Three consulting firm. She loved the work but was less enamored with the travel. She was on the road three weeks out of four. When she did come home, she arrived on a Friday night and flew out on the Sunday evening.

She knew what she signed up for when she went into management consulting. The travel was notoriously brutal. As with everything in life, she quickly discovered there was a difference between theory and reality.

"It doesn't take long for business-class airplane seats and five-star hotels to lose their novelty," she told me when I went on my first business trip for Stanhope. She was right. The gloss wore off quickly.

Amanda's constant absences meant that I had the apartment to myself most of the time. It was a luxury that initially I savored after my awful experience with Stacey, my roommate in Chicago. But after Lucy died, my apartment felt cold and unwelcoming with its assembly-line furniture and mass-produced wall prints that seemed to suck the life out of me.

I took little pleasure in being home. It was a place to sleep, nothing more. I preferred being at the office, or working out at the gym until I was soaked through with sweat. That way, I didn't have to deal with what had happened to Lucy.

I refused invitations from colleagues for after-work drinks and rarely attended parties. On one occasion, Vincent left tickets on my desk to the opening of the Broadway production of *Hair*. I had the impression it was his way of thanking me for helping Lucy's mother. I took the tickets, but changed my mind and gave them to a random couple in the elevator of my apartment building. They looked stunned by their good luck.

"What if?" questions about Lucy ate into my conscience like sulfuric acid. What if I hadn't volunteered to go to Seattle to help out on the bid for a mining company in Alaska? What if I'd been around in those last few days before she died? Would things have turned out differently?

The biggest question related to a call I received a few days before Lucy's death. I was working against a deadline at our Seattle office and didn't notice my phone ringing. It was early morning New York time when I checked my phone and saw two missed calls from Lucy one minute apart.

I fully intended to call Lucy back first thing the next day, but I was caught up fielding one of a dozen minor crises that plagued that deal. When I did find time to call Lucy that evening, she didn't pick up.

What if I'd answered Lucy's calls? Would she still be alive? Lucy wasn't one for phone calls; she usually texted. That she'd called me not once but twice suggested that something was seriously wrong. I should have made an effort to get hold of her. If only I'd thought more about my friend than my career.

I did everything that I could to block out the guilt that gnawed at me. Longer hours. Spin classes or cross-training until I could barely move except to come home, shower, and fall asleep from exhaustion.

One night in the middle of the week, I came home and the apartment lights were on. Mellow jazz music was playing in the living room. Amanda was home. I heard the sound of vegetables being expertly cut in the kitchen. One of Amanda's many talents was cordon bleu cooking.

"I made salmon frittata and salad," she called out as I came in.

"Thanks, but I'm not really hungry."

"Sara, you have to join me. I have enough food here for the cast of a Steven Soderbergh movie."

Amanda was a self-confessed film buff with a particular passion for ensemble-cast movies. She was born in Pittsburgh, the daughter of Vietnamese parents who'd emigrated as children during the Vietnam War, via refugee camps. Her dad worked as a stonemason. Her mother managed the business, growing it into a large company that made stone countertops for kitchens all over the city. Her parents worked hard to send Amanda and her sister to a private Catholic school, where they both were valedictorians of their respective graduating classes.

Amanda had graduated from Columbia Business School. She had a huge group of friends who'd stayed in New York after school. Over dinner, Amanda told me that she'd be back in town for a while. She'd been promoted to associate in record time and had now been assigned to a project three blocks from our apartment.

"How's that for convenience!" she said, as if it was a coincidence instead of the product of months of determined lobbying.

It lifted my mood, having Amanda around. She often made

dinner for us both. When she went out with her friends, she always invited me along. I usually thought up an excuse quickly enough, but Amanda was nothing if not persistent.

"What are you doing tonight?" she asked when I arrived home on a Saturday evening, having spent the entire day at the office, with a quick stop afterward for a boxing class. I was sticky with sweat. I threw my bag and water bottle into my room before heading for the bathroom.

"Showering," I replied. "Then I'll put on a movie and probably fall asleep on the sofa. I've had a hell of a week."

"You've gotta be kidding! It's Saturday night."

"I would never joke about something as serious as my Saturday-night plans."

"They're the plans of a geriatric! Come on, Sara, you can do that when you turn eighty." She stood in the corridor, blocking my path to the bathroom.

"After the week I've had, I feel like I'm eighty," I said, circling around her to get to the bathroom.

"Not tonight," she said emphatically. "Tonight is my birthday and you're invited to my party. So put on something glamorous and let's get the hell out of here."

"Where's your party?" I asked, purely out of politeness. I had not one iota of desire to go partying, though I felt a twinge of guilt, because Amanda always put herself out for me.

"At my friend Nina's place," she said. "In Brooklyn. We'll take a cab over. It's a surprise party so . . . pretend to be surprised."

"If it's such a big surprise, how do *you* know about it?"

"Oh, we're supposed to go out for dinner. Then Nina calls me this morning, asking me to come by her apartment first. She says she needs advice selecting wallpaper for her new apartment." Amanda laughed. "She says she's *desperate* for my help. 'You have such amazing taste, Amanda.' Yeah right. I wasn't born yesterday." She gave a dramatic eye roll. "Sara, please, you have to help me out here. I hate surprise parties."

"I'll think about it," I said, disappearing into the bathroom. I figured I'd come up with an excuse while I showered. I didn't count on Amanda's determination—she was waiting for me outside the bathroom with her arms crossed as I exited a few minutes later in a cloud of steam, a fluffy towel wrapped around me and moisturising cream slathered all over my face.

"I won't take no for an answer, Sara," she called after me as I scuttled into my bedroom. I rubbed body lotion onto my legs while I decided whether to change into my pajamas or put on something cute for a party.

I emerged from my bedroom ten minutes later wearing a short black dress and heels. I put on a long necklace of colored beads and fixed my hair in a topknot. Amanda and I arrived at her friend's house not long after 7:00 P.M.

Nina opened the door, barely acknowledging me, and mumbled something about how the wallpaper samples were in the living room.

"Surprise!" The screams were so loud and sudden that I almost jumped. Even though I'd been well prepped, it scared me silly. Amanda, on the other hand, put on a masterful performance.

"Oh my gosh," she screeched, her hand to her mouth in shock. "I can't believe you guys did this! You are *so* awesome."

Gold and silver helium balloons were suspended in the air, spelling out "Happy Birthday Amanda." There was a table of liquor and another with chicken wings, sushi, and other finger food, as well as bowls filled with the remnants of chips.

The place was so crowded that people were pressing up against one another, struggling to make space for Amanda, who went through the room hugging her friends and jokingly admonishing them for arranging the party. "I had no idea you were so good at keeping secrets! This has to go down as my best birthday ever." She was so sweetly sincere that I almost believed her.

I left the crush of people and went up to the rooftop balcony to chill and check out the view. Upstairs was a table with drinks and mixers. I figured I'd make myself a cocktail. I'd done a bartending course when I was working at Rob Roy. I joked at the time that if I couldn't get a job in finance, then I'd become a cocktail waitress on a cruise ship and try to hook a sugar daddy.

"Do you know how to make a gimlet?" I looked up and saw a man so good-looking that my stomach cartwheeled. He wore a white open-neck shirt and jeans. His light brown hair fell over his forehead in a way that made me want to reach over and flip it out of his eyes.

"I sure do," I replied, to cover for my awkwardness. I felt incredibly self-conscious as I filled the stainless-steel cocktail shaker with gin and lime juice, mixed it, and added a spray of soda at the end before pouring the cocktail and adding a thin wedge of lime.

"Looks good," he said. "Make one for yourself. I hate drinking alone."

"My boss doesn't let me drink when I'm working."

"Then you should sue him, or her, for unfair work practices." He said it with a smile that told me he knew I wasn't a bartender.

"I'm Kevin," he said. "Amanda sent me up to find you. What she didn't tell me is that you make a killer gimlet."

"That's because I've never made her a gimlet. We share an apartment, but until recently, we could have counted on one hand the times we've been under the same roof."

"Tell me about it," he groaned. "It's the first time I've seen

Amanda in . . ." He paused to refresh his memory. "I honestly think it's been over a year. Which is sad, because we used to be really close."

"Did you two date?" I felt an irrational twinge of jealousy, followed by a flash of embarrassment at my blunt question. He didn't seem to mind.

"Amanda went out with my best friend when she was in grad school. They broke up years ago. It was a nasty split. Totally Chris's fault. Anyway, they haven't spoken since, but Amanda and I stayed friends, and we try to get together every now and again."

As he spoke, Kevin mixed a gimlet for me this time.

"There," he said, handing me a slightly lopsided-looking drink. "Now we're even." We wandered over to two oversized egg-shaped chairs and pulled them close together. I slipped my shoes off and curled up in one of the chairs. He sat on the edge of the other, leaning forward, so that our heads almost touched as we talked quietly.

"I'm guessing that Amanda is trying to set us up," I said.

"I presume that was the intention," he said. "But I'm not complaining."

"Me, neither," I replied with a smile.

"Tell me about yourself, Sara. Are you in consulting, as well?"

"I'm in finance, actually. I'm at Stanhope and Sons."

"Really," said Kevin in a way that told me he was impressed. "Stanhope is a tough place to get into."

"What about you?" I asked, trying to take the attention off myself. "Where do you work?"

Kevin told me that he was a lawyer at Slater and Moore, which I knew was a top-five law firm by turnover. He specialized in the technology sector. He was in his fifth year and was determined to become the youngest partner in the firm's history. Kevin was ridiculously ambitious in a city of ridiculously ambitious people.

To be fair, Kevin didn't seem to have much choice in the matter. Every member of his family had been a high achiever. His mom was a judge. His eldest sister was an assistant district attorney. His brother was a pediatric cardiologist. His youngest sister was studying fashion design in Paris and was already making more money than all her siblings by selling funky sleepwear via Instagram. Kevin proudly showed me her account.

The party had started moving upstairs, and someone turned up a hip-hop song. "How about we meet up tomorrow?" Kevin half-shouted.

"Where and when?" I yelled back.

It turned out to be unnecessary for us to make arrangements for the next day. I woke up in his bed sometime late in the morning on Sunday. The sun streamed into the bedroom, so that I had to cover my eyes from the glare. Kevin brought in a tray of homemade brioche French toast with raspberries and crème fraîche, and a glass of freshly squeezed orange juice. I eyed my evening dress hanging off the bathroom doorknob and tried to figure out how I'd retrieve it without taking all of Kevin's bedding with me.

And so Lucy was forgotten amid my burgeoning romance with Kevin. Hotshot lawyer, talented chef, and all-around good guy.

THIRTY-ONE

THE ELEVATOR

In the dark, suffocating world of the stalled elevator, the rules were different. As time passed without any sign of rescue, Vincent seemed more impotent than omnipotent. Even Jules, whose throat was still burning from Vincent's assault, lost all respect for him.

It was apparent to both Jules and Sylvie that Vincent did not have a strategy to get them out, nor did he appear to be trying to come up with one. He sat passively in the back corner of the elevator, clutching his head. Sylvie and Jules didn't know that he had a concussion; they thought he'd given up.

Occasionally, he reassured them that he was certain they were being rescued. "Any minute now," he'd mutter. The silence that followed his words rendered them empty. And so they lost even more respect for him.

They both blamed Vincent for their predicament. He'd brought them there with his text message insisting they all turn up, and he'd failed to get them out when things went awry. It was almost, Sylvie

thought to herself, as if Vincent wanted them there. As if he was testing them.

Sylvie looked at her watch as midnight approached. Her flight was
taking off. Her trip to Paris was over and with it, most likely, her relationship with Marc. There was an outside chance that she could sal-
vage things if she was able to call Marc before her flight arrived in
Paris, seven hours from now, to let him know why she wasn't on it.
Otherwise, Marc would wait for her outside the arrivals hall, just
as they'd arranged, clutching a bouquet of roses—cream, or maybe
pink.

He'd look for her among the stream of arriving passengers. When
she didn't turn up, he'd call her phone and leave her a voice message,
trying but not quite succeeding at disguising his irritation. "Sylvie,
darling," he'd say. "When you come out of customs, look for the
impatient guy with the flowers standing by the car-rental desks."

Eventually, as more time passed, Marc would assume that she'd
stood him up. He'd toss the flowers into the trash and text her that it
was over.

He'd warned her once. They'd been in bed together in Paris, a
week after she'd canceled a trip at the last minute due to a crisis at
work, where a client got cold feet and threatened to pull out of a deal.
Sylvie rescheduled her Paris trip for the following week, thinking that
Marc would understand. He knew that her job was demanding.

"Sylvie," Marc said on that first night back together in Paris, lifting himself up on his arm and looking down at her lying naked under
his white sheet. "I'm not your concubine. If that's the relationship
you want, then have it with someone else. Not with me. I adore you,
but I've never been the type to take second place to anyone, or anything. Least of all a job." He bent down to kiss her breasts.

Sylvie thought about Marc's ultimatum as she stared out into the wall of black, listening to the others breathing softly around her. It was strange how they could barely see one another in the dark and yet they were acutely aware of every aspect of one another—their breathing, their moods, their various positions in the cramped space. They were packed so tightly together that Sylvie could almost feel their hearts beating in unison, as if they were a single organism.

Occasional restless noises scored the silence. Sam whimpering in his opioid-induced sleep. The clearing of a throat. Someone folding and unfolding arms, shifting cramped legs. A hollow cough. The rumbling of an empty stomach. It was an intimacy that Sylvie had only ever really shared with lovers.

The quote on the screen gleamed in the dark. The answer kept slipping away from Vincent just as he thought he remembered where it was from.

It was so quiet that he wondered if the others were hatching a plan against him. They knew that he'd screwed them on their bonuses and that he'd bad-mouthed them to executive management in their performance reviews. There were no longer any secrets between them, and that frightened him.

Vincent stifled a groan of pain from his pounding headache. He couldn't allow them to know that he was injured. His instincts told him they were already hyperaware that he was weak and helpless in the dark without his glasses.

If they knew he was concussed and in danger of passing out, then Jules would come after him. It was with this thought in mind that Vincent realized he could no longer feel the hard metal contours of the pistol resting reassuringly in the back of his pants. He checked his belt and rear pockets. The gun wasn't there anymore.

It worried him that the Glock was missing. He figured he must have lost it when the elevator crashed. He surreptitiously tried to locate it, sliding his feet across the floor when he thought the others weren't paying attention. All he found was broken glass from the smashed elevator mirror that crunched under his shoes. He checked the front pocket of his pants. The magazine was still there. That reassured him.

Sweat poured down Vincent's face. It was from both the heat and the physical exertion of not allowing himself to succumb to the pain. He had to fight a constant urge to take some of Sam's oxycodone. It would make him hazy, vulnerable. He couldn't afford to let down his guard.

Vincent's sense of smell had grown acute in the dark. He could differentiate each person's odor. He could almost taste the antagonism in their rancid, unwashed mouths. He used the touch of his fingers in lieu of sight as he maneuvered around the narrow space with the help of the handrails.

Over time, Vincent's hearing became sharper. He could hear their moods—the hiss of an inhaling breath, the impatient tapping of fingers, their minds whirring as they plotted against him. Only the blackness that cloaked them all protected him.

Jules unbuttoned his shirt to cool down. Vincent's chest was bare. Sylvie still wore her cashmere wool-blend suit—a pencil skirt and fitted jacket. She wanted to look her best when they were rescued. After the humiliating revelations of her meager bonus, and with her face grimy and hair in disarray, all she had left was her dignity.

As more time passed, her clothes began to feel sticky from sweat. She worried that she'd get heatstroke if she continued wearing her heavy winter suit. Slowly, she began to unbutton her jacket.

Vincent and Jules heard her fingers undoing each button and the faint rustle of fabric as she removed her jacket and dropped it in a heap on the floor. Then more buttons being undone and the sound of her shirt coming off her body. They didn't need to see anything to know that the silky ripple hitting the floor meant she had tossed that aside, too. They unwittingly wet their lips as they imagined Sylvie stripping in the dark.

Was she down to her bra? Or did she have nothing underneath that gossamer silk shirt, which she always wore with the top three buttons left tantalizingly open? Their imaginations ran wild as they moved closer to her, drawn to her like magnets.

Jules took a deep breath. He made himself think of Geena. She was a cute redheaded law student whom he'd met at a dinner party a few weeks ago. She was sharp-witted in the endearing way of a graduate student trying too hard to impress. She made him laugh with stories of her professors, some of whom he knew from his time studying at the same law school.

She told him that her parents had pushed her into studying for a JD. While her preference had always been to specialize in international law, she was gradually drifting toward tax law. It seemed more practical.

"That's a good move. Tax is where the money is," he'd reassured her as they smoked on the balcony.

They went on two dates. The first time, he took her to a Japanese restaurant, where a chef grilled a teppanyaki banquet in front of them while they drank sake from blue porcelain cups. The second time, they'd gone to Old Henry's, a jazz bar in Hell's Kitchen that served Cajun food on oversize red plates and had the best live acid jazz anywhere. Geena took a cab home straight afterward, with an excuse that she had a paper to submit the next day. It wasn't exactly how he'd hoped the night would end. Within ten minutes, he'd found a replacement on a dating app. Also a redhead. They met at a bar and had a few drinks before he went back to her place. She was clingy and flaky. Not his type. A poor substitute, he thought, leaving her apartment before dawn.

Jules had arranged to see Geena for brunch on Sunday morning. He'd been looking forward to seeing her again all week. As time dragged on in the elevator, he wondered if he'd make their brunch date. He'd have a hell of a story to tell her about this ordeal.

He ran his hand over the back of his neck. It was slick with sweat. The thick, cloying heat reminded him of Louisiana in late summer. When he visited Lafayette as a young child, his grandmother would press ice cubes into his mouth as they lazed about on her porch swing in the sultry evenings. It was the only way to stay cool in the summer. He thought about sucking ice cubes as he fell asleep.

THIRTY-TWO

SARA HALL

I was in an internal meeting to review our strategy for a new deal when an executive assistant came quietly into the room and whispered into my ear that I had a call. I made my apologies and stepped out of the meeting. Sam looked annoyed at my sudden disappearance. I guess he thought I should have told the assistant to take a message, but my dad was in the hospital again and I assumed the call was from his doctor. And, after two years at the firm, I felt that I didn't need to explain my every move to Sam.

I took the call at my desk while looking out of the window at a gray sky that threatened rain.

"Hello?"

"Hello, Sara. This is Cathy. Lucy Marshall's mother?" A wave of guilt washed over me.

"How are you, Cathy?" My voice rose into a falsetto of false exuberance as I tried to cover my embarrassment. I had promised Cathy to stay in touch, yet I hadn't once picked up the phone in the year since I'd left her standing in the doorway of Lucy's apartment, looking frightened and confused, like a lost child, the day I helped her pack up Lucy's things.

"I'm fine, Sara," she said without a hint of accusation. "I'm calling because the anniversary of Lucy's death is coming up. I was hoping we could get together. That is, if you have time."

"I'd like that."

"How about Sunday afternoon? At my apartment?" She rattled off the address of her apartment in Queens.

"That would be perfect." The timing worked out well. Kevin was away that weekend, which meant that I was free.

If truth be told, I would probably never have seen or spoken to Cathy again if she hadn't called me that day. I don't have any excuse for my lapse other than that work still consumed me. My hours were brutal, and whatever time and energy I had left, I put into my relationship with Kevin, which had become so serious that we were inseparable whenever we weren't working. In my defense, I barely had time to see my own parents, let alone check in on Lucy's mother.

My father's heart and kidneys were in bad shape and he now needed dialysis every second day. Meanwhile, my mother had to give up driving after a minor car accident, which the doctors attributed to residual weakness in her left arm following her stroke. She could no longer drive Dad to his appointments. I told Mom that I'd ask for a transfer to our Chicago office, or quit Stanhope altogether and find a job in Chicago. She immediately put a stop to that idea. "No, Sara," she told me. "I can't think of anything worse than seeing you go backward."

In the end, I insisted on paying for a woman to routinely drive my father to dialysis and help my mother shop, as well as clean their apartment every week. It eased the burden on my mother and assuaged my guilt.

I tried to see them when I could, but it was difficult finding the time. I'd try to steal a few hours to visit them if I was traveling through Chicago for work, but such business trips were infrequent.

The previous year, I'd spent both Thanksgiving and Christmas with them, even though it caused friction with Kevin. He was mad that I didn't go with him to New Hampshire to meet his family over Christmas. They traditionally had a catered Christmas lunch with over fifty guests. His brother and sisters would all fly in with their respective partners. The annual affair was a big deal for his family. That year, Kevin was the only one there without a partner. He couldn't understand why I insisted on going to Chicago for Christmas when I'd already been there for Thanksgiving a few weeks earlier.

I adored Kevin, but he came from a different world. A world in which, for one thing, he didn't carry the burden of expectation that came with being an only child. I tried to shield him from the harsh reality of my life. I was afraid that if he knew my family's situation, he might not want me anymore.

On the really bad days, when my dad was in the hospital and my mother was holding a lone vigil at his bedside, I told myself that at least my job helped cover their medical bills. I don't know what they would have done otherwise.

On the work front, everything was amazing. I was promoted and now had two analysts reporting to me. My salary had nearly doubled, as had my bonus. I'd paid back half my college loans and expected to be debt-free within the next two years. I was even thinking of buying an apartment in Brooklyn as an investment.

My life revolved around the firm. I was fully indoctrinated. I talked the Stanhope jargon as if it were my mother tongue. Dissent was discouraged, no matter what our brochures said about diversity of opinion, and I tailored my thoughts to conform to the consensus of the firm. I kissed whoever's ass I had to kiss and paid the necessary homage in the lead-up to bonus time.

I was as despicable as the rest of them, really, when I think about it. I chased money as if my life depended upon it. I got high on the adrenaline rush of the deal and learned to block out the impact on the lives of ordinary folk struggling to hold it together.

The only people I spent time with were Kevin and people from work. My roommate, Amanda, was transferred to Amsterdam shortly before the lease on our apartment expired. I found a one-bedroom apartment on the same block with a relatively reasonable rent. The Realtor had described it as compact; it was, in fact, tiny, but it was all I needed. I half-hoped that Kevin would insist on moving in, or ask me to move in with him. I was disappointed when he made it clear that, much as he loved dating me, he wasn't looking for a live-in relationship yet.

Weekends, when I had free weekends, were about spending time with Kevin, doing laundry, getting exercise, and shopping for food that I never had time to eat. On the Sunday I was to meet Cathy, I was in the office all morning, catching up on work. I lost track of time and had to rush to Queens in an Uber.

I rang Cathy's doorbell, holding a bouquet of white roses and a box of chocolates I'd picked up at a convenience store near the office. Cathy opened the door and kissed my cheek. There was a welcoming smile on her face, though her eyes were stoic. She looked like someone who had endured great tragedy but never succumbed to it.

Still, she'd aged considerably since I'd last seen her. There were flecks of gray in her thick dark hair. She was thinner than before and moved slowly. She had the aura of a woman entering old age, though she was only fifty-nine. There was something else I noticed as Cathy double-locked the door and then connected the security chain: She looked afraid.

"I'm so pleased you could make it, Sara," she said, gesturing for me to take a seat on a blue-gray sofa that I recognized from Lucy's apartment.

"I'm sorry that I haven't been in touch," I said.

"No need to apologize. I know how busy the firm keeps you all," she said. "I wouldn't hear from Lucy for weeks because of her work schedule. Eventually, I'd panic and leave her half a dozen messages, and she'd text back to say she was fine but very busy and that I shouldn't bother her."

"The hours are long," I admitted. "I travel a lot. . . . Some days I don't know what hemisphere I'm in, let alone what country. But that's no excuse."

"As it happens, this might be the last time we see each other. I'm moving to Baltimore." She paused to let me digest her news. "I've decided to move back and live with my sister. She's alone, as well." I could feel Cathy's pain as she stumbled over those words. "We thought it would make sense for us to live together. Keep each other company. We inherited a lovely apartment, big enough for both of us. I can rent out this place, and I'll find part-time work in Baltimore. It's time I cut back on work anyway; I've had some health issues lately."

"Nothing serious, I hope."

"Enough to remind me that I'm getting older and need to stop over-doing it. And with Lucy gone, there's not much to keep me here." Her voice had a sadness that seemed to reach into the depths of her soul.

"Cathy, it sounds like a good decision. I hope you'll be very happy there."

"I'm sure I will be," she said. "Now, I'm forgetting myself." She disappeared into the kitchen. I heard her clattering about and the stove click on as she set the kettle boiling.

"How do you like your coffee?" she called out.

"Cream, no sugar."

I looked around the living area while she was in the kitchen. Her apartment had large windows with a view of a park across the street. On the wall was a series of framed photographs of Lucy, spanning from her baby photos to one taken a few months before she died.

Cathy came back in and passed me my cup of coffee. She put down a plate with pastries and sat next to me on the sofa. "I just unpacked the boxes I brought over from Lucy's apartment last week, when I began packing for my move. I won't have much space at the new apartment. I've had to sort through Lucy's things to decide what to keep and what I'll donate, sell, or throw out."

"That can't have been easy for you," I said sympathetically. I remembered the tears that rolled soundlessly down her cheeks that day at Lucy's apartment as she put her daughter's most precious belongings into boxes.

"It has to be done," she said, her voice cracking. "Time doesn't heal the pain. It just dulls it. Going through Lucy's things again . . ." She swallowed and paused to compose herself. "It dredged up more questions about her death. The state of her apartment—do you remember the mess we found when we packed up?"

"You thought someone had gone through her closet," I said diplomatically.

"Everyone told me Lucy must have been erratic before she died and that's why her apartment was in such disarray," she responded. "But I wasn't imagining things. In fact, the very next day proved to me that someone had been there."

"In what way?"

"When the movers brought everything here, they were one box short. The missing box was the one that contained Lucy's personal computer. I labeled it myself when we were packing. I told them that they must have left a box behind, but they showed me their logbook and they delivered the same number of boxes that they'd collected from Lucy's apartment that morning. The only explanation I can think of is that someone went into the apartment and took it."

"Did you tell the police?"

"They said it was an insurance matter, that I should take it up with the moving company. But I know that box was stolen. I'm convinced."

"Why would anyone take it? There were plenty of other valuables."

"I don't know." Cathy sighed. "I think it had something to do with the firm. Lucy spoke cryptically about work. She was nervous. She tried to tell me something a couple of times and then stopped herself. The more I've thought about it"—she chose her next words carefully—"the more I think there's a link between Stanhope and her death."

"How so?" I asked.

"I'm not sure," she replied. "There are things I still don't understand about her time at Stanhope and Sons."

"Lucy loved her job," I said, trying not to sound defensive. I got why Cathy needed to find a reason for why Lucy had taken her life, but it seemed to me that blaming Stanhope was far-fetched and unfair. "In fact, Lucy liked her job so much that there were times when she didn't want to go home at the end of the day. It just doesn't jibe with what I knew of Lucy."

"But you weren't there when Lucy died."

"I was in Seattle."

"Maybe something changed while you were away. Something happened to Lucy. Is that possible?" Cathy asked.

"We weren't in touch while I was away," I conceded. "Except for one night, when I received a couple of missed calls from Lucy. It struck me as somewhat strange."

"Strange in what way?"

"Lucy had never been one for calling. She preferred to message me. I'd been in Seattle for almost three weeks straight. I received the calls, oh, two or three days before Lucy died. I was in meetings until late. When I checked my phone on the way to the hotel, I noticed two missed calls from Lucy. It was too late to call back. I messaged her. She didn't respond. I tried to get in touch the next day, but she didn't pick up. I . . . I never spoke to her again."

"Did she leave a message? Send a text? Do you have any idea what she wanted?"

"No, nothing," I said. "I presumed it was a work question, and that she'd found the answer herself."

Cathy took a deep breath. She seemed nervous. Her eyes were fixed on my face, as if trying to gauge my reaction. "I'll be straight with you, Sara," she said. "I think something was going on at Stanhope. I think Lucy was frightened. Do you have any idea what might have worried her?"

"I don't," I told her honestly.

During the silence that followed, I thought to myself that my answer wasn't quite true. I had always found it strange that Lucy wanted to hide our friendship.

And then there was Vincent's request to look out for papers at Lucy's apartment when I went to help Cathy pack. When *he* sent me there, in fact. It seemed like a reasonable request at the time, discretely reclaiming documents belonging to the firm, as they might be confidential. Except there was something about the way that Vincent had acted that unsettled me. That afternoon, when I returned to work, he stopped by my desk and asked if I'd found anything at Lucy's apartment. I told him I hadn't found a thing. He seemed disappointed—and something else that I couldn't quite put my finger on. It was unlike Vincent to be so on edge.

I wandered over to Cathy's living room window. A boy on a blue bike raced another boy along the street until they were obscured by a hedge. A man stood across the way, smoking a cigarette. He stubbed it out when he saw me watching and walked off with his hands in the pocket of a gray hoodie.

"The firm is very competitive. It gets intense," I said, turning back to Cathy. "But I've never seen anything untoward happen. They work us hard, but that's about it. It's a very reputable firm. I don't believe that Lucy's death had anything to do with Stanhope. She would have confided in me if something had been going on."

Cathy pursed her lips. She said nothing as she absorbed my fierce loyalty to an organization that she thought might be responsible for her daughter's death.

"Sara, why were you so secretive about your friendship with Lucy?" Her words pierced me.

"It was Lucy who insisted that nobody from work know that we were friends. To tell you the truth, I never understood why it had to be kept secret. Lucy never explained it to me."

"Maybe Lucy was trying to protect you," observed Cathy. "Here, come with me, Sara." She took me to her spare room. It was lined with floor-to-ceiling cupboards filled with books, records, and CDs.

"I've taken good care of Lucy's record collection for years. Unfortunately, I won't have room for them all once I move. I'm selling them to a collector. All except one," she said.

She handed me a record in its original cover. "Lucy had a Post-it note on here with your name. I think she meant you to have it. I found it when I was going through these last week, before the appraiser came. That's partly why I called."

It was a Fleetwood Mac single called *Sara*, the original pressing. Lucy was obsessive about her record collection, which she'd kept since she was a kid. It would have been something of a sacrifice for her to give me a mint copy of a rare seventies record, even if it did bear my name.

"Thank you," I whispered to Cathy. I had celebrated my birthday while I was in Seattle; I guessed that Lucy planned to give me the record as a present when I returned. I blinked my eyes quickly and looked at the cover while I composed myself. I was about to open it up and take out the record when Cathy said in a strange, thin voice, "Better that you do that at home."

As if to distract me, she pointed out a family photo of Lucy blowing out her candles on her second birthday, her proud parents standing behind her. Intelligence burned in Lucy's eyes even when she was a baby.

"Her father left us when she was three," Cathy said without taking her eyes off the photo. "I think that's why Lucy was a late talker. When she started talking, she told me with her very first sentence that she never talked before because she didn't have anything interesting to say. Imagine hearing that from a child who had barely put two words together before."

We returned to the living room sofa. I put the record down near my bag. Cathy made me another coffee and we talked a little about Lucy's death. She told me about her meeting with Vincent after Lucy died and the way she didn't feel that Lucy's suicide note rang true. She showed it to me so that I could see for myself.

Cathy kept repeating her concerns that something had happened at Stanhope in the days before Lucy's death. It made me feel very uncomfortable. I wanted to sympathize with Cathy, but equally, I was fiercely loyal to my firm. Each time she said anything, I sensed her eyes on me to check my reaction, as if she wasn't sure whether to trust me or not.

"Will you do me a favor, Sara?" Cathy asked after a while. "I have a small box of Lucy's things that I need stored. Would you mind keeping it for me?"

"Of course, I can take it with me now if you like," I offered. I wasn't entirely sure where I'd put it. I had limited storage space in my own apartment.

"No," she said, abruptly. "It's heavy. You'll hurt your back carrying it. I'll have it sent to you when I send my own boxes to Baltimore later in the week. Leave that record, too. I'll put it in the box. It would be a shame if it fell and was damaged on your way home."

I wrote down my address for her and I put Cathy's contact details in Baltimore into my phone so that we could stay in touch.

"I'm so pleased you invited me today," I said as Cathy escorted me to the door. "I very much enjoyed seeing you again."

"Me, too," said Cathy. She gave me a hug. Then she looked through the peephole before opening the locks on her door and letting me out. I felt her eyes on me through that peephole as she watched me walk across the landing to the elevator.

I left Cathy's building and walked the two blocks to the subway. I had a weird feeling that I was being followed. I tried to look behind me as naturally as I could, but it was hard to tell who it might have been. There were quite a few people walking to the station.

When I boarded my train, I saw a man with headphones and a baseball cap sit down at the other end of the car. He lowered his eyes when he saw me watching him. He had a pale, freckled face and a prominent chin. He looked familiar.

It was only that evening, when I walked into my health club for a workout, that I realized I'd seen a guy with the same sharp features in our office building before. He'd been wearing a suit. I'd seen him through a glass-walled meeting room, talking with Vincent.

THIRTY-THREE

THE ELEVATOR

W hat's the longest that anyone has ever been stuck in an elevator?" Jules asked. It was now Saturday, late morning. Everyone but Sam was awake. "We might be breaking a world record here," he added in a feeble attempt at humor.

"We're not." Sylvie's voice was husky from sleep. "A woman in China was found in a stuck elevator after a month. She'd died of dehydration. They found scratch marks on the elevator doors."

"A month! Let's hope that people care enough about us to notice we're missing faster than that," said Jules. "My ex will definitely notice when I don't come to collect Annabelle this morning. Though I doubt she'll send out the search party for me until the child-support payments stop coming through."

"She'll probably be relieved when you don't turn up," mumbled Sylvie under her breath.

"Back in '99, a guy was stuck in an elevator for forty-one hours," Vincent said, pleased the atmosphere had become less tense. "He was a magazine editor working the night shift. He went downstairs to take a cigarette break. On the way up, the elevator got stuck. Forty-one hours. He almost went mad," said Vincent. "Strangely enough, his troubles really started after he got out."

"Oh yeah?"

"A personal-injury lawyer told him he could get a big payout, but first he had to stop working to show that he suffered psychological damage from being stuck in the elevator alone for so long. He quit his job. The lawsuit dragged on for years. Eventually, he received a paltry amount. He ended up unemployed, without anywhere to live. No money. No job."

"At least he got out," said Jules. He was sitting on the floor, his legs crammed between Sam's sleeping body and the elevator wall.

Vincent had held the elevator doors open for a few minutes earlier to allow the ice-cold air from the elevator shaft to waft inside. It was a crude way of cooling the place down, and their only option, given that the heating system couldn't be turned off. Jules and Vincent also used the opportunity to pee through the gap. They listened for sounds of other elevators moving, people talking. All they heard was the howl of wind and Jules's voice bouncing off the concrete walls when he called out for help. Vincent let the doors close again.

That had probably been an hour ago. Jules had lost track of time. He'd turned his phone off to save the battery. The elevator was illuminated only by the white screen of the television monitor, which still displayed the last clue in red letters.

Jules's foot felt numb. He tried to move it gently to restore circulation. It didn't help. The pins and needles were painful. He needed to move around, but when he tried to stand up, he accidentally brushed against Sam. Heat was radiating from his body. Jules knelt down to check on him.

"I think Sam has a temperature," he said. Sam's forehead was hot and slick with sweat.

Vincent scrambled over clumsily in the dark. Sam was clearly running a high fever. Vincent took his water bottle out of his briefcase and poured water straight into Sam's mouth, trickling it down his throat. Sam swallowed in his sleep. Vincent put the cap on tight and returned the bottle to his briefcase. The rest of them could wait to drink. He hoped they'd be rescued before there was a need to ration water.

They all sat back down and listened to the rattle of Sam's breathing. It reminded Jules of his horse, Prince, who'd hurt his leg after being spooked by a low-flying crop duster. Jules had been six. He vividly remembered the evening when the vet came to check the injured horse and a decision was made to put it down.

Jules hid in a storeroom in the barn, not too far away from the stall where the horse lay. He was so close to the horse that the shots were deafening. He'd flinched, as if it were him and not the horse who had been shot. The vet had done a poor job with the first shot. Jules would never forget Prince's horrible whine of agony before the second shot killed him.

"It would have cost us a small fortune to save that horse," he overheard his dad telling his mother later that night as they argued about whether it had been truly necessary. It was Jules's first lesson in the ruthlessness of the adult world.

Vincent put the back of his hand to Sam's pasty forehead and shook his head, much as the vet had done when he'd examined Prince's leg.

"His fever seems very high," said Vincent. He asked Jules to switch on his phone again quickly for light, and then he rolled up Sam's left sleeve. Red threads ran up and down Sam's arm and his skin felt warm and inflamed.

"He has an infection. He needs to get medical treatment soon," said Vincent.

"What happens if he doesn't?" Jules asked.

"He could die." Vincent's voice was raw with worry.

Exhausted, hot, and desperate for a drink, Jules was struck by the uncharitable thought that things might work out in his favor if Sam died. It would certainly improve the odds of his being selected for Eric Miles's old job. Without Sam, there would be one less contender.

THIRTY-FOUR

SARA HALL

I was going through my address book while doing my Christmas correspondence when I came across Cathy's email address. I'd lost touch with her after she moved to live with her sister. I picked up the phone to call her. It was Sunday evening and I figured this would be as good a time as any to call.

"Hello, is this Cathy Marshall?" I asked when an older woman answered the phone.

"No, it's not." The woman's voice sounded like a deeper version of Cathy's. "Who is this, please?" It must have been Cathy's sister. She probably thought I was trying to sell her something.

"My name is Sara," I said. "I was a friend of Cathy's daughter, Lucy. I called to see how Cathy has settled in and to wish her merry Christmas."

A long silence followed. She was still there—I could hear the television blaring in the background—but she didn't say a word. "Is everything all right with Cathy?" I asked. "Can I speak with her?"

"Cathy's not, uh, not here."

"Is she on vacation?" I asked.

"I'm sorry to tell you this. Cathy's dead."

"Dead?" I remembered when Cathy had almost collapsed while we were packing up Lucy's apartment. I'd had to find her medication for her. "I didn't realize Cathy's heart problems were that serious."

"It wasn't her heart," she responded. "Cathy was killed in a hit-and-run five days before she was due to move here with me. She was crossing the street by the supermarket near her apartment. The car came out of nowhere, knocked her down, didn't stop. The coroner said that she was probably already dead before she hit the ground."

When I got off the phone with Cathy's sister, I sat down robotically on the nearest chair. The news was incomprehensible. For months, I'd been imagining Cathy living happily in Baltimore, enjoying a new life away from the tragedy of Lucy's death. Except Cathy had never even made it there. She'd died a few days after I visited her apartment.

When Kevin arrived at my place after the gym to join me for dinner, he found me curled up in an armchair, staring into space. "What's wrong?" he asked.

"The mother of a friend died in a hit-and-run. It happened over the summer, but I just found out."

"That's awful," he said dutifully. He sat down on the arm of the chair and hugged me against his chest. "Anyone I know?"

"No, you wouldn't know her." I stood abruptly. I wanted to be alone. I went back to the kitchen and finished cutting vegetables for a salad while I put the pasta in a pot of boiling water. I had never told Kevin about Lucy; it just never came up in conversation.

After dinner, Kevin booted up his laptop to write emails he needed to send before his early-morning flight to San Francisco. I took out my computer, as well, but I couldn't concentrate on my work, even though it was due the next afternoon.

I was curious about what had happened with Cathy. I vividly remembered the day she'd invited me to her apartment in Queens; her warmth and then the sudden switch to conspiracy theories when she suggested that Stanhope had been a factor in Lucy's death. At the time, I chalked it up to grief. But I also remembered all those locks on Cathy's door and the way she'd carefully looked through the peephole before opening it.

I searched for newspaper articles from around the time when Cathy was killed. A few articles came up. One was a front-page story in a local Queens newspaper: "Shopper killed in hit-and-run." The newspaper illustrated the story with a photograph of a shopping bag filled with groceries lying in the middle of the road alongside a carton of smashed eggs. One of the egg yolks was on the dirty gray asphalt, a splatter of red blood running through it.

One article said the car that killed Cathy had been stolen. Another had a still from CCTV footage, showing the car driving away. The driver wore sunglasses and a baseball cap. Between the hat and the tinted windows of the car, the papers said there was no way for the cops to pull together so much as a rough composite sketch of the driver.

There was something about the driver that reminded me of the man who had followed me to the subway after I left Cathy's apartment.

I found another article with quotes from a cabdriver who'd witnessed the collision close-up. He told the reporter that the driver had swerved intentionally and then accelerated in the seconds before he hit Cathy. "It was as if he'd chosen to hit her out of all the people crossing the street," he said. "It seemed personal."

I could find no other newspaper articles about Cathy's death. It was overtaken by other car accidents, other suburban tragedies. I couldn't find any updates on whether the driver who killed Cathy had ever been arrested. I eventually found a five-page coroner's report on Cathy's death, which was in the public records on a government website.

It appeared that a homicide unit had been briefly assigned to the case. They'd looked into Cathy's financial and personal affairs but found no obvious motive. The coroner said there was no indication that anyone would want to kill a woman in her late fifties with no romantic entanglements, no ties to criminals, no involvement in drugs, gambling, or the sex industry, and no children to fight over what was a relatively insignificant inheritance anyway. He also noted that there was no indication that it was a thrill killing. In the end, the coroner chalked up Cathy's death to a gangbanger in a stolen car, driving too fast and not looking where he was going. I stared pensively at my laptop screen.

"What're you looking at, hon?" Kevin asked.

"My friend's mother, the one who was killed—it made me curious. It's strange that I didn't know she was dead until now."

"Were you close?" Kevin asked. "It's obviously hit you hard."

"No, we weren't close," I said. "But I think we were united by grief. Her daughter, my friend Lucy, she died quite tragically. I felt responsible for keeping an eye on her mother. I did a pretty awful job of it, to be honest. Hell, it took me six months to find out she was dead."

"Don't beat yourself up, babe," Kevin said. "You work longer hours than I do, and I'm no slouch in that department. Ease up a bit."

"It comes with the territory," I said. "If I want to move up in the firm, then I have to work the hours demanded."

"Stanhope won't fire you if you cut back a bit." He lifted up my chin so that I was looking into his bottomless hazel eyes, which were filled with intensity and something else that I couldn't quite decipher. "They think the world of you, Sara. I can't tell you how proud I am of you. The thing is . . ." He hesitated.

"What?"

"If things develop between us, it's just not sustainable that we both work such demanding hours. We'd never see each other."

"What do you mean, 'develop'?"

Kevin shrugged. "We barely see each other some weeks."

"Whose fault is that?" I asked, defensive. "You're on the West Coast two weeks out of four. I try my best to arrange my own travel so that I'm here when you're in town. I know it doesn't always work out, but I really do try."

"I'm not blaming you, Sara," Kevin said softly. "What I am trying to say—in my clumsy way—is that we should coordinate better. I want to spend more time with you, Sara."

He gave me a long kiss. "I have a suggestion," he said. "Let's have a moratorium on computers and phones when we're together. I can think of a lot more interesting things to do."

"I was hoping you'd say that," I said, and he closed my laptop with his free hand.

Later that night, I lay awake in bed, listening to Kevin sleeping soundly beside me. I was still reeling from the news of Cathy's death. I'd met Cathy twice in my life, yet I felt as if I'd lost a close friend. I suppose it was because of the way she was killed, and just as she was trying to get her life back on track.

I wondered whether I should contact the police and tell them what I remembered from my visit to Queens. The way Cathy had been extra particular about her personal safety. Checking the corridor through the peephole, securing the locks and security chain on the door.

I thought that perhaps I should tell them about the hair-raising feeling I'd had when I left Cathy's apartment and walked to the subway. It had felt as if I was being followed, and then someone with similar clothes to the ones in the description of the hit-and-run driver appeared to have followed me onto the train.

On top of all that, there was Cathy's theory that Stanhope had been involved in Lucy's death, though she never said how.

When I woke in the morning, Kevin was gone and I was more rational. If I contacted the police, I'd sound just as paranoid as Cathy had sounded to me when she blamed the firm for Lucy's death.

I didn't get the chance to debate the merits further. It quickly slipped my mind as I became consumed in another high-octane deal that took over my life for a month. And just as that deal was being closed, I received a frantic call from my mother in the middle of the night.

"Dad collapsed," she said. "He's in intensive care at Chicago General. They don't think they can save him this time. You'd better come, Sara."

Dad's doctors said his kidneys were failing. They gave him a week to live, two at the most. I immediately arranged to work from the firm's Chicago office so that I could be with my parents. I didn't have the luxury of taking unpaid leave, which Vincent suggested when I told him what had happened. My parents' basic medical insurance didn't cover the full cost of Dad's treatment. The hospital bill would run into tens of thousands of dollars. I was the one who'd have to pay the bill.

I stayed at my parents' apartment with my mom. Most days, I

headed to the hospital straight after work, usually in the late afternoon or early evening, to sit with Mom at Dad's bedside or give her a chance to go home and rest while I took on the night duty of being by his side.

There is nothing pleasant about a death vigil in a hospital. The man in the room's other bed screamed in pain every time his morphine ran low—sharp-pitched cries that made my father's eyes dart in panic even though he was only semiconscious. I could tell it distressed Dad, and it certainly upset my mom.

I asked the hospital to move my father to a private room. It would balloon the final hospital bill even further, but I didn't care. My dad deserved a peaceful death.

It went on for a couple of weeks. Based on all medical rationale, Dad should have been dead. The doctors were amazed that he was still hanging on. They didn't know my dad. He was a stubborn man to the core—for good and for bad. That's probably why he lasted so long, over all the years of extensive chronic health trouble.

In his last days, I barely recognized him. He had a yellow complexion from jaundice and pain-filled, milky eyes. He seemed a shrunken shadow of a man even though I'd always thought of him as larger than life. He had been whittled away, until there was barely anything left of him.

My father died on a Tuesday night, during the worst snowstorm in Chicago in seven years. It was impossible for me to get from our Chicago office to the hospital in time to be with him before he died. There weren't any cabs until the early hours of the morning, by which time the orderlies had already removed his body from his room and taken him to the hospital morgue.

I hated that I hadn't been with him when he died, but most of all that I hadn't been there to support my mother. That really tore me up. I was so single-minded in my dedication to the job that even though my father was close to death, I'd insisted on going into work that day, despite the blizzard that had been forecast.

It took me a long time to forgive myself. If truth be told, I'm not entirely sure I ever have. It made me reflect on whether I wanted to work at a firm that made such demands on my time that I couldn't take an afternoon off to hold my father's hand as he lay dying.

In the hospital bathroom, washing my tear-stained face after they told me I had arrived too late, I asked my reflection, "Who have you become?" When had making money taken precedence over the people I loved?

We buried Dad in a small ceremony, attended by a smattering of relatives and some old friends going back decades. Kevin offered to fly out for the funeral. I knew that he had to prep for a crucial deposition and told him it wasn't necessary. That was a bald-faced lie; I needed him so badly that it hurt.

After Dad died, I insisted that my mother move to special accommodations. Her own health trouble had made her frail, and there was a real possibility she might have another stroke from the anxiety and stress of Dad's final illness and death.

I was living too far away to check in on her. I worried greatly that she might collapse and that nobody would know until her body was found days later when the lady I'd hired to help her shop and clean came by. I needed someone to check in on my mom every day and make sure that she took her medication. Mostly, she needed company.

I found a place for her at an independent-living complex for retirees. Everyone had a small apartment, and they all came together for meals and daily activities such as music and cards. It was a tiny unit in a complex with well-tended rose gardens and a games room.

The fees were way more than my mother could afford, and she tried to use that as an excuse to get out of it. But I'd already told the management that I'd cover her costs and signed documents to that effect.

My mother remained resistant. She insisted that she was capable of taking care of herself. She told me repeatedly that being in a "home" would kill her. I didn't see any realistic alternative. I convinced her that she'd enjoy the change and explained that it would give me peace of mind. She reluctantly agreed. All that was left was to pack her belongings and move her out.

I ended up taking leave the week after my father died. There was no other way. I had to help my mother with the arrangements for the funeral and her move to the retirement community. I wanted her settled before I returned to New York.

We went through old boxes of family photos and talked about childhood memories, and she told me stories about how she and Dad had met and fallen in love. My parents had their share of troubles—they'd separated twice—but a lifetime of pain had mellowed with age and nostalgia.

On my last night, Mom and I packed up the final boxes for her move. Her new unit was a studio apartment with a half wall that cordoned off a bedroom. It was tiny, with no room for a lifetime collection of knickknacks, dishware, and furniture. We packed away the items that Mom wanted to take with her and sold the rest.

All that remained on that last night was for us to go through the garage storage cupboard. We tossed out things like rusty old tools, and Dad's fishing rod and tackle, which he hadn't used in years. On the top shelf was a box with my name on the label.

"That's yours, Sara," Mom said. I took it out and opened it. It contained my childhood possessions: trinkets, a mother-of-pearl box with some of my baby teeth and cheap silver jewelery that I'd received for birthdays when I was a kid. There were a couple of childhood photo albums and a few of my favorite bedtime storybooks. There was nothing of value; it was all sentimental stuff. I put the box straight into my luggage.

I left the following evening with a gaping sadness in my heart. Seeing my mother settled in her new unit, I felt like I'd lost a lifeline. There was no family home anymore. I had nowhere to return to, no safety net. For the first time in my life, I felt truly alone.

THIRTY-FIVE

THE ELEVATOR

They lay sprawled across the elevator floor, disoriented in the dark and with little hope of a swift rescue. Their limbs were stiff from lack of movement and hours lying on the hard floor. Their bodies were grimy and sticky from sweat.

When the temperature became insufferable, they alleviated the heat by pushing ajar the elevator doors. The blast of frigid air and the nauseating stink of sour urine from the times they'd had to use the narrow gap between the elevator and the concrete shaft as an ad hoc toilet made them quickly pull the doors shut until the heat became unbearable again.

Despite their physical discomfort, it was the boredom that was most excruciating.

To alleviate it, Sylvie turned on her laptop and flicked through a report, barely concentrating on the words. Jules and Vincent followed suit. They listlessly deciphered spreadsheets and typed out emails to be saved for sending later in a bid to block out the claustrophobic reality of their cramped prison.

Mostly, they did it to portray a confidence that everything would be fine, to show they had some semblance of control over the situation and that they would soon be free. When they recounted the story at a dinner party, they wanted to be able to say cockily, "It wasn't all bad; at least I managed to clear a backlog of work."

The light of their screens broke up the darkness enough for them to see one another's silhouettes over their monitors. Vincent used the opportunity to surreptitiously look for the missing Glock.

It was hard to find anything with their coats and bags scattered across the floor. He didn't want to draw attention to his search by rifling through their things, because he didn't want the others to realize that he'd lost track of the gun. He needed them to think that he still had it.

Eventually, when he failed to locate it, he reassured himself it didn't much matter. He had the ammunition clip in his pants pocket. The gun was useless without bullets.

They tried to make the best of a bad situation as they worked. Their fingers tapped away on their laptop keyboards and their work was punctuated by occasional sighs when someone had to do a particularly complicated calculation. It was all a facade to allow themselves to maintain their composure and hide an intense, primal fear that they'd been forgotten; that nobody was coming to rescue them.

No matter how much they tried to be optimistic, they had to face the harsh reality that there had been more than ample time to rescue them.

"Emergency workers would have made contact with us by now," Sylvie said, her voice piping up into the silence. "They'd have called out to reassure us, tell us that they're working on getting us free. We would have heard *something*."

Nobody responded. The silence was their response.

They felt abandoned. Time passed and the batteries of their devices drained. Eventually, their laptops and tablet screens turned as black as their moods. Once again they were shrouded in a blanket of darkness.

Jules had decided sometime during the night that Vincent had lured them here deliberately. That he was the architect of some twisted Machiavellian plot to lock them together in the tiny claustrophobic space—an escape room from which they'd been unable to escape. Why, he didn't know. Who knew what Vincent's motives were; he was always a step ahead of everyone.

"What are you thinking?" Vincent asked. Jules was running down the last of his phone's battery by shining the flashlight at the ceiling.

"There must be an access hatch. Don't you think? If we can open it, then we can get onto the roof of the elevator, maybe get a phone signal to call for help. We can't just keep sitting here like lambs to the slaughter."

Jules was right. If his head hadn't hurt so badly, Vincent might have thought of it himself. Since he was several inches taller than Jules, he rose to his feet and reached up to touch the ceiling. It was made of large decorative silver tiles, mounted into a frame to create a false ceiling. It was easy enough to remove a tile by pushing it from the frame and for Vincent to pull himself up. Using Jules's flashlight, he examined the brushed-steel ceiling until he spotted the square outline of a hatch near the back.

Moving beneath it and removing another tile, Vincent pushed at the hatch door with his hands. It didn't budge. Nor did it loosen when he pummeled it with the metal-tipped corner of his briefcase. Vincent looked around for something he could use to pry open the hatch door. There was nothing that would do.

Eventually, he took the only piece of metal he could find, his house keys. He tried to shove a key under the rim of the hatch door to break open the seal. Deep down, he knew it was pointless, but he felt compelled to make an attempt. He tried several times and almost snapped his key in half.

Once he'd accepted that this wouldn't work, more out of desperation than anything, he wrapped his white handkerchief around his knuckles and punched the latch to try to loosen it.

It made no difference. The escape hatch didn't budge. It must have been locked from the outside to prevent elevator passengers from doing something stupid, like climbing onto the roof, where they might be electrocuted or fall to their death.

Vincent sat down, panting heavily, as he unwound the crumpled cloth from around his fist. The handkerchief was stained red and his knuckles were raw and bleeding.

"This place is like Alcatraz," observed Jules.

THIRTY-SIX

SARA HALL

When I got back to my apartment after Chicago, it was dark and cold, and devastatingly empty. For weeks, I'd been looking forward to being wrapped in Kevin's reassuring arms upon my return home. He wasn't there. He had texted me when I was already at O'Hare, waiting for my flight, to tell me that he had to fly to San Francisco for an emergency meeting with a client. "Sorry," he wrote with a sad emoji. I texted him back an emoji of a broken heart.

"I'll fix it on Friday! Promise!" he wrote back.

I headed to the bathroom, where I had a long, hot shower and luxuriated in being home again. I put on pajamas and made a dinner of a grilled cheese sandwich, which I ate cross-legged on the couch while I watched a mindless reality TV show.

Before bed, I unpacked my suitcase and put everything away except for the box of childhood keepsakes that my mother had given me.

I opened my hall closet to find somewhere to store it. Folded sheets, towels, and blankets jammed up every shelf except the bottom one, which was packed with random junk. I cleared away two bottles of wine and a pack of toilet paper. My box didn't fit in; there was still something taking up space at the back of the shelf.

I pulled it out and immediately realized that it was the box that Cathy had asked me to store for her months ago. I had packed it away out of sight and forgotten I ever had it.

I cut the seals on the box and removed a layer of bubble wrap. On the top was the Fleetwood Mac record that Lucy had left for me. Underneath were a pile of Lucy's sketch pads. I flicked through the top one and found sketches Lucy had done on the streets of New York. There was one of a busker playing saxophone at the entrance to a subway. Lucy had captured the crush of people moving past, and a man lingering behind to listen. She'd drawn a skateboarder riding low on his board in a park, and an old man selling hot dogs from a cart.

At the bottom of the pile of sketch pads was a thickly bound journal with a purple velvet cover. Inside was a handwritten inscription: "Lucy, may you use this journal in good health and with great success as you embark on your new journey in college. Love, Mom."

I was surprised to see the journal contained ink drawings instead of the reams of writing that would usually appear in a personal diary. Rather than describing her thoughts, Lucy had drawn pictures, sometimes with short captions or other writing in thought bubbles. It looked like a graphic novel of Lucy's life.

There were many entries, spanning Lucy's college years and her time at the firm. I found a sketch of Vincent and Lucy sitting by the window of a café, drinking coffee. She'd written "Mentoring my mentor," along with the date, which was around the time that she started at the firm. I found a sketch of me next to a snow leopard, together with the word "Trust?"

Some pages had multiple sketches, made over the space of months. Other times, Lucy had devoted an entire page of her journal to a single event. Every entry, no matter how small, had a date. The last entry was over two facing pages. It was the only entry that was not drawn in black. Lucy had drawn it with a red pen. It was dated two days before she died.

Lucy had drawn herself cowering in the corner of an elevator. Surrounding her were demons in suits and ties with sharp tails that emerged from under their jackets, and twisted, hate-filled faces and claws that seemed to be reaching out for her. It made me shudder. A speech bubble emerged from her mouth. Inside it she'd written "SOS."

The adjacent page was filled with tiny writing in the same red ink. It was completely unintelligible—Lucy's own private language.

Eventually, I prepared for bed, still thinking about that drawing and the strange writing, when it suddenly hit me. I took the journal and held it in front of my full-length mirror. Lucy's incomprehensible words made perfect sense. She had adopted Leonardo da Vinci's mirror-writing technique.

I read her words facing my mirror. When I was finished, I rushed to the toilet and retched until my throat was raw.

We had a meeting with the executive team over the merger. Eric gave them figures that were all wrong. They were going to make the wrong decision and risk eight million dollars in projections that had not been properly adjusted. I had to say something. Vincent wasn't there. If he had been, he might have noticed my discomfort. Sam was, on the other side of the table. I kept trying to catch his eye, but he ignored me. I had to speak up. I tried to be diplomatic. Not my best skill. I said something like "I'm sorry, Eric, but those figures have not been adjusted. The correct adjusted figures indicate a potential eleven-million-dollar loss." Everyone turned to look at me. Eric flashed me a look that frightened me. Nobody has ever looked at me with such hatred.

Later, after lunch, I was coming out of the restroom when he slammed straight into me and pushed me back into the bathroom. It happened so quickly. "Listen, you fucktard," he said. "Don't ever embarrass me in public again." I nodded. I was too terrified to speak. Eric put his hand inside my shirt and squeezed my nipple so hard that it hurt. "You need to learn to shut your mouth." Then he walked out. My legs shook so much that I sank to the floor. Someone came into the bathroom to use the toilet. I pretended that I'd dropped something and left.

Later, I took Sylvie aside and told her what had happened. She told me to play the game, "suck it up." She told me when she was a teen model, a photographer had groped her while arranging her swimsuit, and she'd put up with it. She said no one can go up against Eric Miles, that I should forget about it and move on.

The next night, I stayed back for a late meeting. It ended around 9:00 P.M. I returned to my desk to finish my work. After a couple of hours, my eyes became blurry. I couldn't read my computer screen properly. I figured I was tired and packed up to leave. The office spun as I walked to the elevator. I felt dizzy and unsteady on my feet. The elevator arrived. I stumbled inside. The doors closed behind me. The other passengers pushed me from one to the other. "Fucktard," they kept saying. I wanted to tell them to stop, but I couldn't speak. My throat was paralyzed. I felt hands touching me, tugging at my hair, pushing under my bra. Hands everywhere, touching me in ways I didn't want to be touched. I curled up on the floor and shut my eyes until everything was black.

I don't remember anything else except opening my eyes as the doors slid open. I stumbled drunkenly out into the lobby. I burned with shame that I hadn't fought them off. I didn't say anything to the security guard. All I wanted was to go home and scrub myself in scalding water. After my shower, I went to the closet to find something clean to wear. Everything seemed dirty. Disgusting and dirty, just like me. I tried to call Sara. No answer. Eventually, I called Sylvie and rambled incoherently into the phone. I think I was crying. She said she would come to my apartment. I let her in and told her what had happened. She said it was probably traders who were too drunk to know what they were doing. She told me not to talk to anyone, that Stanhope doesn't like employees who lodge complaints. She told me to stay home. She would cover for me at work. She handed me some capsules she said would make me feel better. I hate medication, but I was desperate to stop feeling this way. I took the capsules. They haven't helped. All I want to do is crawl up in a ball and die.

THIRTY-SEVEN

THE ELEVATOR

It had been almost a full day since they'd been trapped. "A tomb," Jules had called it. The longer they stayed, the more it felt like he was right. They wondered if they'd ever get out.

There was no way to escape. Vincent had established that the hatch to the elevator's roof was sealed and locked. The elevator's steel doors faced the sheer concrete wall of the shaft. The escape-room clues seemed pointless. None of them had the faintest idea what the last clue, which was still on the screen, even meant. They'd called, screamed, shouted, and pleaded for help for hours—all to no avail.

Their best hope was that they would have to wait until Monday morning, when the building would teem with people returning to work. Surely then someone would hear their calls for help. That was almost forty hours away.

"There's nothing we can do for the time being except sleep," Vincent said. That was easier said than done on the hard floor in the sweltering heat.

They envied Sam, who was in a deep oxy-induced sleep, with

only occasional moments of drowsy wakefulness. At which point, Vincent would give him another painkiller to get him back to sleep. They lay in a row, trying to sleep, lulled by the drip of condensation from the ceiling.

Vincent was consumed by thoughts about what they'd need to do to survive until Monday. He had a single bottle of water and two energy bars in his briefcase. If he carefully rationed the water, then it would suffice for the four of them until Monday morning.

The heat, which had worried Vincent for some time, had become a less pressing concern. They'd found a way to control it by intermittently forcing open the elevator doors and letting in the cold air from the elevator shaft.

Vincent's main concern was keeping Jules and Sylvie in line. Their patience was wearing thin. He was relieved when they both fell asleep, because he could let his guard down at least for a moment.

Soft snoring grunts came from where Jules lay in the corner. Sylvie lay with her legs folded under her as she breathed softly in her sleep. Vincent could feel the skin of her legs against his own. Her sophisticated floral perfume was a welcome relief from the stench of the stuffy elevator. He fell asleep to the touch of Sylvie's skin and the sweet smell of her body.

Jules woke in the dark with one thought on his mind. He needed a drink. And not water, though his throat was parched, but a stiff drink. A whiskey. Or vodka. Or maybe even a rum and Coke. Hell, he'd settle for cough syrup if it had a high-enough alcohol content.

He knew he should be thinking of ways to escape. He was good with electronics. If he could concentrate, he could figure out a way to activate the control panel or run a wire to get a cell phone signal. But he couldn't focus without a drink.

He castigated himself for not having taken more of the miniature bottles of booze from the chauffeured car that had brought him over. He'd had many opportunities to drink over the previous weeks and always stayed strong. Client lunches matched with vintage wines. An aged scotch opened at a dinner party. A client meeting at a Russian vodka bar. He'd held firm to his pledge to stay sober.

Surely, he'd thought, if he could resist the temptation of a fifty-year-old bottle of scotch, then he could get through a car ride without being tempted by the relatively mundane contents of a limousine minibar. As time passed in the thick congestion of traffic, his eyes had kept drifting to the drinks cupboard set into the door next to him. What might they have stocked? He told himself it didn't matter; he wasn't drinking anymore. But after another stubborn red traffic light, he figured he'd have a quick look—purely out of curiosity.

He opened the minibar door and saw two dozen or so miniature liquor bottles arranged in neat rows. He figured he might as well see what type of vodka they had. As it happened, there wasn't any. That would have ended things if Jules hadn't noticed an assortment of unfamiliar whiskey. He was a sucker for whiskey, although he drank it rarely, since the smell stuck to him like an oil rag.

He took time to make his selection. He chose a scotch and drank the contents of the bottle in one long gulp. The warmth spread through him as the Town Car made its way through the gridlock of uptown Manhattan. He immediately felt more relaxed, the stress and pressure lifting from him. Four intersections later, he desperately wanted one more drink. He resisted. He had a meeting. The clients would smell the alcohol on his breath.

He wrote an email and reread a report. His eyes kept drifting back to the drinks cabinet. He convinced himself that one more bottle wouldn't make a difference. He drank that down in a single go, too, and placed both empty bottles in his briefcase. He would keep the miniature bottles as souvenirs of the very last alcohol he ever drank. He was contemplating drinking a third bottle when the driver pulled up outside the lobby. "We're at your destination, sir," he said.

Sitting in the dark elevator, Jules regretted not having taken that third bottle. And a fourth. God, he could almost taste the smooth amber on his tongue. He'd do almost anything for a drink. It would make him forget about his empty stomach and aching body. It would drown out Sam's pathetic whines of pain. It would block all the memories that assaulted him in the lonely darkness of the elevator.

He didn't want to think of his dead mother, or his ex-wife, who spoke to him only through eight-hundred-dollar-an-hour lawyers, or his estranged father, or the string of nameless lovers since his marriage breakup, or all the people he'd hurt over the years.

THIRTY-EIGHT

SARA HALL

was sick to my stomach that night as I grappled with what had happened to Lucy. She had been attacked; sexually assaulted in the office elevator. She'd obviously been drugged. From that point on, she had no chance. Lucy had been utterly defenseless once she was in the elevator. She'd have been disoriented, trapped, and terrified.

Eric Miles must have been behind it. It was his revenge on Lucy for making him look like the stupid ass that he was. I knew enough about Eric to know that he was a coward's coward. He would have paid off—or threatened—others to carry out the assault. I doubted he was there in person.

I felt crushed by the weight of the responsibility of finding Lucy's journal. If I brought her assault to light, it would kill my career at the firm. My salary supported not just myself but also my mother in her expensive retirement home. I still had my dad's medical bills to pay off, and his funeral expenses to cover. I couldn't risk losing my income.

Lucy was dead. It had happened a long time ago. There was no way to right the past.

On the flip side, I was outraged by what had happened. Lucy deserved justice. How could I possibly allow Eric Miles to get away with what he'd done?

I dialed Kevin's cell. I badly needed his advice. I assumed that his flight had landed in San Francisco by now, but his phone went straight through to voice mail. I didn't leave a message. Besides, I realized there was no point in consulting him over the phone. Kevin was a cautious lawyer. He would never discuss an issue of this delicacy over the phone. I'd have to wait until he returned on Friday. Five days of waiting.

I arrived in the elevator lobby of our office tower just before 7:00 A.M., holding a take-out coffee from the gourmet coffee truck a half block from the office. By chance, Jules, Sam, and Sylvie were all there, too, holding their own coffees.

We all tended to arrive by 7:30 A.M. to catch up on overnight emails and do any work required to prepare for our first round of conference calls with our European offices, which began at 8:00 A.M. The elevator doors opened. We stepped in, all looking like cardboard cutouts of corporate highfliers. Neatly groomed, in pressed suits and polished shoes, with all the accoutrements and arrogance of our profession.

"You've been gone awhile, Sara. How was Chicago?" Sam asked as he texted on his phone.

"Her dad died," Jules butted in before I could answer Sam's question. "That's why Sara was in Chicago."

"Oh shit, I forgot," Sam said. "My bad. Condolences, Sara."

I noticed Sylvie and Jules, their fingers deliberately grazing as they stood side by side. I wondered how long they'd been sleeping together. I looked up and Sam winked at me as if we shared a secret.

"What's been going on with you, Sylvie?" I asked. Sam smirked. I realized the question was provocative, given what I'd just witnessed.

"I've been in London," Sylvie said. "In fact, I'm heading back tomorrow night. But Vincent and I are presenting to a client this afternoon."

"I thought he was away," I said.

"No, he's here today," said Sylvie. "He flies to Frankfurt tonight. Why do you care?"

Sylvie liked to remind me in a myriad of ways that I was at the bottom of the food chain when it came to the senior members of the team. She could walk into Vincent's office at will; I had to make an appointment with his personal assistant. She and Vincent mixed in similar social circles, attended the same parties. She treated him with a certain familiarity. For me, Vincent was my boss. I was always deferential. We didn't banter, or hang out. I had no idea who his friends were and I never, not even once, ran into him at a party or at a restaurant. I didn't move in his milieu.

Sylvie persisted. "Is there something that you need to talk to him about?"

"Nothing in particular," I said quickly—too quickly. Sylvie's eyes burned with intense curiosity.

I had fervently hoped that Vincent would be away so that I could first consult with Kevin. But Kevin would return only at the end of the week. By which time, Vincent would be in Europe. His European trips sometimes lasted several weeks.

I decided then and there that I would raise the matter with Vincent that day, before he went away. Vincent had been Lucy's greatest ally. He'd be as outraged as I was. He'd know what to do.

I saw Vincent at various meetings during the course of the day. He offered his condolences about my father and asked how my mother had settled into her new accommodations, but there was no opportunity for me to raise the delicate issue of Lucy's journal privately.

I messaged Vincent's personal assistant twice to ask whether he could squeeze me in for a few minutes between meetings. Each time she told me that Vincent was fully booked. I'd have to wait until he returned from Europe.

At 6:00 P.M., a message from Vincent popped up on my screen. "I heard you want to talk. I have a few minutes to spare. Are you free now?"

"Sure. Coming over," I responded.

When I walked into Vincent's office, he was reading a document. He took off his reading glasses and gestured with them that I should take a seat. I shut the office door behind me. I didn't want anyone overhearing our conversation.

"You seem distracted, Sara," said Vincent. "I'm sure the past few weeks haven't been easy. Do you need more time? I lost my father a few years ago. It was tough."

"I definitely don't want more leave. If anything, I've been looking forward to being back at work."

"Okay." Vincent sighed, as if he wasn't convinced. "What's on your mind, Sara?"

"There's something I wanted to talk to you about." I took a deep breath and exhaled slowly. The words that I'd rehearsed dozens of times in my mind poured out in a quick, garbled flow.

"Lucy Marshall's mother, Cathy, died about six months ago," I said. "It was a hit-and-run."

"I didn't know," he said after a pause. "I'm sorry to hear that."

"I saw Cathy before she died. It appears that Lucy kept a journal. In it was an account, from two days before she died, that suggests she was sexually assaulted in the office elevator."

His face turned grim. "Does it say who did it?" he asked.

"She didn't know exactly. I gather that she was drugged. However, I suspect that Eric Miles was involved. Earlier that day, he'd threatened Lucy. She made him look bad in a meeting. He'd given inaccurate figures and she corrected him publicly."

"And how do you know this is true?" asked Vincent.

"It was in Lucy's journal."

"Do you have that journal? I'd like to see it."

"I don't have it. But . . . I've seen it," I replied, trying to be evasive. It was a stupid lie. I could hardly suggest that I go home and get the journal a second after saying that I didn't have it.

"Without seeing the journal, it's hearsay at best. Don't you think?" Vincent spoke quietly, but I could see that he was angry. My face flushed in embarrassment. I didn't know what to say.

"You can't throw around accusations like that without any evidence." I couldn't believe Vincent was making excuses for Eric, of all people. Anyone who worked with Eric knew he was a first-class douche, especially Vincent, who was a good judge of character.

It was because of Eric's connections to the board. Vincent was politically savvy enough to know that taking on Eric Miles would pose an existential threat to his career.

Vincent leaned forward. His eyes were hard. "I can't do anything, Sara, without any evidence and without any corroboration."

"Lucy confided in Sylvie after it happened," I said. "Sylvie went to Lucy's apartment to help her calm down. She gave her medicine. Ask Sylvie. She'll confirm it."

Vincent pressed the intercom button of his phone to speak to his PA. "Ask Sylvie to come into my office. Immediately."

My heart thumped as I sat under Vincent's icy gaze. We waited in silence for Sylvie to arrive, and she walked straight into Vincent's office with her usual self-assurance. She wore a cream suit and a pink silk shirt, open at the neck to display a set of pearls. Her hair was pinned up. She sat down on the chair next to me and casually crossed her legs.

"Do you remember the days before Lucy Marshall died?" Vincent asked her.

"It was a while ago," she replied, noncommittally.

"Did Lucy tell you that she'd been sexually assaulted by Eric Miles, or other men, in the office elevator late one night? Days before her death?"

"Lucy?" said Sylvie, incredulous. "Assaulted in this office? That's ridiculous. Where on earth did you hear that?" She turned to look at me. Her eyes burned with accusation.

"Just to be clear, Sylvie, so there are no misunderstandings. You're saying that Lucy never mentioned to you that she had been assaulted?" Vincent said.

"If that had happened, I would have told you, or the police," Sylvie insisted. Liar, I thought.

"Did you visit Lucy's apartment the day before she died? Did you give her sedatives, or any other medication?"

"I never visited Lucy's apartment. I don't know where she lived. We were hardly friends. You know that, Vincent. Why would I give Lucy medication without a prescription? Who does that?" She looked at him in bewilderment. "To be honest, Vincent, I'm a little offended that you'd even ask."

"Thank you, Sylvie. You can go," said Vincent. He waited until Sylvie left his office.

"What's your angle, Sara?" His voice was cold. "Why make up a story like that? It demeans Lucy's memory and damages Eric Miles's reputation. Not to mention undermining Sylvie by implying she covered up a crime."

"I didn't make it up," I gasped.

"Sylvie just confirmed that it's not true. Lucy never turned to her for help. She's never heard of this supposed incident," said Vincent. "It never happened. It's fiction."

"It's not," I insisted. "It happened two days before Lucy died—it's somehow connected with her death."

"Sara, I can only presume this is some kind of power play," he went on. "To undermine Sylvie and get back at Eric, I don't know, for excluding you from the Bishop deal? I never thought you had it in you to be so manipulative. I don't want to hear of this again."

I swallowed hard, tears of frustration in my eyes. I felt utterly humiliated by his accusations.

"That will be all, Sara," he said dismissively.

I stood up. Trembling, I stumbled toward his office door.

"I'm going to do you the biggest favor of your career, Sara. I'm going to forget you ever raised this. If you like working at Stanhope, then I suggest you be very careful about making unfounded accusations like that in the future." With that, I left his office.

When I arrived home that night, I went through Lucy's other papers to find evidence to convince Vincent that I'd been speaking the truth. Perhaps Lucy had talked to someone else after the assault, someone other than Sylvie who could corroborate her story. I was sure the answers were in the papers that Cathy had sent me. I was determined to show Vincent that what I had said was true and that Sylvie was lying through her teeth.

I went through all of Lucy's sketch pads. Toward the end of the largest sketchbook, I came to a stunning series of sketches from Coney Island, which took up several pages. I turned the pages, expecting to see more of Lucy's street scenes, when I saw something that made me gasp, just as Cathy had. This was the drawing she'd seen when we were packing up Lucy's apartment. Cathy hadn't let me see it then. I wish she had. It would have saved an awful lot of grief. Who knows how things would have played out if I'd seen it then. Cathy might still be alive.

In style and substance, the picture was completely different from the other sketches. The other drawings captured life in the city and its shifting moods. The sketch in front of me was a black ink vignette of life at the firm, drawn with sharp, angry lines. It looked like a panel from a deeply disturbing graphic novel.

It was a sketch of the meeting room where we often worked, the one people referred to as "Vincent's meeting room." I recognized it because Lucy had accurately drawn the view of the city skyline from the windows. She had drawn four people around a table. They were quite clearly caricatures of Vincent, Sam, Sylvie, and Jules. The table wasn't the usual rectangular table in that room. It was round, and Lucy had written "The Circle, Inc." in the middle. I had no idea what that meant.

Sam, with his handsome square face, sat back in his chair with the thoughtful expression that he projected during meetings to show that he was engaged in the conversation. Jules's black hair flopped over his dark, cryptic eyes. And of course Sylvie. Her facial profile was perfectly symmetrical. Her hair was in a chignon and her elongated frame was in the upright posture of a model. Her intelligent eyes cynically mocked them all.

Vincent was the only one who sat with his back to the foreground. I could tell it was him from the shape of the back of his head and his distinctive broad shoulders.

When I looked closely, I realized that in fact Vincent's face *was* in the sketch. It was reflected in the window. Except instead of drawing Vincent's face, Lucy had drawn the face of the devil.

THIRTY-NINE

THE ELEVATOR

Vincent woke hours later, roused by a sense that something was wrong. He was so exhausted and disoriented that it took a few seconds for him to remember that he was in the elevator. He'd awakened because of a scratching noise that he'd heard through thick layers of sleep.

As he became more alert, Vincent realized the scratching sound was someone trying to pick the lock of his briefcase.

"What are you doing, Jules?"

Jules hesitated. "Getting water," he said.

"By breaking into my briefcase?"

"It's been twenty-four hours. I'm thirsty."

"We all are, Jules. You can't just help yourself," said Vincent.

"You were asleep and I didn't want to wake you." His tone was defensive.

"It's still *my* locked briefcase that you're trying to break into."

"Desperate times call for desperate measures," Jules said glibly.

Sylvie had awakened and scrambled into a sitting position.

Vincent had already taken stock of their food and water supply. He had under half a liter of water in his briefcase. It was barely enough for one person, let alone four. He had a couple of energy bars, as well, but they could survive for a week without food. With no water, they might last two days. Three tops.

"Let's be clear. I'm in charge of the water and the food. If you want something, you ask me."

Jules's face reddened in anger. He was tired of having to ask Vincent for every little thing. This wasn't the office, Vincent had no right to talk to him like that. From what he'd seen, Vincent had done fuck all to get them out.

Vincent opened the briefcase and removed the water bottle. With the help of the television monitor, which was still flashing the latest unsolved clue, he carefully poured water into the plastic cap of the bottle. He gave Sylvie her share first. Three caps of water, one after the other. Jules was next. When Jules was done, Vincent poured a lid full of water into Sam's lips, which had parted slightly in his sleep.

"What are you doing?" Jules asked abruptly.

"What does it look like I'm doing? I'm giving Sam his share."

"But Sam's asleep," said Jules. "He'll never know he missed out."

"Plus, he had some earlier," Sylvie chimed in. "We should all get the same amount."

"Sam needs more than the rest of us," Vincent said. "He's running a high fever."

"That's his problem," said Jules.

"I'll tell you what." Vincent's voice was weary. "I'll give Sam my share of water. All right?"

"That's your prerogative." Jules shrugged. "As long as you don't give him my water, I don't really give a damn."

Vincent resisted the urge to point out that he was the one who was sharing his water with all of them. He didn't have the energy to get into the intricacies of ownership of their water supply. He closed the bottle tightly and put it back into his briefcase. He locked his briefcase and put it underneath his head as a pillow. He couldn't leave it unguarded again.

Jules tucked himself back into the corner and returned to sleep.

Sylvie stretched out and pretended to be sleeping, as well. After some time, when she knew that Jules was asleep by the change in his breathing, she wiggled closer to Vincent, until she felt the warmth of his body. She allowed their skin to touch—a brief, flirting touch.

"Vincent, can I have another sip?"

"Not now. We need to ration it."

"Please, Vincent." She moved closer, until the tips of her nipples under the thin fabric of her camisole touched his bare chest.

They were so close to each other that their sweat was intermingling. Vincent's body was tense and his breathing had become audible. Sylvie smiled to herself. She knew that she'd turned him on. She leaned forward toward Vincent's ear and whispered so softly that nobody could hear anything. Then she lowered her mouth and ran her tongue down the nape of his neck. It set off an electric burst of desire in Vincent. He put his hand out to pull her to him. She'd already moved back and was out of reach.

Against his better judgment, Vincent removed the water bottle from his briefcase and handed it to her. "Two sips," he said. Sylvie took three.

Sam lay with his head on the folded jacket, watching Sylvie's interplay with Vincent. He was drowsy, but even through his lethargic daze, he marveled at her opportunism. It was a typical Sylvie move.

Sam noticed Vincent's sideways glances toward Sylvie, who was sitting near him on the elevator floor. She leaned back against the wall, her skirt hiked up and legs slightly apart. Drops of sweat ran down the front of her neck and into the crevice between her breasts.

"I wish we knew why we're here and what we need to do to get out," she said. She fanned herself with her cell phone, which shone filaments of light on the elevator walls.

Sam had already fallen asleep again when Sylvie lay down as close as she could get to Vincent. Within a few minutes, the two of them were curled up in each other's arms, fast asleep.

FORTY

SARA HALL

That night, I paced restlessly around my apartment, looking out the living room window into the neon-lit sky, as if it would provide me with answers. Lucy's drawing of Vincent as the devil left me confused and afraid. I always thought Lucy had worshipped Vincent. I'd never imagined that she thought of him as anything other than her guardian angel. Vincent had hired her, mentored her, watched her back. Why would she draw him as evil personified? What had Vincent done to frighten her?

I barely slept that night. When I did, it was a restless sleep. I thrashed about in my bedsheets until they were twisted and damp from perspiration. I woke with a start, my heart racing. I vaguely remembered dreaming that I was hiding under an office desk while Vincent searched for me with a hunting knife. The office was dark and empty. It was the middle of the night. Vincent's face was demonic, just as Lucy had drawn it.

I had forgotten to set my alarm and woke late. I showered and dressed quickly. There was no time to style my hair, so I tied it up.

As I grabbed my bag and keys, I saw Lucy's sketch pads spread across my coffee table. I tossed them straight into the bottom shelf of the cupboard. I didn't want to see them anymore. I wished I'd never seen them in the first place.

I arrived at work with a strong black coffee in hand. It was all I could stomach; I had no appetite. Vincent's office door was shut. He was in Europe. It was a relief to know that I wouldn't be seeing him for a while.

My phone was ringing as I approached my desk. I grabbed it before I missed the call, still with my handbag over my shoulder. "Hello, Sara." It was Vincent's voice. I swallowed hard and sat down with a stab of anxiety in the pit of my stomach.

It turned out to be a brief call. Completely professional and with no reference to our conversation the previous day. Vincent gave me a list of preparatory work he needed me to do for a meeting he had coming up in Frankfurt.

I was nervous about seeing Sylvie after the confrontation with her the previous day in Vincent's office. When she arrived in the office, she didn't greet me. She then spent the day treating me with her usual benign contempt. Everything was back to normal.

Raising Lucy's journal with Vincent had been a serious miscalculation. I thought he would have been outraged; instead, he seemed intent on covering it up. Without Vincent's support, I couldn't go up against Eric Miles; he would crush me like a cockroach. I couldn't go to the cops, either. There was no way to corroborate what had happened, no evidence. Lucy was dead and Sylvie wasn't talking.

I rationalized my decision to do nothing by telling myself that Lucy must have been delusional before she died. The allegations in her journal were a fiction that she'd created, just as Sylvie had told Vincent with a straight face and steady eyes. I couldn't risk ruining my career by going on a personal crusade about something that might or might not have happened to a friend who was long dead.

I worked late all week so that on Friday night I'd be able to get home early for Kevin's return. I bought steaks and made salad for dinner. I even made tiramisu for dessert. His plane's departure from San Francisco was delayed by storms. By the time he landed, it was already 9:30 P.M. He texted me to say that he was beat and would go straight home.

To say that I was upset was an understatement. We'd been apart for weeks. I became paranoid and decided that he'd met someone else while he was away and planned to break up with me that weekend.

Kevin texted me in the morning to apologize for being too tired to come over. He told me he'd booked a table at Mikado for dinner that night. It was a French–Japanese fusion restaurant that had rave reviews and a two-month waiting list. Kevin had pulled off a near-impossible feat getting us a table at short notice.

It struck me that Mikado wasn't the sort of place for a breakup. The ambience there would turn the most hardened cynic into a romantic: an indoor koi pond, Japanese lanterns on the tables; origami table napkins. I wore a midnight blue evening dress that left one arm bare and an orb-shaped pendant necklace that Kevin had given me for my birthday.

After a dinner of French-influenced sushi and various other delights from the tasting menu, we took a cab to Central Park, where Kevin insisted we take a carriage ride. I'd once confessed to him that it was on my bucket list of kitschy New York things to do. "We're going to work through your bucket list tonight," he said cryptically as he helped me into the carriage.

Kevin gave the driver two hundred dollars and told him to keep going around the park until it was all used up. We stopped only once, when a delivery guy pulled up alongside our carriage and handed Kevin a magnificent bouquet of long-stemmed roses. Kevin had obviously ordered them in advance. There were dozens of red and white roses.

The bouquet was so enormous in my arms that I was barely able to see the small box that Kevin held in front of me. He lifted the lid, and suddenly my world was spinning. Nestled in the velvet lining of the jewelry box was a magnificent emerald-cut diamond ring. I looked at Kevin uncertainly. He nodded his head imperceptibly. We hadn't even moved in together and he wanted to marry me.

"Do you like it?" asked Kevin.

"Like it? It's incredible!"

Kevin put the ring on my finger and asked me to marry him. I spent the following days in a giddy daze of sheer, unadulterated happiness.

The week that followed was filled with excited calls to my mother and Kevin's family to announce the news. We decided that we'd let friends know when we made the official announcement. Still, that didn't stop me from buying a pile of wedding magazines. I fell in love with an off-the-shoulder bridal dress. I made the first draft of my side of a guest list and read several articles about the latest wedding cake trends.

We made plans to travel to New Hampshire so that I could meet Kevin's family. I'd recently met his mother and two of his sisters when they were in New York for a show, but I hadn't met the rest of his family. Kevin hesitantly suggested we have the wedding in his mother's garden, in the fall, when it was at its best, with leaves the color of burnished rust and gold. I agreed without hesitation.

I stayed at Kevin's place the following weekend. We were invited to a dinner party at the home of the managing partner at his law firm. Kevin introduced me as his fiancée. It was the first time that he'd used that term. The following morning, Kevin and I woke late and went for a run along the Hudson. As we ran, we talked about where we should buy our first apartment as a couple.

"I have the name of a good Realtor," said Kevin. "We'll look at places when I get back."

"Get back?" I stopped running. "What do you mean?"

"I have to fly back to California tomorrow."

"Can't you get out of it?"

"I wish," he said. "I didn't want to ruin the weekend by telling you earlier. It's going to be a three-week stretch. But I promise that I'll do everything that I can to come back in the middle, even if it's only for a couple of nights."

"You'd better, Kevin."

FORTY-ONE

THE ELEVATOR

The elevator lights woke them almost immediately. They instinctively covered their eyes. They'd been in the dark for so long that the sudden brightness felt as if it were burning into their retinas.

Sylvie was embarrassed to realize that the soft pillow her head was lying against was Vincent's chest. Her hair was intertwined in his fingers.

"I hope this means that we're getting out of here," said Sylvie nervously, pulling away from Vincent. She could tell that Jules had already noticed the intimate way they'd slept. He smirked at her as if to say, That was quick work.

In the full glare of the fluorescent lights, they couldn't escape their reflections in the mirrored walls. Gray sunken faces, bloodshot eyes. Skewed, crumpled clothes, dirty from grit and perspiration. Sylvie swiftly put her shirt back on to cover the ugly ridges of her burn scars from the car accident that had taken Carl's life.

The destruction was obvious. The displaced ceiling tiles, the discarded clothes. Abandoned laptop chargers scattered across the floor.

The mirrored wall that had been shattered into a spiderweb of cracks, smudged with blood. Jules ran his hand over his rough jaw, where Sam had punched him earlier. His stubble was stained with blood from his nosebleed. The superficial scratch on his throat from where Vincent had hurt him was already scabbing over. There were streaks of crimson on the floor.

Sylvie's hair was tangled and her makeup was smudged. She thought herself garish in the unforgiving light. Something akin to an aging burlesque dancer. She dabbed at her makeup as best she could with a wet wipe from her purse until her face was wiped clean.

She examined herself closely in the mirror. The cut she'd received to her face when the elevator had plummeted was just below her hairline. Sylvie was relieved. It wouldn't leave a visible mark. She didn't need more scars. She already had more than enough.

Sam's homemade sling, which was made from Vincent's ripped white undershirt, had yellowed from sweat. His shirt was unbuttoned and untucked. Sitting up, Sam slowly fastened the buttons of his dress shirt with his one good hand and tucked it into his pants. He, too, wanted to look his best when they were rescued.

Vincent's jaw was flecked with dark blond stubble. His eyes were bloodshot from lack of sleep. His chest was bare and his tattoos were exposed, making him look more like a street fighter than a banker. He'd often thought the two were interchangeable. He didn't clean himself up like the others. He figured he'd do it once he knew for sure they were free.

Their rescue seemed imminent. The elevator lights' coming back on was obviously the work of the technicians who must have been fixing the elevator at that very moment. Time passed. The elevator didn't move. The doors remained shut. They were bitter with disappointment.

They returned to their places on the floor and sat about with nothing to look at in the blinding light but one another. It felt as if they were staring into one another's naked souls. Of all the emotions they could see in the others' faces, it was the fear that scared them most.

Vincent checked his watch. They were due for their next ration of water soon. He would drag it out for as long as possible. He needed to make that small bottle of water last for days, if necessary.

"It doesn't look as if anyone is coming." Sam's eyes were glassy from fever. "How long can we last like this?"

"Three days without water," replied Vincent. "Four if we're lucky. Food is less of an issue."

With the lights restored, everything had reverted to its previous order. Vincent was in charge. They heeded his authority. After all, Vincent was the only one who knew the combination code to access the food and water in his briefcase.

When he removed the bottle and energy bars sometime later, Sylvie looked at the half-empty bottle and said, "If that's all the water we have left, we really are in trouble."

"It should be enough to keep us going until Tuesday morning at the latest," said Vincent. "We'll have to be rescued before then."

"And if we're not?"

"We'll be severely dehydrated by Tuesday night," Vincent said in a tone so clinical that it almost felt as if he was talking about someone else. "Our kidneys will start shutting down and our hearts will go into arrhythmia. Some of us may well be dead by dawn on Wednesday."

"Monday morning is in thirty-six hours' time," mumbled Sam. "I'm sure we'll be rescued on Monday. We can all hang on until then, right Vincent?"

Vincent muttered something affirmative, but he was worried about Sam. His fever was high and they had no medication to lower it, or antibiotics to treat the infection. Under the surface of Sam's clammy skin, bacteria was pumping through his body. Sam was dying before their eyes.

Vincent opened one of the energy bars and divided it among the four of them. He handed out each piece as if it were not a tiny morsel of food, but a lavish meal. He estimated that each piece provided perhaps seventy calories. Hardly enough to stave off starvation.

He carefully poured water into the cap of the water bottle, holding it steady to prevent spilling. They could not afford to lose a single precious drop of water. They all came to him, one after the other, and opened their mouths so that he could pour the water directly into their parched mouths, as if they were receiving Communion. Each of them sat back on the hard floor when they had received their ration of water.

When Vincent was done drinking his own portion, he closed the bottle extra tight and returned it to his briefcase, which he locked. The countdown to survive had begun.

"The most remarkable part of all of this is that we've been able to stand one another's company for this long," remarked Jules, in another clumsy attempt at humor.

"It's not remarkable at all," said Vincent, leaning against the wall with his arms crossed. "I'm sure we've spent more time together over the past seven years than we have with our families. I'd say we have tolerated one another quite well."

"Oh, we've had our ups and downs, haven't we, Sylvie?" said Jules with a sardonic wink in her direction. Sylvie ignored him.

Jules stood up to stretch his legs. Sam followed suit, standing slowly and clumsily. He noticed writing on the escape-room screen and shuffled over to read it. "Let your plans be dark and impenetrable as night, and when you move, fall like a thunderbolt," he read out loud.

"It's another clue," Sylvie explained. "But we haven't been able to figure it out."

"It's Sun Tzu," said Sam, turning around to face them all. "This isn't a clue," he said, his voice trembling. "It's a declaration of war."

FORTY-TWO

SARA HALL

It was several weeks later that I noticed slight, almost imperceptible changes at work. I was excluded from meetings that I would ordinarily have attended. At first, it didn't bother me. If anything, I was grateful. I chalked it up to Vincent considerately allowing me to ease back into work after my father's death.

When it continued for several weeks, I began to worry that it was permanent. I wasn't invited to client meetings, internal meetings, and work lunches that in the past I would have attended without question. Vincent, Sylvie, Sam, and Jules met in a glass-walled meeting room in another part of the office, not the one we usually used. They lowered the blinds so nobody could see inside. They never invited me.

I became neurotic about every glance that came my way; every meeting I wasn't invited to; every quiet huddle in a corner of the office that broke up when I walked past; every phone call that became hushed or was taken out of my earshot when I was nearby.

The usual back-and-forth repartee that we engaged in at our desks was stilted and awkward. Everyone chose their words carefully when they discussed issues related to work, whereas in the past we had all talked openly about whatever we were working on.

Something had changed. It wasn't tangible, but I could sense it in a multitude of ways. My permission to view certain documents stopped; there were even entire share drives I couldn't access.

When I called IT, the technician insisted that it could be rectified in minutes. He made me feel as if I were a dope for not knowing how to work the share drive. After checking things on his end, his tone changed. "Unfortunately, we have an infrastructure issue." It sounded as if he were reading a prepared statement. I knew that he was giving me the runaround.

My computer kept acting up. When I tried to close all the processes running, I found that I couldn't close one of them without an administrator's password. When I searched the name of the application online, I discovered that it was a type of corporate spyware. The firm was watching my every keystroke.

Meanwhile, Sylvie criticized everything I did. It was more vicious and far more personal than the snide little asides she'd made in the past. When she found a single typo in a fifty-page draft report I'd submitted, she said at the top of her voice, so that everyone could hear, "Your spelling needs some work, Sara."

Sylvie and Jules insisted on reviewing every tiny task that I performed, as if I were a new hire requiring close supervision. I bristled at my sudden lack of independence and their obvious mistrust.

When they looked at my work, they tore it apart. Work that had been considered excellent just a few weeks earlier was now slammed. Their criticism was brutal and almost always unfounded. It took a heavy toll on my self-confidence.

"Well, that's an interesting way of doing it," Sam said patronizingly as he leaned over my computer to check a spreadsheet. "It's a shame your assumptions are all wrong."

"I set up this financial model two months ago, Sam, and you agreed with all the assumptions then," I responded. "What's changed?"

"I don't need to tell you that finance is not static. We can't stick to old strategies and models just because we're too lazy to change them." His retort was like a slap in the face.

I held back from telling him that I knew for a fact that he was using financial models from when I first started at the firm three years earlier. I shut up. It wasn't in my interest to start an all-out war.

Work was given to me with ridiculously tight deadlines, with no obvious reasons for why I hadn't gotten it earlier or why it was needed so soon. It was not humanly possible to meet those deadlines. As a result, I was constantly handing in work late and getting emails from Vincent, or Sam, or others on the team, asking why I hadn't yet handed in a report or an analysis they were waiting for.

The situation persisted. I couldn't deceive myself anymore; my position at Stanhope was becoming precarious. I would have confided in Kevin, but he was still in California, indefinitely, dealing with the legal aftermath of a major data breach at his biggest client. The government had opened an investigation, and the company's share price tanked. Needless to say, Kevin barely had time to talk with me on the phone, let alone visit.

When we did talk, he sounded stressed and exhausted. He told me he missed me and mentioned flying back to see me. It never happened. Something always came up. He called me a few days before he was due to return to tell me that he'd have to stay on for at least another two weeks. The following week, I told Kevin that I would fly out to visit instead. He said he'd have to work over the weekend and that it would be a waste of time and money for me to fly across the country so we could spend an hour or two together.

He sounded evasive. My paranoia went into overdrive. It felt as if my life was falling apart. The euphoria of my engagement had disappeared. I still hadn't had a chance to talk to Kevin about Lucy's diary entry or what was happening to me at work. I badly needed his advice. Most of all, I worried he didn't want me anymore.

"Sara, I'd like to meet with you at four P.M. tomorrow, please." Vincent's email arrived not long after I got home from work. Its curt tone threw me into a panic. I barely slept, and arrived the next day bleary-eyed, with a knot of anxiety in the pit of my stomach.

"Close the door behind you, Sara," Vincent said when I entered his office at the appointed time. "It's come to my attention that there have been a number of serious mistakes in your work recently." He reached out for a file and put documents in front of me, like a lawyer presenting evidence in court.

I flushed under his rebuke. In the years that I'd worked at the firm, nobody had ever taken me to task. They'd always been happy with my work. I looked at the documents he presented. Two of the mistakes were minor; the other two weren't mistakes at all.

"Vincent, I'm not sure why this particular work has been brought to your attention, but I can assure you that—"

"I don't need your assurances, Sara," he said, cutting me off. "I simply need you to produce the standard of work we expect from our staff at this firm. I was patient with your absence, dealing with family matters, and its effect on your productivity for weeks after you returned. But that is over now and I expect you to get back on track," he said. "The stakes are too high for you to be distracted or make even small mistakes. These are billion-dollar deals. Do you understand?"

"Yes. But, I'd like to mention that—"

"I don't want excuses or explanations," he said, cutting me off again. "Either your work is of the highest standard or you don't work here. It really is that simple."

"Yes, Vincent."

"I have no choice but to put you on probation. I hope that will encourage you to get your game together."

I turned white at his words. "Yes, of course," I said stupidly.

I walked out of Vincent's office in a daze. I felt his eyes boring into me until I closed the door behind me. I sensed someone watching me. Vincent's personal assistant hastily lowered her head and pretended to be busy.

I don't know how I made it to my desk without falling apart. I felt Sylvie's eyes on me. I refused to give her the satisfaction of seeing me cry. I held it together until I went home that night, collapsing on my bed, too devastated for tears.

I dreaded going into work each morning. The office was cold and hostile; the team was barely talking to me. I felt shut out. Their hostility seemed to influence others, as well. People at work with whom I'd been on good terms suddenly stayed away from me, as if I were anthrax. It was like high school all over again.

I went home at night in tears. They were running me ragged with impossible deadlines and tearing me apart with criticism. I had stabbing pains in my stomach and struggled to sleep at night. I started taking sleeping tablets, but they made me woozy the next day at work, which just fed into the vicious cycle.

They continued to chip away at my confidence in the weeks that followed, until even I doubted the quality of my work. Everything that I did was wrong or substandard, often both. For the first time since I was a kid, I bit my nails so badly that I had to keep them short.

I had no appetite. I lost weight and became so thin that my clothes hung on me shapelessly.

The tasks set for me became even more unrealistic. I was asked on a Friday afternoon to produce an eighty-page report by first thing Monday morning, something that I'd usually have had at least a week to complete. I worked the entire weekend, barely sleeping, and met the deadline anyway.

"Is this your report?" Vincent said, tossing a document across the desk, the day after I'd submitted it.

I picked up the document and leafed through it. The first pages were correct. When I reached the statistical tables, however, the numbers were all wrong. The conclusion section contained glaring spelling mistakes and grammatical errors. It looked like the work of a college freshman, and a sloppy one at that.

"It's my report," I said. "But . . ."

"That's what I thought."

"Some of the things here were changed," I said. "Like here." I turned the report around so he could see me point to a full-page chart. "It's not the same as the one that I submitted. The numbers are wrong. And if you look here," I added, pointing out another page, "there are things that—"

"Do you have any self-respect?"

"About what?"

"You submit sloppy work—riddled with mistakes—and then you try to tell me that it's not yours. Take responsibility for your mistakes, Sara. It's the minimum I would expect."

"These aren't my mistakes, Vincent. Someone's tampered with this document."

"Really? Someone *tampered* with it." Vincent glared at me. "How's that possible?" I couldn't meet his eyes. I felt ridiculous for having said it. Who would do such a thing? I didn't know the answer, but I was certain this was not the work that I'd submitted.

"Go back to your desk, Sara, and bring me your laptop," Vincent instructed. "I want to see the original report that you submitted, as it appears on your computer."

"Of course." I was back in his office within two minutes, my laptop open. I scrolled through my email out-box and victoriously opened the attachment of the report that I'd sent the day before.

When the attachment was open, I quickly looked through the documents so I could point out to Vincent that my original was flawless. I'd reread it and checked the numbers until I was certain there were no mistakes. But now, as I scrolled through my version, I noticed that it had the same errors as the document that Vincent had shown me.

"I don't understand," I said audibly, on the verge of tears. I pulled over my laptop and frantically checked my email again, as well as the documents saved on my computer.

"Well, I understand," said Vincent. "You submitted substandard work and you lied when you were caught. It's fortunate that Sam looked it over before submitting it to the client; otherwise, we would have had an embarrassing fiasco on our hands."

"But I *did* check it," I said. "It was perfect when I submitted it."

"There's nothing perfect about it," said Vincent, pointing at the open document on my computer. "This is the standard we might expect from an intern. I am issuing you an official warning. Sara, if you make any more mistakes, you *will* be fired."

"Someone must have accessed the document on my laptop," I muttered.

"I'd have more respect for you if you accepted responsibility for your mistakes," said Vincent, his voice laced with disgust. "Instead, you insist on lying repeatedly."

"Is this because of what I told you about Lucy?"

He froze at my question. I could feel white-hot anger from across the desk. "You can go now, Sara." His voice was ice.

Kevin was due back at the end of the week. I wasn't sure that he'd recognize me. He'd been gone for almost seven weeks and I'd lost at least eight pounds. I wasn't going to the gym anymore and rarely ran. I was so anxious that my hands trembled. I was struggling to cope and felt perpetually exhausted. I was often late to work. I couldn't seem to get up in the morning. My hair was unruly, my lipstick smudged. I barely recognized myself in the mirror.

"Sara." The receptionist called my name as I walked into the office, an hour late. "Vincent wants to see you in the front meeting room."

I smoothed down my skirt and buttoned up my jacket. I wished that I'd had time to wash my hair that morning and taken more care applying my makeup. I'd done a hasty, halfhearted job because I'd overslept again. My skirt was creased. I hadn't had a chance to iron it. I looked a mess.

I opened the door, to find Vincent sitting at a table along with the Human Resources director. A heavyset man sat on a chair at the back of the room. His face was inscrutable. I remember thinking that he looked awfully uncomfortable in his suit.

"You're late," said Vincent.

"I'm sorry. I had trouble getting a taxi," I replied, lying. "What is it that you need, Vincent?"

"Sara," said the HR director. "As you know from your repeated discussions with Vincent, there has been a steep deterioration in the quality of your work." She looked me over and added pointedly, "And presentation."

I flushed at her pointed comments. A frisson of fear ran through me. I couldn't manage a response or speak up to defend myself in any way. My voice was paralyzed. I was in shock. It was clear where this was going.

"Vincent has done everything he could to help you raise the standard of your work to an acceptable level. Unfortunately, despite all his warnings, the deterioration has continued to a point that is untenable."

"As a result," said Vincent, taking over, "Stanhope will be terminating you, effective immediately. Nick over there"—he indicated the muscular man in the corner—"will escort you to your desk, where you will be allowed to take anything that is personal in nature, after which he will escort you off the premises. It's unfortunate that it's come to this, Sara, but we've given you every opportunity to rectify this situation and you've failed time and time again."

A loud hum filled my ears as he spoke. My legs shook uncontrollably. I had to put my hands on my thighs to stop them from shaking.

"What about my salary?" I asked when I realized that he had stopped talking. "And references?"

The HR director handed me a document. "The firm will pay you two months' severance pay and an additional sum of twenty thousand dollars if you sign this agreement. It contains a nondisclosure clause. You will agree with our assessment of everything that transpired, specifically that you are being terminated due to poor performance. You will also agree that you have no further claims on the company."

"What if I refuse to sign it?"

"It's up to you, Sara," said Vincent. "However, this offer will not be repeated. If you don't sign it, we'll give you whatever is owed by law. I believe that's two weeks' salary. And nothing else. It's a 'take it or leave it' offer. You have two minutes to read it over and sign, or we'll take it off the table." Vincent looked at his watch.

"What about references?" I asked. "It's my first job out of college. I'm going to need a reference."

Vincent sighed. "I can't in good conscience give a reference for an employee who we fired because of sloppy work and a poor work ethic."

"I won't be able to get a job anywhere without one," I said in a panic.

"Sign the form, Sara, and you'll have enough money to tide you over until you get a new job. Your two minutes has started."

I signed the document. I had no choice. When I was done, the HR director gave me a copy of the document I'd signed and an envelope with a check they'd already prepared.

"Nick will show you out," she said, and then she and Vincent left without looking back.

I'd seen employees being fired before. I'd never imagined being one of them. My face was flushed as I followed Nick down the corridor to my desk.

Nick picked up a box that had been left in my cubicle, seemingly in advance preparation for my departure. The firm was nothing if not thorough. He placed it on my desk with a hollow thud that made me shudder.

"You can put your personal items in the box. I need to check each item before you leave," he said loudly. People's heads turned in my direction. I cringed. Whether by accident or design, Jules, Sam, and Sylvie were somewhere else in the office. I don't think I could have withstood the humiliation of going through my things while they watched.

I removed a pair of spare shoes from my bottom drawer and a silk scarf, a shawl, and a jacket from the small cabinet next to my desk.

Nick tossed them all into the box except for the jacket. He put it flat on my desk and patted down each pocket before throwing it into the box. I felt like a criminal.

I handed him a Moleskine notebook with gold-trimmed pages and the firm's logo embossed on the front. It had been in the bag of gifts that we'd been given that first day of our induction.

Nick thumbed through the pages of the notebook to make sure that there was nothing related to the firm. I put a makeup bag in the box. Nick unzipped it and spilled the contents out onto my desk. He checked every item in the bag, including a spare tampon, before tossing them back into the box. I realized that he was making sure there weren't any thumb drives with proprietary information in my belongings. Finally, I put framed photographs of Kevin and my parents in the box.

"I'm done," I said softly.

"No, you're not," he informed me. "I need your security pass, your laptop, and your work phone."

"Of course." My voice quivered. "Can I back up my laptop and my phone first? It'll only take a few minutes. I have photos and personal contact numbers on there."

"No," he said. "You're not allowed to access any of the firm's electronic devices."

"Some of the photos are of my father before he died," I said. My voice was thick. Hot tears streamed down my face. I heard myself sniff loudly. I'd really wanted to hold it together, but realizing I might lose those photos made me fall apart. "I don't have them any-where else. Please," I begged. "Let me at least email myself the photos of my dad."

"That's not possible." His tone became frighteningly aggressive. More heads turned. I flushed bright red. "You're not allowed to touch any electronics. The best I can do is ask HR if they can get IT to send you your photos. No promises, though."

I nodded, incapable of speech.

"Good. Now take the box and walk to reception with me," he instructed.

I picked up the box and walked to reception like a prisoner being escorted into her cell by a warden. I lowered my head so that nobody would see the humiliation on my face. Everyone was unashamedly watching me as I followed Nick down the corridor. I heard a flurry of muffled whispers behind me from those I'd already passed.

When I reached the reception area, the receptionist stopped talking on the phone midsentence as I walked by.

When the elevator arrived, we stepped inside. Everyone knew what it meant for someone to be standing there in tears holding a cardboard box, a burly security guard alongside, even if he was wearing a suit. There was a hushed silence as the elevator descended. I felt eyes burning into my back.

When we reached the lobby, Nick walked behind me, herding me all the way to the revolving glass doors that led to the street. Even then he wouldn't let me go until I was standing on the curb.

"Thank you for your cooperation," he said when we were outside. He clapped his hands together once, as if to signal to me that it was all over. "Now don't try to step foot in the building," he drawled. "If you do, we'll take out a restraining order. Do you understand?"

"Yes."

"Good. There's a taxi heading this way. I suggest you take it."

"No," I said. "I'd prefer to walk."

FORTY-THREE

THE ELEVATOR

Sam stumbled backward, away from the screen. He was still feeling the effects of the oxycodone-induced sleep that he was awakened from when the elevator lights turned on. He didn't know exactly what was going on but after reading the words on the screen, he knew they were snared in a trap that had been baited and sprung with perfect precision.

"I knew it would come back to bite us." Sam's voice rose into a frenzy.

"What would come back to bite us?" Vincent turned Sam around roughly, ignoring his injured arm. He wanted answers. "Why is it a declaration of war?"

"Because of Lucy," said Sam, as if that should have been obvious. "This was one of Lucy Marshall's favorite quotes. She was obsessed with Sun Tzu."

Vincent was annoyed with himself for that lapse in his memory. His head was pounding, but he still should have known right away.

"This isn't an escape room, Vincent. We've been lured here as punishment for what happened to Lucy."

Sam lowered himself to the ground and let his head fall. Ever since Lucy died, he'd been taking blow and Quaaludes and a medicine cabinet's worth of other pills to dull his memory. They blocked out the memories but not the guilt.

Jules and Sylvie both gave a subtle shake of their heads to warn Sam to shut his mouth. But he was too weak and tired to play their games. This was his chance to right a wrong. To do what his father would have done in the same situation.

Sam looked up at them with a stony face and determined eyes. It was time to tell the truth. To break the pledge they'd made as they walked together to the wake for Lucy at the Irish bar after the firm's memorial service for her.

It was Eric's idea. He'd recognized that Jules was the weakest link. He'd taken him aside and told him that he'd seen Lucy's salary— his uncle was on the board and, through him, Eric had access to everything.

"Can you believe that Lucy earns twice as much as you?" Eric showed Jules a screen shot of Lucy's pay slip on his phone to prove it. As he'd expected, Jules was incensed.

Jules would have done anything to get even with Lucy after that. Well, almost anything.

"Who does Vincent think he is, paying that loser more than you? I can't understand what he sees in that weirdo," Eric said, tapping into Jules's darkest emotions. "It's an embarrassment, having someone as ugly as her on our payroll. Stanhope is an investment bank, not a shelter for schizos."

He leaned forward and whispered his proposition into Jules's ear. Eric did the same thing to Sylvie, offering different inducements.

Corrupting those around him was Eric's greatest skill. He'd been doing it since he was in high school, buying essays and book reports from top students so that he didn't have to do the work himself.

"You both thought that Lucy was collateral damage!" Sam's voice rose hysterically, bouncing off the elevator walls, as he looked at Sylvie and Jules. "That she was dispensable. That we got away with it. But we haven't. That's why we're here. I always knew we would pay a terrible price for what happened."

Sylvie and Jules stared daggers at him. The day they walked to Lucy's wake, they all agreed never to divulge a word to Vincent. They couldn't let him have the slightest inkling of what had happened; they had too much to lose. Vincent would come after them mercilessly if he knew the truth.

They'd kept that pledge for years. They'd erased it from their memories, just as they erased Lucy. She was an irrelevant blip. They'd forgotten all about her until Sam connected the dots for them. Lucy kept an out-of-date calendar with Sun Tzu quotes by her desk. That's where they'd seen that quote before.

"What does Lucy Marshall have to do with our being here?" Vincent's eyes searched their faces for answers.

"Everything," replied Sam. "Nothing," said Sylvie at the same time.

"Sam's lost it," said Jules, throwing up his hands in frustration. "It's the drugs. Or the fever. He's hallucinating; he's—"

"I want to hear what Sam has to say," Vincent said, interrupting him. "Nobody has answered my question. What does our being here have to do with Lucy? What happened?" Vincent's question was greeted with awkward silence.

"She died," said Jules. Like the smart-ass he is, thought Vincent. Jules's wise-guy remarks were a miscalculation. It gave Vincent the excuse he needed to act. He struck like a cobra. He pulled Jules toward him by his tie and then shoved him back until he hit the glass wall behind him, crumpling to the ground.

"What did you do to Lucy?"

"It wasn't our fault," said Jules in the whiny voice of a child. "Honestly, Vincent. It was all Eric Miles. He thought he owned Stanhope."

"Eric was an ass," said Vincent. "Tell me something I don't know. What I don't understand is what Eric being a prick has to do with Lucy's death."

Jules and Sylvie quickly glanced at each other. Vincent saw it. He put his hands in his pockets to restrain himself. It was obvious they'd been hiding this secret for years.

"Eric hated Lucy," said Sam. "She offended him because she had the temerity to show everyone what a dumb fuck he really was."

The others could afford to be evasive, but Sam knew he was gravely injured. He had an overwhelming urge to give the confession to Vincent he should have made years earlier. He broke the oath they'd all agreed to keep.

"I attended a leadership meeting on your behalf while you were away. I asked Lucy to join me, in case they drilled us on financials. Eric Miles—remember he was working on that oil and gas deal with us—addressed the leadership team first. When they asked specific questions, he gave them fake revenue projections. He didn't have the answers, so he made up numbers on the spot. Out of thin air."

"Go on," said Vincent. It didn't surprise him. Eric was a bullshit artist to the core. He'd survived purely on his family name. If he'd been anyone else, he'd have been fired on day one. Hell, he'd never have been hired in the first place.

"I didn't say anything. I figured that I'd clarify everything afterward. I didn't want to embarrass Eric publicly. But Lucy, she was incensed. I tried to signal to her to keep quiet. Well, you remember how she was with social cues. She corrected Eric. Publicly. In front of the executive team. She didn't mean to tear him apart, but she basically showed him for what he was. A liar and . . ."

"An idiot," said Vincent.

"Lucy didn't realize that she'd made an implacable enemy. True to form, Eric figured out a way to get back at her."

Jules and Sylvie were completely still as they waited for Sam to recount the rest of the story.

"How did Eric get back at Lucy?" Vincent asked quietly.

Vincent always knew that Eric was a borderline psychopath. Not in the Wall Street sense of the word of a badass banker, someone who would burn everyone to get the deal done. A psychopath in the traditional sense; Eric was capable of hurting people purely because he got a kick out of it.

Sam didn't respond. His hands trembled as he remembered being told what had happened. It shocked him. Not enough to speak up, but enough that he had to numb his guilt with drugs. He always regretted hiding it—Vincent would have taken on Eric if he'd known. Vincent was at his peak in those days, and his ruthlessness was legendary.

"Come on." Vincent thumped his fist against the wall. The elevator rocked. "Tell me exactly what happened. I want to hear every last detail."

"Eric invited two of the more desperate and dumb interns out for drinks one night. He got them plastered. Blind drunk. He had Lucy's water bottle, the one she always kept at her desk, spiked with a date-rape drug."

"Eric raped Lucy?" Vincent's voice was hollow.

"Not exactly," said Sam. "Eric is a coward. He didn't do his own dirty work. He arranged for the drunk interns to get into the elevator with Lucy late at night. Eric fired them up while getting them drunk on vodka shots. Apparently, he told them, 'Penetration is not allowed; this isn't a gang rape. Just have fun, kids.'"

"So what exactly did they do to her?"

"They touched her," Jules chimed in. "Honestly, it wasn't that big a deal. One of them rubbed her face in his crotch. Another kissed her and felt her up. There was some dry humping. It wasn't rape, Vincent; it was a practical joke."

"I'm sure Lucy thought it was hilarious," said Vincent quietly, "because two days later, she killed herself."

Jules was about to say something in his own defense, but he thought better of it. The rage radiating from Vincent suggested that, next time around, Vincent might not be satisfied with shoving him against a wall. He remembered how Vincent had put the glass shard to his neck. He didn't want to find out what Vincent would do if he really lost control of his temper.

"Sylvie, this isn't the first time I've heard a version of this story." Vincent's tone was scathing. "Several years ago, I was told you knew that Eric had molested Lucy and that you did nothing about it. Do you remember that?" Sylvie shifted uncomfortably. She looked at her feet with studied fascination.

"You lied to me," Vincent said. "You covered up what Eric had done."

"If I'd admitted it then, Eric would have come after me next," said Sylvie, not particularly convincingly. Eric was a bully, he went after the weak and defenseless. Sylvie was hardly the type to allow herself to be pushed around.

"I want the truth," said Vincent. "Sara Hall said that Lucy came to you for help. Is that true?"

"Lucy called me," said Sylvie. "In the middle of the night. She'd fallen asleep and woken up confused. Her memory was fuzzy; she was in a blind panic. Hysterical, really. She asked me to come to her apartment, and so I went over there. She was barely coherent. She said she thought she'd been raped."

"And you did nothing to help her? You didn't call the cops?"

"Of course not," said Sylvie. "I knew what had really happened."

"How did you know?" Vincent asked in a voice so soft, they had to strain to hear him.

"Because . . ." She stopped talking as she realized the damage the information she'd already let slip had done.

"Go on," snapped Vincent. "How did you know what happened to Lucy in the elevator?"

"Because Jules was there. He told me what happened. There was no rape," said Sylvie. "Look, Eric made us promises about promotions, but of course he never kept them. We were stupid to listen to him. I agreed to slip the roofie into Lucy's drink; Jules went in the elevator to make sure things didn't get out of hand. We didn't want anyone to get hurt, and that's why he was there."

"It didn't get out of hand," Jules added. "I made sure of that. It was hazing. Pretty tame stuff, really. That's all. It's ancient history."

"No," said Vincent. "It's not ancient history. If it were ancient history, then we wouldn't be locked up in here."

FORTY-FOUR

SARA HALL

For weeks after Kevin returned from Silicon Valley, I kept up a frenetic pretense that nothing had changed. That my career hadn't gone down the toilet. That I hadn't been fired.

On nights that Kevin slept over, I woke at 5:00 A.M. and went to the fitness center, which I couldn't afford anymore, for a workout that I didn't want to do. I'd return home while Kevin was eating breakfast to shower and change into one of my suits while talking to him about whatever made-up story from work came to mind. "Vincent may want me to fly to Hong Kong again in a couple of weeks," that sort of thing.

When I met Kevin after work for drinks or dinner, I peppered my conversation with bubbly anecdotes of whatever fictional event had happened that day at work. What I'd really been doing was sitting home all day in my sweats, watching daytime talk shows and trying to forget that not only was I unemployed but, based on the responses I'd received so far to job applications, I was unemployable.

I was so devastated and humiliated by that final day at Stanhope,

I just couldn't bring myself to tell Kevin. It was the modern-day equivalent of being put in stocks while the townspeople threw rotten tomatoes at my face. I'd lost my self-worth, my friends, my good name, my career, and my livelihood. It seemed easier to pretend it hadn't happened.

If truth be told, my lies were more deep-seated than merely covering up my humiliation. I lied to Kevin because, deep down, I knew that Kevin was in love with the woman I'd been, not the woman I now was. He was marrying an up-and-coming female investment banker at one of the most prestigious firms in the business. I was a foil for his own success. He would have no interest in being engaged to Sara Hall, unemployed corporate reject, whose career was in shambles. Sara Hall, fired for incompetence without a single reference. Or Sara Hall, whose bank account was dwindling on a daily basis. Sara Hall, who would be bankrupt within six months if she didn't find work. Sara Hall, who no matter how hard she tried simply could not get a job.

Success was an integral part of Kevin's image. His mother was a judge; his brother and sisters were all ridiculously accomplished; his dad had been a partner at a large law firm before he died. Everyone in Kevin's orbit was successful. Failure was an alien concept. I was certain that if Kevin found out that I had been fired, it would kill whatever passion he felt for me. It would destroy us.

That's why I pretended that my life hadn't changed in any way once he got back from California. I kept my apartment, despite not being able to afford the rent, to prevent Kevin from finding out that I'd lost my job. I stupidly fooled myself into thinking that I'd quickly find another job. Then I'd tell Kevin that I'd decided to move to a new firm. I hoped to swing things so that he never found out the truth.

That was pure fantasy, of course. It was impossible to get a job without a professional reference. Nobody would look at me. Headhunters didn't answer my calls once they knew that I'd left Stanhope without a new job in hand. It was a surefire indication that I'd been kicked out. Recruiters pulled me from interviews they'd set up once I had to admit that my only reference was an old college professor.

"But you've been working for several years. Where are your references?"

"My former boss is now in Shanghai, and I haven't been able to get hold of him," I'd tell them, unable to meet their eyes. It was like saying "The dog ate my homework."

I tried repeatedly to contact Vincent by phone and by email to request—to beg, really—that he give me a letter of recommendation. Surely there was something positive that he could say about my work after those years I'd been at Stanhope. He never responded. He put a block on my emails and declined my calls.

I waited outside the Stanhope building several nights in a row, until one evening I saw Jules walking from the revolving glass doors out onto the street.

"Hi, Jules," I said, approaching him. "How's everything going with you?" He looked up in surprise.

"You shouldn't be here," he said, hailing a taxi. "Vincent won't like it."

"I need a reference, Jules. Nobody will hire me."

"It's not going to happen, Sara," he said as he stepped into his cab and closed the door.

Two days later, a courier delivered a cease-and-desist letter from Stanhope's lawyers, threatening that they'd take out a restraining order against me if I contacted anyone from the firm again.

Between paying my rent, my mother's retirement home fees, and my dad's medical bills, my savings were disappearing fast. I was well on my way to being flat broke.

My biggest mistake was that I'd forgotten that while I lived in a city of eight million people, there were at most three degrees of separation between Kevin and my colleagues.

One night, a few weeks into this charade, Kevin had arranged for us to meet for a drink after work at a place called Clancy's. As my taxi turned the corner, I could already see Kevin standing outside the bar. It was a cold night and the yellow glow of streetlights was reflected on a sidewalk slick with rain.

The driver pulled over and I opened the door to get out. My heels were unsteady on the slippery sidewalk. I had to watch my footing, so I didn't see the expression on Kevin's face until I was standing on the curb, the taxi still waiting behind me.

"Sorry, hon. Vincent's meeting dragged on and on tonight." I spoke with the polished tone of a practiced liar.

I was wearing one of my best suits and still acting as if I'd come straight from work. In reality, I'd spent the afternoon interviewing with second-rate recruiters, all of whom immediately cut me off when I told them that I couldn't provide them with a reference from my previous employer.

Kevin stared at me with a strange expression. Then he asked me the question that I'd been dreading.

"Why didn't you tell me you were fired?"

I didn't know what to say. I just stared at him, wide-eyed, my heart slowly breaking.

"Why?" he insisted. I could hear the disgust in his voice.

"I don't know." It was the most truthful thing that I'd said to him in weeks.

He said something else. I couldn't hear the words, though I saw his lips move. All I could hear was the rapid beat of my heart as my world fell apart. The taxi driver broke through my trance by honking his horn and sticking his head out of the window. "Lady, I'm a taxi driver, not your dad. Where's my money?"

"I'm sorry." I leaned through the window and handed him cash. I wasn't sure whether my words were directed at the driver or at Kevin. It didn't much matter. By the time I turned around again, Kevin had gone.

I don't know how long I stood on that sidewalk, soaked by the rain, listening to raucous laughter coming from the bar where we were supposed to have spent the evening together. My life was irretrievably broken.

The truth is, Kevin was bound to find out. On the night we'd arranged to meet at Clancy's, he had come from an alumni event at his law school. It was the same law school that Jules had graduated from a few years ahead of Kevin. When I remembered that connection, I realized what had probably happened. They'd seen each other there and, knowing how Jules liked to throw a cat among the pigeons, he'd almost certainly beelined to Kevin and asked him something along the lines of: "How's Sara doing with her job search?"

Jules would have said it with some delight, enjoying Kevin's shocked reaction. After that night, I imagined that scene a thousand times in a thousand ways, each more excruciating than the last.

Kevin sent me an email the morning after he'd abandoned me outside Clancy's. He told me that the wedding was off, and that he wanted the ring back. He wrote it in polite legal language that suggested I'd find myself in court if I refused. I had no intention of refusing. I went to his office to return the ring, but Kevin wouldn't come down to see me. He sent his personal assistant to the foyer and I put the ring in her manicured hand.

I never saw Kevin again.

That day, after our engagement was officially broken off, I gave notice to my landlord and began packing. Among the things to pack were Lucy's sketch pads and her journal. For the first time since the day I raised the allegations against Eric Miles with Vincent, I was curious to look at them again. I was certain those notebooks had something to do with my dismissal.

I flipped through the pages of the journal repeatedly. I couldn't find the red ink drawing of Lucy being attacked in the elevator, nor could I find Lucy's mirror writing on the page alongside it. At first, I thought that I'd flipped the pages too fast. I started back at the beginning and slowly went through every single page in the journal. The red ink pages weren't there. It was as if they'd never been there.

I went through that journal a dozen times, and all of Lucy's sketch pads. There was no trace of the red ink drawing. It made me question my own sanity, until I found Lucy's drawing of the team in the meeting room, with Vincent's face drawn as the devil. Etched into the round table, Lucy had written "The Circle, Inc." I still had no idea what that meant.

Though I was disturbed by the disappearance of the journal entries, I was overwhelmed by the stressful task of moving back to Chicago, especially under such painful circumstances. I had to get rid of the bulk of my stuff virtually overnight. I reduced my apartment to two dozen boxes and sold all my furniture and TV for some extra cash.

Ten days after breaking up with Kevin, I was back in Chicago, living much the way that I had before starting at Stanhope. Except it was worse, because now I had no prospects and no expectations.

I rented a small room on a short-term lease in a dingy apartment above a burger joint. During the evening rush, the whole apartment smelled of grease. When I went to job interviews, I had to spray myself with perfume so that my clothes wouldn't smell like a grill.

My roommate, Fiona, was a college dropout whose deadbeat friends hung out in the living room on a semipermanent basis, watching television at full volume.

I'd wake up in the morning to an apartment smelling of stale cigarette smoke as well as grease, and littered with dozens of empty beer cans. Dirty plates filled with cigarette butts were scattered around the room. The bathroom stank like a public urinal, filled with the stench of sour urine from guests too drunk to aim properly.

I took sleeping pills to get through the nights, and sometimes to get through the more difficult days, as well. They left me in a haze, so that I lost track of time and missed job interviews, or arrived late, or looking ill-kempt and exhausted. Often both.

I searched for work by every means possible. I answered job ads, went to agencies to speak to recruiters, and tried to leverage my old college network. I couldn't find a job in the financial industry without a reference. Nobody wanted to touch me. They treated me as if I had the plague.

I lowered my expectations. Instead of applying for top-tier firms, I applied to smaller ones. When nothing came of that, I applied for low-level jobs at family-run firms, at a fraction of my previous salary. They'd ask me why I wanted to move from a high-flying job at the top of my profession to a two-bit outfit in a strip mall. It was a reasonable question. I'd tell them it was to be near my mother. They'd almost believe me—until they found out I couldn't offer them a single reference from my old job.

I lowered my sights again. Eventually, I found a job as a bookkeeper at a sleazy debt-collection agency run by a small-time loan shark, Rudi. It was in a part of town filled with auto junkyards and run-down office buildings offering cheap rent to dodgy fly-by-night businesses, like the one I was now employed by. They didn't care that I had no references; they were happy to milk my experience at minimum wage.

I couldn't cover my mother's retirement village fees beyond the next two months. I was pulling my courage together to tell my mom that I'd have to move her, when I received a call from the facility. My mom had had a massive stroke while sitting out in the garden. They'd found her collapsed on the grass. "She wouldn't have felt a thing," they told me.

It almost broke me having to bury my mother so soon after my father. I was more alone than I'd ever imagined it was possible to be. There was nobody left for me. Nobody who gave a damn if I lived or died.

I stood at my parents' graves with an ache in my heart for a long time after my mother's burial. Perhaps it's better this way, I thought to myself. It would have devastated my mom and dad to have known that my life had fallen apart. Mom's funeral expenses took up the last of my savings. I was broke and my life was shattered.

After that, the months passed in a blur of depression and pills. I'd drifted away from my best friends, Jill and Lisa, as well as from my closest friends from college. Working at Stanhope had been so all-consuming that it had been hard keeping up with anyone outside work. They were hurt that I'd never made much effort, and eventually they stopped reaching out. I was too proud to contact them now that my life was in ruins.

I was isolated and lonely. Every day was a struggle; both financial and psychological. I would stumble out of bed and go to work and then return in the evening and go straight to bed again. I'd fall asleep to the smell of greasy fries cooked in rancid oil which wafted into the apartment from the fast food joint downstairs, and the shrieks of drunken laughter from Fiona's friends partying outside my thin bedroom walls.

My old life faded into a surreal blur, like an old movie that I'd once seen—faintly recognizable but out of sync somehow; a tripped-up remake too fantastical to be the real thing.

There were days when I almost believed that I'd never left Chicago to work at Stanhope. Days when it felt as if my life in New York had happened to someone else and that I'd awakened from a deep coma, only to find myself trapped in a hellish existence that I couldn't escape.

Sometimes, when the medication wore off, my memory would come back into focus. I'd remember the injustice. The public humiliation. The way they'd chipped away at my self-esteem until there was almost nothing left of me. The way they'd ruined my future with Kevin.

It was during those moments that I thought about revenge.

FORTY-FIVE

THE ELEVATOR

The ceiling vent that had been chugging out thick streams of heat suddenly shifted, of its own accord, to pumping ice-cold air into the elevator.

Vincent was so cold that he put his blood-splattered shirt back on. Over that, he put on his jacket and his cashmere overcoat, all buttoned up. Other than the faint shadows of a beard and the cuts to his knuckles, he looked much as he had when he stepped into the elevator all those hours earlier. Sylvie shivered uncontrollably because of her bare legs. She wrapped her arms around herself to keep warm.

If the men noticed that she was shivering, they didn't care enough to offer her a jacket or overcoat to keep warm. They huddled under their own coats as the elevator turned from a sauna into an arctic wasteland. They didn't want to be near one another, but it was so cold that they were slowly drawn to one another's body heat. They became less focused on their meager water supply and more focused on staying warm. They knew hypothermia would get them long before dehydration.

"Sam, you're wasting our energy rehashing what happened in the past with Lucy. We can do that another time. We need to work out who locked us in here," Jules stuttered through chattering teeth. "Seems to me that might be our best hope of figuring a way out."

"Don't you understand?" said Sam wildly, his face flushed. "It's all connected to Lucy. I knew that we'd never get away with it. That one day we'd have to pay for what we did."

"It's Eric Miles; he lured us here," said Sylvie, ignoring Sam. "It's exactly the sort of thing he'd do. He did it to Lucy and now he's doing a version of the same thing with us. Didn't he have a beef with you, Vincent? I heard he blamed you for being kicked out of Stanhope, and by extension he blamed the rest of us."

The Stanhope rumor mill suggested that Eric was let go over his conduct with female graduates and interns. It was an open secret that Eric was incapable of keeping his hands to himself and acted as if female interns were his personal harem.

Vincent was the only one among them who knew why Eric was really dismissed. It was because he'd provided false information to help nail a deal, in return for kickbacks. Straight-out corruption. That was why the firm had lost its biggest account right before Christmas. Stanhope could handle sexual harassment with payoffs and nondisclosure agreements, but fraud was another matter entirely. It crossed a red line. Eric had to go.

"Eric didn't lure us here. He's not smart enough. If he wanted to get me, he'd have hired a goon to beat us up," said Vincent. The elevator rattled slightly as a draft of wind blew up the shaft. "And anyway, I heard he checked into a clinic in Switzerland, for sex addiction. His wife threatened to leave him if he didn't get treatment."

"If not Eric, then who's behind this?" Sylvie said. "What do they want? Because I sure as hell want to get out of here. I've never been so cold in my life."

"Let's look at the clues again," said Jules. "They're telling us *something*."

"Rubbish," Vincent said. "They're random. Unconnected. They were meant to fool us into thinking this was an escape room."

"Then how do you explain the anagram that formed Sara Hall's name, or the Sun Tzu quote?" said Jules. "It's obviously connected to Lucy. Only those who worked closest with Lucy knew that she hero-worshipped Sun Tzu. And we're all here. Except for—" He stopped talking abruptly.

"Except for who?" Vincent asked.

"Sara Hall," said Jules. "She used to sit near Lucy's desk. She was part of our team when Lucy was alive."

"It can't be Sara Hall," Sylvie said. "Sara Hall has been dead for years."

FORTY-SIX

SARA HALL

Through my thin bedroom door, I could hear Fiona and her friends getting drunk and increasingly rowdy. I would have gone out for the evening to get away from the noise, but it was raining and, frankly, I had nowhere to go.

I stayed in my room, a prisoner to the torpor that had infested me for months since being fired and dumped.

Someone put on trance music. The beat was so loud that my room vibrated. I tidied up my bedroom while I waited for them to leave for the club they were going to. Cigarette smoke wafted into my room. It was soon followed by the distinct smell of weed so strong that it overwhelmed the greasy hamburger odor that usually infused the apartment.

The doorbell rang; more people arrived. I restrained myself from going into the living room and yelling at Fiona for having a party on a work night. I couldn't risk another blowup with her, especially with a dozen drunk friends taking her side. We were one argument away from her kicking me out. I needed that room until I sorted out my life.

I tried to find some peace in the mundane task of tidying up my closet. I was folding a sweater when I noticed the cover of the vinyl record *Sara* that Lucy had left for me. I honestly don't know why I'd kept it. I guess it was as a keepsake to remember Lucy, because it was unlikely that I'd ever actually play the record. I'd never owned a record player and wasn't planning on buying one.

Someone in the living room threw an empty beer can at my door. Laughter erupted. "It's raining," someone shouted. "Let's party here instead."

Great, just great, I thought to myself. I pulled out the liner notes from inside the record sleeve to read the lyrics, in lieu of actually listening to it. The back of the lyrics sheet was filled with small, precise handwriting. I sat down slowly on the corner of my bed to study it more closely. It was Lucy's writing. She'd written formulas and mathematical calculations and other information in upside-down mirror writing.

It took me ages to decipher the sheet. It was well into the early morning by the time I was done.

From what I could understand, the formulas determined the impact on the shares of one company from a sudden shock in another. For example, the effect of an acquisition of a car manufacturer on shares in a company that supplied car parts for them. If someone could accurately predict such effects, then serious money could be made. If they worked at Stanhope and had inside information, then they could make exponentially more money. They would also be breaking the law.

Halfway down the first page, Lucy had meticulously recorded a list of securities traded, with the prices, profit, and dates of the transactions. Alongside each, she'd detailed a deal that our team at Stanhope had been handling, which wouldn't have been public knowledge at that time. It was the smoking gun, proof that insider trading had taken place. The crime carried a maximum sentence of twenty years in a federal prison.

Lucy had pulled together a complete trail of evidence. It had been her insurance policy and she'd entrusted it to me. She knew that I had enough inside knowledge of the firm to piece it together pretty quickly, but I bet she'd never imagined it would take me so long to find it.

Someone had harnessed Lucy's brilliance to make an awful lot of money, using a highly sophisticated scheme that, at best, skated on the edge of the law. According to Lucy's notes, the trades were conducted by a shell company called The Circle, Inc. I remembered that name on her sketch of the team in which she'd drawn Vincent as the devil. A quick internet search came up with nothing except for an address for a company by that name at a serviced office in the Cayman Islands.

I remembered how Cathy was convinced that Lucy's personal computer had been stolen after she died. She must have been right. Whoever had done it was probably trying to erase any trace of The Circle. What they hadn't realized was that Lucy had written down all the information by hand before she died. She had a photographic memory and must have memorized every document that she'd seen over the years. Knowing Lucy's lateral thinking, she figured that nobody would look for a handwritten copy of the information, hidden inside the sleeve of an old-fashioned analog record, no less. They'd look for digital copies on USB drives or on her computer's hard drive, or even in the cloud.

As it happened, Lucy's plan almost failed. I had come close to throwing out that record with all the other stuff that I got rid of when I moved back to Chicago. It was saved in a moment of sentimentality.

At the bottom of the page was more upside-down mirror writing, which I soon realized included the bank details and codes for The Circle's bank account. When Lucy had written these notes, there was well over ninety-five million dollars in the account. The signatories to the account were listed as Jules, Sam, Sylvie, and Lucy. Vincent was listed as the principal signatory and he was the only one with the master password to the account. Lucy had somehow found out what it was and carefully documented it in her tiny writing at the bottom of the page.

Lucy's drawing of Vincent as the devil finally made sense. He was the ringleader of a massive insider-trading conspiracy.

FORTY-SEVEN

THE ELEVATOR

They huddled together, pressing close for warmth despite their distaste for one another. They were in survival mode. They weren't worried about whether they had enough food or water anymore, or whether they'd be able to alert the throngs of office workers who arrived on Monday morning that they were stuck in an elevator. They worried whether they'd be alive on Monday morning. With no other recourse, they crammed together to share body heat, clutching one another in an intimate embrace.

It was ironic, thought Jules, that they were helping each other survive when it was not really in their individual interests. They all had good reason to want one another dead. Here in the elevator, it would be easy. Sylvie in her skirt and without a proper coat could easily die of hypothermia. Sam was getting weaker by the hour; his eyes were sunken and his face ashen. It wouldn't take much for him to lose his battle to stay alive. It would be so easy to gently press a hand over his nose when everyone was sleeping. Sam would be too weak to struggle. He'd die of suffocation and nobody would ever suspect anything.

If Sam and Sylvie were gone, there would only be two of them left—him and Vincent. If there was only one survivor, he would get to claim the greatest prize of all: The Circle's assets, all neatly tied up in their Cayman Islands bank account.

When they'd formed The Circle, they'd never expected it would be around this long. They were working on a deal and realized they could all profit from inside information without actually breaking the law. It was a deal on behalf of a global mining company, and they knew the announcement would affect palladium prices. They formed a company in the Cayman Islands to take a joint position on metals options ahead of the news of the deal breaking. It netted them just under three million dollars.

It was supposed to be one trade. But a few months later, another opportunity presented itself, and that time they made close to five million. By the third trade, they'd become addicted.

Vincent insisted on complete secrecy. He put into place a series of measures to protect them from any government or law-enforcement investigation. He knew that by sharing the money via The Circle, it would be in their collective interest to keep their mouths shut. He made sure they all had too much at stake to go to the authorities.

They weren't happy when Vincent brought Lucy into The Circle. It meant they had to share the profits five ways. None of them trusted her. She was unpredictable, weird. Vincent wouldn't listen to their concerns; his only concession was that Lucy would be the last member. Nobody else would join.

"Lucy's brilliant," Vincent reassured them. "She'll make us a fortune."

Jules had the impression that Lucy went along with it out of intellectual curiosity rather than greed. She'd never struck him as the type to put much store in money. The formulas she devised were sheer genius; her algorithms made them millions. The more money they made, the more they threw caution to the wind. Insider trading, tax evasion. They were in deep. If they were caught, they could spend the rest of their lives inside a federal penitentiary.

"It's a victimless crime," Vincent told them, "but technically we're still breaking the law. We have to be discreet and, most important, we have to be patient."

Vincent said they'd have to wait a decade to access the money, in order to ensure they went under the radar of law enforcement.

Then Lucy died. They started losing money. They hadn't realized just how much work Lucy did to fine-tune the algorithms to make smart investment decisions. When the market dropped, they took significant losses. As The Circle's bank balance went south, dropping down to fifty million dollars, their relationships became more fractious. They wanted to cut their losses. Vincent refused. He said it was too soon; that it was dangerous and might alert the authorities.

They worried that Vincent would find out the role they'd played in Lucy's death and punish them by refusing to give them their share of The Circle's assets. Vincent had a soft spot for Lucy. He had a thing for strays, and a ruthless streak underneath his urbane exterior that made him capable of almost anything when he was crossed.

The recent uncertainty at Stanhope meant they might all soon be without jobs. It created a fresh impetus to break up The Circle so they could finally access their money. Jules's divorce had nearly killed him financially. Ironically, Sam's marriage had done the same, thanks to

Kim's extravagant spending. As for Sylvie, she was tired of fighting for her place at Stanhope. She was more than ready to live the rest of her life with Marc and a passive, tax-free income from her share of The Circle's assets.

Vincent insisted the safest course of action was to leave the money alone for another few years. He was more cautious than the others and less in need of cash. Crucially, he had the master password required to close The Circle's accounts and distribute its assets. It helped cement his iron grip over them.

"How did Lucy really die?" asked Vincent without warning. It had been weighing on his mind ever since Sam had broken ranks with the others and begun his rambling confession. "I know that some questions are better left unasked, but I never believed that Lucy killed herself."

Sam's body trembled from the cold, or nerves, or perhaps both. His tongue felt thick and unwieldy amid his chattering teeth. When he finally spoke, it was rapidly, as if he welcomed the opportunity to relieve himself of a terrible burden.

"Lucy came to work the day after the elevator incident, even though Sylvie had told her to stay home," Sam recounted. "She pulled me aside. She was distraught. Slightly crazed, really. She said that something horrible had happened to her the night before. That it made her realize she'd become a terrible person and that it was time to make amends.

"She said we should all come clean about The Circle. I told her that was out of the question. She insisted that it was inevitable the feds would find out. That if we confessed, the punishment would be far more lenient than if we were caught."

"So you three killed her?" Vincent asked. "Just like that." He snapped his fingers to emphasize his point. "Because she was hysterical after being assaulted in an elevator and made a few empty threats?"

"No. Not the three of us. Sam is the one who killed her," said Sylvie.

"Lucy knew enough about The Circle to destroy us financially. To get us sent to prison." Sam was quick to defend himself. "I tried to reason with her, Vincent. I really did. I reassured her that we'd covered our tracks so well nobody would ever find out unless one of us blabbed. I reminded her that she was implicated as well, that she'd go to jail, too, but she said she didn't care. Lucy wouldn't listen to reason."

"She was probably in shock after what happened. She wasn't thinking rationally," said Vincent.

"I thought so, too," said Sam. "I convinced her to go home and sleep on it before making a decision. I went to her apartment later that night to talk it over with her."

"And what happened?"

"She threatened to bring us down. Me, you, The Circle. If anything, she was more agitated. She said the money we'd made was blood money and she'd see us all in hell, where we belonged. Or failing that, in a federal penitentiary. She was serious, Vincent. She was going to the cops, the SEC, the feds."

"Jesus, Sam," Vincent muttered.

"Lucy left me with no choice," Sam replied. "I put a roofie in her drink to make her compliant. The drug worked within minutes. She was almost robotic. I dictated the suicide letter to her and she wrote it down. Then I told her to take a bath. I figured she'd fall asleep and drown. It would look like suicide. The drug I'd chosen metabolized quickly. There would be no trace by the time they did an autopsy."

"Except that's not what happened," said Vincent.

"No," said Sam. "She sat upright in the tub like a zombie. I realized that I hadn't thought it through very well. One capsule wasn't strong enough to knock her out. I switched to plan B to help things along a little. I put on my leather gloves. Up until then, I'd kept my hands in the pockets of my jacket." He glimpsed a skeptical expression on Vincent's face. "Look, I wasn't sure how things would turn out when I went into that apartment. But I realized at that point that there was no choice, I had to take matters into my own hands. I plugged Lucy's tablet device into the bathroom socket. The cord was badly frayed. I put the device in her hands as she sat in the tub. I knew that she'd drop it sooner or later, electrocuting herself."

"You left her like that," Vincent said.

"I washed out the glass to remove any traces of the drug I'd given her, and then broke it and dumped the shards in the trash. I broke a couple more glasses and messed up her cupboards, too. I figured it would look as if she'd been caught in some sort of mania before she died. After that, I climbed down the emergency stairs on the side of the building. I was halfway down the street when I turned around and saw her entire floor had gone dark. The power was out. That's when I knew that Lucy was dead."

Vincent looked at him in disgust. "You stupid bastard," he said. "Didn't you realize that by killing Lucy you were endangering The Circle? Lucy was our golden goose. We've barely made any serious money since she died. If anything, we're worth less now than when she was alive. You should have come to me. I would have talked sense into her. She always listened to me."

"You were in London. I couldn't get ahold of you, and anyway, we certainly couldn't discuss the details on the phone. I did it to save us, Vincent. I did it to save The Circle's money. I had no choice. I was cleaning up the mess left by Jules and Sylvie. It would never have come to that point if they hadn't helped Eric Miles torment Lucy. You should blame them before you blame me," he whined.

"Don't pin Lucy's murder on us, Sam," snapped Sylvie. "You just admitted to it. We didn't kill anyone. You're lucky that nobody ever suspected it was murder."

"Oh, someone suspected it all right," Sam said, almost to himself. "Lucy's mother found documents when she was packing up to move to Baltimore, and she could tell there was something off about them. She called the office to speak with Vincent, but he was abroad again and his PA put her through to me. Cathy said the papers she'd found had something to do with a company called The Circle. Her tone was suspicious—she was testing me." Sam paused to let the implications of his words sink in. "I thought we were safe when we took Lucy's laptop, but it turned out that she'd left information behind some-where else. Well, I had to do something. Cathy would have gone to the cops."

"You killed Lucy's mother, too?" said Jules.

"What choice did I have?" Sam pleaded for their understanding. "I met with her first and gave her a convoluted explanation for the notes she'd found. I thought it sounded legitimate, but I could tell that she didn't buy it. I hired a guy; Marty. An ex-broker who was fired for screwing up trades while on a cocaine binge. You knew him, Vincent; you threw him work on occasion. He was seriously down on his luck. Two ex-wives, killer alimony, no regular work. I offered him ten grand to break into Lucy's mother's apartment and find those papers. He broke in twice but found nothing. In the end, I paid him forty grand to run her over. I told him to make it look like an acci-dent. He did the job and went to Thailand to cool his heels. An all-expenses trip, paid by me. He died in a Bangkok brothel from an overdose or a heart attack. It was never clear."

Vincent ran his palm down his face as if hoping to wipe away these revelations.

"It was never supposed to come to this," he said. "The Circle was our retirement fund. No one was meant to die."

FORTY-EIGHT

SARA HALL

Finding Lucy's information on The Circle snapped me out of my stupor. It gave me hope when I had none. That's all I really needed to get out of the medicated haze, out of the listlessness and self-hatred that had allowed me to surrender life's possibilities.

Lucy's information gave me the opportunity to destroy the lives of those who had destroyed mine. I considered my options carefully. If I leaked the information to the authorities, Vincent and the others would come under investigation. With the evidence I had, they'd lose their jobs and go to jail. That's if their high-priced lawyers couldn't get them off the hook, and if they didn't catch wind of what was happening and flee the country before they were arrested. But there was another option—one that I liked better.

I stopped taking sleeping pills that night. I woke early the next morning and went to a local gym to work out for the first time in months. I ran on the treadmill for thirty minutes solid and spent the rest of the time doing free weights. While I worked out, I planned my revenge. I would no longer be passive. I would no longer accept the fate they'd given me. I would get my life back—on my terms.

It's harder to kill yourself than you might imagine, especially when you don't actually intend to die. But for my plan to work, Sara Hall had to be dead and buried.

I disappeared one night when Fiona was out with her friends. I left a note saying that I was going away for a few days to visit family. I enclosed a check for the next rent payment, so that she'd have no reason to chase me down.

I took a few sentimental items that wouldn't be missed and a small selection of clothes and shoes—enough to fill a backpack. Other than that, I left behind everything I owned in the world.

A few days earlier, I'd bought an old sedan for cash at a dodgy used-car lot. The salesman allowed me to keep the papers unchanged after I slipped him an extra five hundred dollars.

The night I left, I drove for hours. I stopped at an all-night pancake joint in Des Moines for free refill coffees and a short stack. When I was done, I removed the SIM card from my phone, crushed it, and threw it down a drain. I climbed back into my car and drove through the night, heading south.

In the following days, I stuck to cities rather than small towns, losing myself in faceless crowds of strangers. I paid for everything in cash. I didn't use my credit cards and didn't risk touching the meager savings in my bank account. Dead people don't withdraw money. At night, I slept in a sleeping bag in the backseat of my beat-up car.

A week after leaving, I went to an internet café and sent Fiona an email from an account that I set up in the name of a fictional aunt, explaining that Sara Hall had been killed in a car accident. I told her that she could donate Sara's things to charity, even though I knew that she'd probably keep what she liked and sell the rest for booze or drugs. I'd left my best suits behind, but the sacrifice was worth it if it helped me cover my tracks.

I sent a similar email to my employer, Rudi, the loan shark. I was touched when he wrote back asking where he could send flowers. I gave him the address of the cemetery in Woodland, Iowa, where I interred an urn containing the ashes of Sara Hall. I'd actually filled that urn with cigarette ashes from Fiona's all-night parties, which I'd taken with me in a Ziploc bag.

I only ever stayed in one place for a few weeks at a time. I found waitressing jobs at restaurants with high staff turnover, where I worked for tips to pay for food and gas. When I felt like indulging myself, I stayed in strip motels. I'd stand under the hot shower for ages, wash my laundry in the bathroom sink, and then collapse on the bed for the rare treat of a night of undisturbed sleep on a proper mattress.

A month after Sara Hall died, I bought a cheap laptop at Walmart. Using a VPN, I submitted the necessary documents to get Sara Hall's Facebook account changed to a memorial page. They wanted proof of death. I gave them a receipt from the cemetery where Sara Hall's ashes were interred.

Within hours of the memorial page going live, a tumult of comments from old friends filled the feed, expressing sorrow at the tragic death of Sara Hall, who was hit by a truck in Des Moines and died immediately. "For those who loved her, it may be some consolation to know that she did not suffer," I posted in the guise of my fictional aunt.

I was surprised at the number of likes and heartfelt comments on the Facebook memorial site from people at Stanhope, as well as old friends with whom I'd lost touch. Nobody could deny that Sara Hall was dead after reading my memorial page. The way I figured it, if Facebook said I was dead, then I was dead.

Driving through Utah, I received a job alert matching the filters I'd set up. "Atomic Lounge Bar, Las Vegas. Waitress wanted. Immediate start. Great tips. Must have experience making cocktails. Sense of humor essential."

I stopped to get gas and called the listed phone number. The guy who answered pretty much indicated that the job was mine provided I got there in time for that night's graveyard shift, beginning at 10:00 P.M. One of his regular waitresses had done a runner on him, he said. I told him I'd be there.

I drove for five hours straight to get there in time. As I steered my clunky car through heavy traffic on the Strip, blinded by bright fluorescent lights against a midnight blue desert sky, I knew I'd found the right place to disappear.

I parked in a car lot two blocks from the bar. The interior was red and black, dimly lit. There were dancers writhing on the dance floor. Strobe lights revealed them in split-second flashes. In the shadows along the sides were red fake-leather booths. The music was EDM. Loud, hypnotic. The beat reverberated as I made my way toward the bar, where a guy with dyed white-blond hair and a piercing in his lip was pouring drinks.

"You the new girl?" he asked as he worked the beer tap. I could barely hear him over the throbbing music.

"How'd you know?" I yelled back at him.

"Look around you." I turned back to the dance floor and strained to get a proper look at the people in the manic light. I realized everyone was wearing a costume. I stuck out in my jeans and a button-down shirt.

"Friday night is fantasy night," he said, indicating a woman approaching the bar dressed as a French chambermaid. "This is the biggest night of the week for us. Which is good for you, little lady, because the tips are sweeeet."

He looked me up and down. "But not half as sweet as you," he said. "Your shift starts in ten minutes. Get ready."

"Don't you need to interview me? Check my references?"

"Darling, I know everything I need to know. You need money, but not so bad that you're out on the street. More important, you're a size six, bust thirty-eight inches, and you'll look smoking hot in the number I have in mind for you."

He asked a girl with pink cropped hair to take over at the bar. He escorted me down a dark corridor, also painted red and black. There was only one working light, its bulb flashing on and off, about to die. He opened a door at the end of the corridor and I entered the storeroom with him, unnerved by being in such an isolated place with a total stranger.

In the corner was a rack of clothes and a chipped mirror with a fluorescent light above it. Under the mirror was a wobbly table with an assortment of makeup thrown about.

"Try this on," he said, handing me a black leather dress and a red-and-gold masquerade mask, which I soon discovered was the same as the masks worn by all the waitresses that night. The dress was tight on me and it showed more cleavage than was decent. I was dubious about wearing it and had to hold back the urge to walk out. I didn't have that luxury. I barely had enough money to cover one night's accommodation and a breakfast special. This was the only job that I had and I had to make the best of it.

"That dress is a tip-making machine," the bartender muttered when I emerged from the room. Once he'd shown me which tables to serve, I quickly realized he was right. The tips were phenomenal. When I left at dawn, I shoved a wad of bills into my purse—$780 worth.

I found myself a spare bunk bed at a crummy hostel, sharing a dormitory room with seven other girls who'd come to Vegas to work in bars and casinos and needed a cheap place to lay their heads between shifts.

I worked every graveyard shift for three months. I hated every second of that job; the sleazy customers and their lascivious comments. But I put up with it because it was a means to an end. The tips were unlike any I'd ever earned before as a waitress. I needed the money to move to the next part of my plan, and so I swallowed my bile, swatting patrons' hands off my ass or politely rejecting explicit requests for sexual favors.

I got to recognize the regular clientele, including two heavyset men with tattooed necks who conducted some sort of business from a back-corner booth. I had a pretty good idea that whatever they were doing wasn't exactly legal. They both had beards and wore black biker T-shirts and jeans. Those two scared the hell out of me. Their eyes were hard, like they'd seen it all and didn't give a damn. One of the bartenders confirmed my suspicions, telling me to watch myself around them. They were, he whispered, lieutenants in a motorcycle gang that ran drugs all over town.

One night, I was serving them kamikazes in their regular booth. They were talking about something or other connected to their business. I wasn't listening. I was anxiously trying to figure out how to broach a subject I'd been wanting to ask them about for weeks.

"I'm looking to get some fresh IDs," I blurted out as breezily as I could. I collected their empty beer glasses, my hands trembling slightly.

It had taken me weeks to work up the courage to ask them that, but despite my intention to sound brash and experienced in such matters, I came off as nervous and uncertain. "I mean, I don't suppose you have any idea where I can find someone who can do good-quality papers? You know, a driver's licence, Social Security card. That sort of thing?"

Before I could move, the guy to my right grabbed my arm and forced me onto the seat next to him. "What makes you think we would know anyone? Have you been eavesdropping?" He looked at me as if waiting for an answer. I gulped and shook my head. "Good," he said, "because in this town it's plain dumb to overhear things you shouldn't."

"Dangerous, too," snarled his friend.

"I'm sorry. I promise I wasn't listening," I said, rubbing my wrist. "I just . . . I need a new identity. To get away from my ex. I thought you might be able to help me find someone who can do it. I've asked people and nobody seems to know."

The two of them exchanged a look that I couldn't read.

"You've been working here for a while, haven't you?" said the one next to me. I nodded. "Thought so. I don't forget a pretty set of legs that easily," he said with a smirk. "Faces, too. I never forget faces."

His friend leaned over the table. "It's true; my buddy here is *real* good with faces. You understand what I'm saying? If you try to screw us, if you go to the cops—"

"I'm after a new identity," I said, interrupting him. "The last thing I want is the cops on my case."

He tilted his head, weighing up the truth of what I'd said. "All right," he said finally. "You want to go to a place called Mick's Tattoos. Ask for Darryl. He'll take care of you."

I thanked them and beat a hasty retreat. The next day, I went to the tattoo parlor right after it opened. It was in a run-down section of Old Vegas, between a cheap strip joint and a twenty-four-hour wedding chapel.

When I walked in, there was only one guy, sitting by the cash register with his feet on the counter, playing a game on his phone. I told him I was looking for Darryl and he gestured toward a back room without looking at me.

I walked through a half-open door into a small room. Inside was an old fridge that hummed loudly and an oversize aquarium filled with tropical fish. Watching the fish from a rickety chair, his feet propped up on a wall, was a great brute of a man. He was covered with tattoos from head to foot, with a beefy face crisscrossed with scars.

"Are you Darryl?" I asked. He smiled in answer, revealing gold front teeth. "I'm looking for new IDs. Social Security card, passport. The lot."

He didn't blink. "I can get you a Nevada driver's licence, fake birth certificate, old high school ID, anything else you need to get a legit Social Security card," he told me. "But first you need to do some research."

"Research? Like what?"

"Well, you got to figure out a name," he said, looking at me as if I were dumb. "Something not too common. Not too rare. Go to the library. Check out high school yearbooks, social media, genealogy records. The secret of a good identity is that you already need to exist." He threw a bit of fish food into the aquarium. "Find someone with a history, a social media fingerprint, someone who resembles you in age and appearance. If anyone looks you up one day, you want them to find a bunch of stuff about you online. Old high school photos with your name tagged, college photos. When you have all that, come back and I'll get you the documents you need. Once you've built up a bit of history with your new identity, you'll be able to apply for a legit Social Security card and passport."

"And how much will all that cost me?" I asked.

"I like you; you're straight to the point," said Darryl. "I'll do it for fifteen K. But go do your homework first. And if you're really serious about a new identity, you might need to get some work done."

"Work?"

"Yeah, you know, plastic surgery. Facial recognition these days is a killer. Lucky for you I know a guy." He rooted around in a drawer and then handed me the card of a craniofacial plastic surgeon.

I tossed the card once I left the place. I had no intention of going under the knife. But I did find a hairdresser who specialized in makeovers. When I went into her salon, she gushed that she'd make me look like a million dollars.

"Actually, I want a makeover that makes me look like a wallflower. Completely forgettable," I told her. "I've left my ex and don't want him to ever find me," I added to quell her curiosity.

She dyed my hair a mousy brown, along with my lashes and my eyebrows, which she suggested reshaping. "People don't realize how much eyebrow shape affects a woman's overall look. What do you think? I'll tell you what. I'll throw it in at half price."

"In for a penny, in for a pound," I muttered. She flashed me a blindingly white smile, though I could tell she had no idea what I was talking about as she reached out for a pot of hot wax.

I spent hours at the local library, searching for names in records and yearbooks and anything else I could get my hands on to create the authentic identity that Darryl had asked for.

I settled on the name Stephanie Anderson. I'd found thousands of women by that name in my searches. Several were around my age. I chose a Stephanie Anderson from Indianapolis and memorized scraps of her biography that I dug up in research so extensive, I might as well have been stalking her.

I'd managed to get her date of birth, her parents' names, and even the names of her high school and college, together with her graduation years. I went back to Mick's Tattoos a week later with passport photos and the details of my new identity all neatly scribbled down. Darryl was in the same place where I'd seen him last, watching those tropical fish swim around in circles.

I handed him a sheet of notepaper with the details of my new identity. He snatched the paper and examined the information approvingly. "I'll see you in two weeks," he said.

When I returned to get my documents, Darryl was in the front of the store, tattooing a cobra across the belly of a college kid with a try-hard wispy beard. The kid's face was red as he tried not to scream. His girlfriend sat next to him, checking her phone.

I handed Darryl the money in an envelope, which he quickly glanced into before shoving it into a console next to his tattoo inks. He pulled out an even larger brown envelope from a bottom drawer.

Inside I found a new Social Security card, birth certificate, and various other forms of identification, all for Stephanie Anderson.

"Nice knowing you, Steph," he said as he bent over the kid to resume work on the cobra.

I knew that it was best if I left with no trace at all, so with my new identity in my purse and a duffel bag of my paltry possessions, I headed to the bus station.

FORTY-NINE

SARA HALL

As I came up with my plan, I asked myself how Lucy would have done it. She was a master strategist. She would have thought ten steps ahead of every move. That's how she played chess, and that's how I was going to play my own version of the game.

I'd found an elevator company in Houston that was advertising a number of jobs. I managed to get an interview, but that would be in person, meaning I had to endure a twelve-hour Greyhound ride, with three transfers, to get there. When the bus pulled into the bus station in downtown Houston, it was not long after dawn. I found a room in a run-down hostel nearby, where I showered and had a nap on a narrow single bed in a room not much bigger and probably more spartan than a prison cell.

By the afternoon, following two interviews, I was hired as a service assistant at the Cortane Elevator Company. My starting salary was $37,350 a year.

I was thrilled. Once I started the job, I rented a dingy one-room apartment near the office to build up some more history for Stephanie

Anderson. I was done with roommates, and didn't want anyone keeping track of how I spent my time.

At Cortane, I worked hard and kept my head down. I was the fastest learner they'd ever had, or at least that's what my supervisor told me, admiring how quickly I'd learned the ropes. He didn't know the half of it. He thought I was supermotivated when I asked if I could go out with the installers and repair technicians in my free time to see what it was like in the field. I explained that it would make my job working with customers so much easier.

I spent the better part of a year asking endless questions of the technicians, studying blueprints of the elevators, and reading anything and everything I could get my hands on relating to elevator design, electronics, and installation. I signed up for courses in programming and electronics at a community college. I loved the coding. It was the first thing that I'd done in a long time that challenged me intellectually. I quickly learned C, C++, and Java, and within months was writing my own code for a program that allowed me to hack into an elevator system and then control it with an app on my phone.

In between semesters, I attended drama classes. I learned how to alter my walk and gestures to suit my new persona. They taught me how to change my speech, too, and I adopted a lower pitch and different intonations, which became second nature over time. I even picked up a slight Texas drawl.

A year after moving to Houston, I went back to Vegas on a weekend trip. I found Darryl working on a tattoo of intertwined initials on the arms of a couple who'd just married at the all-night wedding chapel next door. They were too drunk to feel any pain, I noticed as I flicked through the well-thumbed pages of a celebrity magazine while I waited for Darryl to finish.

When he was done, we went into the back room. I paid him five

grand for a fake bachelor's degree for Stephanie Anderson and another five grand for fake references from an ex-lawyer who'd spent
time in jail on drug charges. The arrangement was that the lawyer
would take whatever calls came his way from prospective employers
and talk enthusiastically about my work.

He had a deep voice that sounded impressive on the phone and an
ability to speak with authority on topics he had no idea about. In
short, a typical lawyer. When I met him in person to explain the sort
of questions he might be asked, he didn't look at all how I'd expected.
He had a graying ponytail and a face sunken from too much weed
and acid. He told me that he was on the wagon after a cancer scare
and had become a holistic vegan. Whatever that meant.

When I got back to Houston, I quit my job at Cortane with the
teary-eyed explanation that I needed to go back home to nurse my
dying mother. They threw me a party on my last day; there was a
pink-iced cake with a message in chocolate-cream piping.

Again I traveled by bus, crisscrossing through the Midwest, all
the way back to New York. I didn't want my name appearing on any
flight manifests.

Getting a job at Stanhope was easy enough. I built a fake résumé
that detailed a work history in IT support going back two decades.

I applied for a back-office job in the network-support department, where I would be tucked far away from my former colleagues
in the rabbit warren of desks three floors below the main Stanhope
office suites.

Stanhope struggled to keep support staff because they stiffed them
on pay, unlike the executives, who made small fortunes. That worked
in my favor, as the firm always had vacancies for qualified candidates.
My references from the Vegas lawyer—he claimed I'd been an exem-
plary IT service manager at a boutique West Coast firm—and the

fake degree I'd bought from Darryl were enough to get me through a screening call and two interviews with IT-support supervisors whom I'd never met before.

For the interviews, I bought a bland wardrobe that made me look frumpy and pounds heavier and wore brown contact lenses and round gold prescription glasses that added years to my age. Just to be safe, I applied thick makeup and a lipstick in an unflattering shade. I barely recognized myself in the mirror.

My references checked out and I was hired to start the following week. They had a vacancy they needed to fill quickly.

My job gave me access to all the information that I needed on the firm's computer system without ever having to leave the safety of the back-office cubicles.

One afternoon when I'd been there for three months, my supervisor asked me to deliver a laptop to the main offices. I tried to make an excuse, but he wouldn't buy it. For the first time, I was back among my former colleagues and teammates.

It was nerve-racking. Just as I was heading out, carrying a pile of computer cords and a broken laptop, I spotted Sylvie walking down the same corridor. I tried to duck into an office, but there was no way to do it without drawing attention to myself. So I kept walking. I held my breath as she strode past me.

She didn't even look in my direction. That's when I realized that the lowly administration staff were invisible to the high-fliers in the firm. They noticed the furniture more than they noticed us.

My ordinariness was camouflage. It allowed me to blend into their narcissistic corporate lives. I became less cautious. One morning, I was standing in a crowded elevator when Vincent stepped inside. The sharp tang of his aftershave hung in the air like an acid cloud.

It burned my lungs and seared my resolve. It was almost like old times, standing shoulder-to-shoulder in the confines of the elevator with the man who'd destroyed my life as casually as he pressed the elevator button for the executive floor. For over a minute, we dangled together hundreds of feet above the ground. If something went wrong, we'd share the same fate. Death, after all, was the ultimate equalizer.

I flirted with danger and stopped taking measures to avoid running into my former teammates. When they stepped inside the same elevator as I was in, I'd push myself into the back corner, with my oversize handbag pressed against my stomach and my eyes downcast.

I stared at the floor not out of fear, but to hide the ice-cold rage I could never fully disguise. The lack of recognition on their arrogant faces amused me. If they'd known who I was—what I was planning—none of them would have lowered his guard so easily.

If they took any notice of me, it was only to throw me a pitying glance—a hint of distaste that warned me off bringing my ordinariness into their privileged space. They acted as if mediocrity was an infectious disease. I didn't mind. It allowed me to get up close and personal, to study every nuance of their regimented lives without raising any suspicion.

Nothing had changed. They were creatures of habit. They arrived a few minutes before 7:30 A.M. holding take-out coffee with their names written crookedly in black marker by baristas serving the impatient early-morning Wall Street crowd.

With their free hand, the men in the elevator texted the girl from the night before or their wives, often both. Or they swiped through dating apps to find a date for the evening ahead, pausing occasionally to check if London's FTSE had rallied in the afternoon.

Sylvie texted her latest squeeze in Paris, Marc, while setting up her trades before the morning bell. Sylvie had great instincts when it came to predicting market movements, but she'd never been as astute when it came to picking men. I found it remarkable that she never noticed me standing behind her, practically looking over her shoulder. But then, Sylvie never truly had eyes for anyone except herself.

They were like capitalist soldiers in their two-thousand-dollar suits, pressed razor-sharp. Impeccably groomed. You'd think they'd never been touched by perspiration, dirt, or excrement. But no one gets to make the kind of money those four did without tarnishing his soul. Their hands were soft, and clean, and free of calluses. But only because they never touched the blood they spilled.

Over many months, I gradually accessed their email accounts and internet browsers and took note of the most mundane snippets of their lives. I knew how much money they had in their bank accounts, the state of their investment portfolios, as well as a myriad of seemingly inane details: restaurant preferences, their next holiday destinations, their taste in alcohol, lovers, and food. The names of their cleaners, dry-cleaning services, and their burglar alarm codes. I looked for their soft underbellies, prodding and poking until I found a weakness. Over time, I built a comprehensive picture of every facet of their lives.

I found out enough about the team's business deals to leak information about the bids to a competitor. Stanhope lost key deals twice in the space of six months—almost sixty million dollars in lost revenue. I couldn't resist the temptation of undermining them, even though it was dumb to risk blowing my cover. But I enjoyed seeing Vincent, Jules, Sam, and Sylvie's panicked faces as things went wrong in their otherwise-perfect lives.

They thought I was no better than the janitor who mopped their urine splatter off the restroom floor. I consoled myself with the thought that they'd find out soon enough who I was and what I was capable of. The key was patience. And I was very, very patient.

After much trial and error, I was able to use an app to turn the webcams of their laptops into a scanner and took biometric scans of their irises. That's when I knew that I was ready to strike.

Not long after, I arranged vacation leave and went to Switzerland, Hong Kong, Singapore, Antigua, Lichtenstein, and the Channel Islands in the space of twelve days. In each country, I set up bank accounts in Stephanie Anderson's name.

By the time I got back, all that was left was setting and baiting the trap. I sneaked into the building I'd carefully selected and rigged up an elevator, including climbing into the elevator shaft to leave a transponder on the roof of the elevator's cabin, allowing me to control it remotely. While I was there, I tightened the screws on the escape hatch so there was no way in hell any of them were getting out.

Crucially, I made sure they wouldn't be able to use their phones. No way messages or calls could be made or received by anyone in the elevator. For my plan to work, I needed them all totally incommunicado for at least twenty-four hours.

When every part of my plan was in place, I sent them a fake meeting invitation, using the generic Stanhope Human Resources email address. I sent the emails to Sylvie and the others midafternoon on a Friday so they wouldn't have time to ask too many questions. In the email to Vincent, I added a line stressing that attendance was compulsory and that he'd be held accountable if anyone didn't turn up.

They all arrived, just as I knew they would. They always did when Stanhope snapped its fingers. With the layoffs in the offing, I figured none of them would have the guts to disregard the meeting invitation, even if it was at an inconvenient time.

Once they were inside, I was able to control the elevator remotely by using my app on a burner phone. I had full control over the elevator's movement, thermostat, and lights.

I imagined what it might be like if I were locked inside—the emotions that I would have felt, the stress and fear as time passed without rescue. Then I amplified that feeling, because I knew the four of them would get on one another's nerves in no time at all. When I thought of what Lucy had endured in the elevator that night, it hardened my resolve further.

I came up with the escape-room ruse to keep them off balance and buy me time. It would keep them distracted while I executed the most crucial part of my plan. Coming up with the puzzles was the most fun. Stupid, meaningless clues that would turn them against one another and keep them confused.

The bonus letters were the coup de grâce. Stanhope had an ironclad security procedure for bonus letters. But as a trusted member of the IT team, I had access to everything.

It was easy enough to find out the bonuses for the people on Vincent's team, and to produce a letter listing the amounts. When Vincent and his personal assistant were both in a meeting upstairs, I marched into his office with a new set of computer cables and quickly slipped the envelope I'd prepared into the outside pocket of his briefcase.

If there was anything guaranteed to turn those four into enemies, it was finding out one another's bonuses. They'd be weak if they were divided. That would work to my advantage as I played them all.

At midnight that Friday, when they were still locked in the elevator, I walked through a metal detector at La Guardia and boarded my flight. I was still using my burner phone to torment them but also to implement the most beautiful part of my plan.

Meanwhile, the four of them would be found on Monday morning, alive and well. I wasn't too worried about them. How much trouble could four investment bankers get into in a locked elevator?

FIFTY

THE ELEVATOR

Vincent sat bolt upright, still half-asleep. He sensed a brooding shadow looming over where they lay huddled, clutching one another to stay warm. His heart quickened. His eyes were blurry from sleep as he stared at the hazy silhouette. It took on a familiar appearance.

It was Jules, standing over them. The remote expression in Jules's black eyes sent a chill down Vincent's spine.

"What's wrong, Jules?" Vincent's breath turned into vapor in the cold.

"You set this up, Vincent."

"What the hell are you talking about?" Vincent scrambled to his feet. When Vincent was halfway up, Jules pushed him in the chest with his foot. Unbalanced, Vincent immediately toppled clumsily to the floor.

"Not a good idea," warned Jules. He gave a faint shake of his head.

It was only then that Vincent noticed Jules's outstretched arm. In his hand was a gun. Jules's grip was tight. It didn't waver. The barrel was aimed at Vincent's chest.

"How . . ." Vincent began to ask. He'd spent hours looking for the Glock, even through the blinding pain of his concussion. It had worried him greatly that he hadn't found it.

"I took my gun back when you were knocked out," said Jules. "Don't give me that look. It is mine, after all."

Vincent felt the reassuring weight of the metal ammunition clip resting in his pocket. As if anticipating what he was thinking, Jules moved his grip so that Vincent could see the clip of ammunition he'd pushed into the gun. Jules pulled back the slide with a loud metal click, pushing a round into the chamber.

"You think I carry only one clip with me? I had a spare in my bag. This thing is locked and loaded and I have no qualms about using it."

The noise of the two men talking roused Sam and Sylvie from their sleep. Sylvie looked up at Jules and quickly processed the situation, much as Vincent had done a moment earlier. Sam lay feebly on the floor, too weak to rise, or speak, or do anything other than watch them helplessly.

"What are you doing, Jules?" Sylvie's voice was hoarse from lack of water.

"It occurred to me," said Jules, "that it was Vincent who lured us here. We got a vague email from HR, but Vincent was the one who texted us to tell us it was a compulsory meeting."

"I thought the email from HR was authentic," said Vincent angrily. "I truly thought it was a team-building activity to help the firm make its final decision on the layoffs and maybe choose Eric Miles's successor. I had no idea about any of this," he said, looking around at the blood-smeared elevator, the cracked mirrors, the exposed ceiling, the rubble of discarded silver ceiling tiles and broken glass scattered across the floor.

"Then why did you stash food and water in your briefcase? Why come dressed in your thickest overcoat?" Jules said. "No. You knew it would be like this. You planted the clues—about Sara Hall, about Lucy and that Sun Tzu quote—to divert our attention. You pretended it was a game so that we wouldn't realize your real objective in bringing us here: to kill us."

"My objective," Vincent responded, "is and has always been to get us out of here alive. To do that, we need to work as a team, we need to trust one another. Jules, put the gun down."

"He's right," Sylvie said. "Put it down. We need to work together. Otherwise, we'll all freeze to death long before Monday morning comes around."

"Not all of us," said Jules. "Vincent won't. Not while he's wearing that overcoat. You could survive a Siberian winter in that thing. You know what? Vincent, take off your coat. I want it."

Vincent slowly unbuttoned the overcoat and removed it. He threw it to Jules awkwardly, so that it fell on the floor. It was deliberate; he was looking for an opening to disarm him. Jules knew what he was thinking. He left it lying on the floor even though he felt the bitter cold terribly through the thin fabric of his own coat.

"It's my standard winter overcoat," said Vincent. "And I always keep food and water in my bag. It's for my blood sugar; I'm prediabetic. It was good luck for all of us that I had supplies, no matter how small. You may recall, Jules," he added sarcastically, "that I didn't keep it for myself. I shared it."

"He has a point," said Sylvie.

"Can't you see what's right in front of your face, Sylvie?" Jules hissed. "Vincent wants us to die. From exposure, or dehydration, or whatever. He'll get out and keep all The Circle's money without having to share it."

"There's a flaw in your argument," Vincent said. "The money will be of no use to me if I'm dead. If I really had lured you here, I would have been smart enough to make sure that I *wasn't* here. Because the way things are at the moment, I can't see a way out for us."

"Then who could have possibly lured us here and given us clues that only a member of our team could know?" Jules asked. "Lucy Marshall? Sara Hall? They're both dead. I've kept tabs on the two interns who were in the elevator with Lucy. One died of a ketamine overdose and the other was transferred to our office in Sydney. Eric Miles—you said yourself he's in a clinic in Switzerland. That leaves the four of us. I know it's not me, and Sam doesn't have the brains to set this up. So that leaves Sylvie or you."

"It wasn't me," Sylvie said.

"I know," said Jules. "I know it wasn't you, Sylvie, because I have indisputable evidence that it was Vincent."

He held up Vincent's phone. There was an email open on the screen, but it was too far away for them to see what it said. "I accessed it while you were all dozing. I've seen Vincent input his phone pass code hundreds of times over the years." Jules threw the phone to Sylvie. She caught it and looked at the email.

Sylvie's head snapped up as she looked at Vincent accusingly. "You booked a flight to Grand Cayman for next Friday night?"

"That's right," Jules said, lifting the barrel of his gun so that it was aimed at Vincent's head. "What a coincidence! Vincent books a flight to the place where we keep The Circle's bank account, on the evening the retrenchments are due to be announced. I don't need to connect the dots here. Vincent probably arranged a generous payout for himself, and then planned to take all our money from The Circle's account and run."

"I was going there on a vacation. It's the Caribbean! People do go there on vacation."

Jules exploded. "Fuck you, Vincent." His face flushed with anger. "You were planning on robbing us blind."

"You're not thinking straight, Jules." Vincent spoke quickly. "We have plenty of money in the account. My share is more than enough for the rest of my life."

"You became greedy," said Jules. "You were about to lose your job and you needed the money."

"I don't need the money," Vincent said. "I don't do drugs like Sam. I don't drink like you. I don't have a wife, or an ex-wife. No kids. No alimony. You all saw my bonus. Seven figures. Out of all of us, I'm the one who least needs the money," said Vincent. "Jules, you're projecting your own greed onto me. Maybe you're the one who set this up!"

Jules hit Vincent across the face so hard with the Glock that Vincent's face smashed against the wall, leaving a deep gash near his temple.

Sylvie jumped up in the confusion, trying to pry open the elevator doors, screaming for help through the thin crack. Her screams were deafening. Jules stumbled over to her, pulled her around, and slapped her hard across the face with the back of his hand. Her head swung around and hit the control panel, which lit up.

"The problem with you, Sylvie, is that you don't know when to shut up," Jules said. "You were the best tail I ever had, but even I couldn't stand being around you for long."

"Leave her alone," Sam slurred. Jules swung his head around in Sam's direction. Vincent used the distraction to kick Jules's legs out from under him. Jules slammed to the floor so hard that it jolted the elevator. He pulled the trigger in panic. The gun went off as he fell. The single shot ricocheted through the elevator. Vincent wrestled with Jules for the Glock. He smacked the gun out of Jules's hand and punched him repeatedly.

"You know," said Sylvie in an icy voice, "it's been a long time since I fired one of these." Vincent and Jules stopped struggling and looked up at Sylvie. She'd picked up the gun and was now testing its weight in her hands. "I hear that shooting a gun is like riding a bike. Shall we put that to the test, gentlemen?"

"Hand it over," said Vincent.

"Jules made a very good point," Sylvie said, shaking her head. "He was always good at making arguments—he should have been a trial lawyer. That's why we lasted so long. I only broke up with him when he got drunk and punched me. Do you remember that, Jules? I should shoot you right now, just for that black eye. I couldn't go to the office for a week; I had to pretend that I had a bad flu."

"It was an accident. I apologized at the time. I bought you earrings."

"Diamonds don't make up for black eyes," said Sylvie smoothly. "But I have to hand it to you, you did make a very persuasive argument earlier."

"About what?"

"If three people die in here, the fourth will get to keep everything. The Circle's money. His job at Stanhope. Maybe even the promotion to Eric Miles's job. If you three were gone . . ."

Sylvie's hands trembled from the cold. Her legs were bare and her jacket was impossibly inadequate. She dragged over Vincent's overcoat with her shoe. She bent down and lifted it up while keeping the gun trained on Vincent and Jules.

As she put on the coat one sleeve at a time, she didn't notice Jules sliding out a broken shard of glass from the cracked wall behind him. She wasn't expecting it when he lunged toward her, but he wasn't fast enough to overcome her instinctive reflex. She pulled the trigger and fired twice. Two thunderous shots. One hit its mark, the other missed and ricocheted across the elevator, causing damage wherever it hit.

His eyes wide, Jules coughed blood and collapsed to the floor. A trickle of blood ran from his mouth. Sylvie was stunned by the hot pain rising in her abdomen. She looked down and saw blood seeping between her fingers and dripping down to the alabaster floor. She crumpled to the floor and stared blankly as a thick puddle of blood began to form around her. Vincent knelt nearby, bent over, his hand against his chest. His white shirt turned crimson as he breathed raggedly.

Sam picked up the gun. He scrambled to the back corner of the elevator and pointed it all around, as if to warn the others away. He was so delirious that he wasn't sure what danger he was protecting himself from. All he knew was that he had to do whatever was necessary to survive.

When the elevator doors opened, Sam stood up, waving the Glock excitedly. He was finally getting out. His ears were still pounding from the gunfire in the confined space. Through the pulsating numbness, he didn't hear the cops telling him to drop his weapon. He walked toward the open entrance of the elevator in a trance, focused only on getting free, a smile of relief on his face.

The shots from the police propelled him against the back of the elevator. His body slid down the mirrored wall as the bullets kept coming. His eyes were open. They registered his shock.

When the ambulance crews arrived, they almost couldn't find Vincent's pulse, it was that weak. But he was alive. He was the only one to leave the elevator on a stretcher instead of in a body bag.

FIFTY-ONE

SARA HALL

George Town harbor is crowded with water taxis dropping off day-trippers from the gleaming white cruise ships anchored in deep water offshore like pods of giant whales. I pause to watch tourists posing for selfies in front of the colorful array of washed-out buildings that line the harbor. I head toward the main branch of the Cayman Capital Bank.

I wear a cream jacket and black business pants, my hair scraped back into a tight blond chignon. I have done everything I can to look like Sylvie. I wear custom-made green contact lenses that are imprinted with the exact pattern of Sylvie's irises. My hair is salon-dyed caramel blond. I lost a heap of weight and spent weeks practicing Sylvie's elegant walk in her trademark two-inch heels. I almost give myself a fright when I catch my reflection in a store window. I've clearly mastered Sylvie's arrogant swagger. "You'll do," I say to myself with a smile.

The bank is in an old colonial building, worn down by the sun and the salt of the sea. It opened ten minutes ago. Already a queue is forming at the cashiers. I stride over to the VIP desk with Sylvie's entitled expression on my makeup-tinted face.

"I need to see Mr. Russell," I inform the clerk. I reel off the details so fast that he can barely keep up.

"Please come this way," he says deferentially.

The bank manager, Mr. Russell, shakes my hand warmly as I enter his office. He shows me to an antique chair on a pale pink Persian rug. I tell him that I'm closing an account and wish to clear out the safety-deposit box.

"Of course."

He speaks in the emotionless voice of a banker, but his curious eyes give him away. He's seen the zero balance in the account.

Last night, I cashed all The Circle's investments and transferred everything to a new bank account. I didn't have to worry about any of the other signatories receiving notification texts or emails from the bank, or a verification call from the bank manager, because they were all locked up in the elevator, with no phone access whatsoever. That's why I put the four of them there, to get them out of the way while I emptied The Circle's accounts into my own.

I spent the rest of the night enjoying a beer and a burger on my hotel room bed, a random cop show playing in the background, while I toyed with the elevator controls on my burner phone and pushed through another "clue" onto the elevator screen to keep my former colleagues occupied while I drained their finances.

By breakfast, I'd split the bulk of the money into another two accounts. By nightfall, it will be moved to yet another set of accounts; another bank, another country. It's my own private shell game.

Mr. Russell slides over a pile of documents. He points with his index finger to the various places where I have to sign. Learning Sylvie's distinctive signature had been a piece of cake. I reproduce it effortlessly on his form. When we're done, his assistant escorts me to the safe-deposit boxes in the basement of the bank.

To be allowed into the safe where the security boxes are kept, I have to scan my iris on a device on the wall. I press my right eye against it, thankful one last time for my old friend Darryl, who was able to direct me to a guy in Amsterdam who created the contact lenses from the scans I took in the office.

Mr. Russell's assistant brings me the safety-deposit box in a private booth, unlocks it, and then retreats to a respectful distance. When I finally open up the box, I expel a sigh of pleasure so loud that my escort inadvertently turns his head in my direction.

Inside the metal safety-deposit box are neat stacks of gold bullion and a pile of treasury notes. I fill my oversize handbag. The rest goes into a woven tote bag. As I walk out of the bank and slide into a waiting taxi, I am carrying over one million dollars in solid gold and another million in treasury notes.

My hotel is a small, mid-range establishment in the middle of town. There's no sea view. Downstairs is a kidney-shaped swimming pool filled with sunburned British and American tourists vying for poolside loungers. They're loud and seemingly permanently soused.

I head straight to my room, where I close the curtains and lock the door, with the DO NOT DISTURB sign turned to face the corridor. The hotel is one of those places that awards itself four stars on its website, though it's barely worthy of two. My room has a dated peach decor and smells of stale cigarette smoke. The towels are threadbare and the soap comes in white plastic wrappers.

I arrange the gold bars on pieces of newspaper and spray-paint them red and blue. When they're dry, I put them in an empty box of children's magnetic blocks, which are a similar size and weight to the gold bars. I wrap the box in colorful wrapping paper and attach a birthday card. "Dear Jonny," I write. "I'm sorry I couldn't make your party but hope you have lots of fun building with your new blocks." I roll up the treasury notes tightly with an elastic band and put them in an inside pocket of my handbag.

I shower, take out the contact lenses, and dye my hair from blond to a forgettable brown. When I'm done, I dress in jeans and a loose linen shirt. I wear oversize black sunglasses and a large straw hat so the hotel staff won't notice my appearance has changed so dramatically.

I pack the wrapped present in my suitcase under a pile of clothes and lock my suitcase with a combination lock. I catch a glimpse of myself in the mirror as I leave the room. I look like any of a thousand tourists walking the streets of George Town. Another shell game.

I toss the spray-paint cans and the hair dye box into a garbage bag hanging off a cleaner's trolley in the corridor outside my room, then roll my suitcase toward the elevator.

"We hope you had a pleasant stay," says the receptionist when I hand her my key card.

"Very much so," I tell her with a smile.

The cruise ship is due to sail in less than an hour. The staff are effusive as they examine my ticket. I'm headed for Miami, with stops at various Caribbean islands. I see none of these islands; instead, I stay inside my cabin, with the excuse that I've come down with a stomach bug. The crew is happy for me to remain inside—the last thing they want is a gastro outbreak. I'm busy on my laptop anyway, getting my finances in order. It takes time. Fifty-eight million dollars is an awful lot of money to invest.

I take a break that first evening on the ship to use my mobile app to turn down the temperature in the elevator to freezing. Just to shake things up a little. I don't want them to get too comfortable while they wait to be rescued.

When we reach Saint John, I tell the bursar that I will be disembarking early and flying home due to health issues. His sympathy barely masks his relief at being rid of a sick passenger. He arranges a place for me on an express boat taking VIP passengers to shore, which fast-tracks passport control.

I stand at the stern of the boat, wearing a crimson sundress, as it speeds toward land. Sea foam flicks onto my skin and the wind ruffles my hair. I bubble with excitement as we approach the pier. Not long now, I tell myself. Almost home.

My driver, Anthony, offers me a newspaper, but I decline. I don't feel like a dose of reality yet. I tell him that I'd rather enjoy the view. He drives off, with me comfortably seated in the back, looking out at the throngs of cruise ship passengers heading out on a half-day bus tour until the ship sets sail in the late afternoon. Anthony takes a bumpy back road to the other side of the island, where I catch teasing glimpses between palm trees of bright blue sea in the distance.

We turn down a narrow dirt road and continue until we reach a steel gate, which he opens with a remote control fob so that he doesn't need to stop. We drive toward an expansive ultramodern low-rise house of slate and walls of glass, overlooking the sea.

My housekeeper, Jasmine, greets me with an ebullient welcome and a glass of iced tea. She takes my suitcase from Anthony and wheels it to my expansive bedroom, which is dominated by a king-size bed with white bamboo sheets and a cotton net canopy that sways slightly in the breeze from the open terrace door.

The house spills onto a timber deck that leads to my private beach, pristine white sand and azure water hugged by coconut palms. A bottle of champagne awaits in an ice bucket, just as I'd requested.

I pour myself a flute of champagne and wander in my bare feet to the water's edge. The sand is warm under my feet and gentle waves lap at my toes until it tickles. I raise my glass in a silent toast toward the horizon, acknowledging Lucy for her role in bringing me here.

I slip off my dress until I'm wearing only a bikini. I leave the dress alongside my champagne glass on the sand and walk into the water. The water is so translucent that I can see a colorful school of fish dart about playfully before scattering when my shadow gets too close.

I swim underwater for as long as I can last on one breath and then rise to the surface. There are yachts in the distance and a seaplane flying low. I look for more fish or a sea turtle, which can occasionally be spotted in the cove for those who are lucky. I look back at the house and watch Jasmine setting up lunch on the balcony. She waves to me; I wave back.

I float for a while as I think about everything I've been through to get here: the loneliness and the overwhelming sense of helplessness when I felt trapped by seemingly insurmountable obstacles; all those times when I thought there was no way out. And yet here I am. A lifetime of worry and stress dissolves as I watch the sun's rays glint against a cloudless azure sky.

As I emerge from the sea with water running down my skin and my long hair all slicked back, I feel as if I've been reborn. My mother used to tell me that the best revenge is to live well. I couldn't agree more.

ACKNOWLEDGMENTS

I wish to thank my agent, David Gernert, as well as Anna Worrall, Rebecca Gardner, and Ellen Coughtrey, of The Gernert Company. I'd like to extend my deepest appreciation to Charles Spicer, Jennifer Enderlin, and the fabulously talented team at St. Martin's Press. Special thanks to Ali Watts, Johannes Jakob, and Nerrilee Weir, for their support and encouragement. To my parents, my siblings, and my wonderful husband and sons, I am forever grateful.

TURN THE PAGE FOR A SNEAK PEEK

at Megan Goldin's new novel

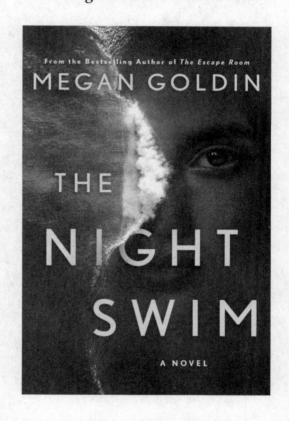

From the Bestselling Author of *The Escape Room*

MEGAN GOLDIN

THE NIGHT SWIM

A NOVEL

AVAILABLE SUMMER 2020

1

Hannah

It was Jenny's death that killed my mother. Killed her as good as if she'd been shot in the chest with a twelve-gauge shotgun. The doctor said it was the cancer. But I saw the will to live drain out of her the moment the policeman knocked on our screen door.

"It's Jenny, isn't it?" Mom rasped, clutching the lapel of her faded dressing gown.

"Ma'am, I don't know how to tell you other than to say it straight." The policeman spoke in the low-pitched melancholic tone he'd used moments earlier when he'd pulled up and told me to wait in the patrol car as its siren lights painted our house streaks of red and blue.

Despite his request, I'd slipped out of the back seat and rushed to Mom's side as she turned on the front porch light and stepped onto the stoop dazed from being woken late at night. I hugged her withered waist as he told her what he had to say. Her body shuddered at each word.

His jaw was tight under strawberry blond stubble and his light eyes were watery by the time he was done. He was a young cop.

Visibly inexperienced in dealing with tragedy. He ran his knuckles across the corners of his glistening eyes and swallowed hard.

"I'm s-s-sorry for your loss, ma'am," he stammered when there was nothing left to say. The finality of those words would reverberate through the years that followed.

But at that moment, as the platitudes still hung in the air, we stood on the stoop, staring at each other, uncertain what to do as we contemplated the etiquette of death.

I tightened my small, girlish arms around Mom's waist as she lurched blindly into the house. Overcome by grief. I moved along with her. My arms locked around her. My face pressed against her hollow stomach. I wouldn't let go. I was certain that I was all that was holding her up.

She collapsed into the lumpy cushion of the armchair. Her face hidden in her clawed-up hands and her shoulders shaking from soundless sobs.

I limped to the kitchen and poured her a glass of lemonade. It was all I could think to do. In our family, lemonade was the Band-Aid to fix life's troubles. Mom's teeth chattered against the glass as she tilted it to her mouth. She took a sip and left the glass teetering on the worn upholstery of her armchair as she wrapped her arms around herself.

I grabbed the glass before it fell, and stumbled toward the kitchen. Halfway there, I realized the policeman was still standing at the doorway. He was staring at the floor. I followed his gaze. A track of bloody footprints in the shape of my small feet was smeared across the linoleum floor.

He looked at me expectantly. It was time for me to go to the hospital like I'd agreed when I'd begged him to take me home first so that I could be with Mom when she found out about Jenny. I glared at him defiantly. I would not leave my mother alone that night. Not even to get medical treatment for the cuts on my feet. He was about to argue the point when a garbled message came through on his patrol car radio. He squatted down so that he was at the level of my eyes and told me that he'd arrange for a nurse to come to the house as soon as possible to attend to my injured feet. I watched through the mesh of the screen door as he sped away. The blare of his police siren echoed long after his car disappeared in the dark.

The nurse arrived the following morning. She wore hospital scrubs and carried an oversized medical bag. She apologized for the delay, telling me that the ER had been overwhelmed by an emergency the previous night and nobody could get away to attend to me. She sewed me up with black sutures and wrapped thick bandages around my feet. Before she left, she warned me not to walk, because the sutures would pop. She was right. They did.

Jenny was barely sixteen when she died. I was five weeks short of my tenth birthday. Old enough to know that my life would never be the same. Too young to understand why.

I never told my mother that I'd held Jenny's cold body in my arms until police officers swarmed over her like buzzards and pulled me away. I never told her a single thing about that night. Even if I had, I doubt she would have heard. Her mind was in another place.

We buried my sister in a private funeral. The two of us and a local minister, and a couple of Mom's old colleagues who came during their lunch break, wearing their supermarket cashier uniforms. At least they're the ones that I remember. Maybe there were others. I can't recall. I was so young.

The only part of the funeral that I remember clearly was Jenny's simple coffin resting on a patch of grass alongside a freshly dug grave. I took off my hand-knitted sweater and laid it out on top of the polished casket. "Jenny will need it," I told Mom. "It'll be cold for her in the ground."

We both knew how much Jenny hated the cold. On winter days when bitter drafts tore through gaps in the patched-up walls of our house, Jenny would beg Mom to move us to a place where summer never ended.

A few days after Jenny's funeral, a stone-faced man from the police department arrived in a creased gabardine suit. He pulled a flip-top notebook from his jacket and asked me if I knew what had happened the night that Jenny died.

My eyes were downcast while I studied each errant thread in the soiled bandages wrapped around my feet. I sensed his relief when after going through the motions of asking more questions and getting no response he tucked his empty notebook into his jacket pocket and headed back to his car.

I hated myself for my stubborn silence as he drove away. Sometimes when the guilt overwhelms me, I remind myself that it was not my fault. He didn't ask the right questions and I didn't know how to explain things that I was too young to understand.

This year we mark a milestone. Twenty-five years since Jenny died. A quarter of a century and nothing has changed. Her death is as raw as it was the day we buried her. The only difference is that I won't be silent anymore.

2

Rachel

A single streak of white cloud marred an otherwise perfect blue sky as Rachel Krall drove her silver SUV on a flat stretch of highway toward the Atlantic Ocean. Dead ahead on the horizon was a thin blue line. It widened as she drove closer until Rachel knew for certain that it was the sea.

Rachel glanced uneasily at the fluttering pages of the letter resting on the front passenger seat next to her as she zoomed along the right lane of the highway. She was deeply troubled by the letter. Not so much by the contents, but instead by the strange, almost sinister way the letter had been delivered earlier that morning.

After hours on the road, she'd pulled into a twenty-four-hour diner where she ordered a mug of coffee and pancakes that came covered with half-thawed blueberries and two scoops of vanilla ice cream, which she pushed to the side of her plate. The coffee was bitter, but she drank it anyway. She needed it for the caffeine, not the taste. When she finished her meal, she ordered an extra-strong iced coffee and a muffin to go in case her energy flagged on the final leg of the drive.

While waiting for her takeout order, Rachel applied eye drops to revive her tired green eyes and twisted up her shoulder-length auburn hair to get it out of her face. Rachel was tying her hair into a topknot when the waitress brought her order in a white paper bag before rushing off to serve a truck driver who was gesticulating angrily for his bill.

Rachel left a larger than necessary tip for the waitress, mostly because she felt bad at the way customers hounded the poor woman over the slow service. Not her fault, thought Rachel. She'd waitressed through college and knew how tough it was to be the only person serving tables during an unexpected rush.

By the time she pushed open the swinging doors of the restaurant, Rachel was feeling full and slightly queasy. It was bright outside and she had to shield her eyes from the sun as she headed to her car. Even before she reached it, she saw something shoved under her windshield wiper. Assuming it was an advertising flyer, Rachel abruptly pulled it off her windshield. She was about to crumple it up unread when she noticed her name had been neatly written in bold lettering: *Rachel Krall (from the* Guilty or Not Guilty *podcast).*

Rachel received thousands of emails and social media messages every week. Most were charming and friendly. Letters from fans. A few scared the hell out of her. Rachel had no idea which category the letter would fall into, but the mere fact that a stranger had recognized her and left a note addressed to her on her car made her decidedly uncomfortable.

Rachel looked around in case the person who'd left the letter was still there. Waiting. Watching her reaction. Truck drivers stood around smoking and shooting the breeze. Others checked the rigging of the loads on their trucks. Car doors slammed as motorists arrived. Engines rumbled to life as others left. Nobody paid Rachel any attention, although that did little to ease the eerie feeling she was being watched.

It was rare for Rachel to feel vulnerable. She'd been in plenty of hairy situations over the years. A month earlier, she'd spent the best part of an afternoon locked in a high-security prison cell talking to an uncuffed serial killer while police marksmen pointed automatic rifles through a hole in the ceiling in case the prisoner lunged at her during the interview. Rachel hadn't so much as broken into a sweat the entire time. Rachel felt ridiculous that a letter left on her car had unnerved her more than a face-to-face meeting with a killer.

Deep down, Rachel knew the reason for her discomfort. She had been recognized. In public. By a stranger. That had never happened before. Rachel had worked hard to maintain her anonymity after being catapulted to fame when the first season of her podcast became a cultural sensation, spurring a wave of imitation podcasts and a national obsession with true crime.

In that first season, Rachel had uncovered fresh evidence that proved that a high school teacher had been wrongly convicted for the murder of his wife on their second honeymoon. Season 2 was even more successful when Rachel had solved a previously unsolvable cold case of a single mother of two who was bashed to death in her hair salon. By the time the season had ended, Rachel Krall had become a household name.

Despite her sudden fame, or rather because of it, she deliberately kept a low profile. Rachel's name and broadcast voice were instantly recognizable, but people had no idea what she looked like or who she was when she went to the gym, or drank coffee at her favorite cafe, or pushed a shopping cart through her local supermarket.

The only public photos of Rachel were a series of black-and-white shots taken by her ex-husband during their short-lived marriage when she was at grad school. The photos barely resembled her anymore, maybe because of the camera angle, or the monochrome hues, or perhaps because her face had become more defined as she entered her thirties.

In the early days, before the podcast had taken off, they'd received their first media request for a photograph of Rachel to run alongside an article on the podcast's then-cult following. It was her producer Pete's idea to use those dated photographs. He had pointed out that reporting on true crime often attracted cranks and kooks, and even the occasional psychopath. Anonymity, they'd agreed, was Rachel's protection. Ever since then she'd cultivated it obsessively, purposely avoiding public-speaking events and TV show appearances so that she wouldn't be recognized in her private life.

That was why it was unfathomable to Rachel that a random stranger had recognized her well enough to leave her a personalized note at a remote highway rest area where she'd stopped at a whim. Glancing once more over her shoulder, she ripped open the envelope to read the letter inside:

Dear Rachel,
  I hope you don't mind me calling you by your first name. I feel that I know you so well.

She recoiled at the presumed intimacy of the letter. The last time she'd received fan mail in that sort of familiar tone, it was from a sexual sadist inviting her to pay a conjugal visit at his maximum-security prison.

Rachel climbed into the driver's seat of her car and continued reading the note, which was written on paper torn from a spiral notebook.

I'm a huge fan, Rachel. I listened to every episode of your podcast. I truly believe that you are the only person who can help me. My sister Jenny was killed a long time ago. She was only sixteen. I've written to you twice to ask you to help me. I don't know what I'll do if you say no again.

Rachel turned to the last page. The letter was signed: *Hannah*. She had no recollection of getting Hannah's letters, but that didn't mean much. If letters had been sent, they would have gone to Pete or their intern, both of whom vetted the flood of correspondence sent to the podcast email address. Occasionally Pete would forward a letter to Rachel to personally review.

In the early days of the podcast, Rachel had personally read all the requests for help that came from either family or friends frustrated at the lack of progress in their loved ones' homicide investigations, or prisoners claiming innocence and begging Rachel to clear their names. She'd made a point of personally responding to each letter, usually after doing preliminary research, and often by including referrals to not-for-profit organizations that might help.

But as the requests grew exponentially, the emotional toll of desperate people begging Rachel for help overwhelmed her. She'd become the last hope of anyone who'd ever been let down by the justice system. Rachel discovered firsthand that there were a lot of them and they all wanted the same thing. They wanted Rachel to make their case the subject of the next season of her podcast, or at the very least, to use her considerable investigative skills to right their wrong.

Rachel hated that most of the time she could do nothing other than send empty words of consolation to desperate, broken people. The burden of their expectations became so crushing that Rachel almost abandoned the podcast. In the end, Pete took over reviewing all correspondence to protect Rachel and to give her time to research and report on her podcast stories.

The letter left on her windshield was the first to make it through Pete's human firewall. This piqued Rachel's interest, despite the nagging worry that made her double-lock her car door as she continued reading from behind the steering wheel.

> *It was Jenny's death that killed my mother* [the letter went on]. *Killed her as good as if she'd been shot in the chest with a twelve-gauge shotgun.*

Though it was late morning on a hot summer's day and her car was heating up like an oven, Rachel felt a chill run through her.

> *I've spent my life running away from the memories. Hurting myself. And others. It took the trial in Neapolis to make me face up to my past. That is why I am writing to you, Rachel. Jenny's killer will be there. In that town. Maybe in that courtroom. It's time for justice to be done. You're the only one who can help me deliver it.*

The metallic crash of a minibus door being pushed open startled Rachel. She tossed the pages on the front passenger seat and hastily reversed out of the parking spot.

She was so engrossed in thinking about the letter and the mysterious way that it was delivered that she didn't notice she had merged onto the highway and was speeding until she came out of her trancelike state and saw metal barricades whizzing past in a blur. She'd driven more than ten miles and couldn't remember any of it. Rachel slowed down, and dialed Pete.

No answer. She put him on auto redial but gave up after the fourth attempt when he still hadn't picked up. Ahead of her, the widening band of blue ocean on the horizon beckoned at the end of the long, flat stretch of highway. She was getting close to her destination.

Rachel looked into her rearview mirror and noticed a silver sedan on the road behind her. The license plate number looked familiar. Rachel could have sworn that she'd seen the same car before over the course of her long drive. She changed lanes. The sedan changed lanes and moved directly behind her. Rachel sped up. The car sped up. When she braked, the car did, too. Rachel dialed Pete again. Still no answer.

"Damn it, Pete." She slammed her hands on the steering wheel.

The sedan pulled out and drove alongside her. Rachel turned her head to see the driver. The window was tinted and reflected the glare of the sun as the car sped ahead, weaving between lanes until it was lost in a sea of vehicles. Rachel slowed down as she entered traffic near a giant billboard on a grassy embankment that read: "Welcome to Neapolis. Your gateway to the Crystal Coast."

Neapolis was a three-hour drive north of Wilmington and well off the main interstate highway route. Rachel had never heard of the place until she'd chosen the upcoming trial there as the subject of the hotly anticipated third season of *Guilty or Not Guilty*.

She pulled to a stop at a red traffic light and turned on the car radio. It automatically tuned into a local station running a talkback slot in between playing old tracks of country music on a lazy Saturday morning. She surveyed the town through the glass of her dusty windshield. It had a charmless grit that she'd seen in a hundred other small towns she'd passed through over her thirty-two years. The same ubiquitous gas station signs. Fast-food stores with grimy windows. Tired shopping strips of run-down stores that had long ago lost the war with the malls.

"We have a caller on the line," the radio host said, after the final notes of acoustic guitar had faded away. "What's your name?"

"Dean."

"What do you want to talk about today, Dean?"

"Everyone is so politically correct these days that nobody calls it as they see it. So I'm going to say it straight out. That trial next week is a disgrace."

"Why do you say that?" asked the radio announcer.

"Because what the heck was that girl thinking!"

"You're blaming the girl?"

"Hell yeah. It's not right. A kid's life is being ruined because a girl got drunk and did something dumb that she regretted afterward. We all regret stuff. Except we don't try to get someone put in prison for our screw-ups."

"The police and district attorney obviously think a crime has been committed if they're bringing it to trial," interrupted the host, testily.

"Don't get me wrong. I feel bad for her and all. Hell, I feel bad for everyone in this messed-up situation. But I especially feel bad for that Blair boy. Everything he worked for has gone up in smoke. And he ain't even been found guilty yet. Fact is, this trial is a waste. It's a waste of time. And it's a waste of our taxes."

"Jury selection might be over, but the trial hasn't begun, Dean," snapped the radio announcer. "There's a jury of twelve fine citizens who will decide his guilt or innocence. It's not up to us, or you, to decide."

"Well, I sure hope that jury has their heads screwed on right, because there's no way that anyone with a shred of good old-fashioned common sense will reach a guilty verdict. No way."

The caller's voice dropped out as the first notes of a hit country-western song hit the airwaves. The announcer's voice rose over the music. "It's just after eleven A.M. on what's turning out to be a very humid Saturday morning in Neapolis. Everyone in town is talking about the Blair trial that starts next week. We'll take more callers after this little tune."

ABOUT THE AUTHOR

MEGAN GOLDIN worked as a correspondent for Reuters and other media outlets, where she covered war, peace, international terrorism, and financial meltdowns in the Middle East and Asia. She is now based in Melbourne, Australia, where she raises three sons and is a foster mom to Labrador puppies learning to be guide dogs. *The Escape Room* is her debut novel.